ALL THAT MONK BUSINESS

All That Monk Business

a novel

Barry Kennedy

N₁ O₂ N₁
CANADA

Publisher's note: This book is a work of fiction. Names, characters, places and incidents are either the product of the author's imagination or are used fictitiously, and any resemblance to actual persons living or dead is entirely coincidental.

Library and Archives Canada Cataloguing in Publication

Title: All that monk business : a novel / Barry Kennedy.

Names: Kennedy, Barry, author.

Identifiers: Canadiana 20200384252 | ISBN 9781989689202 (softcover)

Classification: LCC PS8571.E62725 A75 2021 | DDC C813/.54—dc23

Printed and bound in Canada on 100% recycled paper.

Now Or Never Publishing
901, 163 Street
Surrey, British Columbia
Canada V4A 9T8

nonpublishing.com
Fighting Words.

We gratefully acknowledge the support of the Canada Council for the Arts and the British Columbia Arts Council for our publishing program.

To Tracy, who taught me that writing need not be a lonely business, and keeps me laughing and loving so I don't ever forget it.

Prologue

Resuscitation

After turning turtle in the storm and ditching her skipper in the Strait of Georgia, on the way down the fishboat consoled herself with the prospect of an early retirement. But the years of labour could not so easily be shrugged off, and when the inactivity began to wear on her, she set up shop as an artificial reef. Rooming house to the bottom dweller, hostel to the finned traveller, refuge to the lost and the scared, the sheer overwhelmed.

Attractive enough to fishy types, the old troller has little to offer the visitor from dry land. On the day she hit the bottom inverted most of the superstructure was raked off, leaving her a rather humdrum destination spot alongside the more dramatic wrecks of the coastal waters. To undersea adventurers the decomposing vessel hasn't much of a story to tell, a common enough take on things and people with no obvious utility. But then comes the day two scuba divers find a third.

To the young divers who chance upon him, it looks as though the unconscious man tried to squeeze underneath the port gunwale to see what he could see. They have no problem freeing his gear from where it hooked on a cleat, nor in identifying as blood the tendrils leaking from a gash over his eye. But restarting his breathing is another matter, and in their borderline panic they simply stuff the regulator back between his wasting blue lips and haul him to the surface.

When the call comes, the fishboat's former captain is enjoying a coffee and wrestling with a crossword. Louie Zimbot—eighty years, full head of hair, lives alone, eats just enough to keep upright, smokes unfiltered Pall Malls he gets cheap from a friend in Bellingham. Hobbies? A little sketching, just for himself, don't even ask.

By the time he gets his truck started and makes his way to the marina, the recovering diver is under the care of the paramedics. His vitals are fine, but as a precaution he'll be medevaced down-island to the hyperbaric chamber in Victoria. Louie's familiar with most everyone connected with the sea along this stretch of Vancouver Island coast, and he recognizes the survivor as a middle-aged man from up-Island who hits town the odd weekend for supplies and to idle away the time out on the pier coaxing songs from his guitar. And this time, apparently, to ignore safety standards by diving solo on a wreck. Nice enough fella, blind to caution is all, something Louie can't quite bring himself to condemn—to his way of thinking, risky business is nothing but the primordial urge to call the more heedful part of oneself out of the shadows to see how much it can handle.

The medevac chopper descends with a concussion of blades, throwing up a funky cyclone of grit and rotting kelp. Survivor aboard, it hustles off on its mission.

Farther along the spit, the day's heroes are arguing with one of the RCMP constables. The policeman's wharfside manner isn't helping matters and he soon retires to his cruiser, leaving the young adventurers sputtering with frustration. For a time after the boat went down, divers would periodically present Louie with mementos from the wreck as though delivering dog tags to the parent of a fallen soldier, a ritual he eventually put the kibosh to in that certain way he has. But this time it isn't about salvage, and the two lads are leaping over each other to bring him up to speed:

Hey, Louie, thanks for coming. I knew something stupid would happen, man, I knew it—Yeah, if that cop would just stop treating us like beach bums and listen—See, our video camera was on a wrist strap and when we swam over to help the trapped dude it was running the whole time. The clip would like totally go viral, except the cop's impounding the camera—Yeah, he's calling it evidence, can you believe it? Evidence of what? Nobody died, thanks to us—And it's like a proven fact cops keep everything they confiscate—Yeah, so we're like getting totally ripped off—Fuckin cop, man—Yeah, fuckin dude.

Louie commiserates in the way he does at a funeral for a distant relative, and when pressed to look into the matter issues a promise vague enough to leave unfulfilled. Halfway back to his truck the incident has already been leached of detail, which can be said for pretty much all his memories. Alone in sharp remembrance is the long-gone day when a bit of mischief out at sea changed another man's world. But that was then. There's nothing these days to disturb his peace. His old fishboat has it right—park yourself somewhere easy on the eyes and roll with the tides.

Louie continues along to the small central area of town just up from the harbour. He wouldn't turn down a beer, but ever since the Lorne Hotel burned to the stumps there's been no place in downtown Comox to have a pint without tourists snapping selfies for evidence of their existence. Maybe there's a beer or two left in his fridge. And he forgot his smokes at home anyway. So that's where he goes.

Chapter I

He Don't Bother Chasing Mice Around

"You can't keep wild animals in your apartment." If not completely reconciled to her son's behaviour, June at least finds his justifications amusing enough to cut him some slack. But this latest thing, no, it would be abdicating parental responsibility.

At Buddy's second-floor desk overlooking the street, the pleasure drains from the day aborning. Sunrise is his personal time for strategizing, and his mother normally respects his regimen by waiting for a decent hour to strike. But of late he's been sensing something astir in the old life-guardian who brought him into the world, and here she is again, pouncing just as the sun lips the horizon with its inverted smile.

"Do you hear me?" she says. "Mice are wild animals."

"Having trouble with my land line. Gimme a sec and I'll call you back on the cell."

Buddy rocks his phone in its cradle and scans the street below. It's one of the rare mornings this spring when Vancouver isn't being irrigated from on high. Songbirds dip and soar on test flights, shaking out the kinks for another day on the wires and ledges, the rooftops and hedges of Commercial Drive. The crows, hungover and unapologetic, scour curbside for pizza scraps, jacking around, screeching at dirty jokes, buoyant with the joy of being an unfavoured species and therefore free to behave in any manner they please. A biker on a Harley thunders past, drawing from the crows happy squawks, the whole raucous caucus sympathetic to any confederate in public unrest and disorder.

Buddy clasps and unclasps his hands, a pair of crooked grapplers that, like the rest of him, harbour less fat than a Haida totem pole. He isn't as attractive, of course, as carved red cedar, not really a pretty sight at all—hair cropped close to the scalp, carcass hard-used, face interesting enough maybe but a good few notches short of handsome. Built less for flash than the long haul. "All right," Buddy says to his mother, "I'm back. But we have to make this quick."

"You sound hollow on that old flip phone," June says. "I hate the tone it gives your voice."

Most people do. Precisely why Buddy won't even dream of ditching it.

"Promise to get rid of the mice," June continues, "and you'll never have to hear from me again."

"Not plural, Mum. There's no herd. One mouse. My guess is he was being harassed by his mother and bolted for the arms of someone who can relate."

Good person that she is, June ignores the comment. "How do you know it's a *he*?"

"Male mice have a greater distance between their genitals and anus."

"You measured. Who measures that? What else do you do to wild animals?"

Her son flips over the sympathy card: "And he's deformed." Buddy doesn't lie reflexively, but often it's the only way to cleanse the air of criticism. In this case, however, he's giving his mum the straight goods.

The mouse popped up a week before at three in the morning, gnawing at the plaster behind the bookshelves. Buddy awoke instantly alert and pulled out his old Carl Yastrzemski baseball bat from under the bed. When he tugged away a double handful of books, expecting the usual rodent behaviour of either freezing in place or scurrying for the nearest cover, a darkish blob spurted into space, landed at his feet and sat there unfazed. Buddy, unable to credit such behaviour in any rodent short of a starving wharf rat, was most impressed. Brave little rascal. No doubt panicky and confused, but brave nevertheless. Buddy isn't one to shy from confrontation, on the contrary spends a significant portion of each day actively seeking it out. Yet he could hardly stomp the helpless nightstalker, at least not with bare feet, and to scare it off only to set out traps or poison the next day reeked of dishonour. So Buddy got on his knees and squinted, studied. A broad, slightly squashed head in lieu of the normal tightly tapered snout of a house mouse. Rear legs splayed reptile-like. A strange patch of long hair on his back. A freak. A loser. Buddy jerked out a hand, freak mouse sat. Banged on the floor, loser mouse sniffed. Hooted like an owl, freak loser mouse sashayed off for the passageway leading to the bathroom, taking his leave as easily as he had arrived. Like a long-time widower with a rescue puppy, Buddy Monk fell in love.

"What do you mean by *deformed*?" June says.

"Probably an X-linked genetic disorder that's passed on exclusively through the mother."

No reaction, so on Buddy forges: "Besides, he has to be easier to live with than Nita."

"Don't start on Nita," June says. "The trouble with you, mister, is you think everything about human beings can be explained by science."

"Seven years of study."

"*Pff!* A bunch of semesters spread over three universities that cut you loose the minute they caught on to your bullshit."

"I walked out of each one on my own two feet," Buddy says.

"And straight into jail."

"Please. Three days isn't jail."

"What do you call it then?"

"The school of hard knocks."

"Right, just like the other schools—the only thing you came out with was what you already believed going in."

While Buddy assays the merits of veering off in this new direction, his mother finds the ruts her wheels previously carved and lurches back on track. "What about the defecation?"

"I've never had a problem with that."

"You're a riot. I mean the mouse droppings."

"Hard dry flecks," Buddy scoffs. "You probably inhale worse just walking down the street. And don't try to tell me you find something like that disgusting. You served tables at the Steveston Hotel when the canneries were running full tilt. The old Buccaneer Pub should have permanently suppressed your gag reflex."

"People can change, for your information."

"So why don't you change into someone who likes mice?"

The hitch while June mulls this over gives her son his first gleam of hope, and both contestants recognize the shift in advantage. A few more exchanges might see Buddy in the clear. While casting around in his mind for an outflanking manoeuvre, a sound penetrates that doesn't immediately register as his mother's voice.

"Are you even listening?" June says.

"Sorry, what was that again? I was surfing mouse porn."

"Hantavirus," his mother repeats. "Vancouver Coastal Health dropped off a pamphlet at the restaurant. A group of viruses carried by rodents. Fever, respiratory infections, you don't know what you're letting yourself in for with that thing running around defecating everywhere. It can have lethal consequences."

"Thanks for the concern," Buddy says with an earnest timbre that brings pause to the exchange. He leans back in his Value Village springback chair. An unofficial tally of points has them roughly even, precisely when his mother is at her most dangerous. Never content to safely protect a slim lead or play for a draw, at this juncture she'll often abandon frontal assault for distraction, counterfeit weakness like a killdeer with a bogus broken wing trying to divert a predator from the nest.

"Anyway," June says, searching for fresh footing, "if you're going to refuse good advice I'm not going to waste any more time on you. Some people have to work for a living."

"Me included," Buddy says. "Don't pretend it's news to you that barbers close Mondays. World-wide phenomenon, I think. Guild solidarity or something."

"Only barbers who keep a proper schedule take Mondays off."

"I've been busy lately."

"*Pff!* That ridiculous lawsuit."

"Ridiculous? Civil liberties, human rights—I learned all that from you and your precious daughter-in-law."

"And look how you've perverted it."

"All right, all right, I'll get rid of the mouse. Maybe put it on eBay."

"Now you're lying just to shut me up."

"Exactly." Buddy waits out a spell of dead air, almost able to smell the predictable alteration in his mother's voice.

A whisper: "What time are you coming by today, son?"

"What time works for you, Mum?"

"I'm going to be tied up the whole morning, a thousand-and-one things, better if you wait till later."

"Anything you need me to pick up?"

"Ohh, I don't know right now. Nothing I can think of."

The tone gives Buddy pause. Lately his mother has been showing signs of wear, a certain tapering off of spirit. But is this reason enough for him to slacken the pressure? If anything he ought to be applying himself more ferociously to the contest. Then again, June has a long day of work staring her in the face, a face that's been beaming protectively upon him these forty-one years. What to do, what to do. One heartbeat, two heartbeats, three heartbeats, four.

June checks in: "Are you still there?"

One heartbeat, two heartbeats, three heartbeats, four. "I'll see you later, Mum."

Buddy downs the phone and rakes his eyes around the bachelor apartment, four-hundred square feet of press-on vinyl tiles applied so poorly as to leave evidence of each previous layer, prompting images of past generations like the regress of strata in an archaeological tell. Off the main room with its kitchenette and futon, a short hall leads past a closet attached as an afterthought to the wall and ends at a curtained-off bathroom with a clawfoot tub and a toilet from the Middle Porcelain Age. Meager digs, but since the studio is directly above the barbershop Buddy can't get any closer to work, and there's that large window overlooking Commercial Drive, a stretch of East Vancouver that supports a range of lifestyles sufficient to allow him personal free rein while maintaining a healthy level of outrage at the behaviour of others. True the arrival of the mouse threatens his sense of good order and domestic discipline. But that's just to be expected when one starts a family.

He transfers his attention to the outdoors, where the street is starting to flush as its arteries swell with the long and the short and the tall, the rooted and the rootless, the immigrants and the migrants, the upwardly mobile and the succumbers to inertia, the new parents and the never-wills, the caregivers and the care-for-nothings, the poets and the performers, the bookish and the booksellers, the Eye-Ties and the Port-oo-geez and the Ell-Gee-Bee-Tees, the freelivers and the freebooters, the bums and boozers and streetcombers, the militants and the pacifists, the lawyers and the scofflaws, the dentists and the flossless, the bullies and the buskers, the shopowners and the shopworn, the native carvers of wood and the many carvers of place.

There, better now. He sets the shower running for the full five minutes it takes to coax a few degrees from a hot water heater that might as well be in Seattle pumping through a stone aqueduct, strips, throws off a couple of poses in the mirror, returns to the main room, against the wall slings furiously through twenty handstand pushups and promenades back down the hall toward the billowing bathroom cumulus, mind alert, electric and entirely given over to the pleasant business of slapping some sense into the new day.

Chapter 2

The Dunmow Flitch

Now June will have Buddy on the brain till closing time. Whatever lately has been causing her son's lightning leaps and drops in mood, he's leaving no clues. While toying with the foolish notion of calling him back for an explanation, it dawns on her she's forgotten to let Al know she's on her way. He opened the restaurant for her twice last week when she was either too tired to drag herself out the door or was at some early paperwork and lost track of the time, and she hates interrupting his morning devotional with the boys.

Al and his cohorts launch each day with caffeine and complaints, sports scores and small wagers, crabgrass-roots political analysis and a laugh or two, patronizing whichever coffee shop fits the mood of the morning. Up and down Commercial Drive they go, checking on the early overseas soccer matches, greeting the folks setting up the outdoor produce stands, trying not to be caught ogling the young women in yoga wear that shows their you-knows and their what-alls, pausing periodically to gauge the mood of the Drive while punishing passersby with broadsides of tobacco smoke. June phones, assures him the situation is well in hand and that he can hang out awhile yet. But wouldn't you know it, by the time she freshens up and hikes the short distance from home, there's Nita at the front door waiting to be let in.

"Sorry," June says, pawing through a ten-kilo tangle of keys. "Your first day on the job and I'm late."

"Nothing to apologize for," Nita says.

June leads, snapping on lights while wondering what's come over her lately. For years a meticulous planner with the attention to detail of an antique watch mechanic, she seems to have lost this specific life skill and been deposited into the free-range confusion of, well, Nita's world. "Have you ever been in the kitchen?" June says. "Take a look around, I'll just drop this in the office."

She returns to find the new employee exploring the doubtful possibility of fitting a hairnet over her mass of prematurely grey-streaked dreadlocks. "You won't need that for working the floor," June says. "And you look just fine."

Nita does look fine, in June's estimation. There's an unidentifiable exoticism about her son's ex, a nonspecific not-from-around-here feel. Dramatic tangled hawsers up top, cut-glass eyes, a long sweep of arms and legs. Her breasts are perfectly fried sunnyside-up eggs—in contrast to June's, which look ready at any moment to spring free and commence a general pummelling of anything within reach. Not that June isn't proud of her tits, mighty fine for sixty-four and same goes for her legs. Her hair, though, so much thinner than Nita's. But then whose isn't, and pulled back from her face the way June wears it allows the character of her large eyes, serious nose and strong jawline full stage on which to strut their stuff. A woman poised between slightly frowzy beauty and stern handsomeness, June Monk both attracts and cautions. Nita Randolph attracts only, yet of the two may require more caution.

"Where do you want me to start?" Nita says.

"For now just follow me around. Coffee on first, we can gab as we go."

Over the seven years they've been together, Al and June have been divvying up responsibilities and shuffling their hours with whatever in the way of staff that hasn't yet found something better and quit, stolen from them and quit, gotten pregnant and quit, broken bones in a snowboarding accident and been forced to quit, gone back to school and quit working, quit school but also quit showing up for their shifts, or nearly overdosed again and can't quit that. June's feeling the weight. It's hard on the nerves and harder physically. Since the latest cook was caught rolling a full barrel of Kokanee draft beer to the curb and trying to load it onto the 20 bus, June's been splitting shifts—open the restaurant for breakfast, the bar for lunch, home for a quick break then back for the after-work crowd—and it'll be nice if Nita can take up some of the load.

June guides her through her duties, thankful for not being saddled with another dewy-eyed sprout. Bless his heart, but Al can't resist hiring the most untried of innocents, just out of school and inquiring after benefits and time off before they've even learned how to balance a tray, fiddling with their iPhones for ski conditions while customers slowly starve and desiccate. But though Nita can be scattered, and June hopes that isn't understating the case out of desperation, her daughter-in-law learns new things with an effortless grace. Besides, she's plain good to be around. They aren't tight in a sisterly sense, but the friendship is solidly grounded. As for taking sides in the recent breakup, the mother could never actively lobby against the son, but Buddy certainly makes it easy to afford Nita equal consideration.

"Hey," June says, "I just realized I've been going on and on and haven't asked whether you have any experience in the service industry. You've done so many things. If all this is old news, tell me to button my lip."

"It was way long ago," Nita says. "Happy to be brought up to date." Also happy for the job. If she has to do something to pay the bills, better it be here. She likes June and Al's story, a later-in-life love affair that seems, barring unforeseeable mischance, ready and able to carry on right the way through. Naturally that was Nita and Buddy's expectation too, though what they used as a basis for such a forecast is a monument to the power of fantasy. Consistent, their marriage, she'll give it that, a three-year catalogue of miscues and misunderstandings from the celebratory heaving of the bridesmaids into Trout Lake to the last pitiful deception.

Nita excuses herself to go to the Ladies, and there above the sink in Buddy's handwriting is: *Caution! Objects in Mirror Are Slower Than They Appear.* What's this, is the message directed at her personally? He's not supposed to know she's working here till she gets settled. Peering closer, she revises her evaluation. The jab was applied with a more self-possessed hand than Buddy's, whose impatient scribbling is rarely legible. She commands herself to settle down. No reason to be paranoid. He handed over what little savings they had in the joint account, is helping her out with the rent on her new place, and he isn't one of those post-breakup lunatics who calls at all hours to drunkenly argue his case before collapsing into a puddle of grief. But he's just so . . . Buddy, so fucking Buddy. Liquid soap from the dispenser and a bit of rubbing with a paper towel removes the graffito, and by the time Nita's finished her husband has been wiped as cleanly from her mind, at least till she exits and catches June lowering her cell from her ear with that look on her face.

"How did he find out?" Nita says resignedly.

"What can I say?" June shrugs. "He's an alien. I mean, we're talking about an adult man intent on suing a lawn bowling association for ageism. But don't worry, he doesn't own this place."

"It doesn't worry me," Nita says. "Just makes me tired." More than tired, the fatigue of sadness, of regret. She wonders whether it's over the loss of a partner or the depleted reserves of emotional energy from having pumped so much of it into a doomed enterprise.

"Come on," says June, ready to apply the dubious folk remedy of banishing the blues with work, "let's prep for Al before he gets here so we don't have to go rushing around at the last minute."

Al Esposito's occupies the main floor of a two-story building with four apartments up top. On the right, viewed from the street, is the entrance, which leads the visitor into the cafe-restaurant, furnished with out-of-date but somehow appropriate furniture and the bare minimum of wrought-iron curlicues, amateur frescoes and other decorative Mediterranean atrocities common to East Van. June herself disposed of the white plaster lions abandoned by the previous owners. At the back, around the corner from the service counter, is the office, which does double duty as a storage room and looks the part, packed with dry goods, napkins, broken appliances and the like. Anyone in the mood for a cocktail and a chin-wag can turn left in front of the kitchen and pass through the archway into the bar, licensed capacity of forty-nine. Over the years, the room has morphed from a jazzy-bluesy snug with a small stage for live music to the familiar catchall pub, the walls filled with plastic beer signs and half of Samsung's annual flat-screen TV production, normally tuned to sports from around the world. Al Esposito's—half beverage room and half restaurant, if not exactly, as Buddy never tires of calling it, half-ass.

Nita trails into the kitchen, and after distractedly dropping a pound of fresh butter from the wrapper and dripping a few tears into the pancake batter, she feels June's hand on her shoulder and follows along till they're out back in the delivery area.

At their arrival in the alley, a rump neighbourhood council of crows deliberating over the day's upcoming activities scatters before cautiously returning when one of the honourable members spies under the dumpster a paper plate with scraps of lamb donair and drags it out to the enthusiastic beating of wings and shouts of *Hear hear! Hear hear!*

After lighting a cigarette and exhaling downwind, June says, "I can bar him till you get used to the job. Say the word."

Nita shakes her head. "It'd just give him an excuse to . . . "

June has no idea whether this is the right time to ask. "He never told me. About the end, I mean. The last straw."

"I should have told you myself. But by the time we broke up I was so tired of everything. Trying to out-do each other, arguing even about things we agreed on. To tell you would have looked like I was trying to top his story or excuse myself. You knew it was coming anyhow. And I was embarrassed, felt like a dumb kid falling in love for the first time. Afraid, too, I guess, of making you take sides. I didn't want to lose you, on top of everything else."

"That wouldn't have happened then any more than it will now."

A leakage of cigarette smoke undulates through the air like the notes from a pan flute and loses itself in the creviced maze of

Nita's dreads. She dips into her canvas purse and hands June a folded piece of paper. "This is how it all started."

June unfolds the sheet.

In England connubial contentment could win the Dunmow Flitch—a side, or flitch, of bacon awarded to any couple who could come to Dunmow in Essex after a year of marriage and truthfully swear that they never quarreled and did not regret the marriage and would do it over again if given the chance.

The light hasn't gone on, but June has firm enough grounds for misgivings, that unnerving tingle of watching a young actress mount the attic stairs in a horror movie—unaware of exactly what's waiting at the top but damn certain it's nothing to which the girl should be exposing herself.

"It started, I don't know, centuries ago," Nita says. "They revived the tradition and hold trials in this Dunmow place every four years. It's a fun thing, people dress in period costumes and play-act and socialize. Buddy had been paying for everything with the barbershop VISA to build up Air Canada points so the tickets to England wouldn't show on our bank statement."

"To surprise you?"

Nita shakes her head. "I told him flat-out at the first mention of it that we couldn't be spending that kind of money on one of his games."

"And . . . ?"

"He said in that case, he'd take another woman. A substitute. I wasn't to worry, there was nothing emotional involved, he just couldn't pass up the opportunity. He wanted me to write a love letter swearing to all the conditions in the rules—never quarrelling, no regrets, all that."

"So let me get this straight." June fires another cigarette to replace the one she just jettisoned half-smoked. To keep track of her summary, she flips out each digit of her free hand, starting with the thumb. "One, wanted you to write a fake love letter. Two, ran up an enormous VISA bill to collect Air Canada miles. Three, so he could fly to England. Four, with a fake wife. Five, for a chance to win bacon." Free hand fully occupied with fanned fingers, she rips a stream of smoke through the cigarette held in the other hand, the hand she'd rather be using to knock a knot into her son's stupid head.

Nita laughs with a sound unrelated to humour. "You know him and competitions."

June looks at the end of the smoke and flicks it into the lane. "I don't get the letter."

"It was for the judges. To build up his case for a successful marriage."

"I mean, why the letter if he was going to have the phoney wife along?"

"She was supposed to fake a recent throat operation. He didn't want her speaking."

"Are you going to make me ask?"

"Sally," Nita says. "Sally From the Alley."

"Jesus."

As the steel door whispers closed, the crows fill the abandoned space. The senior office holder hops diagonally over to June's wasted cigarette, stabs the filter with his beak, and on confirming its inedibility turns to his fellow representatives, squawks *Once! Twice! Thrice!* and the council meeting is adjourned.

CHAPTER 3
MULLETS TO MOHAWKS

It's dark in the narrow stairway leading to the street and not much lighter outside. Clouds have stolen in, uniform stratus advancing from the North Shore Mountains as though transpiring from a hidden refuge over the ridgeline. The lights are on next door in Take-A-Number Deli, but Old Kim, the long-time Korean owner who weighs less than some of Buddy's darker thoughts, won't open for another half hour.

The sidewalks are filling. People on their way to work, dog-walkers, espresso sippers, newspaper junkies. Several new mothers are airing out their infants, mummified bundles strapped into double-wide strollers the width of road graders with room for wine cellars and second-story guest suites, the monstrosities that cause wicked havoc in the stores and around the outdoor produce stands. Buddy growls in his throat before lightening up when a young woman walks past with a baby dangling in a striped cotton sling against her belly. Much better. Contact, connection.

When his dad was away on the boats, Buddy would crawl sleepy-scared in with his mum in the middle of the night, rest his forehead on her strong back and pull the flannel sheets up over his head. They'd walk hand-in-hand through Steveston to buy prawns, sit leaning against each other on the docks watching the heavily-laden fishboats wallowing up the Fraser estuary to the canneries. When he was on his own, he was on his own. Fall out of a tree? Don't come crying. Get hurt throwing rocks? Don't come crying. Makes sense you have to touch and feel. No expectations back then of protection from cradle to car seat to coffin. He would never have learned anything of value insulated from his environment.

The barbershop window has been tagged again by the same vandal, *YOULYSSES*, a flourish in silver with a ragged black border. At least he—or she, but Buddy guesses *he* for the sheer fuck-you-ity of the persistence—has refrained from spraying the brick surround, instead carefully decorating the plate glass below the shop's name and proprietor:

MULLETS TO MOHAWKS
BUDDY MONK, KING OF THE BUZZ CUT
YOULYSSES

The tag is easily removed with the window scraper Buddy has taken to carrying, and he does so now, sliding out the half-razorblade from its sheath and with careful strokes stripping the patch of paint. *Dingle,* giggles the bell over the door, and the barber's inside.

Buddy's been at it since his days in Toronto when he scored a small government grant to learn a practical skill. Barbering had the advantage of being a skill he planned to teach himself, leaving him free to apply the grant to a start-up shop of his own, wise strategy for a man less than masterful at playing well with others. Alas, there would be no grant outside of his registering in a recognized program, but by that juncture the very novelty of the thing had him by the throat, so with a ten-dollar pair of clippers and the accompanying instructions, Buddy set out in preliminary reconnaissance of the craft. Thankfully, he had on hand a head on which to practise—his own.

Judging the taper to be the trickiest bit, that's where he started, coming up quickly with the clippers along the sides. Next, with his back to the bathroom mirror and a hand mirror held in front, he had a go at the neckline. Upon reflection, the problem was the reflection. Each time his hand or the clippers blocked his view of the cutline in the double-mirror arrangement, the natural reaction was to move his head the better to see, grinding it one way or another into the vibrating teeth, in turn necessitating another few passes to even things up. Over and over he cut with smaller and smaller clipper guards, and just as he was starting to get a handle on the technique the game was over—to proceed any deeper would be to encounter grey matter. On top was the remainder, a roughly circular pad looking something like a yarmulke of yak hair, and the only thing for it was to shave that too down to the scalp. Short of using a razor, he was now officially bald. But that was all right, he could appreciate the advantages of his new condition. Sanitary, easy on maintenance, he'd save money on gel, and there were bound to be other positives he could dredge up with some willful self-deception. Never mind, he'd do a better job as soon as his hair grew back. Till then he'd take advantage of the look popular among the younger crowd by wearing a pulled-down toque day and night, indoors and out, particularly to barber school, which he commenced immediately.

To call Mullets to Mohawks atypical would be accurate without being insulting. It has the mandatory mirrors, sink at the back, two barber chairs, one of them a spare, but there ends any similarity to the iconic neighbourhood barbershop. No striped pole, and the furnishings are a miscellany of castoffs and recycled pieces from various used-merchandise outfits in the East End. Angled in the front corner of the shop is an antique brocade armchair, witness in its time to countless generations of backsides and legions of dust mites. Opposite stands the reception counter, formerly a jewellery display case, its glass top piled with the *Georgia Straight* and a raft of local business brochures. Around the room can be found a bookcase packed with *National Geographics* and *Scientific Americans,* a coffee table strewn with newspapers and unwashed mugs, three '50s-style kitchen chairs aligned beside the armchair along the front window and a wheel-less bicycle frame kept upright by a pedal wedged in the umbrella stand. The quiddity of the place is best represented by a tent card on the front counter: Hair Cut—Price Determined by Attitude.

The King looks out on the Drive through the letters of his shop window. Was it really only three years ago Nita stood on the other side? He was staring out like this with his mind on autosearch when the wild-looking woman skipped across the street from Happy Thyme, inched up till they were nose-to-nose through the pane of glass, cradled a mass of dreads in each hand, canted her head and hollered, "Anything you can do with this?" before laughing and vanishing northbound. She was moving fast, long legs carrying her away, away, away . . . it took a flat-out sprint, but Buddy caught up before she hit the East End Food Co-op.

"So you're the King of The Buzz Cut," she said back in the shop with the CLOSED sign hung on the door and a beer apiece.

"I was going to go with King of the Flat-top," Buddy said. "But that's a guitar."

"Why do you have to be the king of anything?"

"A name ought to reflect the owner's status. What do you want—Buddy Monk the Buzz Cut Peasant?"

"Isn't a barbershop supposed to have haircut pictures? The different styles, The Cosmopolitan or The Windsor or whatever?"

He followed her inspection of the walls with their shots of sports stars and generals, heroes and conquerors, financial titans and Everest climbers, winners all. Good-looking woman, no question, with a strangeness he found all the more attractive. Lemony-olive skin, sharp clear eyes over prominent cheekbones, a crooked smile, a certain foreign stamp that called to mind no specific nationality.

"This is quite the place," she continued. "Looks like one of those coffee shops you find in the American southwest that serve booze at six in the morning to damaged Vietnam vets and meth lab entrepreneurs."

"Hey!"

"Why Mullets to Mohawks? When you're the King of The Buzz Cut, I mean?"

"Why all the questions?" He rolled his empty the length of the floor till it bonked into the door of the storage closet, then cracked another. "Look, I don't like scissors, okay? I mastered clippers early and believe in emphasizing your strengths. Besides, to get your mohawk you more-or-less buzz everything except the strip down the middle. And your mullet, well, some barbers use scissors, and some customers want something froofy on top as long as it's way shorter than the back, but my technique is to leave the back pretty much alone and buzz the rest with a long guard, a Number 8 or something."

"Mullets to Mohawks." Nita rolled it around in her mouth, washed it down with a stream of beer and repeated it with the same sceptical tone.

"I considered some others. Bowl Cuts to Beehives, Crew Cuts to Cornrows. Even," he said, nodding at her clotted coils, "Ducktails to Dreadlocks. But there was always at least one of the pair that required major scissor work."

"Why does it have to be double-barrelled? *Da* to *Da*?"

"I don't know, it's catchy."

"Mullets to Mohawks. Hmmm . . ."

"What?"

"It might lead people to think that's all you have on offer. Limited as far as marketing goes."

Buddy Monk is not, was not and never will be limited. "First off, that's why the *to*. Mullets *to* Mohawks, get it? A range of options."

"A range restricted to the letter *M*. Actually, to hairstyles between *Mu* and *Mo*. How many cuts fall within that spread?"

"I suppose you'd prefer something boring like Buddy's Barbershop."

"Sounds good to me. And you should try losing your fear of scissors. It's perfectly all right to emphasize your strengths so long as you work on your weaknesses."

Fear. Weakness. Clearly he was wasting his time and beer on an imbecile. Nothing but trouble this one, confusing him just by being there. And who asked her opinion anyhow. So he threw her out.

Buddy leans his head on the glass and squints up the street in the direction she disappeared that day. Southbound, as if her initial route toward the mountains had been selected only to satisfy the need for motion. Always lightly positioned, Nita Randolph, apt to spirit off in a new direction at the slightest outside influence or internal whim. Which is why Buddy's unconcerned about her working at the restaurant with his mum and Al. She can't possibly last long, not at something for which she has to be punctual or plain predictable. Besides, she'll need help from a supernatural agency if she expects to fit the job in with her volunteer work with Greenpeace, Carnegie Centre, Pivot Legal, however many others.

Here comes the rain. Not serious, mist punctuated with drizzle. Enough, though, to dampen the sidewalks and imperfectly reflect the man across the way at the bus stop, he and his mirror image joined at the feet like Chinese acrobats, the lower standing on his head and coarsened by the irregular surface of the pavement, the real-life partner sharper edged and balancing upright sole-to-sole-to-soul. Buddy's eyes well up. Nita Randolph. And everything else. Jamming him up.

It's Monday. Shop closed. Buddy doesn't know what the hell he's doing here. Not here in the shop, just here, you know? Maybe he's used up all his potential. Pissed it away is more like it. But no, that's not right. He's still got it. Tired to the marrow, he flops in the spare barber chair where she'd been sitting that first day and idly rotates a little to the left, a little to the right, staring with detachment out the window, unable to dredge up enthusiasm even when one of the local sidewalk terrorists catches a wheel in a crack and rockets off his skateboard into the side of a parked delivery van.

He checks the time on the big wall clock. Too early for most things, too late in life for others. Movement, that always does it. And not a stroll, either, but a hard driving power walk through the streets. Flush out due thought and process, leaving only the core. Yeah.

Chapter 4

Surely He Jests

The Jester's bells enliven the morning air. Intrigued by the light-hearted dingling, a few weary overnighters angle out of the ticket line to glance up the sidewalk. Those who aren't immediately captured avert their eyes and feign disinterest, but it can't be sustained. Like people unable to tear themselves from a public hanging, they turn again to regard the fantastic character.

In the eye of the beholder, the Jester is either endearingly unique or repulsively ugly. Coarse hempen hair, brow ridge shading close-set eyes, lightly cratered nose. Spanning most of the gap between cauliflower ears, the lips form a rubbery surround for a few randomly arranged teeth visible when he smiles, which he does often, serving up a wide grin that raises the urge either to pet him or bolt for cover. Unable to compete with the visual force of the face, the torso and appendages appear to dwindle away till encountering large feet jammed into fabric boots with upturned toes, belled to match the hat. Naturally he isn't an actual jester, no more than he is a pirate, a fireman, a swordsman or any other of the characters from stage, screen and Halloween whose costumes he cobbles together from thrift shops. His real name is Robert Fairchild, known to his sister and a few others as Bo.

Bo has trouble gaining admittance to public places. Too broke, too startling, people in uniform or with nametags just being who they are. He takes a long look at the straggly line of music fans, drooped and hunched from hours of waiting, and nods at their dedication to things of the heart. He can sink a little into loneliness at times, but lovers of music and plays and movies and stories make him feel part of an extended family. They're blocking the poster on the wall, and Bo scuttles this way and that trying to see who's performing. If he had a coupon he might try to get in no matter who it is. Coupons are the best, he has a whole boxful at home, but the pockets of his costume are full of other stuff and he didn't want to crinkle the valuable pieces of paper by shoving them in.

He's hungry. Hungry enough to confuse, and the line of people with tickets casts him back to his childhood, a trip with his father to a Renaissance Faire where people were dressed as kings and queens and princesses, jugglers and balladeers, knights in shining armour. The man at the gate didn't want to take the tickets, just smiled at him and waved them through. His dad got awfully mad and shoved the tickets into the man's hand, but it was a nice offer all the same. Every since, Bo has made particular note of the occasions when he's been let in free somewhere—shelters, small art galleries around town, the 20 bus when the driver's having a good day. But he'd better get moving. A couple of youngsters have stopped a short distance away and are looking at him the way young men do when they're getting ready to punch somebody just for fun.

Wait a minute, the dizziness is coming on again. He should try to get inside. For some reason it's way easier to get help from people if he goes down inside. Out on the sidewalk like this, most people just keep walking. So people won't be scared, he smiles, mouth shakily turning up at the corners, eyeballs skittish dots down leathery tunnels. He starts forward, the queue parts, a slew of camera phones raise and point in his direction, but before Bo reaches the door to the theatre he's done.

Time takes its time till he realizes a policeman and policewoman are helping him to his feet. He collapsed, they tell him. They smell his breath and ask how he feels and decide between them there's no need to call the paramedics. Someone from the line passes him a bottle of water and he drinks a little. The police give him a ride home and escort him to his room. Eat something, they urge, and he assures them there's no problem there, he's well-stocked with graham crackers. He invites them to join him, but after a peek inside they go back downstairs, where he can hear them yelling at the building manager.

Bo's second-floor chamber is a miasma of mildew and bad dreams. The lone window is distorted, fly-blown, allowing scant light to penetrate. A two-ring hotplate sits on the counter. Over the sink juts a horizontal copper pipe stoppered against vermin, and each time Bo uses the pipe he marvels at the ability of hamsters and gerbils to drink from similar contraptions without soaking their fur. In one corner is a small wood cupboard beside a half-fridge. Kitty-corner is a mattress covered with a patterned counterpane he picked up at Value Village. On the wall opposite the window is a trunk for his costumes and a worn leather satchel holding his sketches. Piled in front of the trunk are several newer drawings glued to stiff cardboard. The latest is always left propped up facing the mattress where he can see it in recline if he spreads his feet a little.

That's where he is now, stretched out on the mattress. He hopes nobody from the lineup goes away without a ticket after waiting so long. A concert, how wonderful, always someone new coming to town, something new happening. New things are all he's sure about these days. Only a few of the older things stick—the Renaissance Faire with his dad, a hazy image of his mummy before she went away, trouble at school but also an academic prize. A few more things take on substance when prompted by his big sister, Sally. Don't get him wrong, though. Lacking a full history isn't all bad. For one thing, it frees him from the pressure to agree with other people's versions of it.

The mattress is gritty. He didn't eat a thing yesterday till getting home late and gorging on a whole box of graham crackers, his all-time favourite food, methodically stuffing the rectangles into his mouth till sneezing near the end of the second row and blasting the mattress with crumbs. He'll keep his costume on as protection against the scratchy bits. Some wiggling fits his joints into the permanent indentations in the thin pad. There, that's pretty comfortable. He thinks a little while of Sally, the best sister anyone could ever have. It's always been them two, even if they don't see each other all the time. He peeks between his feet at his latest sketch of Vancouver, and after a little burp he nods off.

★

The manager's wearing the indignant expression of a man refused seconds at a cruise ship buffet. Bo slumps. Before going out, he washed, shaved and changed into his cleanest costume, the trekking ensemble featuring a green alpine hat, lederhosen and a pair of hiking boots. He's proud of the Bavarian rig—jaunty feather, ginormous leather shorts, snappy suspenders. It makes him feel sort of like . . . Heidi. If she was a man, he means. And if she came from Bavaria instead of Switzerland, although he's pretty sure the Swiss wear leather shorts too, maybe not day-to-day but at least when they get together for some yodelling.

When he woke from his nap, in his impatience to investigate the new grocery store he left home without the cheque from his handyman friend and didn't catch on till he was at Pigeon Park Savings. Beverly, his favourite teller, called up his account and told him his chequing balance was only a little over two dollars, and though his savings account held almost twelve, that's for major emergencies and he didn't want to start dipping into it just for food. So it was back home to retrieve the cheque and start all over.

It was fun roaming the aisles of the new supermarket and poking his head into the frosty coolers. Everything looked so good—the long green cucumber, the round red tomato, the crisp skinny loaf of bread, the sweaty carton of milk with a cow on the side. He could have spent hours there, but some of the other customers were mumbling to one other, making funny noises in their throats, avoiding whatever aisle he happened to be in. Same old story even in a new place. He wasn't surprised when the manager showed up at his elbow.

The manager looks very young, and is being urged on by a shopper jabbing the air with his finger. Bo issues a blanket apology and starts for the exit with the manager close behind. On the way past the side counter where they sell lottery tickets, a lady with sparkly fingernails smiles and says, "Feeling lucky?" No, not really. Besides, Bo tries to stay out of luck's shadow. He's never been comfortable with how good luck for one can be bad for another. And there's too fine a line between good and bad luck in the first place, too many things at play that can switch one to the other. Before he can respond to the nice lady, he's rushed out the door by the manager so quickly his hat falls off. While bending to retrieve it, through the glass he can see the young man receiving thanks from the people in the checkout line. When someone claps their hands, the manager bows.

Bo learned long ago that the best thing to do in a situation like this is nothing. When confronted by people with no centre to their circle, causing a commotion only makes them stagger around more wildly on the perimeter. Best to lie low and hope they stumble on something good to believe in. He'll remember the lottery lady, though. Her smile was for real and cancels out all the stuff the manager said.

He's tired again. Maybe he'll rest on this planter wall for a few minutes. That's better. The confrontation has him overheated and the cold air rushing in from the ocean feels good. The mist is thick—he can barely see the North Shore Mountains. Still pretty, though, in any weather Vancouver's pretty. Except lots of traffic, way more than where he used to live. That place didn't have so many cars and trucks, mostly just ginormous trees and lots of water. Sometimes Bo and his dad could walk right down the gravel roads for hours without seeing even one car.

Sleepy, drifting off, he's brought around by the sight of someone bustling up the sidewalk. Oh! It's Walker-Talker Man. Bo has seen him on the Downtown Eastside a lot lately, just the other day cutting through Oppenheimer Park and another time near the end of Main Street where he looked to be heading for the overpass to Crab Park. He must like parks. Really like them, because he's always moving fast and talking to himself like he's full to the brim with wild things that can be safely released only in the forest or over open water.

The store's automatic door slides open, releasing the manager. "You can't sit there," the young man says, bare arms goosebumping in the breeze. "You can't panhandle here."

Bo wasn't planning on it. But how do you talk to someone who just used *can't* twice in eight words?

"You can't come in the store anymore," the manager adds. "And you can't loiter out here and pester people on the street."

Two more *can'ts*. Bo gets to his feet. He has to find something to eat. His stomach is pulling his bellybutton back so far it might touch his backbone pretty soon. He'll go to the Washington neighbourhood market and check out the specials. They often have excellent deals and he's never been kicked out, not even once. Moving along as directed, he barely has time to register a slash of colour in the corner of his eye before feeling a hand on his arm.

It's Walker-Talker Man. He looks ready to explode, but Bo reads no threat, maybe because the man's looking right into his eyes instead of focussing over his head or off to the side like most people. Honed by the need to be continuously cautious, Bo's good at reading people, but this is a lot even for him. He seems to be in Walker-Talker Man's head, like he went in right through the eyes. And what a mind to play in—smart but silly, crazy and contradictory, reflections and refractions and inventions everywhere. Before Bo can make sense of the whole, quick as a stray cat Walker-Talker Man slips around him.

"What's the problem here?" snaps Buddy Monk.

"None of your business," the manager says. Backpedalling, he inadvertently steps on the store's pressure mat and a half-dozen Nosey Parkers abandon the checkout line and cluster around the open door for a gander. "I have every right—"

"Keep it to yourself," Buddy interrupts. He cocks his head Bo's way. "Doesn't look to me like this guy's being aggressive, and he's obviously not vending without a license, so before you start exercising your power as palace eunuch of this shithole, Google up the bylaws."

"I'm calling the police." The manager darts a hand to the cell phone holster that's clipped to his belt like a weapon.

"Call up a whole squad," Buddy says, waving Bo to join him. "And while you're at it, keep in mind that cops hate being bothered by bullying little pricks even more than we do."

The manager assesses his position. His supervisor training included a seminar on conflict resolution, but he's found that dealing with the actual public has a way of frustrating the application of lecture notes and role-playing exercises.

Buddy lays a hand on Bo's shoulder. "Tell this guy where to get off. I mean it, go ahead. Call him a name or something, give him a piece of your mind, you'll feel better."

Bo wouldn't know where to begin. The absolute all-time worst thing he's ever said to anyone is *Up your bum with bubble gum*—and that was to a man holding a knife on him.

"All right," Buddy says. "We'll let him get away with it this time."

The manager needs no further encouragement and hustles inside, where's he's cooed at and cosseted by his sympathetic audience till regaining a portion of self-importance sufficient to see him through his shift.

Buddy pulls out a business card. "If you're ever in the neighbourhood."

Bo doesn't get many business cards. Hmmm, let's see . . . it's for a barbershop on Commercial Drive and . . . hold on, not a business card, a coupon! Coupons are the best! It's good for One Free Haircut. Even more exciting, the shop's run by the King of The Buzz Cut. Other than following visits and weddings and watching *The Crown* on the free Netflix that came with his sister's basement apartment, Bo has had few dealings with royalty. There was that man who hung around the Carnegie Centre who was the King of Hardwood Floors on TV before he got into crack and meth. And there was the Queen of Reptiles who used to dance with a snake at the Drake before it closed. Both of them treated him badly, the King by stealing his stuff and the Queen by making fun of him. But that's okay. Bo understands that being addicted to drugs or getting beaten up by customers right after you've given them oral sex behind a dumpster aren't the best incentives to start loving the world. Still, Queen Elizabeth must have tons of people bugging her, and she's always nice.

He adjusts his hat so the feather's sticking straight up again. What a world to produce a day that starts out so badly and turns around so quickly. One minute half-starved and bounced from the grocery store, the next a coupon from a king's representative.

And you never know, Walker-Talker Man might be more than that, he could be part of the royal family, a prince or something, even the King himself!

Hey, wait a minute . . . if the barbershop's on Commercial Drive, then Bo could tie in the haircut with a visit to his sister. Sally loves surprises. Oh, and hey, wait another minute! Even if she's a girl and doesn't go to barbershops, wouldn't it be something if Sally and the King knew each other? It'd be like that actress who went to England and married a prince. He'd check with Walker-Talker Man, but to Bo's great disappointment, when he looks up his new friend is gone.

Gone and moving fast. Heel-and-toeing it slippery-hipped as a race walker, Buddy whips around the corner northbound before hauling up for a red light at Cordova. While monitoring the light and the vehicles streaming one-way eastbound, waiting for the first to change or the second to spring a leak, his mind slews back to the strange little man. The eyes, the way they smacked Buddy with the conjunction of enchantment and exposure, attraction and fear. The only parallel for effect he can draw was his first meeting with Nita, and while any further comparison between the two individuals would be absurd, Buddy's point stands.

He glances at his training watch, up at the light, down to the three lanes of traffic ripping along Cordova, up at the light, down to the vehicles, up at the light, and enough already—Buddy Monk's on the fly, slashing behind a faded blue Econoline van, stutter-stepping to let a deliriously honking BMW zip past so close the side mirror flicks his shirt, sprinting in front of a Cadillac Escalade and finally fetching up on the opposite sidewalk, where he turns toward the fleeing vehicles he's just bested in fair combat and raises his fists in triumph.

Chapter 5

Mum and Al

"Guess what Lippy said this morning." Al's using his feeling-good voice, tender as a bruise.

June wouldn't consider guessing. Lippy has a line for everything from funerals to fortune cookies with fart jokes in between, and she's roundly tired of them. Lippy Delillo she can do without. Last year at a public meeting June rebutted his proposal to ban loiterers from Grandview Park—as if loitering isn't what parks are for, and as if a lone businessman should be able to dictate to the community, and don't get her started all over again—and his response was so demeaning she was compelled to escalate her own argument, which naturally called for counterattacks from Lippy and so on and on, till by the end of the exchange their relationship was a smoking hole in the ground. She hasn't said a word to him since, the prick.

Al knows better, all right, but he'll explode if he can't get it out and there's no one else to serve as an audience. "He said the Arabs invented the zero, so if it wasn't for them, his son's bank account would at least have some numbers in it." Al loses himself in a bout of snorting—*No zero! That Lippy!*

Al's not surprised at June's lack of reaction. She goes all stone-faced at anything to do with Lippy. But he's okay in Al's books. Over the past few years half the shops on the Drive have been brought to their knees—fighting against lease increases, being priced out of the area—and wow, did Lippy ever see that coming. His shop, Cicalone, is a class operation right down the line, no deals or gimmicks or any of that dollar-store baloney. It says it all on the sign: Workout Wear for the Weekend Warrior. Top-of-the-line recreational clothing for everything from capoeira to sailboarding to happy hour at the Cactus Club. To coordinate with the tights, tops, shorts, cross-trainers, suede boxing shoes and stationary-bike gloves, at the end of each aisle is a small glass display case of imported jewellery—delicate chains to weave through the strap of the athlete's GPS watch, onyx flip-lid boxes to store heart monitors, authentic replicas of past Boston Marathon pins, all of it kissed by old-world craftsmanship. Lippy claims his greatest pride comes from never having held a sale in his life, something Al can appreciate. Big numbers on the stickers make for big profits, no? And all this in less than a year in town. Lippy's five other businesses around the country well illustrate his belief in diversification—real estate, footwear, electronics, formal wear for infants, and the Toronto flagship store, Suck It Up, a vapour lounge on the street-level of Canada's highest condo building.

Lippy has money up the you-know-what, yet what really gets Al is we're not talking a snob here. Everybody's family to Lippy Delillo, and that goes for the guys who work for him. No one's beneath his notice so long as they're ready to put in a full day and don't expect the benefits that crush the life out of business. On top of it all—killer jokes. Come on, name another guy who'd have this on the window of his Edmonton footwear boutique: *I Shod the Sheriff But I Didn't Shoe No Deputy*. Of course June doesn't find it funny, even after Al explained it's from that song, that singer, Al forgets his name, one of them Jamaican guys with the hair all scrunched up like Nita's.

Anyways, Al could use some of that. Esposito's—sure, his own name right there on the sign, but look at this place, another day like the one before and probably tomorrow. A small spurt at lunch then crapola till happy hour. And evenings, don't bring it up. Wasn't for the odd hanger-on at the bar who might want a bite, Al would shut down the kitchen as soon as the after-work crowd wandered off. Already they operate off a bare bones menu after five, sometimes pulling the plug by six or seven. After that, Al either heads home if June has help, or if they're short of staff, like way too often, he pitches in while trying to ignore the bar conversation so he isn't up all night with an upset stomach.

Al likes to think of himself as a respectful man. And you know why? He'll tell you why—because he is. One of those guys the country's supposed to be about. Mostly Italian, Al, but some Catalonian in there, bunch of other stuff, even some Slovene. Multi-ethnic is what he's saying, polite for dog's breakfast, a mongrel, and Canada's a good place to be for all that stuff.

He's thankful, he'll tell you that out loud to your face. Living in a free country, though they could tighten the rules on protesters and troublemakers, Al's getting a little tired of some of them bums; a social security net, not so good as it used to be, lots of holes in the net and he's not betting on how it'll work out for the next generation, but still; a house to call his own, but good thing he got in when the getting was good, no way now in Vancouver; a professional police force except okay, some of the guys get out of hand now and again, just to be expected; a good first wife who passed far too young, had a red-hot temper, a real spitfire always embarrassing him in public but good in her heart; and now later in life a partner he'd run in front of bulls for like them crazy Spaniards. He's made a few mistakes along the way, he'll admit that, but even the Pope don't pretend to be infallible no more. So you won't catch Al complaining. He has no time for the whiners, the letters-to-the-editor people. Can't escape it in his own establishment, if you can believe. Every day it's the same thing, having to listen to Buddy and the other local baloney artists tear down a world they done nothing to help build. Talk, talk, alla time talk. They should find some place where they can all be mayor at the same time.

Al stops at the full-length mirror on the wall under the archway to the bar. Sheesh, he's putting on weight. He can barely jam his thumbs behind his belt, seems like he just bought it and already on the last hole. He'll take a look sideways . . . not so good. He's starting to look like one of them inflatable punching-bag clowns, you know the ones, you clobber 'em and they bounce back up. Strong nose, though, and no flabby neck, and a good head of hair, thick and full of real colour, none of that purply-black gunk some of the guys put in to hide the grey.

All of a sudden Al remembers another great line Lippy came up with this morning—he has to charge the prices he does so he can support his wife in the lifestyle to which she's become addicted. Addicted. That Lippy!

Al might never understand how June can turn up her nose at a guy like that yet find Buddy so funny. Her son's jokes are sick, in Al's opinion. Sick. He's no monster or nothing, and he loves his mother even though sometimes you gotta wonder, but he's one of those guys with a position on everything. Backwards position is what Al means, always the other direction from what's tried-and-true. Feed Buddy an idea and before you know it good solid traditional thinking ends up twisted in so many kinks and knots you can't recognize what you were talking about in the first place. That *manga cake* Joseph Smith never went to town on the scriptures the way Buddy can with a simple newspaper. Grocery list, even. And sure enough, now that the subject's in Al's head . . .

"Afternoon, Al," Buddy says. "How're things at the old E. Coli Café?"

See? Sick.

Buddy balks at entering the bar area. "Nita still around?"

"Your wife?" says Al, hoping this is one of those days Buddy's down in the dumps enough to wince at the term. Don't get him wrong, Al's not a mean person, but with Buddy you gotta get a leg up when you can.

No wince from Buddy, a correction: "Ex-wife."

Al gives it another try just in case: "Your wife was gone when I got in. Probably out rescuing killer whales off a beach somewhere, pushing around seal pups in wheel chairs."

"When was that?"

"Ten about. I was a couple hours late. Lippy needed some help at his warehouse."

"Lippy needed help."

Al throws a one-shoulder Italian shrug—hand palm up, shoulder and ear trying to meet halfway. "Friends help friends, simple."

"Lippy Delillo, friend to the world. Two-hundred dollar running pants for sale and his employees make minimum wage. So cheap he hires illegal immigrants to recycle his ass-wipe."

Sick.

"But I couldn't care less," Buddy continues. "Water off a duck's back."

Off a duck's, maybe, but it clings to Buddy's back so tenaciously it could resist a high-pressure air hose. On those occasions when the barber gets around to elevating his snap judgements to considered thought, he admits the greatest irritant is the way Al and his small-business pals hang on Lippy's every word like indentured labourers in hock to the company store.

"He does good around here," Al says.

"Doing good and being a menace aren't mutually exclusive. During the reign of Suleiman, his Head Gardener doubled as Chief Executioner."

"Suleiman? What are you talking? You're just mad about your wife."

"Ex. When's she due back?"

"Ask your mother," Al says. "Anyways, today was just supposed to be a short training session."

"Two-hour shift. Better get used to it."

Al's afraid he'll have to. He likes Nita the way he does certain movie stars—never met any of them, doesn't understand them, but picks his favourites and hopes they don't end up on the news full of drugs and tearing their clothes off at a White House party. Nita's all over the place, and Al's not expecting any proper work ethic, but she's part of the family so far as it stands for now. As for her volunteer stuff, good for her, though in Al's opinion they run a little too much to pie-in-the-sky. He's all for helping people, but he's been around the block enough times to realize charities need an eye kept on them as much as big-shot CEOs. Too many stories about bad apples making off with the funds or taking advantage of their position, mixing up private stuff with public.

On top of that, he's gotta admit Nita makes him a little nervous. Jittery, you know? Like when she walks past with that smell of hers and gives him the beginnings of one of those things guys get between the legs. Or the other way, the bad way, when she's so caught up in a project or civil action it reminds Al of that old movie he saw about the Mau Mau Rebellion, cut-off heads and everything. Anyways, June has a point, they'll be better off even if all Nita does is not rob them blind. It was Al who caught the last employee trying to load the keg of Kokanee onto the 20 bus.

Buddy heads through the arch into the bar area and Al follows. Behind the bar itself along the back wall, June watches her son approach with what she calls Early Years, a look of diffidence he slides into when he's after something, a remnant of his boyhood ability to slick himself up and margarine his way into her good graces. But since it's clear what he wants is information on Nita, his mother parries before he can thrust. "If it isn't the mouse wrangler."

Buddy checks out a stranger under the old picture of the 2006 Italian World Cup Champions, nods down the hardwood to a local and lugs two bar chairs out of the way, depositing them beside the ATM. His mother pushes air out between clenched teeth. Same thing every day. Why he insists on standing when there's a perfectly good place to sit drives June loopy. Little enough thing, she supposes, but the world is made up of little things.

Without looking, Buddy calls, "*Annyeounghaseyo*," loud enough to carry to the front window, where Old Kim has parked his boney, almost non-existent behind. For ages he's been a fixture on the Drive, but had never stopped in at Esposito's till three years ago after his wife died. June worked her usual magic, and since then the friendship has grown till Kim has become as close to being part of the family as his enigmatic personality allows. The dried-leather Korean shop owner is invariably in place minutes after his granddaughter takes over for the last two hours at Take-A-Number Deli, confirmed today when a squeaky laugh spurts out of him like particles from a high-energy collision. "*Annyeounghaseyo,* Mr. Buddy. I think you owe me one beer for the olives yesterday."

Buddy nods, June pours, Al walks it over. "Here you go, sir."

"Fank you, Al," Kim says. "Doan hi-fi me, please."

"What?" Al says. "I never high-fived anybody in my life, why would I start now?"

"Okay. Just I have sore shoulder from unloading big steamship round into cooler."

"By yourself? Aren't the meat delivery guys supposed to handle that? Lemme know when your next order is. The guys I use are the best, I'll steer 'em your way."

Old Kim smiles, raises his glass to both Al and the two Monks at the bar, and sips like a connoisseur.

Our barber responds with a trial mouthful of the pint in front of him. He doesn't much feel like drinking, and he ought to have known there'd be nobody here to talk to about the lawsuit. Even his own mother throws a fit at the mere mention. Particularly his own mother, he should say.

June leans on the bar, arms spread wide. On this subject her son has forfeited any reasonably claim to privacy, and June's going to come right out with it in front of anyone who cares to listen. "I heard all about your plan to take Sally to England."

The local lad down the rail spins on his chair, then quickly reverses the rotation at a look from Buddy. June gallops her fingernails on the bar. Al was filled in earlier and hurries back from Old Kim's table, eager to see the chief baloney artist try to talk himself out of this one.

"Sally?" Buddy says.

"Don't play dumb. Nita gave me the whole story about trying to win bacon at the Cornrow Switch."

"Cornrow Switch. Never heard of it."

"Whatever it's called."

"Dunmow Flitch. And I was just blowing wind up Nita's skirt. Does it sound like something I'd be interested in?"

"It's a competition," June says. "And you're Buddy Monk."

"And Nita's losing her mind."

"You two. I'll never get you two."

"And before you continue your daily summary of my shortcomings—I've given up on the lawyers. Came up empty again this morning. No one left to ask, no interest, no case, no lawsuit. That should keep you happy for the rest of the year. Don't expect a birthday or Christmas present."

June holds her tongue. She's so utterly exhausted by the subject that she feels no sense of triumph. She shouldn't even have tried. How would any mother deal with an adult son intent on suing a lawn bowling association for ageism? But showing satisfaction could easily set him off, so she'll just slide him another beer and plaster on a moronic smile.

Al watches Buddy and his mum yak away awhile before heading to the kitchen. They get it. Al doesn't know how to explain in words what it is, and probably they don't either, but they get it anyways. He's been watching them together for seven years now, and it's like watching those dancers doing what's it called, the lady with the whirling skirt and the snapping fingers overhead and the man stamping his feet—flamenco, that's it—Al doesn't have a clue what the flamenco movements are all about, but wow! the mystery of the dance.

Al's in it for good. That was a foregone conclusion from the minute he saw June Monk on her hands and knees scrambling on the sidewalk in front of Santa Barbara Market. Her bag had split, tumbling her purchases to the ground, and she was grabbing at rolling Roma tomatoes and corralling runaway apples and oranges while keeping up a conversation with someone picking over produce in the outdoor stand. Maybe it was Al's shadow as he stood over her too paralyzed to offer help. Or maybe she sensed him. She raised her beautiful face, looked him right in the eyes, laughed out loud and tried to juggle three oranges. Al's not making this up, she tried to juggle these three oranges and kept at it till they all rolled away. And it was just for him. Other people stopped to watch, sure, but that was for him. He looks at her again behind the bar, where she's laughing with her troublemaking son, and feels shy and mushy and a little bit stupid, the good kind of stupid. He'll tell you this—don't matter how bad she is at juggling oranges, with everything else June's got the best touch around.

CHAPTER 6

YOU NEVER KNOW WHO YOU'LL RUN INTO

Nita's long mantis legs have been propelling her around the track for thirty minutes. She lost count of the laps almost immediately, but that's no issue. Since she's running for the release of the movement, a strict tally of distance is unnecessary. Round and round she goes.

The track lies on Britannia's western flank, far from the madding traffic. Britannia is a miniature village of its own with elementary and high schools, a public library, youth and seniors centres, ice rink and weight room, community programs, job boards. Along with Grandview Park, the northern edge of which it probes with a finger down a back alley, Britannia constitutes the education-recreation nerve centre of the neighbourhood. This late afternoon the track's infield hosts a trio of Frisbee players, a man and his two dogs, individual loungers and strollers, but is empty of organized student activities. Nita has the oval to herself.

Not long after she learned to walk she ran, as if born for rapid motion. She seemed to spend more time running than anything else done upright. She remembers one of Buddy's pet numbers: 11.2 km/sec—escape velocity from Earth. To break free from gravity you can't ease away, you have to put your head down and bolt. Her plan for lifelong fitness was to increase her longest run to match her age, adding a mile a year, aiming for twenty miles at twenty, her first marathon at twenty-six, over time graduating to ultra-marathons. For years she kept to the schedule with little effort, but now she's thirty-eight and her plan has outdistanced her. Maybe she begrudges the time it takes to stick with it. Nita spends her money on time. She works until she has enough to buy another batch—a week, a month—and stops working. The very idea of tying herself to the mast of a job in the middle of a perpetual storm is ludicrous. *What do you do?* is the constant nagging question she's been assaulted with half the days of her adult life. What do I do? I live, dopey.

She's finished another lap, and on reaching the northern end of the oval departs the track on a tangent. She has no firm destination in mind, but with a pile of loonies and toonies from her coin jar, her phone and the key to a roof over her head all wrapped in a sock to keep everything from jingling in her fanny pack, the destination is immaterial. At Clark she cuts north. Ahead at the port are the orange loading cranes, crustacean-looking creatures straight out of a horror movie that cut the mountains into iron-framed patches of forest. At the foot of the overpass to the port lands Nita swerves left and hauls down to Powell, where she stops. No, she'd better walk at least. With the onshore wind, it won't take long for her body heat to dissipate and her hamstrings to tighten. The Gassy Jack statue is just ahead, and she continues along the cobblestones of Gastown till cutting up the slight hill to Hastings.

From half a block away she spies the strange costumed man under the sign for the defunct Loggers Social Club. They're not acquainted, but she's seen him at various fundraising and Downtown Eastside events. There's no telling what he's dressed as today. Dirty bare legs sprouting from oversize boots and disappearing into overlarge shorts, suspenders dangling from one clip as if they've been ripped off his shoulders, white shirt torn and dirty. One eye is swollen, rendering his bizarre features all the more rebarbative.

Bo watches her approach. Her name's Nita. He read it on her nametag at a Pivot Legal Society party in Strathcona Park where they had bands and food and free water. She was running around all day helping out, greeting everyone with that smile people have when they don't really know what they're doing but are happy to keep doing it. Bo understands. People who feel out of place have misplaced their friends, that's all. It's why sometimes they get scared and make mistakes. She looks like she recognizes him, too, so he raises his Bavarian hat to be polite. His suspenders broke earlier and he has to clutch his shorts to keep them from sliding down, and he's a little embarrassed about the hat because the feather's missing and the brim is torn. He still feels like Heidi, but after a good working over with an alpenstock. He's dizzy, and before the lady gets close enough for him to say anything to her, he collapses.

"Are you okay?" Nita says. "Are you hurt?"

Sure. He just dozed off.

Nita helps him to his feet.

What's important now is how to fix his suspenders. Without them he'll have to walk around holding up his lederhosen, and they're so big he has to use both hands. More important, he can't find his feather.

"Don't worry," Nita says. "It'll be around here somewhere."

A small crowd at the nearby bus stop is watching. Bo would wave hello, but there'd go his shorts.

The downtown folks idle in neutral observance. Nothing serious seems to be going down. Bo with his various costumes is a familiar, garden-variety neighbourhood weirdo, and longlegs there volunteers at the Carnegie and anyhow is too exotic and noticeable to be working undercover. They'd be on their way if the bus would just show up, and the second the issue's raised two people step into the street and crane their necks while the rest launch into an informal panel discussion of the matter: *How come every time you want to get somewhere important the bus is late?—Yeah, the more important the date, the later it's late—Hey, that rhymes, the lady's a poet—Thanks, baby—Welcome for sure—Happens to me all the time, want a bus there's no nuthin, but start walkin to the next stop and one streaks past showin you its tailpipe like sayin, "Stick your dick in here, loser"—Who's got a light?—Can't tell me about buses along Hastings, been ridin this route thirty years—Know what drives me to drink is you wait and wait, finally the bus comes along and there's three of the fuckin things piled up behind it in a row—Yeah, yeah, anything drive you to drink—You offerin to do the drivin?—Heh!—It's all the new drivers, they keep losin their poles offa the electric cables, gotta stop every two blocks to run around back and reattach 'em to the lines—God, don't get me started on that, I was right there the day that lady driver got smooshed, end of the pole wouldn't grab onto the overhead cable, right? Kept slippin, and this car or truck, right? It all happened so fast, this car or truck ran her into the back of her own bus, mashed her flat as my wife before the tit job—Man, never heard about that—I forget the year—You forget the year cause it never happened, numbnuts, that's one of them urban myths—Well, it could happen is all I'm sayin, all kinds'a things in the universe could happen while you're jerkin off callin people liars—Hey, it's the bus—Which one?—The 20—Fuck me, right on time.*

"Let's take a look at that eye," Nita says.

Bo's sore all over, especially right here. Hey, where's his . . . oh-oh, his money's gone. Quickly he checks around his feet and in the doorway. He didn't spend it in the Washington market because he never made it that far. Let's see . . . he was asked to leave the new grocery store, he remembers that, then . . . right, he met Walker-Talker Man. But what came after? He was going to sketch the ducks and swans in Lost Lagoon but changed his mind or something. Wait, he didn't have bus fare, that's why he didn't go. So he must have lost the money before. Maybe he laid down for a nap and somebody robbed him. What's the lady saying? And what's her name again? She helps out at the Carnegie Centre, and he saw her at that concert in Strathcona Park, the party with free water and bands—Justice Rocks, he remembers now, it was called Justice Rocks—where people got up on the stage and made speeches. He likes speeches, school for free is the way he looks at it, and—

"I'm Nita. What do you like to be called?"

That's a tough one. Robert is what welfare and Pigeon Park Savings and all the other official places use. Devona uses Bob, or Bobby, and sometimes Mardi Gras. His mummy's favourite name for him was Bo, and that's what he likes the most. It has a nice round sound—Bo, trying saying it, Bo—and that's his sister's name for him too. He'll use that one with the lady.

"As in *Beau Geste?*" Nita says.

No, he's seen that old movie and they spelled it different. Wait a minute, if it was earlier this morning before he put on the Heidi costume, he'd be Bo Jester, which is pretty close to Nita's guess. He laughs at his own joke, a hellish gargle that jets through his teeth—*Yaksputz-figsack-korfle!* The sound has Nita close to pounding him between the shoulder blades before identifying the spitting and wheezing as connected to humour rather than asphyxiation. She's glad she caught herself in time. From the looks of him, a slap on the back could propel his lungs clear out onto the sidewalk.

"Let's get something to hold up those shorts." Nita begins scouring the vicinity for a piece of rope or some wire, anything.

Bo saves elastic bands and has a few in his pocket. He'd reach in himself, but then his shorts might fall down. He cocks a hip.

Nita hesitates. "I'm not going to stick myself on anything in there, am I?"

Yaksputz-figsack-korfle! He'd never use drugs. Nita must be joking.

Carefully she fishes around in the pocket. "A pencil stub."

That's for sketching.

Again into the leather pocket, and Nita emerges with a golf ball-size sphere of multicoloured elastic bands. She rolls it in her fingers. "I don't think these little things will do it."

Bo slants the opposite hip.

Nita pulls out a tangled gillnet of fine string, heavy twine and monofilament ensnaring another stub of a pencil and a business card. Once the mess is sorted, familiar words rise up from the card and deal her a body blow. "Where did you get this?" She fans the card in the air like drying a Polaroid print.

The coupon for a free haircut? From Bo's new friend. He's a prince.

"Yeah," Nita says. "A regular Prince Charming."

Funny, for a while Bo had a Prince Charming costume. He made the high riding boots by taping black garbage bags to his shoes and holding them up over his knees with tape. But when his plastic cape and the big floppy prince hat were stolen, he just looked like a fisherman with homemade rubber boots, and that was the end of that outfit. The story makes the lady laugh.

Nita pokes the card back into his pocket and goes to work. Five minutes of looping and knotting has the lederhosen and suspenders re-mated and Bo ready for his next expedition. Nita steps back, assesses the package and hands him another card. "It'll do more for you than the one from that barber."

Bo brings the card in close. It's from Pivot Legal Society, the people who put on the party in Strathcona. On the face in red bold-faced capitals: STATEMENT FOR POLICE. Inside is a list of charter rights and the procedure for their exercise if stopped and questioned. At the top of the list is the right to silence, already Bo's default position. The remaining points are more detailed, and once the swelling around his eye goes down he'll go over them more closely.

"I hope I haven't made you miss your bus," Nita says.

No. He was thinking of going to visit his sister but remembered she went out shopping for a used pullout couch for when he was staying overnight.

"Good," Nita says. "Because I have a great idea." She turns to the brick building and gestures at the far boarded-up entrance. "This was where The Only seafood place was. Remember the sign? That cool neon seahorse above the waves? And their famous chowder? Before they closed, my mum and dad would take me there whenever we were downtown. I know another place like that not far from here, and I've run a long ways and can't make it home without eating. So what do you say we have an early supper together. I started a new job this morning, so I can treat."

Bo would like that. But only if next time the treat's on him.

"Fair enough," Nita says, and along the street they go.

At the restaurant, Bo allows Nita to hold the door for him, though it should be the other way around. Respect for ladies is one thing Mummy taught him. He wishes he could remember more about his mummy. He's asked his sister a million times, but Sally doesn't like it when he brings the subject up. It's just the two of them, she keeps saying, just them two and Devona.

The fish-house warmth wraps him up in its arms. Some Monday—a free haircut coupon, a free meal, and two new friends, a prince and a sort of princess. All that's left is how to explain to the princess that he's allergic to seafood.

Chapter 7

Monk Business

Aside from some activity at the markets, there's no rush left on the street. Only a few folks, the grind of Monday's reacquaintance with work behind them, are still on the trail home.

Buddy's moving as slowly as the rest, tired players slogging their steel-toed way along the sidewalks, stickered hardhats strapped to backpacks, hi-visibility vests, boxes of beer in split-nailed hands. Others roll past and around, step out of Range Rovers and BMWs, happily up to their armpits in the waters of lifestyle maintenance. Those from the outdoors are putting in overtime, hands out, caps extended, samples of carved wood going cheap, used paperbacks for sale, magazines.

Locals with rolled mats under their arms and various models of asses and reproductive parts cradled in spandex are passing Buck-A-Slice on their way to the adjoining Yogi Bear Yoga studio. Buddy keeps an eye out for Nita. He can't summon enthusiasm for yoga, maybe if it involved tackling, but on those days he catches Nita on her way to or from class he's somehow reassured. Physical activity of any kind was a safe topic between them. And how pitiful is that—to think a topic had to be certified safe before they wrestled with it.

Agitated, he leaves the citizens to their activities and ducks into Esposito's. Through the empty restaurant he goes and right to the empty bar.

"Back again," June says to her son while wiping the hardwood for the sake of the motion. "You and the mouse have a fight?"

The closer Buddy gets, the more she regrets the crack. June was wondering when the bottom would fall out. A split after many years of marriage is one thing. Despite the freight of sorrow, it requires a complete life overhaul, opening a door to a new world of possibilities. But her son and Nita are too close to the start to forget what it was all about. The beauty of the beginning and the ugliness of the end haven't enough intervening years acting as an analgesic. For once, Buddy uses a bar chair for its designed purpose and slings himself aboard. June finds it strange to see him sitting down. It makes him look short and awkward, a trained chimp hamming it up for the cameras. She's changed her mind. When Buddy hang-dogged through the arch, she considered letting the Lawnmower Glitch incident slide for the time being. But he'll never recover without facing up to the inglorious episode. "Shall we pick up from where we left off earlier?"

"We were talking about how slow business is getting." Buddy swivels to the empty room and spreads his arms.

"No, we were talking about you trying to win bacon in a foreign country. The Marlow Witch or whatever that bloody thing is called."

"Dunmow Flitch," Buddy says. "I told you that was all a bunch of bullshit to needle Nita."

"And you were lying. At least on some level. Well done. My son lost his wife trying to win bacon."

"Any idea how many pigs have lost their lives over bacon?"

"Yeah, yeah, joke. I can hardly wait to tell the girls at Bingo."

"You always use that Bingo line, but you don't go. You never compete in anything. That's why you can't understand the joy of winning."

"What joy do you experience? The only thing I've ever seen is that wolf grin like you just dragged down a crippled moose."

"There's no fun in competing just for fun," Buddy says.

"That's your dad talking."

"That's you saying he was wrong about everything."

June swallows her next comment—wasn't CC wrong? Wasn't he as wrong as a man can be? Half a lifetime on the fishboats bucketing along on his own course, coming home between contracts only to take her to task for everything that went wrong in his absence. She was wrong? The only one holding the household together was wrong? It hurt bad and it hurt often, even before she learned he had more experience than she did with households. "I started a list yesterday," she says.

Buddy doesn't ask. He's going to get it regardless.

"At the top is your eating contests, probably because in a city of soup lines and with half the world starving they're so vulgar. All I have down so far is pie, hot dog, rib, oyster, meat ball and perogy. The time you had your stomach pumped—was that oyster or perogy? Never mind, I'm recording them all. Games, that's another category. Cheating to win the Grade 6 crokinole championship, I put that one at the top. Sports has its own page, might take up a whole binder. Remember your local semi-pro wrestling debut? You haven't forgotten that. At the Russian Community Centre where you were thrown over the top rope by the cook from the old Avanti's Pub. The whole thing had been scripted and you still ended up with a broken nose and a concussion. And how about when you went you tried to gain an advantage by going out for the Scribes over-forty rugby team when you were thirty-two? Banned from the club for life."

Buddy waves it off: "Old news. So long ago The Captain and Tennille was her and a sergeant."

"It doesn't matter how old the news, you haven't changed. The Dunsmuir . . . aaaaagh!"

"Dunmow Flitch."

"Dunmow Flitch, Dunmow Flitch, Dunmow Flitch . . . was just three months ago. And as we speak, you're in the process of suing The East Vancouver Lawn Bowling Association."

"Just because I'm not in my dotage? Ageist bastards."

"There's a pattern here. When you were younger, you tried to sneak into a rugby league so you could compete against middle-age men, and now that you're middle-age yourself, you want to play bowls against seniors. What do you have against people older than you? Should I be watching out for my job?"

"You're missing the point," Buddy says. "The B.C. *Human Rights Code* guarantees equal treatment. Age discrimination may happen when, I quote, '. . . a rule, condition, policy or practise that is the same for everyone has an unfair effect on a person because of their age.' We let this slip and the next thing you know—"

"The next thing you know," June cuts in, "people like you will nitpick the legal system to a standstill. And besides, when did you climb aboard the social justice bandwagon? You used to say Nita was gunning for the Nobel Peace Prize while you were gunning down food for the table. Or in your case, clipping and shaving."

How would Buddy's father have answered? Not a single thing springs to our barber's mind. For all CC's talk of fighting his way to the top in a dog-eat-dog world, he hadn't an ounce of fight in him.

"I should have gone home when Al closed the kitchen," June says. She examines the place as though seeking an obvious flaw. It isn't the menu, nothing wrong with the service, decor's not repellant, no phony theme, never major trouble at the bar. Maybe that's it. She's just described it to herself as a series of negatives. The place isn't one specific thing, has no sense of what to do with itself beyond its primary function. But what's the solution? They're not about to turn it into one of those wannabe-swank clones with half-brainless cheerleaders for staff and a bar area full of businessmen playing characters from *Mad Men*.

Buddy joins her look around. "You need an attraction, a hook, something to make the place stand out."

"I suppose you have a plan."

"People love competitions."

"You love competitions. If we brought in midget wrestling, you'd cut off your legs to sign up."

"Depends. Senior midgets?"

"*Pff!*"

"I'm outta here."

"I'll join you. Let me lock up and I'll do the cash in the morning."

Buddy struggles off his chair, banging an ankle on the foot rail—see what a man gets for sitting down?—and makes his way outside, where he waits for his mother to set the alarm. "Walk you home?"

"Partway," June says. "I think I'm going to duck into the Libra Room for a little light jazz and a drink. It's so seldom I get off the path between home and the restaurant. I don't even buy groceries if I can't get them on the way." A short distance down the street she pulls up. "This is far enough. I'll go on alone from here."

"Positive?" Buddy says.

June lights a cigarette and inclines her head toward the building beside them, where through Yogi Bear Yoga's pastel window coverings blurred silhouettes are sliding from one posture to the next. "Mondays she takes the evening class. They'll be letting out soon."

Buddy watches the coolest old broad he knows jaywalk through the gloaming before shaking himself like a drenched retriever and turning toward the studio.

*

The class is winding down. Fragrance of sandalwood overlying the light perspiration from bodies supine on their mats, subdued lighting, subliminal message of peace. The instructor, sitting cross-legged at the head of the room, is looking through him with a hazy expression that somehow translates as a smile. When a gentle tinkling of bells emerges from a hidden speaker, the participants rise like spirits and begin returning their various pillows and pads to a storage area in the back.

The ambience is transitory. By the time the class has filtered out back to the parking area, the instructor is speculating on whether she's going to get laid tonight, a young woman is lighting a cigarette and a slender dreamy-eyed man in a skullcap and purple caftan is loudly motherfuckering whatever shit-lover ticketed his car for the second time in a week. Nice while it lasted, though.

Nita leads the way down the street. "You don't have to add your two cents' worth," she says.

"I like it," Buddy says. "Who wouldn't need a release after all that calming down?"

She has to laugh. "Great activity, but it's like any group, made up of all sorts. The only unanimity seems to be a love of Lululemon."

"I've often wondered about how a company can make millions upon millions of dollars on yoga wear. I thought one of the attractions of the discipline is the simplicity of the gear, that you don't need to go broke buying equipment."

"What do you know about yoga?" she says.

"Not much. But I figure once you get your mat and helmet, you should be good to go, right?"

Maybe it's the pacific high from the hour of concentration that sends Nita into a fit of giggles. Buddy keeps his mouth shut and lets her roll, enjoying the sound, bathing in the lightness. He risks a longish look at his ex-wife—in fact it's only a separation, a term they avoid for its connotations of wishy-washy resolve and false hope—and his heart drops a little. So good, so close, yet scored into his memory is the view of her at her laptop, hair pushed up with a scarf into a mobcap of furry tentacles, face hidden down close to the keyboard, elbows out, tirelessly assembling another tract for another cause, patiently protesting, doggedly determined, while he sat across the room by himself or rolled through the place alone.

Nita's laughter is cut off when an awkward footstep raises a twinge. After the day's long run she thought of skipping class, but decided the extra exercise load would be offset by the benefits of the stretching. She almost missed the session as it was, rushing from the hospital only after Bo was out of danger.

They'd finished their chowder and were sharing an order of mussels when he flung back his head, trachea visibly spasming through his parchment skin, narrow chest heaving in streaky scraps of air. While Nita was punching 911 a customer ran out and hailed a cab, and they hit St. Paul's in under ten minutes. Once Bo's condition stabilized, he apologized for putting her to all the trouble and made her feel smaller than she already did by thanking her profusely for the meal of what turned out to be pernicious allergens. The doctor decided to keep him overnight, and once Bo dozed off Nita quietly left.

Nita stops. She's slightly taller than Buddy and goes up on her toes to emphasize the difference. "What's this scam you're running? Tell me you're not papering the Downtown Eastside with those things, that you're not scrounging for suckers among the homeless."

Her leaning into him like this, smelling of sandalwood and herself, provokes his cock into uncoiling from its sleeping position and raising its head cobra-like to see what all the hubbub's about. "What?" he croaks. "I have no idea what you're talking about."

Betrayed by her weary calves, Nita settles onto her heels without settling down. "A friend of mine had one of your so-called free haircut cards."

"What kind of scam could I possibly run off that?" He's so genuinely aggrieved that both Nita and his cobra wind their necks in. "Contrary to what you believe . . . no, it doesn't matter, you don't listen to anything I say that doesn't agree with your preconceptions."

"Not *pre*conceptions," Nita says. "Actual conceptions derived from experience."

"It's just marketing, trying to shake things up a little at the shop."

"You can't fool me anymore. Not anymore, you can't."

"This friend of yours, fairy-tale-looking guy? Like he lives under a bridge waiting to spring out at billy goats?"

"He can't help how he looks."

"Never said he could."

"Bo, his name's Bo."

"As in *Beau Geste?*"

"Bo Derek, Bo Diddley," Nita says. "Look, I have to get home." He's like fibreglass insulation under a flannel shirt, itching so bad all she wants to do is rake her skin with her nails till drawing blood. She wants home. Home, take a shower and curl up in front of a roaring . . . well, a roaring plug-in heater.

"How's work going?" Buddy says.

"June showed me the ropes. I can handle it awhile, I guess. Oh, and she told me about your mice."

"Singular. One mouse."

"Do you have a name for it?"

"Don't be ridiculous."

The second appearance by the visitor was the night after their first introduction. By then Buddy had found its entry point, a hole in the baseboard behind the clawfoot tub. Mice sweep their heads in the back-and-forth search pattern even if food is placed directly in front of their noses, but this little nightstalker just gulped the hard scrap of cheese rind Buddy had set down and continued on its merry splay-footed way, canvassing the apartment as if evaluating its merits as a summer home. Naturally the naming would have to take into account the deformities—the strange patch of long back hair, the partially flattened head, the reptilian rear carriage. In olden days, special forces were associated with the disfigured and misshapen, and if on the downside deformed slaves were sometimes kept by wealthy Romans for entertainment, it said more about the wealthy Romans than anything else. More uplifting is that at many times in history the afflicted have been associated with good fortune and were allowed wide licence in behaviour.

Buddy cracked a beer, and as he watched the miniature rover his mind skipped through history, thoughts of the Romans and their slaves narrowing to the image of Caesar, leading to his horse, which was deformed with polydactylism—extra toes—the same condition borne by Alexander's horse, Bucephalus. And just like that Buddy had the name. On his hands and knees he leaned over the mouse—by now investigating a stack of DVDs, likely looking for the latest Pixar release—and rained down a single drop of beer on its head. Using the translation for Bucephalus, he pronounced, "I christen thee *Oxhead*." Then they partied, Buddy doing most of the drinking, Oxhead most of the squeaking.

"I'm glad you haven't gone completely psycho," Nita says. "Don't name it. Once it has a name it's in your heart for good, and I don't see any future for you and mice."

"How did we get here?"

"This isn't the time."

"I mean geographically. We're almost at Venables."

They pivot this way and that like travellers having miraculously survived the plunge from a disintegrating Boeing. "We got turned around," Nita says, and back they go down the street, fully aware they're retracing the route of three years ago, when the love and the tears began.

Their second meeting was vastly more satisfying than the first. True, the initial encounter had wrapped up with Buddy throwing Nita out of the shop, so anything after that could hardly fail to be an improvement. Nevertheless.

He was shopping in Santa Barbara Market when his eye was caught by a collection of twisted hanks of hair above the shelves of pasta. He opened with an apology disguised as an explanation, an overripe bit of blather that veered off topic immediately. Nita let him ramble on, and by the time she paid for her groceries and was halfway down the block, he'd talked himself out. She asked him on a date. The exact word wasn't used in case it stirred him to thoughts of dinner, dancing or anything else stereotypically romantic that has never failed to leave her flat. Instead she proposed a walk. That's all, she stated emphatically, a visit to Lynn Canyon for a walk over the suspension bridge and through the forest. They could talk along the way. Buddy accepted as though it were his proposition, and an hour later they met up back on the Drive.

When a large urban area is so situated that major trailheads are serviced by public transit, taking a car seems more like commuting than recreation, so they hopped on the bus. Not that they had much choice. Nita doesn't own a license and Buddy's has been revoked. Nita has never learned to drive; Buddy has learned never to.

Their route was a section of the Baden-Powell Trail in North Vancouver, and they went at it with a will. The jaw-dropping lookouts, the pungent evergreen musk, the silent duff-padded footpaths, the drama of the Lynn Canyon Suspension Bridge—all of it was missed by the two chatterboxes fairly race-walking their way along the trail, carving past other hikers without comradely acknowledgment, ranting about the self-obsessed society they were coming close to epitomizing, in their hearts reverential but imposing themselves on the wilderness like turncoat forest gods. Nita's long legs and distance-runner's constitution gave her an advantage, allowing her to pull slightly ahead on the uphill portions, but she hadn't been seriously training and on the descent had to slow so much to recover that Buddy, chugging and blowing, would catch up. Both would have liked nothing more than to stop for a rest or a look-see, but that would be to admit that, well, you see how it was. Once out of the forest and on the 210 Vancouver bus arching its way over the hump of Ironworkers Memorial Bridge, mild panic began to set in. Two fiercely independent souls, already into it over their heads, silently calculating the costs of compromise.

Near dark now. The sidewalks are fullish but you wouldn't know it by Buddy and Nita. They're blocking pedestrian traffic at the corner of Graveley, hearts as confused as minds, each of them sad in his or her unique way.

"I have a favour to ask," Nita says.

"I have a few ideas to generate more income," Buddy says. "And business is bound to pick up. No matter how bad a recession, people need to get their hair cut if just to apply for a job."

"What? No, no, that's not the issue. You help out plenty and I appreciate every bit of it. I do."

"You're having a hard time getting it out," Buddy says. "Is it that bad?"

Nita shakes her head. "I want you to drop the lawsuit. I'm calling it a favour because if you think it's advice you'll freeze up. I want you to drop it—let me finish, I won't bring it up again . . . Thank you. Now, this has nothing to do with me, okay? We're not together. I don't have to go through things like this with you anymore. Lawn bowling for godsake, but I promised myself not to . . . I just want you to let it go. For yourself."

"I gotta get home," Buddy says. "Busy day tomorrow."

"All I'm saying is you don't have to try so hard. You don't have to try at all."

By the time he's climbing the stairs to his apartment, Buddy has manufactured three or four, eight, a dozen, twenty-plus, fifty-or-more exceptionally good responses for the crazy woman he made the mistake of getting involved with, all of which will have to wait.

Halfway through a third set of handstand pushups, a miniature beastie enters the top of his sightline and stops to watch. Buddy kicks off the wall. "It's my main man, Oxhead. Hang on a minute, mister." He grabs a beer from the fridge and a pinch of steel-cut oats from a glass jar and jabs on the computer. From semi-recline in his Value Village springback, Buddy rains oatmeal manna down on the creature, whose spread legs preclude sitting back on his haunches like a normal mouse, forcing him to tie into his feed like an iguana.

Buddy turns out the apartment lights to see out the window. Air dead calm under a sky monochrome and featureless. The occasional car slides past, parcels of foot traffic. Maybe he's fooling himself, maybe Nita's gone forever.

"Look at me," he says with the unselfconsciousness of a man with a rodent audience. "My mum and Nita, both of them. Getting so I can't walk a girl home anymore."

Oxhead nods. Tell him about it.

Chapter 8

Thoughtful Crossing

The judder of the screws biting into the salt chuck is felt clear up to the cafeteria, sending tremors through Louie Zimbot's legs and prompting a merry dance from his coffee mug. He makes no attempt to arrest its traverse of the laminate tabletop, hoping the dreadful brew skips over the retaining edge and dashes itself to the deck.

Almost missed the boat. He left Comox with plenty of time to spare, but an accident on the inland route diverted him to the Old Island Highway along the coast. Was a day he'd fuel himself with a belly full of brave and go barrel-assing down the sinuous two-laner in the pitch dark with the pedal floored, the radio jacked and his arm around a lady of similar worldview. But shenanigans like that are long behind him.

In Nanaimo, the crew for the last ferry of the night out of Departure Bay was waving on the final few cars when Louie slung his rusty half-ton around the curve at the bottom of Brechin Road and took aim at the ticket booths. Once through, he was faced with an expanse of empty boarding lanes and could have driven right into the mouth of the big Queen if the truck hadn't gone all sulky and quit for the third time in a month, which is to say the only times he's had it out over that period. He stumped his way aboard, thanked the lower-deck crew for not making him go up and around to the foot passenger gangway, and through fumes of gas, grease and steel made his way to the stairwell.

Abandoning the coffee, he picks up a ticket at the Pacific Coach desk and heads for the night air. Alone against the railing, a smoke going, gentle exhalations being torn from his mouth by the wind and dumped astern above the chuck. Pulling fifteen to eighteen knots by Louie's reckoning, though he finds it hard to tell from five stories off the surface. He's never been fond of large vessels, not after so many years of hugging the water in the troller. A thousand-and-one days and nights of remembrance on the old tub out in the swells. How about the season he hit big off the Charlottes, got greedy and overloaded, coming into the mainland met the fresh water of the estuary and thought they were headed right to the bottom, riding lower and lower in the decreasing buoyancy till the water came up over the deck, there they were wallowing along with no more than ten square feet of freeboard forward and the cabin awash till the engine finally waved the white flag and they had to be towed in. Short, it's a short season, fishing, and who can tell when you go out how long the run will last. You just go out, that's all, go on out and make what money you can.

The old boat served him right, he'll give it that. First craft he owned, first and last, and considering it doubled as his living quarters during the season, a bargain it surely was. He laughs at how big his balls were at that age to plunge into it the way he did. He'd fished recreationally throughout his teen years and wasn't a stranger to boats and the sea, but didn't really know what he was getting into, what the difference was between fishing and being a fisherman. If not for the older men willing to help out with advice and teach him about engines—that part's always been his short suit, just ask his truck—he might have starved. All right, that's stretching it. Only passable with a boat, but he sure could catch fish. No fish-finding sonar, no bugger-all, just a gut feel for bringing in a catch, likely could have done so out on the chuck with water wings and a dip net. Took him awhile to learn the boat though. Hell, it wasn't till the first overhaul with the engine pulled and hanging from chains in the hoist that he discovered the false bottom.

The hidden hold averaged twenty inches deep running from the engine compartment bulkhead to somewhere short of the bow, and next time he was in Victoria, Louie did some checking at the records office and the archives. Turned out the troller had spent its early years as a rum runner. It was fully licenced and geared up to fish, and did so, but along the way had undergone elective surgery to illegally haul booze. The limited storage capacity would suggest a modest operation, probably confined to small towns on the Olympic Peninsula and throughout the San Juan Islands, cut short when the vessel was impounded shortly before the Volstead Act was repealed. It raised his status some, owning a vessel with a history. Skippering something with a rep of any kind, especially unsavoury, had a cachet all its own. Probably does to this day.

Ferry deck now. Moon and stars shrouded in cloud, ocean furrowed by their passage as though for planting, bow wave a-sparkle with bioluminescence—comb jellies and dinoflagellates and other invertebrate sea critters tossing Louie Zimbot flickering winks and nods. All so beautiful from here on deck, but cold, can't take it like he used to. Once back inside, and after a stroll past the gift shop and the kids' play area, the snack bar and the computer tables—the whole time yakked at by TVs, the play-by-play of a game of some kind and news updates on this and that, he can't escape it even on a ferry—Louie eases into a leatherette seat and opens his satchel. His former deckhand's informal will and testament is there, Louie's shaving kit, and look at this—the sandwich and banana he forgot about. In his last-minute dash he left the suitcase with a change of clothes in the truck, but he can pick up whatever he needs in the city.

With the ship stealing up on Horseshoe Bay, Louie heads back out to the railing. From this angle the lights of Vancouver shine diffusely from behind the mountains as from an outdoor concert bowl, a dull radiance illuminating the underside of the cloud cover, lightly pulsing as the moist air reflects and refracts.

His mind slews to Charlie's will. Two weeks back, after the medevac chopper whisked the resuscitated diver from the harbour, the young men who found him switched tanks and went down for another look. Poking around at their leisure, they discovered the false bottom, which was partially detached from the boat. They assumed it was it from natural decomposition. Had it torn loose on impact when the troller sank, anything that tumbled out would surely over the years have been found, buried in sediment or displaced by the current. But sitting out in the clear was a waterproof lock box the size of a large cookie tin. The divers apologized for having opened it, but Louie assured them that to have done otherwise would have shown an abnormal lack of curiosity for adventurous explorers such as themselves. The flattery raised a pair of humble grins and the passing over of the only items found inside, two sheets of paper. They hadn't disturbed the site any more than scooping up the box and, well, okay, sorry, they couldn't resist removing the cleat the trapped dude's regulator hose had snagged on. Of course they considered the cleat Louie's property, but after having their video stolen by that fuckin cop, it'd be nice if, you know, they had a memento. To their great pleasure, Louie agreed.

When the call comes for bus passengers to proceed to the lower vehicle deck, Louie fingers his ticket and makes his way below. The smell of mingled oil and sea advertises itself as he boards the coach and takes a seat in the very back, where the blue disinfectant from the washroom is pitching a competing fragrance. The ferry docks, without so much as a touch of the wooden guides. The bus growls to life and rolls off.

Partway up the climb to the Upper Levels Highway, a long-lost but instantly placeable feeling insinuates itself into Louie's private musings. How many years? How many years of mucking around the Comox Valley, meals alone, beers with anyone willing to stand at the bar and help him pile fresh lies on stale stories, hours upon hours on the flats of Kye Bay poking around the tide pools? He's been content in a sort of numb unchallenged way, but now in the space of two weeks here he is with the travel gear of a hobo heading for whatever the hell this is he's getting himself into. Maybe he's dropping a line into waters intended for younger men, but what of it? Wouldn't be the first time he's been called a halibut short of a fish fry. He has a job to do, a duty, and that's all that needs to be said. As with anything of weight, failure is in attendance, ready to swoop and foul the works, a state of affairs Louie Zimbot accepts with grace. He's a man on a mission. Mighty fine.

Chapter 9

Coupon For a Cut

Buddy's scraping the daily *YOULYSSES* tag from the window when the simultaneous arrival of three customers announces the kickoff of his work day. He waves them in, and fifteen minutes later two of them have been dealt a cropping that would satisfy a drill sergeant—tight to the scalp with barely a lick on top. Just like that the lineup is down to one, a nearly bald senior with the air of a man satisfied to spend the rest of the day sitting exactly where he is.

"What'll it be today?" Buddy says after the gentleman has creaked across the tile and eased himself into the chair.

The customer takes a minute to study himself in the mirror, turning this way and that as if expecting the scarcely detectable hair fringing his head like a victory wreath to suggest something novel. Chuckles. "Just get it up off my shoulders."

In contrast to the previous rehearsals, what ensues is full-dress theatre. Twenty minutes later Buddy's still caught up in superfluous business, clipping near-invisible segments, swooping and darting the scissors in great exaggerated arcs. Between the two men pass tales of much swagger and little truth. A tidal flow of TV references, neighbourhood gossip, results of recent boxing matches, off-colour jokes, in-house badinage, old-fashioned joshing, nickname calling, the pulling of pissers. After an elaborate manufactured argument over the size of the tip, the old man leaves happily cackling.

Barely into the work day, Buddy's already weighing the merits of locking up and poking a stick at what the street has to offer. But comes the dingle of the door's bell, and in walks a customer whose particoloured hat and floppy boots are doing some dingling of their own.

Bo's feeling pretty good. He was told by the nurse at the hospital last night to drink plenty of water, so when he got home he nursed from the copper pipe over the sink till his belly bulged. After that, he scrunched under the covers on the mattress and was soon dreaming of the Renaissance Faire. Not the old dream of his dad getting angry at the ticket man, no. In this one they strolled through the crowd of lords, ladies, princes, knights, troubadours and minstrels and ate meat with their fingers off metal plates and drank root beer from big mugs with glass bottoms. Then they went for a walk up the small river that ran through the park, following the twists and turns through picnic spots toward the mountains. They hit thickets and scrub bush low in the valley, and before the ground started to rise they stopped and sat beside each other on the cool grass at the edge of the water. His dad smoked a cigarette and flicked the butt into the river, where it swirled near the shore until being pulled away downstream. When they got up, their bums were wet and his dad joked about it. First time ever for that dream, and on awakening he put it down to something he ate at the fish place with Nita, a pretty harmless side effect considering what he'd eaten almost killed him.

His head is clearer than it was yesterday, and it takes only a few minutes of searching to find the new coupon in his yodelling shorts. By now he's shaken the notion that the King of the Buzz Cut is true royalty, but a king is a king is a king. With his interpretation of a courtly flourish, Bo presents the coupon for One Free Haircut.

Buddy scrutinizes the card as though unsure of its provenance and hands it back. "Your name's Bo, that right?"

How would Walker-Talker Man know that? It's like magic! He pats down his pockets. Don't tell him he forgot . . . ah, here it is.

"A picture of John Travolta in *Grease,*" Buddy says. "This is the haircut you want, a pompadour?"

Bo nods. Yes, please, if His Majesty would do him the favour.

Buddy laughs like hell. "Okay, get the hat off and let's take a look. Turn around. Turn back to me. All right, Bo, there's a big steel sink in the back. I want you to get your head in there and wash your hair. Use a whole bottle of shampoo if you need to, and it wouldn't hurt to get some on that clown bodysuit thing you're wearing."

Not a clown, a jester. They're different.

"I'll take your word for it," Buddy says.

Thank you.

"Hang on—I'll be back in a minute."

On Buddy's return from upstairs, Bo's still messing around at the sink. "Never mind about that," the barber says, "Put this on." Buddy hands him an old UBC sweatshirt that nearly reaches his knees. "If you're comfy, climb aboard the chair and let's see what we can do."

Bo rolls the sleeves up till they're bunched around his arms and settles in.

Buddy's ready to launch. Clipper guards aligned shortest-to-longest on the narrow shelf under the mirror, scissors close at hand, three combs in the breast pocket of the Hawaiian shirt he uses as a barber jacket. His first pompadour. Hmmm . . . cut the sides shorter than the top and pull them to the rear . . . pare down the back by eye . . . for the all-important hump over the forehead leave the hair long, mash in a goodly amount of gel, comb appropriately, adjust accordingly. Make it up as he goes, is what he's saying.

He begins the affair with his favoured implement, the #8 clippers, that vibrating darling with the gnashing underbite. For a time all goes well. He is, however, dealing with the relatively manageable corona, and soon enough is faced by the main body of hair, a forest in a matrix of sand, street grit, sweat, dark memories, sorry news and a wad of Juicy Fruit. An experimental run is aborted when the clippers grind to a halt. The overheated implement is put aside, and with a hand callused from the weightlifting bar the barber clamps onto his largest shears.

Preliminary topping clears elbow room for the full harvest, and Buddy works his way deeper into the woods, with wholesale abandon falling stands of old growth and secondary timber, hacking, hewing. To bring his weight to bear he leans in, severing one clotted bundle after another, the larger ones impacting the tile floor with audible thumps. The violence of the affair pushes Bo over sideways, forward, to the other side, round-and-round the mulberry bush. Panting, the barber steps back to assess his progress on a head that at this stage looks like an aerial view of a mixed-crop farm.

Bo feels good. Other than being a little dizzy from all the shoving, this is the most comfortable he's been in a long time. The barbershop's warm and dry, and because the sweatshirt leaves room for two more of him in there, the extra fabric presses down with the reassuring weight of a greatcoat. The chair is solidly padded and spins smoothly and silently. The shop is warm and dry, if he forgot to mention that. And it's quiet, the only sound the crunching of the scissors.

Renewing the campaign before he starts to cramp, Buddy recaptures the clippers, reduces an acre of gorse to stalks, roots out patches of bulrushes from around the ears, and abandons the clipper guard to deal with a dense underlying mat of moss that's mated like Velcro. The buzzing blades twice need unclogging, but eventually he horses them around the back and sides and returns to the scissors. Easier going now, the small pair will do just fine. Snip-snip, a snip here, a snip there, snippety-snip, a snip at anything with the nerve to poke its head above the crowd. Right. Styling time. Once an island of manoeuvring space amid the shaggy deadfall on the floor is swept clear, the barber applies half a tub of gel to the customer's head and finishes up with the styling comb.

Bo turns his head this way and that, and with the help of King Walker-Talker Man's hand mirror gets a look at the back. His head feels no lighter—the weight of the gel almost matches that of the lost hair—but he's sleeker, that's for sure. In the mirror he looks like a seal. Well, a seal in a motorcycle helmet. When he leans his head down for a better look at the top, a hand-sized wedge of shellacked hair detaches from the main coif, pivots as on a hinge and flops out into space. He straightens his head and the gummy forelock slaps back into place. Bo giggles and tries it again—head down and the gelled mat flops forward, head up and the mat whaps back. Head down, flop. Head up, whap. *Yaksputz-figsack-korfle!*

"You having a good time with that?" Buddy laughs. He runs the comb through a few more times to cut the concentration of hair product before sliding off the cape.

Bo pulls on his belled hat, now far too large but thanks to the styling gel more securely fastened to his head than ever. Then his eyes widen and he takes a step back from the window.

On the sidewalk, Old Kim is sweeping. Three times a day he whisks the pavement in front of Take-A-Number Deli and the barbershop. Bent in the back to start with, hunched over the broom the deli owner looks like a question mark mugging an exclamation point. Sweep and shuffle forward, sweep and shuffle. From across the street, head down, wraparound sunglasses, blind to his trajectory, comes a cyclist in thrift store camouflage. In a whirl of spokes he vaults the curb and finally looks up. Slewing on locked-up brakes, at the last possible second his rear tire loses purchase and the wheel flicks out, knocking Old Kim on his boney behind and tipping the rider from his bike. In a jumble of metal, pedals and army surplus khaki, the shabby soldier of fortune hits the concrete. Immediately he's up, screaming at Kim and remounting his bike. Buddy has already hurdled a table and is out the door as fast as it's possible to cover the distance. The grubby guerrilla has crossed the street to the far sidewalk and the barber gives chase, sprinting hard through traffic. Tires screech, horns blare, Buddy runs. The cyclist turns into Grandview Park, almost creaming a pedestrian in front of the cenotaph, leaps one of the curved concrete benches, and with middle finger raised behind his back sails off toward the horizon. Buddy gives up the unequal chase and pounds the flats of his hands on the concrete, which as a tranquilizer works about as well as it ever does.

Back on the sidewalk, Old Kim is dusting off his pants. "Lot of people in big hurry," he says. "Should stop and smell a flower."

"I stop and smell and there goes the neighbourhood." Buddy tips up his chin and looks down his nose as though expecting to see the enemy disappearing over the horizon. "I'm going to start setting out those spike strips the cops use to keep cars from fleeing. Blow that bastard right off his bike."

"I invite him in some time. Any customer good customer. I sell almost nuffing yesterday. Maybe change name of shop to Old Kim, King of Meat. Two king side-by-side, big tourist attraction. Get haircut while waiting for slice cold cut. Any idea be better than now. Water slide in alley. Poker game in back room. Stage in basement, dancer show her bare bum." He screeches one of his torturous laughs and returns to his broom work, scratching out short strokes over and over.

"Hey, did you see where that little guy went?"

"Man with giant sweatshirt? Number 20 bus come, he get on."

Buddy stares up the street as though following the route to Hastings. He could use a beer. Maybe he should lock up for a couple hours, cruise over to Esposito's, see what's up. Check that thought—what's up is Nita's first full shift. And he's barred from his other regular spot, The Dime, for the incident with the fridge. On the the off chance of corralling a stray, he checks the storage closet at the back of the shop, but comes up empty. Hmm, now what?

Chapter 10

Deal Him In

"Like the pirate said to his freeloading son, 'Prepare to be room-and-boarded.'" Judging by the look on June's face, Al should have kept Lippy Delillo's latest joke to himself.

"When are we going to replace the cook?" June says. "Lunch was madness. Nita's just finding her footing and you weren't answering your phone. Have I ever complained about your early mornings with your friends? Never. But it's one-thirty and this is the first breath I've taken."

Al risks a glance around. Three people at a table nursing their coffees. What, a busload of tourists ran in, ordered all at once and ran out? Lunch might have been a little busy but it's never madness, not around here. He leads June through the archway before she starts yelling and clears the remaining customers. "Lippy called a meeting," he says with a whiff of self-importance. "Just a few of us."

"Lippy calls a meeting every day."

"He wants a few of us to work together. Mix things up, compare ideas. You gotta pay attention to a guy who nails things so tight. Here's something—everybody knows being on time's important, right? Lippy, the guy's like a wizard. He calls and tells you he'll meet you at so-and-so exactly seventeen minutes from now. Nails it on the nose. Not sixteen minutes, not eighteen, walks in at seventeen on the button. Or thirty-six, or an-hour-and-four, anything. Who do you know has time appreciation like that? So when Lippy makes a suggestion about how to be more competitive, you listen."

"He doesn't want to compete, he wants to dominate."

"Times are hard," Al says. "When life gives you lemons, make lemonade, no?"

"Sure, the way Lippy would—slash the pickers' wages, coerce a sweetheart deal out of the orchards and bribe a scientist to advertise the weight-loss benefits of citrus. Lemons. I don't want to hear about lemons, Al. To sell lemons that prick would spike the city's water supply with scurvy."

"You can actually do that with scurvy?"

"Let it drop."

Al lets it drop. Maybe it really was madness around here. But probably not. Probably she's just being June. It happens sometimes, as bad as her son. One thing is, Al better stop with Lippy's jokes. If June could see how funny he is maybe she'd lighten up, but that'll never happen. She'd absolutely go out of her mind if she heard any of Lippy's raw stuff, like last week when he said about that dynamite girl who teaches yoga . . . nope, no way, Al better purge his memory completely of that one in case it ever slips out. June would burn him in his bed.

He summons his best make-nice voice: "So business was up for lunch. That's good."

"Oh, Al."

He's caught the tone before. It makes him sadder that you can believe, but what are you gonna do? You can't stay ahead of the crowd anyways. It seems like only yesterday anybody with a downtown sidewalk cart or a food truck serving plain boiled wieners with squeeze mustard was a lunchtime hero like a chef with his own TV show. Swarmed like flies, the office workers. Then one season somebody started with sausages—German, Italian, Polish—and that trend swept the streets. Japadog came next, *Japadog* if you can believe, people standing in lines halfway around the block. Now you can buy wraps, pitas, sushi, anything. Shawarmas you can get, something no two people in the whole town can even agree on the spelling. People plan—he's not making this up—they plan on what cart to meet at for lunch and hang around on the sidewalk stuffing their faces instead of sitting down like human beings. Or pack into a food court in a mall, plastic scrunch-up-your-legs tables surrounded by holes-in-the-wall serving so much grease, salt and nitrates, why don't you buy lunch right from Monsanto. Him and June are supposed to come up with an answer to that foolishness? Anyways, he better put a lid on it. June's off her head today and one of them's got to hold it together.

Out of sight of the customers, he sneaks a hand around her waist. "Why don't you take an extra hour or so. I'll handle it till the bar starts filling up. By the way, where's Nita to help, what's with that for a new employee? Out there teaching whales how to hold protest signs?"

"On a break. She was good at lunch. Most of the customers knew her so maybe they'll tell their friends, who'll tell their friends, who'll tell la-la-la, ha-ha-ha . . . what a laugh."

"Here, take my jacket, they're calling for showers."

June's looking another direction, or out the window, or into the future, or nowhere at all. "Al, am I old or young?"

"What are you talking?"

"I don't feel old. Sure, I hurt in places and my tits and ass sag. But inside. They say it's good to feel young, but what scares me is maybe I'm young in all the bad ways. I make the same mistakes, I reach decisions for reasons I can't back up, I keep on at things that scream *wake up* right in my face. I tell myself I've learned along the way, but whatever I've picked up doesn't seem to have affected my behaviour. So do I have an old body with young thoughts and feelings that never caught up? The worst of both worlds?"

"Aww, if you're old, I'm really old."

That's all she's going to get out of him today. June kisses him on both cheeks and the mouth and he rushes to hold the door for her. "The jacket," Al says, but is left with it clutched in his hand as she steps out into the rain, holds her face up to the sky and starts down the sidewalk. Al shakes his head. She's something, that one. He wishes he could snap his fingers like that and lift her up when she's down. But he's working on it, you bet, that was one heck of an interesting meeting with Lippy this morning, best one so far. He watches June on her way down the sidewalk until she penetrates a wall of umbrellas tipped forward against the wind.

The last table wants to pay. Good, it'll be dead for a couple hours and Al has some thinking to do on Lippy's proposal, mostly about how to raise the subject with June. And it better be soon. If she finds out before he can turn the trick, she'll have his nuts for gnocchi. It's hard on him, you know? Al's not even one of those little-white-lie guys around his wife—yeah, yeah, everybody calls it *partners* when you're not officially married, but he figures you love as much then you call it as much—and it's giving him ulcers trying to keep the secret. If June could just appreciate Lippy Delillo's what would Al call it, genius? Is that too much? Luck, for sure. Name one guy you know who won a house playing poker. Not just a little bungalow neither, but two floors and a whole bunch of bathrooms. Talent, that's another thing. How many local shop owners you heard of competed for Italy in the Olympic Games? Sure, this was back in the '70s when Lippy was involved romantically with a certain East German swimmer had a back as wide as Europe and a trainer could've opened a drugstore, but still. So when Lippy Delillo's dealing the cards, best to be sitting at his elbow.

What's that, he just got a whiff of incense, all spicy and smoky, and sure enough it's Nita right behind him.

"Hi, Al."

"Hey, how you doing, kid? You okay with the job so far? It's Commercial Drive. A few characters in the neighbourhood not so, uhhh, polite, drop in. You good with that?"

"You ask me the same thing every day."

"A boss is allowed to be concerned for his staff. You never heard?"

"Yes. And thank you. But come on, Al. When I worked up north, just to see some bar band me and a Cree guy drove two snowmobiles twenty miles across the tundra. On mushrooms."

She slips around him to the front desk and opens the pebbled black ledger. "Why do we need a reservation book? The last entry was written with a quill."

"Two reasons. One, it looks professional. Two, you never know. Don't walk in and start changing already." Great girl, Nita, but too much Buddy rubbed off on her.

When Nita moves away from the counter, Al sees a sticker he knows for sure wasn't there yesterday:

The revolution has to proceed at a furious pace. Whoever gets tired has the right to get tired, but not to be in the vanguard.

"Huh?" Al chuffs. "What's that all about?"

"Che Guevara," Nita says.

"Yeah, yeah, we knew a little bit about kicking out the big shots in Italy too, in case you never heard. But when we tear down, afterwards we build up. Not like them bearded bums."

"Al, remember the last time we talked politics?"

"I'm with you, let's leave it alone. But take off the sticker, please. And if you want a rule of thumb to go by, anything you get at hippie shops, don't hang it here."

"Hippies. What year is this, Al?"

"You know what I mean."

"Hey, you," Nita says in a shaky but recognizable impersonation. "Name's Al Esposito, call me Al. You wouldn't be one of those what is it, a hippie, would you? Got a camera here. It's okay you make a peace sign while I take your picture in front of this VW van?"

"Go ahead, have your laugh," Al says, laughing. Mother of God, if he was twenty years younger . . . no use thinking.

"Would it be okay to take off for half an hour?" Nita says. "I'm having some used furniture delivered to my place and I absolutely have to be there. Three months without even the basics is driving me mad."

Nita took over the second-floor apartment in an old Victorian on Graveley after a law student serving an internship with Pivot Legal Society returned to her studies. Unfortunately, the one-bedroom had been furnished by the owner of the house, who had use of his own for the furniture after his wife bounced him from their main-floor suite downstairs for unpublicized misdemeanors. Buddy offered all Nita wanted from their old place, but that would have been dragging memories. A fresh start should be fresh, although other than brief gusts of oxygenated clarity there's been nothing fresh about the polluted air of confusion and second-guessing Nita's been inhaling since the breakup.

She wasn't looking for much, a flop would do. Well, that might be overstating it. She's no hippie. But the basics have always been fine. Somewhere to sit, a proper bed, working fridge and stove, decent water pressure in the shower. When possessions build to a certain point Nita feels their physical presence as a threat, an aggressive contraction of the space around her. She has a friend who styles herself a professional organizer, and though Nita's happy for anyone who finds a way to turn talent into money, she wonders what kind of pathetic society creates people who have so lost their individuality and trust in their own wants and needs as to hire professionals to help clean out their houses. To actually spell out for them what they don't need. A truly special type of helplessness.

Her few personal effects she's been transporting from her and Buddy's shared storage locker as they occur to her, and that will be the next step, to clear it out once and for all. The last time, while rooting around for her hiking boots she came across his sound gear. At the end of each day, whether coming home straight from the shop or stopping off for a beer, he'd park himself with a microphone in their living room and through a concealed outside speaker boom out warnings and critiques to passersby for transgressions ranging from walking their dogs off-leash to illegal parking to sporting bad haircuts. *Unwinding*, he called it. Jesus H., how did she ever?

"As long as it takes," Al says. "You deserve a decent place. But maybe could you help out with the bar later? Makes for a split shift but it's a couple hours overtime."

"Happy to help," Nita says, already crossing the floor.

Al's happy too. Business should work out like this all the time. The boss gives a little, the employee gives a little, a civilized way to go through life. Except Al's left to tend to the table, where an argument has broken out over the bill. June usually handles this part, the complaints and all that baloney. He loves that woman, loves her heart and soul, plus they're a good match in practical matters. He's convinced that's what everybody tries to do even if they don't realize it—gather around them people well-equipped in the areas where they fall short themselves.

All three customers are looking at him now. From their indignant faces, Al might have been caught spying on them in the shower. He's been here ten minutes. Ten minutes, and this is what he has to deal with. June and Nita better not be long or they'll be cutting him down from a rafter like drying prosciutto.

Chapter 11

Duty is the Great Business of a Sea Officer

Louie manages to blow most of the smoke out the window, and with a couple of flaps of his hand sends the surplus wafting in tight eddies to the four corners of the room.

After the bus rolled off the ferry last night, all he could call to mind was an indistinct image of a bus station near an armoury and drew a blank on nearby places to bunk. But to his relief, the operation had moved to the old Pacific Central Station, western terminus for VIA Rail and northern for the Amtrak Cascades passenger run up the coast from Washington State. Conveniently bordering the station grounds was the Ivanhoe, and ten minutes after arrival he was checked into the hostel above the pub. He ponied up for a private room, which set him back less than a third of what he'd expected this close to downtown.

At a chair pulled up to the window, Louie drowns his butt in a half-glass of water and casts an eye down on Main Street. It's been rare over the years that he's bothered with the city, and even then for only a day or two at a time. He found this stretch of Main in the mid-'70s and revisited at intervals when in the mood to marble his fun with a little trouble. The Ivanhoe, the American, the Cobalt. Fancy enough hotels in their day, he guesses, but by the time he started darkening the doorways they'd deteriorated precisely to the level with which he was most comfortable, dispensing cheap drinks, cheap food, cheap entertainment and cheap dates. He himself couldn't have changed much over the years, because here he is in the same spot and worse situation—no luggage and no woman. So much for the alleged age-wisdom correlation.

★

The trouble began in forty feet of water. Louie remembers the details as though he lived them more than once. Midway through the season they were on the home leg of their worst outing yet. The previous three trips had been only marginally better, and the trend was as obvious as it was ominous. Poor catches were becoming so common they had lost their appeal among fishermen as the primary subject for bitching, and with the rapid decline of west coast fish stocks all variety of turbulence was swirling around the industry. Catastrophic collapse was forecast as often as predictions for natural rebound, and every faction—commercial, sport, aboriginal, environmental—was in righteous high dudgeon, clamoring for reform running through open access to exclusive rights to unconditional moratorium.

For ethical reasons Louie used hook and line to keep bycatch to a minimum. The indiscriminate nature of seining never did sit well with him, and you didn't dare promote bottom trawling or drift netting to his face unless you had your hands up protecting your face. Beyond that, he ignored the politics. His days were full with trying to make a living. Fishing paid the bills and fed a few other needs not so measurable, and all he could honestly contribute to the argument was what he counted in the boat's hold, which is to say that if the trend continued, he'd soon be the skipper of a boat secured permanently to the dock.

It was Charlie who spotted the crab pot buoy and suggested they give the line a tug. The new deckhand had been cut loose by several owners up and down the coast before Louie snagged him as an emergency mid-season replacement. His reputation was of someone prone to error, had repeatedly been let go for pissing in the pickles over some matter or other. But Louie found him competent enough, admittedly mild praise for someone who'd been at it over twenty years. Nice enough fella, bit of an enigma, quiet and didn't cut up ashore and all that. Worked hard, just not much of a fisherman. Didn't have that special feel. But that was okay. Louie didn't need some wise old salt, just someone smart enough to take directions and game to put in an effort. But as for his calling attention to someone else's crab pot and suggesting they haul it up, the ancient world's entire collection of oracles couldn't have forecast the fallout from that.

Louie had never stolen anything in his life, not even as a kid, and to this day can't sufficiently reconstruct his state of mind to explain why he gave in. A weak moment, maybe. Demoralized by decades at a profession that was being blown against the rocks and without the strength to turn into the wind, could've been that. Pathetic and misdirected protest, who knows. He'll not dwell on the psychology or his state of mind at the time, for the action says it all—at Charlie's urging, Louie reached for the rope to help. It didn't strike him as terribly bad, hardly a capital crime, no worse than filching a few apples from an orchard and as easy to dismiss. Until they hauled up forty feet of rope, at the end of which was a crab trap filled with airtight cans holding polyethylene-wrapped parcels full of white powder.

On those occasions when Louie settles on the subject of religion, he considers himself either a pantheist, seeing God in all things, or a pagan, in the pejorative sense of believing in bugger-all. Christian he most definitely is not, neither is he Jewish, yet having a load of cocaine to deal with was some serious retribution for disobeying the OT Commandment to not steal.

He and Charlie reacted in synch, dropping the trap on the deck and ducking down to hide. But when the sea air cleared their minds, they allowed as how the few small sailboats in the vicinity and the Powell River ferry likely weren't about to charge down on them with decks awash in RCMP officers brandishing firearms. Likewise the Boston Whaler roaring at full power twenty yards across their stern posed no threat, unless the topless woman standing at the wheel and the bottomless man lurching on the deck pitching empty bottles into the chuck were professional associates of Pablo Escobar. So skipping the Hollywood Moment wherein the two principals squabble over the best course of action, Louie and Charlie snatched up the trap full of coke, heaved the fucking thing back over the gunwale and headed at full power for shore, not without, it must be said, hunching their necks into their shoulders with every bang of the hull against a wave.

On the dock, they laughed nervously about the incident and Charlie made a joke about swearing off crab for fear of becoming addicted. They parted in the parking lot. With the abysmal fishing, Louie had decided to break the run of bad luck by heading to Port Alberni for a few days to see a longstanding friend, a lady highly skilled in transferring to Louis her own inner peace. As for his deckhand, Charlie spent the off-season at a place not far south of Comox and Courtenay, somewhere close to Fanny Bay or Bowser from his description of it, and in Louie's absence would be staying on the boat to take care of minor repairs and gussy the old girl up a tad. His personal life was near blank. Louie gathered there was a woman in the picture, and a boy Charlie referred to infrequently. Gossip and rumours did their small-town best to fill in the gaps with details, which expanded with the retelling, widening the cracks like frost-heaved pavement—bad-news mother, a boy with behavioural problems—but in the end adding nothing of value to the family biography. Truth be told, to Louie it all sounded like a bunch of malicious face-scratching by people empty of anything interesting in their own lives.

Strange how the past can overwhelm the present. And the nose can trump them both—banana, he smells banana. Louie went straight to bed when he got in last night, and forgot got all about the snack he'd packed. He pulls away from his view of Main Street to root through his satchel. The banana was too ripe to begin with and hangs in his hand like a sea cucumber. The sandwich sniffs out okay, and with that side of his mouth home to the most teeth he tears out a crescent.

Charlie Monk. After all this time. They called him a loser back then, but CC was just one of those people who thinks big while being unarmed for the fight. One hand slowly staining with squeeze mustard oozing from the white-bread sandwich of dry cheese and mystery meat, with the other Louie retrieves the Last Will and Testament from the satchel. A document written in a desperate rush. One page of anguished, non-specific apologies followed by: "I kept all of it. I leave it to my family. Ask the boy." On the second page, the names. Charlie would have stowed the waterproof lock box in the false bottom before they came for him. He must have known they'd come, must have realized from the get-go. Louie reads the key passage one last time: "I kept all of it. I leave it to my family. Ask the boy."

Look at this, almost two in the afternoon, how long has Louie been staring out the window peeling away the years? He'd better get on it. If the old Army & Navy is still open, he'll pick up a package each of socks and underwear, a pair of pants and a shirt, running shoes in case he has to spend as much time on his feet as seems likely. And he'd better run through his story a few more times. With the buffer of distance, he'd almost talked himself out of the difficulty of the mission, but now that he's in the neighbourhood he has to admit it's one helluva thing to be dropping on unsuspecting heads.

Chapter 12

Trolling

"Between you and Al," June says with just enough draw-down on the humour to screw home her point, "I'm starting to feel like a disease carrier. Are you two afraid to be around me?"

"Didn't he tell you?" Nita says. "I had to be home for a delivery."

"Four hours ago."

"Four hours?" Nita checks her bare wrist.

On the move toward the bar, June spins and in a tone uncomfortably close to being authoritarian flings: "Finish straightening these tables then start in here," before vanishing through the archway.

Nita jumps to it, rushing about with pointless energy, micro-aligning chairs, patting and picking at her clothes as though readying livery for a lord's inspection rather than fussing with a pair of black jeans and a plain white blouse. The flurry of activity lasts for all of thirty seconds, the time it takes her to start wondering how four hours vaporized. The furniture delivery was right on time, so no holdup there. She must have been on the phone with the hospital longer than she thought.

With Bo's condition stabilized, the doctor had recommended he be kept overnight as a precaution. When Nita called later as a follow up, the duty nurse seemed understanding but couldn't elaborate, explaining she hadn't been on duty at the time and all the records showed was that the patient had made a complete recovery and was released in his sister's care. Nita was transferred to a nurse more familiar with the incident, who explained that given the intensity of the allergic reaction and Bo's less-than-robust condition the recovery was on the level of "amazing." The good news went only partway to alleviating Nita's concern. Where does he live? Sorry, the hospital wasn't free to release that information. Phone number? Sorry. The sister then, what about her? Sorry. The exchange continued in this vein until Nita told the nurse that yes, she was sorry, a sorry excuse for a health-care professional and not to expect support next time she was out on the picket lines.

Maybe the episode took longer than Nita's estimate. But still, four whole hours can't be explained, even factoring in the trip to the post office and the bakery. And it's impossible her nap could have accounted for more than a fraction—she barely closed her eyes. But she's here now, and at least in possession of Bo's full name. She'll check at the Carnegie Centre and a few other places on the Downtown Eastside. It's a close community, he'll turn up somewhere. She could probably have tracked him down already if not for having to rush to work.

"Nita! Little help in here!"

"On the way!"

June too is scrambling, though her version is less imagined than Nita's. A slow day in the restaurant has given way to a bar crowd seemingly determined to compensate, on a Tuesday of all nights. Several new faces, a few that haven't been around in months, a party of eight already into the shooters. At her new employee's appearance in the archway, June snaps, "Table six."

Nita waves that she's on it and wades into the crowd without the foggiest notion of how the tables are numbered. From all quarters people are crying for attention, petulantly raising empty glasses, flapping hands. Every television is tuned to a game of some type, a different one apiece or so it seems, a montage of brightly uniformed players slamming into one another, impairing Nita's concentration on faces, numbers, drinks. The fans banging down shooters are being pulled in all directions, shouting encouragement or hurling abuse at first one screen then the next, and even those patrons who couldn't tell a football from a footstool are jazzed with sympathetic animation. Nita feels trapped in that scene from *A Clockwork Orange* where the subject has his eyelids pinned open, forcing him to absorb waves of shocking visual stimuli.

Nothing sets her going like the sound of pro sports fans in a bar. Citizens in a country on the verge of another recession, a good portion of them laid off or already part of the working poor, yet huddled in a cave with other truant husbands cheering themselves sick for multimillionaire twenty-year-olds. If war is politics for the bloody minded, then pro sports is war for the feeble minded.

She's surrounded by noise these days, constantly assailed. She needs to get away, anywhere so long as it's away, a place without hypersensitive car alarms and vehicles that beep and honk when they're locked or unlocked and people who frantically press the chirping crosswalk button a thousand times thinking it makes the light change faster. Just quiet. A place where a celebration is singing silently to the moon rather than howling drunkenly at hired mutants in a stadium trying to permanently rupture one other.

All that aside, over the next two hours she does a creditable job. Filling every order, swallowing every complaint, joking with her personal heroes—those with the grace and common sense to do as advised and go to the self-service area—overall behaving as a boss would expect. And marvel of marvels, eventually a customer sympathizes.

"They're running you right off your feet tonight."

It's one of her helpful heroes returning with a fresh pint from the bar without waiting for table service. The old man looks to have undergone a bargain-basement makeover—thin, ill-fitting cotton shirt still creased from the package, too-long green workpants rolled up into bunched cuffs. Dark, very dark eyes, skin as weathered as any street person's. Nita rips him a smile, a dazzler, and says, "Thanks for helping yourself."

Louie Zimbot smiles and returns to his seat at the window.

When the last game ends, the fans lapse into the bewilderment of unexpectedly released gulag prisoners until one of their number, sulkily eyeballing Nita, proposes to his mates a sojourn to any place where waitresses don't respond to flirtation with a threat to stab you. For all the earlier obnoxiousness, their departure bleeds whatever energy the room had, and in short order Al Esposito's is near empty and back to its normal inertial resting state.

June has likewise lost her flush of anger, and smiles apologetically. "You handled that perfectly," she says. Nita slides her tray onto the bar and slumps onto a stool. "Shame they left," June continues. "It's been ages since we've had a good stabbing in here, barely a poke with a butter knife."

Nita's laugh holds no energy. She cranes her neck around. "Didn't I see Sally earlier?"

"Yeah, she came in to tell me she got a job."

"Really? Good for her."

Sally has an apartment one street over with an entry off the alley, a location from which she periodically sets sail for city parts and purposes unknown, a spectral figure leaving a bewildering trail. She likes cleaning things. Off and on she's discovered washing dishes in some local restaurant at which she doesn't work, having snuck in unnoticed, and can be seen street side pulling down expired event and entertainment posters or sweeping butts off the sidewalks.

"She found a cleaning job," June says, "a real one. Down at the Grandview Legion. It's just now and again, but they're throwing in work clothes and she'll even be getting a small cut of the tips."

"Good on them and her both."

"How about you?"

"Me? Simple—I'm turning into a bitch."

"Maybe you're spread too thin," June says.

"You could give me an argument about it."

"Seriously, how many non-profits are you involved with? It has to be frustrating beyond belief."

"So you give up? Is that the solution?"

"I was a romantic once," June says. "Now either side gives me the shivers. The other day I saw a T-shirt that read: "Stop the Extinction of the Whales—Remember the Dinosaurs." Do people actually think humans wiped out the poor dinos?"

Nita laughs tiredly and June gives her a quick four-squeeze shoulder massage before calling an end to the night. Nita was clearing and cleaning as she went, and June has to say that once she got moving there was no stopping her. It greatly eased the burden, and that's the term for it all right, a bloody burden. At an age when the load should be lightening, June's stooping ever lower under the weight. And Al's up to something. She knows it and he knows she knows. Everything about him when he rushed out the door spoke of a man this close to crapping his pants, from the anguished look on his face to the pinched waddle. Whatever it is, June hopes it's bad news. Whenever Al's hiding something meant to be good—birthday present, surprise overnight getaway, house renovation scheme—the gods of Olympus knock themselves silly to be first in line to punish the poor thing for his folly and hubris.

Nita makes eye contact and cocks her head toward the back, a few dreads slipping loose from their tiedown. "Go have a smoke. I'll keep an eye."

Five minutes later June's back, and she slides in beside Nita at the bar. They're turned toward each other and partially into the room, not looking straight at the last customer by the window, but keeping him in view while attempting, through sheer will, to force him out the door.

"I was little," June says apropos of nothing.

Accustomed to her friend's abrupt way of introducing a notion only half-conceived, Nita chips in to help the story along: "How little?"

"Not an exact age. A few years when I was growing up in Winnipeg. There was a man who worked the neighbourhood. He'd walk up and down the streets pulling a cart with a grinding wheel attached to it. A bell on a spring would let everyone know he was around, *dingle-dingle* with every bump. The housewives would bring out their carving knives and scissors and he'd sharpen them right there. He'd do a horrible job. The knives would come back so dull they couldn't cut skim milk. It didn't matter. No one could stand to see him pounding the pavement for hours on end without results. The women would sharpen them over again themselves so their husbands wouldn't find out."

"Good for them."

"He killed himself. I can't remember, I think it was gas in his apartment, or maybe pills. He'd been living alone in a room full of *Free Press* newspapers and *Star Weekly* magazines."

"How sad," Nita says, and after a few seconds of dead air adds: "Uh, I don't really know where you're going with this."

"Just once. Maybe if someone just once said listen, this isn't working, it's wrong, wrong, fucking wrong! It isn't working for any of us. Just once made him face up."

"Are you okay?"

"Good question." At the last customer's approach, June rises. "All done then?"

"I suppose I am," Louie says. "At least so far as the bill goes."

It's Nita's hero. She gives and gets a smile and goes to bus his table. The window adjacent to his seat is ajar, and while pulling it closed she spies on the sidewalk below a small volcano of cigarette butts. That sneaky old . . .

"Cash or card?" June says, swinging behind the bar. No immediate response. The old man looks uncomfortable. God almighty, he's not about to hit on her, is he?

"I was wondering whether I might have a word."

"Was there a problem tonight?"

"No, no, nothing like that." A few barks of smokers cough. "My name's Louie Zimbot." The disclosure is delivered with an exploratory uplift at the end, a sliver shy of a full question.

"I'm sorry, have we met?"

A shake of his head. "June Monk, is that right?"

"We're trying to close up here."

"You have a son. Bernard. Or Buddy, maybe you call him."

"Where I'm from," June says, "anyone who dances around what they're trying to say gets kicked out of the kitchen to go sit with the people in the fancy living room."

"Charlie and I fished together. Charlie Monk."

"My husband."

"Husband?"

"What else would he have been?"

"I'm sorry, just trying to get things straight."

"CC died twenty-five years ago."

"Ah, so it was soon after. I didn't know exactly when."

There's no threat here. June regards him with wary interest. "You worked together?"

"He was my deckhand. Half a season, the last season. Up to the final . . . accident on the boat."

"The boat? CC was injured in the bush, so unless your boat was left up a mountain like the ark I'm going to get out of here and off my feet."

"There's an explanation."

"There always is," June says.

"Can we sit? There have been developments, some news. Documents have been found. Please, a few minutes of your time."

"Follow me. I'm going out back for a smoke. That's how long you have—the time it takes for one cigarette. As soon as this butt hits the alley, yours hits the road."

Chapter 13
Engagement

Wednesday morning, 0520 hours. The gym opens in ten minutes.

Buddy spent last night at the Ivanhoe catching up with an old university classmate, now a UBC physics prof who calls himself "Schrödinger's Boozer," explaining that at any given time he can be considered both drunk *and* sober until being observed by his wife and collapsing into one state or the other. They eventually broke out and roamed far and wide to other sloughs, drinking and talking, lying and laughing, pissing in alleys. Buddy made it home all right and remembered to set out a ration of leftovers for Oxhead. It went untouched, so maybe the pygmy moocher had a time of it last night himself.

Buddy picks up the pace, pushing steadily along the sidewalk in the indirect light. He started lifting weights the summer his father came home for the last time. CC's hiking accident was only roughly explained, a loose account of a fall down a mountainside, but whatever the details he was sorely used. Buddy was sixteen, and with a spanking new drivers licence in his wallet was tasked with ferrying his father each day to rehab. Bored with waiting around for the sessions to end but impressed by the motivation of CC's fellow patients, Buddy drifted into a local gym. Hooked.

No coach, no teammates, no overseer, and the gym was 24-hour, allowing Buddy to align the workouts with his mood. Oftentimes he preferred to go through the repetitive motions in the middle of the night with no one around, plates and bars his only dance partners, *clanks* and *clunks* his only music. His father encouraged him, at least in CC's customary way of speaking out to contradict Buddy's mother, who was starting to cast a skeptical eye on her son's fixation on poundage, sets and reps, and was getting tired of searching for her sewing tape, which Buddy borrowed to measure the growth of individual body parts and never replaced. Tired of her husband, too, it seemed.

Frost-nipped by the chill between his parents, Buddy shut his mouth and poured more hours into the gym. He was gaining size and strength, each incremental accretion of mass spurring greater tenacity. At rehab, his father showed no such progress. While he was breaking through the lesions and becoming more flexible and ambulatory, his internal injuries were the determining factors in his overall recovery. The finishing touch was another fall, minor in itself—a trip on a parking lot curb—but deadly in its aggravation of a head trauma from his accident. Cerebral hemorrhaging set in, he lapsed into a coma, and Charles Clarence Monk was gone in three weeks.

The day after the private service a ghostly connection arrived for Buddy in the mail, the first issue of a muscle magazine subscription from a father no longer around to accept thanks. The feature article was on the guns, bodybuilder-speak for the arms. A program for the dedicated lifter to grow the largest biceps and triceps possible. Freshly motivated, indeed aroused, Buddy barely took the time to copy out the routines before switching his membership to a gym patronized by serious bodybuilders and powerlifters. Compared to this new batch of beef, Buddy was a strip of jerky. But he loved being in the thick of the action as the iron heads went at it, goliaths wrapped and belted, hands chalked, bug-eyed with lab testosterone, popping smelling-salt caps under their noses, shaking the walls with primal grunts and screams amid pulsing surround-sound. He completely overdid it, of course, allowing nowhere near proper recovery time between workouts, day after day lifting through stiffness and injury, illness and stress, and in the sixth week ruptured his left bicep tendon so badly the muscle tore free of the bone and rolled into a lump under the skin, keeping him out of action for months and putting a permanent ceiling on his progress.

Buddy's hustling along Commercial, chock full of hangover and trying to talk himself out of it. The gym, Spartacus, is just around the next corner, and for this time of the morning there's an impressive amount of noise curling around the bend. On arrival he slows to take in the action.

Arf-Arf, a pit bull puppy, is at the end of her leash near the gym entrance barking playfully at a half-dozen crows trying to make off with a scrap of donair at the limit of her reach. The birds reconnoitre, feint, probe, retreat, confer, dart, distract, attempt to outflank, retreat once again. Nervous elation spreads when one of their number dares a solo charge, but he too is beaten back, minus a few feathers. The confrontation is complicated by the input of two women in identical tights who seem uncertain about which animal should shoulder the blame for blocking the door. They tssk, they fret, they hiss, they fuss. Disgusting as they find crows, the dog's breed counts against her. They couldn't possibly take the side of a well-documented devourer of infants and innocent passersby, not as they would automatically with, say, a fluffy Wheaten Terrier. They agree that the young pit, on the cusp between puppyhood and serial killer, seems tame enough. She's obviously enjoying the game with the birds, and is cute if you don't think of the teeth or look at the jaw muscles even at this age tracking up the sides of her head. But evil surely lurks in her heart, and even when an inbound crow on final approach strafes the women with an impressive streak of greenish-white birdshit, support doesn't swing to the dog.

The arrival of Sally From the Alley puts the kibosh on the morning carnival. Arf-Arf rolls back on her haunches, lolls her tongue and ducks her head with a grimace of a smile as though fessing up to bad behaviour. Keeping a nonchalant eye on breakfast, the crows stroll peg-legged to the curb and feign disinterest, shouldering and shoving one another like adolescent boys showing off at a public pool. The women dash through the doorway and down the stairs to the gym.

"Sorry, Arf-Arf," Sally says, squatting so the dog, after butting her in the leg, can rasp the breath from her in a licking frenzy. "I couldn't wait for the gym to open to go pee and there's no place around without being a customer."

"Hey, Sally."

"Oh, hi, Buddy. I couldn't wait for the gym to open to go pee and there's no place around without being a customer."

"I know what you mean."

"Funny, isn't it?"

"Uh, sure. I guess that's pretty funny."

Sally's in her early forties, a wan elfin spirit with lank blonde hair, eyes reminiscent of the round-eyed orphan prints Buddy's mother used to have hanging in the family kitchen, and a heart so big it might have an extra chamber. When not pressed by circumstance, Sally can stand disturbingly frozen for great periods of time, head tilted skyward, gazing up and away as if wrestling with weighty philosophical puzzlers, or perhaps petitioning a personal saint for direction. At the moment she's being thoroughly mauled, licked and rammed. Arf-Arf is the first dog Buddy's encountered that butts by way of friendly greeting, bashing into any available body part, thrashing its head back and forth and all around as if taking horns to a fallen matador. Arf-Arf is the runt of a litter of six whose mother, Arf, was Sally's first pit.

"Did you hear the good news?" Sally says through a cataract of canine slobber.

"You got into co-op housing," Buddy says. "Congratulations. What's it been, eight years?"

"Can't move in for another month. But not that." Big breath. "I won bigtime Saturday at the Legion."

Buddy's hangover instantly dematerializes. "The Legion? What can you win there?"

"Meat. I won a ham, five kilos of Italian sausage and a package of little porky baby ribs."

Rapid fire: "How do you enter? What does it cost? Is it open to everybody or do you have to be a member?"

"I can check. After I won, I helped clean up and Donna offered me a job. Not every day, except for today, but after special events. It's going to be a really great place to work. The only trouble is now I'm an employee so I can't play the meat draw anymore. But that's okay. I'm a vegan anyway, and Arf-Arf is allergic to meat—pretty weird for a dog, eh?"

"Is there another one this Saturday? Meat draw, I mean."

"Yup, three draws."

"What time?"

Sally has drifted off, looking aloft as though evaluating the counterpane of clouds for moth holes. She returns to earth with a shadow of sadness. "I wonder if I should keep the job. What do you think?"

"I say it sounds good. Close to home, you know most of the staff and the people in there, leaves you time for other things you like doing. I can't see any downside."

"But if I quit they'd let me play the meat draw again. This time I gave the meat to my brother 'cause he doesn't always eat right."

"There's that to consider, but if you're making money you can help your brother out with groceries."

"He sure was sick."

"Too much all at once?"

"Allergic, really allergic, he could have died. Seafood can make him stop breathing."

"You won seafood too?"

"No, that was different. He didn't even get to eat the meat. Somebody in his building stole it. The ham, the sausage, the porky ribs and everything. But if I could win again, this time he could come over to my place and eat it there. So I don't know about the job."

As always, Buddy's unable to keep pace with Sally's sorties from the main subject and is still trying to splice the seafood sidebar story into the rest of it. But that can wait for now. "I better get into the gym—are you going to be around later? There's something I'd like to clear up."

Sally pulls away from the dog and purses her lips. "If this is about breaking our engagement, you don't have to apologize. I'm over it, I have closure. Let's move on with our lives, 'kay?"

"Uh, it wasn't really an engagement. Just for a game, remember? When I thought about it some more, I decided

England was too far to go just to try to win bacon and, uh . . . well, sometimes I like playing games a bit too much."

"Yeah, your mum says you're nuts."

"I'm glad she shared that with you."

"Like *really* nuts. She said even in Grade 5 you cheated just to win a crokinole tournament."

"There was a little more to it than that."

"She said once in school, on a bet you ran from the back of the room and slammed your head into the blackboard. With the teacher still at her desk."

"I was younger then."

"And after, the teacher made you stand in the hall with your stitches and bandages."

"The world's full of cruel people."

"And the principal made you give the bet money to the food bank."

"I've always cared about charities, just like Nita."

"Anyhow, like I said, I have closure. And I'm glad to hear you're okay with everything."

"We'll always be friends," Buddy says. "Don't ever worry about that."

"Thanks again for letting me keep the spending money for the trip when we didn't even go to the bacon game. Oh, and one more thing—Nita's not still mad at me, is she?"

"She was never mad at you, Sally. You didn't do one thing wrong."

"'Kay."

Down the stairs. After scanning his key tag, Buddy grabs a towel and lifting straps from his locker and heads out to the main room. Spartacus began as a hardcore gym back in the '70s and has morphed into a community facility for the average fitness fan. Later in the day a few serious lifters drop in, but though some of them work out as hard as Buddy, none of them gets quite so worked up.

Just past the cardio section he halts, stands at attention and breaks into his pre-workout, psych-up chant:

In Lewis isle with fearful blaze,
the house-destroying fire plays,
to hills and rocks the people fly,
fearing all shelter but the sky.
In Uist the king deep crimson made
the lightning of his glancing blade;
the peasant lost his land and life,
who dared to bide the Norseman's stride.
The hungry battle-birds were filled
in Skye with blood of foemen killed,
and wolves on Tiree's lonely shore,
dyed red their hairy jaws in gore.

The preposterous hooey draws from staff and morning fitness folk the usual rolling of eyes and tossing of heads. But never you mind, our neighbourhood Viking is oblivious to anything outside his zone. It's time to give 'er.

Chapter 14

Message From a Bottle

June's treading wearily down Grant Street and warily in her mind. After exhausting all avenues last night trying to wring more information from Louie Zimbot, details it became clear the old fisherman couldn't supply, by the time she hit home Al was asleep. When she woke this morning, in his place on the pillow was a note urging her to sleep in, that it would be his pleasure to open for her. She's glad for the reprieve, but it would have been nice to feel his physical presence, relax in his goodness, pretend it was a rare day when they didn't have to work and could cuddle awhile, rub her nose back and forth on his chest hair and hear him laugh as he did every time.

Showering, she twice dropped the soap, forgot to rinse, toweled off incompletely, dressed distractedly, shoes didn't match the slacks, cruddy old shoulder bag but where was the new one, what's with the goddamn hair, makeup looked applied with a lacrosse stick, boiling kettle scorched the pad of her thumb, here there and everywhere and finally out the door. On the sidewalk she checked her jacket pocket for keys, shoulder bag for the same. Disoriented, vertiginous, if not in a hurry she would have laid flat on her back and prayed for rain to wash away her sins and misapplied eye shadow both.

Past the entrance to Spartacus, she checks out Caffè Roma's patio and squints through the plate-glass windows in case Al and the boys have reached this far in their rounds. No sign of him, and maybe that's good. She wouldn't know where to start. Only then does it occur to her Al's at the restaurant. That's what his note said, didn't it? That he was going to open? God, her head's splitting. Waves of the past are sloshing against the shores of the protected years, throwing up driftwood, eroding her foothold in the sands of time, her grip on buried truths. She turns to go, and there across the street by the hardware store is her son and Sally.

Sally sees her coming and raises from her crouch over Arf-Arf. "Buddy, it's your mum. Hi, June."

June returns the greeting, and to protect her shins presents the back of a leg so the pup can ram into the fleshy calf.

Buddy's propped against the wall of the Home Hardware building, bent at an acute angle, awkwardly supporting himself with one hand. To all appearances spellbound by the window display of French press coffee makers, rice cookers, safety vests, hand tools, eco-bags, seed packets, painters drop clothes and dis-associated bric-a-brac, in fact none of it registers. Alert to his mother's mood, he holds his position, content to let the encounter play out in reflection.

"How did you hurt your back?" June says right off. "And don't lie, I can tell by the way you're standing. Let me guess—you were lifting weights."

"He was lifting weights," Sally says. She holds up Buddy's gym bag as though introducing evidence at court.

June captures her son's eyes in the glass. "Who were you trying to out-lift?"

"Nobody," Buddy says. "Going for a personal best."

"My brother says that all the time," Sally adds. "Be the best you can be, you know?"

June's going to get nowhere with her son so shuts down the inquiry. "Am I ever going to meet this brother of yours, Sally? Doesn't he ever come to the Drive?"

"Bo likes it downtown. He knows everybody, and that's where a lot of agencies and the Carnegie Centre are. He can get in trouble when he goes too far. Sometimes he thinks he said things when he was really just thinking them, and other times he says things out loud he wanted to keep to himself. People don't understand and get mad."

"One of these days maybe."

Sally nods vigorously and says, "We better get going. I said I'd help Buddy to the clinic."

"*Ow.*"

"Arf-Arf!"

"It's all right," June says, "she missed the bone. And I can take over from here if you want."

"Really? Sure?"

"Positive. And sweetheart, how about this—I'd like to treat you both to dinner at the restaurant. Make it a . . . celebration. Talk it over and let me know when it's convenient. It'll be fun."

Slowly Sally raises her face to the heavens, and after a few billion virtual particles wink in and out of existence, says, "Umm, that's really nice. But there's some bad news. I don't know how to say this but things didn't work out the way we thought. We're still friends, though. Maybe Buddy can explain everything, 'kay?"

June checks the window again, but her son's scrutinizing the pavement and all that's visible in reflection is the top of his head. "Sally, the invitation is for you and your brother."

"Oh. Whew! Sure, that'd be great." Of course her and Bo. She and Buddy were just going to England for a game. Too bad the trip fell through. She always has fun around Buddy and she'd been looking forward to visiting Lady Di's grave. But on the other hand, what if something happened to Bo while she was running around England looking for where the Beatles were born or something? Just thinking about it makes her shiver.

"So let me know," June says. "Here, I'll take the gym bag."

"There's more news," Sally says. "I won the meat draw at the Legion. A ham, Italian sausage and those little porky baby ribs."

"Good for you." She'll burn hell for it but June's powerless to stop herself: "No bacon?"

"Nope," Sally says. "I'm not so lucky at bacon."

"Ah."

"Anyhow, thanks for taking over, I have to get home and get ready for work later. Bye June, bye Buddy, c'mon Arf-Arf."

June watches them cross Commercial Drive before turning back to her son, who has unstuck himself from the building and is picking his way along the sidewalk.

Shuffling raises too many vibrations, creeping's too slow. Buddy experiments till settling on a technique that covers ground at an acceptable rate with minimum pain, gliding with bent knees to avoid the jolting of his heels while holding his upper body stiffly vertical. The injury isn't anything he could have prevented. He hadn't been deadlifting anything close to his personal best. True, he raced through the warmup, but lack of preparation or faulty form had nothing to do with it. An old rugby injury is all, a spasm that recurs infrequently and unpredictably, the last time initiated by no more than reaching for a top shelf. It clears up of its own accord and normally remains localized, though on occasion it will trap the sciatic nerve, prompting a cascade of electric twitching that spirals around his leg right to the top of his foot. This time it seized hold after Buddy had straightened and locked out with the bar held at arms-length across his thighs. Just as he started to bend to lower the weight his *erector spinae* cramped, and in the fraction of a second it took for him to realize he'd lost control, gravity pulled the weight from his hands, slamming the loaded barbell onto the hard rubber mat and tipping him over the bar into the floor-to-ceiling mirror.

At the clinic, Buddy pulls up his shirt and flattens his lumbar region against the exterior wall to feel the sweet cool concrete on his overheated erector muscles. "I'm not waiting two hours for this place to open."

June lights a cigarette. "You stink. I mean it, you reek of booze, no wonder you injured yourself. What were you up to last night?"

"Working on a plan to boost the restaurant. A promotional type of thing like we talked about. I might be able to set it up for Italian Day this weekend."

"Should I be asking?"

"A meat draw."

"Brilliant."

"Yeah, funny how things can just pop into your head."

When her son pulls off the wall, June says, "You're not going anywhere."

"I don't need a diagnosis, just a prescription for muscle relaxants. This'll disappear on its own, and if not I'll come back later."

They set off up the sidewalk, June on the curb side, which with its trees and newspaper boxes, trash bins and bus stops, parking meters and bicycle racks, would pose too much of an obstacle course for her son. The open sidewalk he has no trouble negotiating, feet shooting flatly forward just high enough to miss the butts and coffee cup lids and vomit and bloodstains and other detritus and fluids that have accumulated overnight, reminders of that other city from which the sun withholds its beneficence, the city of dreary nightshifts, of bars, fights, threats and shaky reconciliation, the search for after-hour engagement with the world, the search for love and a place to sleep, no place to sleep then love will do.

"By the way," Buddy says. "Sally's brother, did she call him Bo?"

"She might have, I missed it. Why?"

"Just wondering."

To keep from exciting the rapidly firing muscle fibres in his back, Buddy's tooling along with his arms held straight down and tight to his sides like a pensioned-off Riverdancer. This combined with the smooth bent-knee glide makes his upper body appear to be moving along on a conveyor belt. The unorthodox form of travel is harvesting sidelong glances from visitors to the Drive, whereas the locals treat the sight as one more manifestation of Buddy's erratic behaviour and on passing avert their eyes to avoid riling the peevish skull pruner.

"Come to the restaurant with me," June says. "There's something I want to talk to you about. It's important. Or could be important."

After a brief examination of his mother's face, Buddy nods.

"You can have breakfast when we get there," she continues. "By now Al will have everything ready to go. And don't be scared—she won't be in till nine."

"Who?"

"Very funny."

Buddy glide-steps around an unconscious urban camper who's jutting from a recessed doorway, buried headfirst in his sleeping bag as though having fallen asleep while rooting around the bottom for the day's socks. When they pass Mullets to Mohawks, the barber considers a detour up to his apartment to see what in the way of leftover painkillers he can find in his basket of supplements, but can't bring himself to face the stairs.

June, noticing the hitch in his stride on the way by, intuits accurately and says, "I might have some Tylenol 3s left from when I spilled that hot oil, but they're so old now they probably have all the strength of chalk."

"Worth a try," Buddy says. "I can always jazz them up with a beer."

"I'm not serving you beer at this time of the morning. You wouldn't have injured yourself if you weren't half-pissed. Never mind the long-term effect of all the drinking."

"You know what has a worse long-term effect? The accumulated stress of never doing what you want in the short term."

"*Pff!*"

As they near the restaurant, June lets another formless syllable pop out and for the last few steps picks up the pace. The blackout blinds are down, lights off, door locked. Once inside, she surveys the room as if half-expecting a squad of merrymakers to spring out from behind the counter with a cake and shrieks of *SURPRISE!* But no, just the foetid air of Al's absence.

"Bad move," she says from deep in her chest. "Very bad move, Mr. Esposito."

Buddy helps out by saying, "Maybe Lippy needed help with his child prostitute ring."

"We're supposed to open in ten minutes. I was hoping he could keep an eye on things so you and I could . . . what are you doing?"

"Locking the door."

"There'll be people wanting breakfast."

"It's a city of options. I locked up the shop once mid-head and booted the guy out. I'm sure the customer didn't spend the rest of the day with half a mullet."

The definition of futility would be trying Nita this early, and in any event there'd be no talking to Buddy with those two in the same space. So June figures what the hell, bar the door against the whole world. She tells her son to take a seat and aims for the kitchen.

Once Buddy's insides are busy processing four poached eggs, a grapefruit, two slices of toast and three Tylenols, the stage appears to be set. In the interim one person has come to the door, by way of investigation offering only a timid rattle of the handle before moving along. Buddy's been watching his mother. Whatever's on her mind is straining so hard to get out he's surprised it's not expressing itself as hives.

"Let me take the dishes," he says, easing sideways off his chair and carefully rising. "If I don't keep moving I'll stiffen up."

June follows, wiping the table on the way by. As Buddy's ditching the plates onto the stainless-steel counter, his mother undergoes radical decompression and blurts, "He left a will! CC left a written will."

Buddy could have guessed it had something to do with his father. No other subject can coil her so tightly. Buddy was sixteen when CC died, and was preoccupied enough with his own confusing sentiments to miss the actual forms of his mother's grief, not just failure of interpretation but of basic recognition. Only later did he see the anger, which may have always been there, anger manifesting itself in broad self-deprecation smelling a little too much of shame. As if it were her fault.

"That was twenty-five years ago," he says carefully, towelling off his hands. "He had nothing to leave anyhow, just our old furniture and some junk. So what's the big deal?"

"The big deal is I just found out last night."

"Last night? What, Dad passed you the news at a fucking séance?"

"There was a man at the bar. The will has our names and our old Steveston address."

"This is looking good, Mum. A stranger tells you—"

"Can we sit down?" June interrupts. She leads the way, passing through the restaurant and the archway to the bar as though needing to recreate the telling's physical setting.

Between seasonal fishing and off-season ventures back to the Island for spells of repair work on the boats, CC was gone over half of every year. His intervals home naturally had great impact on their son, which June considered a reasonable trade-off for his absences. It wasn't till after the accident brought him home fulltime that she began to seriously question the validity of her own argument. Only high quality can compensate for low quantity, and her mistake was in relinquishing oversight. With her husband's hold on their son tightening, one day it struck her that she'd been reduced to moderator, her only apparent purpose to make the two of them comfortable. How sad. And how very unlike the woman who with half a husband had reared a son. It was the start of her own transformation. *But so late, so very late.* If she was a minority of one, she could, should, would cast her ballot. *So late.* The rules of life are in perpetual development so the majority must only rule provisionally. Her own father, a partially closeted Maoist, was serious when he used to say, "A billion Chinese can't be wrong." But Daddy, yes they can. Any number of any people can. *Too late.*

She feels she failed Buddy in those days, and questions how she's made out over the years, whether her efforts have paid off to any great degree. Buddy's Buddy, for what that's worth. But she's in there, yes she is. Who knows, maybe the packets of sane guidance she's been inserting over time are all that have kept her son's wilder oscillations confined to a finite envelope.

Without thinking, she assumes her position behind the wood bar top. Buddy, bad back and all, works two chairs aside for manoeuvring room and takes his regular spot. "Old habits," June says, and maybe it's the tension that makes their laughter carry on much longer than the remark can justify.

"All right, " Buddy says. "Let's have a look."

"I don't have the whole will."

"What's that all about? And how did some stranger get hold of it in the first place?"

"I won't be able to do this if you're going to yell. I'm really serious, I need you to . . . just don't yell." A few seconds of silence serve as a trial run. "Thank you."

"You're welcome."

"First, he wasn't a stranger to your father. His name's Louie Zimbot. He came over from Comox Monday night. CC worked for him on his boat."

"Let's say it's true, who can guess how many men Dad worked for? He bounced around all over the place. You know how he was about variety, how much he liked working on different boats and for different skippers. What makes this guy special? I'll say it again—how did he get his hands on the will? If there really is one and this isn't a con. Seriously, hasn't it at least flashed through your mind that all fishermen are congenital liars?"

"Buddy, don't . . . don't! . . . All right, then. Louie wanted to check with me—with us—before proceeding."

"*Louie* already," Buddy mumbles. "First name basis with—"

"How would you like to be barred?" She pours him a defensive half-glass of draft to bevel his edge. "Apparently the will was written in a rush, and it looks like it. Just a minute." She rummages through her shoulder bag. "He left me a partial photocopy . . . here. Christ, I can barely read it in this light. 'I kept all of it. I leave it to my family. Ask the boy.' Then our names."

"Gimme." Buddy snatches the paper and scans it at record speed. "Meaningless. There was nothing to leave except what we already talked about. Why would he bother writing anything down?"

"It's the phrasing," June says. "Louie pointed it out. CC didn't say 'all I have' or 'all I own,' one of those standard lines, but 'I kept *all of it.* I leave *it* to my family.' Doesn't that sound like he's referring to something specific?"

"Getting pretty picky, aren't we? Let's not try to strain fish shit out of ditch water."

"He thinks there's money involved. He'll tell us more once he checks on a few things and gets the will authenticated, but for now he has reason to believe CC came into money near the end."

"Near the end. This Louie . . ."

"Zimbot."

"He wasn't around when Dad died, at least I don't remember him."

"What he means is up to the accident. Which, by the way, apparently has more to do with the boat than the bush."

"More fantasy. Dad was smashed up so badly hiking on that mountain it led to his death. Why would he lie about how it happened?"

"The will was found on the boat. Just two weeks back a couple of scuba divers found it in a box that had been hidden onboard."

"Let me guess—with it was a pirate's eye patch, a peg leg, a parrot skeleton and a hand-drawn map with an X on it."

June hadn't expected it to be easy. "You can see for yourself. Our names are right there, along with the Steveston address. And obviously, 'Ask the boy' means you."

Buddy drifts the sheet onto the bar. "You got the goods on me. I've been sitting on a pile of treasure since I was sixteen waiting for you to croak. I thought you were getting suspicious so I hired Oxhead to guard the stash whenever I had to leave the apartment."

"Oxhead?"

"The mouse, Mum. The one with hantavirus."

"This is starting to get insulting."

"What's insulting is that instead of relying on your own judgement or god-forbid trusting your son, you parade some stranger's sleight-of-hand as gospel."

"I have a feeling it's your dad's will. The handwriting is right on. The money part, who knows. And that's all I'm going to say till we learn more."

"You have feelings, the fisherman has reason to believe. I'm not hearing any evidence, and I want to be there when any comes out. No, first I'll squeeze the lies out of him. Where's he staying?"

"Downtown somewhere."

"Somewhere. I'm guessing the slippery bastard didn't leave a number either."

"He's not trying to dodge you. According to the will, you're the one who's supposed to know something. I gave him your number and told him where your shop is. He said he'd call today and can drop by right after you close."

How far does June go with her own additions? Does she let it all out? Full disclosure or damage control—either one would break the healer's injunction to do no harm. Before her eyes Buddy's transforming. Radiant, he raises his arms overhead in the stick-em-up position, steps away from the bar, folds in half and touches his forehead to his knees.

"Look at you," June says. "Back to normal."

"Nothing compared to later," he says, shadow boxing in a small circle, "once I've had a short dance with a long liar."

"Good plan. Why bother hearing him out when getting barking mad for no reason is so productive."

Buddy doesn't hear. The pain has vamoosed and he's back in the game, shuffling across the floor, messing with some Kingsmen lyrics while popping out jabs and crosses, hooks and uppercuts:

> *Louie, Louie, ooohhh yeah, you gotta go—*
> *Yeah, yeah, yeah, yeah, yeah, yeah.*
> *Louie, Louie, ooohhh baby, said you gotta go now—*
> *Yeah, yeah, yeah, yeah, yeah, yeah . . .*

Chapter 15

His Heart Soars Like a Beagle

In the space of six bus stops, Nita's been drawn into as many conversations.

Hastings is a workplace street, an artery to trundle down with bags and shopping carts of cans and bottles, a sidewalk market for salvage and castoffs, this and that. It's all on sale here—who's holding, who's looking, ass, hash, trash, no returns, no guarantees. Also a living space street, a spot out of the rain under an awning against the wall, sleeping bag as a cushion, rummage through the shopping-cart closet for a change of clothes, reach into the plastic-bag fridge for the other half of the sandwich. Scattered on corners and cross-streets are urban gardens, churches, secular drop-ins, because without nature and faith and a leg up of some kind, that's where it all ends. So Nita considers it only natural for people who spend their days and often nights on the pavement to start up with other transit riders. The bus is in-house transportation, that's all, a horizontal stair lift running down a roofless hallway, and ignoring fellow riders would be as rude as stiffing your partner in your own house.

The drizzle started just as she was leaving the Carnegie Centre, and after a dozen blocks the 20 bus is a humid hothouse of recirculating poverty. Representatives of the urban middle class are opening windows, but the inrushing air doesn't seem to be diluting the funk so much as carving it into discrete units all the more pestilent for the concentration, and when the bus pulls up at the next stop the reek spreads and settles.

Nita's listening to an apple-nose man in a frayed sharkskin suit years out of style, dirty and bunched but somehow appropriate for the stage from which he's preaching. He's working the crowd, dreamily rapping and bopping, keeping the passengers high with unattached observations, at the moment inveighing against the city in which they live, explaining any place that constantly feels the need to refer to itself as Cosmopolitan and World Class must be well aware of how short it falls in both departments. As the bus looks about to pull from the curb the apple-nose man starts for the rear exit, raising from his fellow passengers cries of "Back door! Back door!" The driver dutifully halts, and now that the man has regained control of the space he takes the time to admire the fine lady he's been sitting beside. Slowly he reaches an exploratory hand toward her dreadlocks, and when the move draws a smile rather than a tropic jerk away, in return for the kindness he proffers a page torn from a book and explains to the beautiful lady it's a poem written by a friend, a dear friend. By now the crowd's growing restless. If the show's over they'd as soon get going, things to do people to see. The wheelman, too, has had about enough—he must, after all, answer to the higher power of TransLink—and he sends down the length of the bus an amplified directive that pops the ears. The apple-nose man bows to the crowd before gliding out the rear doors, and as he vanishes in a cloud of spray Nita looks down at the page with its small haiku:

who do you
panhandle
for real change?

The rest of the trip can't measure up, and the crowd travels in silence.

Real change, yes. Nita would never admit it, but maybe Buddy has a point about spreading herself too thin across the sea of social causes. So much to do, and all of it handled not by God or angels but people in all their tints, the good and the bad, the high-minded and the low. The factions and splinter groups splinter again and again, breeding redundancy and overlap of interests, diluting the funding, the attention. She feels non-profit workers would profit from specialty gear, a survival kit with something for emotional relief, foam earplugs, bicarbonate for food on the fly, prism glasses to keep an eye on things while flat on their backs from sheer immobilizing frustration. The pettiness and the all-too-human selfishness, the politics, the *tribalism* of it all. Still, they persevere despite the outside assaults and the internecine spats and squabbles. What do you do but keep at it, what do you do when you're the one with clear sight other than work to open the eyes of those who would ever after have the world's banquet table keep tipping their way while they crouch at the end with arms spread to collect and maws agape to swallow?

Earlier at the Carnegie Centre, where Nita started her day's quest, as always plenty of people were slo-mo milling around the corner. The question was barely out of her mouth when she caught the rebound.

"What you looking for'm for?" Late-middle-aged woman, in her sixties maybe. Nita had glimpsed her from time to time, strong and broad abeam, from a distance identifiable by her ever-present salmon-pink shoes, lustrous as patent leather. Closer up revealed a face with a twist of suspicion from half a lifetime of getting watery answers to meaty questions. "And his name's Bob. Robert, if you want to go ahead and call'm that, or Bobby, that's mostly what I call'm. But not *Bo*. Nobody calls'm Bo anymore except, well, Bob is what he's called."

"Sorry," Nita said. "Bo is the only name he gave me."

"He told you that?"

"Is something wrong?"

"What did you say you were looking for'm for?"

"I'm a friend. I was with him when he was sick Monday night and I want to make sure he's okay."

"You got ID?"

"Nothing that lists my friends." Nita immediately regretted the little joke, but the woman chortled in her belly like an after-firing jalopy and said, "I can't tell you nothing unless Bobby gimme the green light. It's a privacy thing."

"If you can wait a few minutes for the Carnegie to open you can check me out. I help in the library and the theatre when they need somebody."

"I know who you are. Not calling you a cop or a goofy or something."

"I understand," Nita said. "It's a privacy thing."

"You got it."

"I'm Nita."

"I'm Devona."

"Pleased to meet you."

"That's some bunch'a hair."

"I like yours," Nita said. "Curly and full of colour. Mine's been going grey since I was thirty."

"This perm and dye better last," Devona said. "I tried'm both together and fell asleep with all the stuff in, woke up thought my fuckin head was on fire." A burble of laughter shook her body. "Thought I was Richard Pryor freebasing." That one bent her over with stomach cramps, howling at the pavement. "Michael Jackson in that Pepsi commercial!" A scream of laughter and Devona staggered to the iron fence for support, head lowered between her arms, shoulders heaving, belly emitting feeble squeaks as though stuffed with kittens. "Oh, oh, fuck me, fuck meeheeheeheeheeheehee . . ." Around them on the corner was a hemi-circle of snaggletooth smiles, men and woman drifting in from the perimeter, the electricity of the moment converted by Devona's laughter to lines of magnetic force. When she finished wiping her eyes she waved and clapped her hands to disperse the crowd of snoops pushing in on her before returning her attention to Nita. "I can tell you one thing," she said. "Bobby jumped on the 20 a few minutes ago, that's only what. You want to find'm he'll be at the Value Village on Hastings and Vic or the SPCA."

"The SPCA?"

"Got friends there."

Nita bobbed her head. "Thanks so much, glad we finally met. I'm sure I'll see you soon. You know how it works—once you meet someone, next thing you know you're running into them all over the place."

"Bobby, he don't really have a costume on today. He's dressed up sort of but . . . it's not important, I guess I'm just used to seein'm with, you know."

"I think he's got a pretty good friend in you."

"That horn toots out of both ends."

When Nita turns, the 20 is cruising to a stop, and on she gets for the ride back the way she came.

At her destination, back along Hastings east of Commercial, Bo is on his second turn of Value Village. For the first time in ages he's out of costume. Other than the belled hat and booties he's dressed as an ordinary everyday citizen—vintage bell-bottom jeans, an orange paisley shirt with floppy lapels like a sniffer-dog's ears and a cowboy bolo tie featuring Willy Nelson's face on the plastic slide. He considered a couple of classics—his lion tamer ensemble hasn't been out of the trunk for months, and he hasn't dressed as a pirate since everyone at the Carnegie started calling him Johnny Depp—but after the loss of the bodysuit, nothing feels right.

Home from the barbershop yesterday afternoon, he was visited by his handyman friend, who showed up with a cheque for a job clearing blackberries. Bo still has the scratches, if anyone wants to see. For private jobs like yard work the money often arrives late and is less than what was agreed on, but in this case it was hardly short at all. After depositing most of it in his account at Pigeon Park Savings and tucking five dollars in his pocket for food, he splurged on a mechanical drawing pencil for his sketches. It's not much good for shading or filling in, but is excellent for precise lines, and he loves how easy it is to recharge the barrel with the needles of graphite instead of fumbling with a sharpener. So things were looking up till the sick feeling returned.

He ached all over, and his ankles and feet were swollen fit to burst the skin. He obviously hadn't recovered fully from his allergic reaction, and swore from now on to be extra-extra careful with seafood. Keep his distance from the aquariums in the pet store, stay off the seawall in case he's splashed with fishy spray, in Chinatown detour to side streets to avoid a whiff of the squid and other fresh and dried products in the sidewalk stands. His overall diet, too, will receive some attention. He won't fast, since it's very close to what he does on a regular basis, but he'll carefully read food labels, drink plenty of water, cut down on the graham crackers, that sort of thing.

To be on the safe side he went to bed early, but he couldn't stop thinking of the trip to the barbershop. He's never had an experience quite like it. Around three in the morning he finally gave in and turned on the light. He drank from the copper pipe and dragged the trunk across the floor so he could kneel on the mattress and inventory the contents. Some of the stuff was just taking up space—a lambswool neckpiece, a toque from Québec's Carnival, other accessories that had once contributed to long-gone costumes. These he set aside for anyone on the street who might need them to complete his or her own outfit.

Next, he retrieved the leather satchel and went through his sketches. Many of them transported him back to the source of the inspiration, or to be more accurate aroused the emotions of the time. The flashbacks weren't necessarily good for his peace of mind, but maybe important because of that. All this, how would he describe it, *nostalgia*, left him no closer to easing his inner commotion. He knows in his heart that life is all about patterns and coincidences, as much those you miss as those you recognize.

He's at the rear of the store again and decides to cut up the middle to the front. Bo likes thrift stores, recyclers of history, of memories. He wrote a story about it once in his last year at school, about the notion that most everything for sale has at one time been important to someone else. A gift given or received, clothing that kept people warm or made them feel special. These things provide a sense of identification with the past, continuity. Teapots used by mothers to make tea for their family and to serve visitors, dishes eaten from by children now parents themselves, books read and records played by those after myth and laughter and knowledge and purpose. His teacher entered the story in an essay contest for him, but the judges said he must have copied it from someone else and disqualified him.

"Bo! Over here!"

Uh-oh, it's Nita. A forced upturn of his rubbery lips is the closest he can get to pretending he's happy to see her. She's the best person he's met in forever, but how's he going to surprise her now? He has to get her gift today while he has money, and anyway when someone does something nice like buy you supper you don't wait around for Christmas to thank them.

After wrapping him in a hug Nita says, "You look great. How are you feeling? I only left the hospital because they said you were going to be kept overnight. They told me your sister came and made sure you got home all right. Does she live close? Hey, is that a new haircut? Don't be shy, take off the hat and let's see."

She keeps on at this clip till Bo's thoroughly bewildered. His mummy taught him always to answer people's questions, but at the rate they're piling up he'll have to write them down, and would if he wasn't saving his new pencil for his artwork. When Nita peters out, Bo tries to address each query in turn, skipping the first one about how he's feeling. He'd rather avoid talking about himself. It's what people do when they're scared and Nita somehow makes him feel, well, not brave but something like it. So he starts with his big sister.

"Her name's Sally?" Nita says. "And she lives on the Drive? Does she have big round eyes and stringy blonde . . . not stringy, but not as thick as my mine?"

She sure does.

"I run into her all the time. She's nice, really nice."

She sure is.

"Don't let me interrupt your shopping, I can't stay long. I just wanted to see that you're okay."

Bo has forgotten the rest of the questions, so it's a good thing Nita's still talking. Maybe she'll get to someplace where he can hop on. But when she asks what he's looking for, he's stuck for an answer. He can't say he's trying to find her a present for buying him dinner and taking him to the hospital. And he sure can't tell her about the hunt for a new Jester bodysuit. The selection of a costume, the fitting together of parts that add up to a whole, can only be done alone. It's all in the feel. Like him and Sally, they just know they belong together, brother and sister. In the same way, he and the parts of his ensemble have a way of recognizing when they belong. He settles for saying he's just browsing, but that doesn't even slow her down.

"I ran into a friend of yours," Nita says partway along an aisle of long-sleeve men's shirts, "Devona. She told me you'd either be here or the SPCA. She said you have friends there."

He sure does.

"I used to volunteer at an animal shelter before everything else took over. I keep on with the World Wildlife Fund and Greenpeace."

Bo stops so abruptly Nita bumps him from behind, almost propelling him into a forest of hangars with their branch loads of droopy T-shirts. His eyes travel over a set of shelves stacked with folded red squares.

"Long underwear," Nita says. "Who in the world buys used under—oh, these are all new. Is that what you're looking for? Let's take a look." She ignores the X-Larges and Larges, and after sizing him up concedes the Mediums look suitable for conversion into an overcoat with sufficient leftover material for a good start on a tent. The solitary set of Adult Small long johns likewise looks too big, but she tries it against his frame in case all that's needed is a tuck and a fold. Not a chance.

Bo's seen enough. He won't find the right piece here. There's no vibe of recognition. Many other items—dishes, books—have caught his eye, but he doesn't want to spend his money just because he has it on him. It's such a funny thing, money. He remembers that day in the record cold winter he made $25 working outdoors and later in the afternoon a friend won twice as much doing nothing except scratch a lottery ticket. That night, a lady downtown climbed into her shopping cart, set something on fire to keep warm and the poor girl burned to death. Which taken all together says something to him about money, fairness and luck. Uh-oh, now what?

"Impossible," Nita shouts over the rack into the next aisle. "It can't be. How about you over there, what does yours say? Quarter after ten, shit, Bo, sorry, I'm late for work, I'll call. Do you have a phone? . . . Okay, I'll find you, I'll ask Sally. Bye."

Bo watches with admiration as she hurdles a child sitting on the floor sucking on a large SALE tag, jukes through the shoppers and exits at high speed. Wow. If he could move that fast he'd keep running just for the different places it would take him.

He'd better fold the long johns and put them back on the shelf. Too bad he had no luck here today. But the good news is that it's after ten, so the SPCA will be open. He's still for a few seconds, feeding on the chatter and movement of fellow shoppers picking through the merchandise, the hustle and bustle carrying him back to his favourite day of all time, the day with his dad at the Renaissance Faire. Averting his face to keep from scaring the little girl on the floor, he aims for the door in the big wall of glass at the front, on his way to the animal shelter to spend time with his friends.

Chapter 16

Fell Deeds

The SkyTrain dopplers past him on its straightaway down Terminal, and Buddy picks up the pace. The end of the drizzle has allowed the more bashful sounds of the city to reassert themselves, and our barber's ears absorb every vibration. His eyes, too, are into the game, sending hyper-sharp images to his brain for translation. On the far side of the street hunkers a large brick storage building, where Unit 409 holds the remains of his and Nita's married life. The locker is the last remnant of their shared turf and acts as both scourge and memento. Moving at a good clip, lips a-flap rehearsing opening remarks to his upcoming adversary, Buddy hits Station Street and rounds the corner.

Louie Zimbot's call was a straight-forward offer to drop by after the shop closed, and Buddy chose to see through it. Stands to reason a grifter would try to soften up his mark with an offer to go out of his way. No deal, mister. Buddy would establish right off the bat who the big tusker of this walrus colony was, and told him straight that they'd meet wherever Louie was staying. Our barber has entertained the contrary thesis, that he's dealing with an honest man with no hidden agenda, but dismisses it as unsupported by the facts, said facts to be determined once he meets this bogus fisherman, this preyer upon widows and half-orphans.

Buddy cuts under the SkyTrain line, a dreary overhead of water-stained concrete, and chugs along the pathway through the greensward fronting the Pacific Central Terminal. A hole has opened in the clouds, a tatter-edged patch of blue drawing out longitudinally that allows a blast of sunlight to rake the south face of the Ivanhoe Hotel. Even from a distance where the eyes can't be made out, Buddy senses that the old man smoking on the sidewalk is very much aware of his presence. He looks comfortable with himself, no question about that. Casual, too casual.

Louie was caught smoking in his room and took it outside. It's pleasant against the brick wall out of the wind, and he's looking at nothing in particular when he notices an approaching pedestrian staring at him and picking up speed. He guesses this would be the son, the barber, and since it doesn't look like he plans to stop till Louie's part of the wall, he pushes off to meet him, hand out. "Louie Zimbot."

The meeting's almost a collision.

"Where do you want to talk?" Louie continues. "What time is it, nearly two, let's do this over a beer."

Buddy's left a couple of steps behind. Having had a visual in his head of some slick piece of business, he'll need a second to adjust to this weather-coarsened geezer who looks to have been dressed by his mother for the first day of school. When Louie disappears through the door without checking to see whether he's being followed, Buddy lingers a good twenty seconds to assert his independence.

Inside, Louie's already at a table against the right-hand wall, opposite the pool tables. His outsized cotton shirt bulges over his belt like liposuction's excess skin. The cuffs on the workpants saved him from littering the sidewalk by trapping a couple of inattentively dropped cigarette butts, only one of which burned through the fabric. Louie has already downed a large mouthful from the pint and stretches back comfortably in the chair, legs outstretched, new sneakers crossed. "I told the waitress we needed some privacy," he says and indicates a full glass on Buddy's side of the table, "so after this we can self-serve."

"You seem to be calling the shots here."

"Call away. This is your show, I'm just a messenger."

"Before we start—I don't like the idea of you talking to my mother without me around."

"Fair enough," Louie says. "In future I won't."

Buddy hitches. "Is that all you have to say?"

"You want me to argue with you about it? Or was I too brief. I can drag it out, repeat myself in French, whatever makes you happy."

"Don't get smart."

"That's going to be a tall order to fill," Louie says, and gets his elbows on the table. "Because I am smart. Just as I assume you are. I'm not your enemy, just a fella who hired your dad a long time ago and finds himself involved again by luck of the draw—whether good luck or bad yet to be determined." His hand goes into the green workpants and comes out with a folded sheet of paper, which he opens, pats flat and slides across the table.

"I saw this last night," Buddy says. "A photocopy, and it looks like only a piece at that, partial information, meaningless."

"Like I told your mother, the will has to be authenticated, but I wanted to lay the groundwork with anyone involved before I see a lawyer. I've already talked to one, just waiting for a call back. This is a copy of the pertinent part. Look, right there you can see—"

"Yeah, yeah—'I kept all of it. I leave it to my family. Ask the boy.'" Buddy slips the refolded sheet into the breast pocket of the Hawaiian shirt barber jacket he was in too much of a rush to change, and which now that he thinks about it didn't shake out and is itching like a homemade hair shirt. "'Ask the boy.'" he repeats. "I don't have a clue what it's referring to. And notice I said *it* and not *he*. There's no proof my father wrote this. If this was about a family heirloom or some interesting photos or lost personal correspondence, I probably wouldn't question your motives. But . . ."

"I have no legal or ethical standing and I'm not asking for any. I'm not named in the will, it just came into my possession."

"How did that happen?"

"My boat sank years ago. Little while back two scuba divers were rooting around and found it in a waterproof box."

"And you think there's money involved."

"Maybe none at all. But there's something he thought important."

"How long to authenticate it?"

"I wouldn't think very long. There's just one more page besides what you have. Basic document with no specific mention of cash or property."

"You have all the answers, don't you?"

"Exactly what you'd expect from someone telling the truth."

"The money, then. What, he had a bunch of loot socked away and never told his family?"

"It's complicated."

"Uncomplicate it while I'm taking a piss."

Buddy returns to fresh beers on the table and a serene Louie Zimbot.

"What's got you looking so satisfied?"

"I find it interesting," says the fisherman. "When my boat sank I didn't immediately recognize the personal good luck in it. We plug away all our lives at things as ingrained as the way we brush our teeth, with little satisfaction and for reasons long forgotten. When our hand is called we're forced to deal with a new world, one we haven't grown up with, and while it can be painful it's also a new start. I'm afraid the wreck happened too late in life for me to totally adjust, so you could say that right now I'm happy for another chance to feel the blood flow. And if this doesn't disturb the modern sensibilities—it's the right thing to do. Your father and I were together when the whole thing started and I'm seeing it through to the end."

Buddy's anything but sure he gives a shoemaker's shit about Louie Zimbot's need to forge a late-life turnaround, but at present it's all he has to work with. "You knew him pretty well?"

"On a fishboat you end up spending time."

"So you'd say he was a friend."

Louie picks up on the nudging and says, "Is there something you want to ask me?"

Buddy pushes away his empty glass, pulls his hand back quickly to disguise the minor tremor, and in a voice strained with offhandedness says, "What was he like? Away from home, I mean."

"I doubt I can answer that in any way that'd satisfy you."

"Did he have friends over there on the Island? People he was close to?"

"We didn't talk all that much."

"At least fill me in on the other."

After an appreciable pause to weigh the consequences, Louie says, "I'm going to tell you a story here. Last night I only roughed things in for your mother. I left this part out. Whether, when, or how you share it with her is your decision."

For the past two weeks Louie's been rehearsing, but now with the son across the table all that falls away. How to tell the story of a dead man a quarter-century after the fact? A man little comprehends his own biography. With personal history hammered half-shapeless by interpretation, what's left to judge beyond what the art of imagination reveals? We choose, is what Louie is saying, we tell one story among many and pack it with fudges and recursions to hedge the bet. So he jumps in without a life jacket, opening with that day on the water when Charlie spotted the crab pot buoy. And just as well Louie abandoned his prepared notes, for relating the story aloud to an audience shines a spotlight on the flagrant inadequacy of the arc. The straight and simple narrative of hauling up the trap hoping to steal a few Dungeness crabs shimmers with the reflection of time, and once he and Charlie reach the dock in the old fishboat the story fairly explodes into speculation. Louie chops it short, ending on neither a bang nor a whimper but a mouthful of beer.

"There's not a lot you're sure of," Buddy says.

"Can't argue with that. After we docked, it's mostly guesswork. But the drugs we pulled up, yes, I'm almost positive he went back for them. He was seen heading out with the boat not long after I left, coming back in a short time later, and two sport fishermen spotted him idling in the vicinity where we had stopped earlier. Three days later he was found in the bush."

"What were you doing all this time?"

"After we docked I took off for the west coast of the Island to visit a lady friend. I left Charlie to take care of some minor repairs."

"Couldn't that explain it? When he went out later maybe the drugs had nothing to do with it. He could have been testing the engine or whatever."

"Nothing was done to it. Same old boat next time I saw it."

"So he went and hauled up the trap planning to what, sell the stuff himself? I can't see my father as an aspiring drug dealer."

"Probably no plan, making it up as he went along. Least likely in my opinion is that he tried to keep the drugs. They'd be too complicated to get rid of safely without experience. And I don't take him as a dealer any more than you. More likely he was hoping to ransom it to the people who dropped it. There could have been a buyback of some kind, or attempted buyback. Something like that anyhow, an exchange, maybe just a deal gone bad. It's all mixed up, quite possibly he never got his hands on any money at all."

"But you think he did."

"Why else leave the will?"

"People leave wills."

"He hid it on the boat in a waterproof box, and you don't go to that trouble unless you're running scared. The only reason a will exists is for people to know about it. The troller had been fitted out as a rum-runner with a false hull. Two weeks ago a couple of scuba divers found a box, and inside—"

"Yeah, yeah, my mum filled me in on all that."

"So he hid it in a place only one person would know to look. I was the one person, but of course I didn't know there was anything to look for."

"The thing of it is, he ended up in the bush . . ." Buddy tails off, feeling uncommonly lost.

"You're safe here."

"Why would they leave him alive?"

Louie replies with a gentle surge of his shoulders. "Probably thought they didn't."

"How about you?" Buddy says. "Why were you spared? It was your boat after all, natural suspicion would zoom in on the captain. You'd be as much of a target as he was."

"I was living to fight another day." Louie chuckles with no warmth. "I was with my lady friend in Port Alberni, got a call from the manager of the marina telling me Charlie was in the hospital. That's also when I heard about him heading back out with the boat the day I left. Two-and-two together, and I didn't have to be any conspiracy theorist for my shorts to freeze. I told the marina manager to keep my friend's number to himself and didn't leave Port Alberni for a month. At that point I couldn't have done any good back in Comox anyhow, and you'll excuse me if that sounds like self-justification. Or plain cowardice."

Buddy shakes off the implication. "What about later?"

"He was gone. The hospital said he was convalescing in Vancouver. I was eat-dirt broke by then and picked up fishing where I left off. As for you and your mother, Charlie and I never talked about you. Until I read the will I didn't even know your names. Sorry if that's being blunt, but the circumstances call for it."

"How about the cops?"

"All they got out of your dad was a hazy story of a fall down a slope. Climbing, hiking, a fall, same story he gave your mum it sounds like. The Mounties accepted his version and why not? Accidents and mountainsides aren't strangers to each other."

"For argument let's say you're right. The will makes you think either there was the payoff you guessed at or that the drugs were hidden somewhere, so why wouldn't the rightful owners—if that's the term—keep after it?"

"They might not have been local players. Presuming Charlie dead, they cleared out. And if they knew he was alive, they'd also know that by then the police were at least in contact with him. With their offshore drop blown, they would have considered themselves well gone and out of it. To you and me a crab pot full of drugs is big league, but it would be a walk-away for a large outfit concerned with protecting the organization. All I know for sure is there was never any news about it. Nothing on TV, the papers, not even local gossip."

"You've done some thinking on this."

"You wouldn't believe."

"And you still don't know the truth."

"Not within a mile."

Buddy sweeps the room with his eyes, registering nothing of the physical space. Louie waits patiently, as though tracking the barber through the virtual hedge maze of possibilities, a labyrinth the fisherman himself has thoroughly explored without breaking into the open.

"'I kept all of it.'" Buddy finishes his beer. "Anyone familiar with him would know 'all of it' might mean forty bucks in his wallet."

Louie smiles in accord. The mood lightens appreciably.

"Over his head," Buddy continues. "Way over his head."

"I left out these details with your mother. Obviously it's up to you whether to tell her, but she seems well able to handle it."

"I wouldn't think not to tell her. But before I do, I'd like to see a full copy of the will."

Louie nods and says, "This isn't exactly my regular line of work. I don't doubt I'll make a few mistakes along the way but I'm trying to keep everyone's feelings in mind. After twenty-five years, for this to surface . . ."

"Yeah."

"Your family—brothers and sisters?"

"No, just us, me and my mum."

"Cousins?"

"No."

"I see."

A long pause till Buddy rises. "I have to get going."

"One more thing. I feel uncomfortable saying this, and you don't have to give me an answer now or ever. But it might help if you could think back to that time, or ask your mother, whether your father was going through a bad patch. A particular period of pressure that would have made him take a risk like he did. Anything. Family problems, personal, like that."

"Of course," Buddy says. "Anything we can think of."

"I'll keep you up to speed as much as I can. The number I reached you at, was that the barber shop?"

Buddy nods and scribbles his cell number on a corner of the photocopy. Louie tears it off, makes a grateful sound and tucks it into his wallet. Buddy smiles soft-easy-like, but the scene has grown impossibly homey. This will require peak performance, teeth and edge, and he deliberately fastens onto dark thoughts before leaving without a goodbye.

Chapter 17

Where There's a Will, There's Waves

This morning Lippy did it again. Said he'd be at the meeting in exactly twenty-three minutes and nailed it on the nose, to the second. Al looks down the bar where June and Nita are still doing everything but physically circle each other. They've been arguing off-and-on all day with the creepy smiles of friends finding themselves on opposite sides of a divide.

How can he get through to his wife how important this deal with Lippy is? Al and the three other guys are like most small business owners these days, told they're the backbone of the community but have been ground down over the years till you wonder how much a guy can stand. Leases and taxes sky-high, wondering every day whether you'll be able to cover your payroll, out of credit so you can't afford even to spruce the place up, and he'll not even get into the younger people trying to raise families. Al's read up on the larger picture and has a good freshman's grasp on the philosophy—neoliberalism versus market protection, regional and national openness to investment and expansion, trickle-down theory, all very interesting but on a neighbourhood level neither here nor there.

Al and the boys view it as simply as it was proposed, four small businesses combining under the umbrella—a large, successful and waterproof umbrella, Al doesn't have to add—of Cicalone and Lippy's other five out-of-province shops. With six solid high-end stores to their four average local joints, naturally Lippy Delillo will have overall control. And who'd want it different? Not all of them together comes close in sales to any one of Lippy's outfits. And the cherry on top of the icing that's on top of the cake—wait a sec, did Al get that right, yeah, it'll do—is that while Lippy and his board members will be applying their expertise to all ten businesses, Al and the new boys will have a combined forty-percent say. And since major policy can only change by two-thirds vote, the four of them can block anything that sounds too drastic. As if they would! The attraction in the first place is Lippy's business genius.

Al leans his back on the bar so he can see out to the street. Rain again. With the buyout, him and June'll never have to stick it out through another crappy spring or Canadian winter in their life. Pick their spots to come back for a visit. Another glance down the bar. Nita, there's another one. Al said to her once that she treats Lippy like a cockroach, and she said when it comes to greed it's broader than just Lippy. She told Al to keep in mind that even the cockroach starts off clean—it ain't unhealthy till it starts spreading around human filth. What's that all about? Lippy's a clean cockroach? Society's all filth? So this is what Al said to her, he said if her friends and family are a little dirty, does she prefer a clean cockroach? You can bet that shut her up. Well, it didn't, but that's Nita.

Al's gotta tell June, and soon. Bad enough he's been keeping it secret this long, but now that he's actually got the papers in his hand, that's it. He hasn't signed yet, but he's promised, and that's as good to Lippy.

Another glance down the bar to where the *miracolo* of his life is filling Nita's order. Seven years ago they at least had the thrill of the future to keep them going. If in another seven years they're in the same position—fighting for every dime, half glad when an employee quits so they can save on a salary, June wearing the same pair of shoes so broken down her knees and back are going out—wait, no chance, they're not going to be in the same position. He can talk till he's blue in the face about Lippy and everything else, but it's Al's job to fix this. His idea in the beginning, his experience, his start-up cash and now his responsibility. He's not looking to be some billionaire tycoon with the boats and the jets or nothing. Good enough for him if he's hero to June Monk so she doesn't have to work her fingers to the bone and buy clothes that fall apart before the year's out.

Everyone wants to be a hero to people they love, and never mind scoring no winning goal in a game or having a monster house looks like a castle in the suburbs. No, the best way is just doing whatever it takes for the one with the high, hard hold on your heart.

June's returning Al's glances, trying to decipher the series of facial expressions that flicker and flash as he tries to digest what's going on in his head.

". . . how scared I was."

"Sorry?" June says.

Nita's across the bar at the staff service area and hasn't turned to check on the floor for ten minutes. "He almost died," she says.

June's close to screaming. She's been making no more progress getting Nita off the subject of Sally's brother than she does with Buddy when he's on a mission of clearing his name of some self-inflicted stain. She asked Nita to stay late for a large group that had just arrived, but they dawdled over one drink apiece, off they went, and now it's different, now June's getting fed up, now there might be a little spite. She loves Nita and believes their variety of understanding to be rare among men, whose younger-older friendships are usually more teacher-pupil than communion. But there's no realism in Nita, a lack of recognition that certain things in life cannot be massaged. When it blows, you shelter. When it floods, you sandbag. "I keep telling you I don't care if you were late this morning. I thought we were done with this."

Nita would like to be done with it, but everything about June from her tone of voice to the jerking of her hands screams of a woman who hasn't let one thing go. God, what does Nita have to do? She could have pulled a hamstring in her sprint from Value Village and now this, forced to make up the time by working past five. Detention, that's what it is, school-age punishment plain and simple. She wonders whether she's blundered into the wrong job. Or the wrong boss. Working for a stranger is easy. There are no hard feelings if you need a little time for yourself. She's learned often enough it eventually gets you fired, but that's a price willingly paid. "Okay," she says, "consider the topic closed. Next time I see someone fighting for their life I'll walk on by."

"Thank you. That would be fine."

Al pulls away from the bar and takes to the floor. He doesn't know about this will-and-testament business, but already he'd like it to be over one way or another. What's the deal with this CC character anyways? It'd be nuts in the noodle of Al to be jealous of a dead guy all this time, and June's never given him reason to be, never gone around staring into space or nothing like that, but this is the most upset Al's seen her in maybe forever. You'd think the chance at some surprise cash would have her interested, but no way, it's just packed her full like a sausage you forgot to poke on a grill, ready to burst its skin. And she can't quit talking about Buddy this and Buddy that, although right this minute Al can see the sense in worrying. The baloney artist is supposed to be meeting this old fisherman from Comox so there must be all kinds of scary-movie crapola running through June's head. Wouldn't surprise nobody she gets a call from the police about Buddy going to town on some ancient mariner and put him in the hospital, she's gotta go down to the cop shop and bail the idiot out.

Humming a little tune, he wanders the room looking for something to keep him occupied, but the few customers are nursing their drinks, looking unsatisfied with themselves for sitting in the same spot every day. When June cracks his name, Al jerks and bangs his knee on a table. Nobody can blame him for making the most of it by putting on a limp on the way to the bar.

"I didn't say nothing to nobody," Al says. "Not a word, honest."

"You don't even know what I want you for," June says.

Nita replaces Al on the floor and begins working the room.

"Look at her out there," June says. "Little Miss Innocent."

"Did you tell her to keep it to herself?" Al says.

"She doesn't need to be told."

"Aww."

"Don't *aww* me," June says. "I wish we'd never heard. The wording's vague and probably doesn't mean anything."

"That's not what you said before," Al corrects.

"Thanks for your help, you're a goddamn pillar."

Money. Last week June passed a luxury automobile showroom, and with the cost of any single car through the glass she and Al could wipe out the accumulated debt of seven years. June won't fool herself into thinking she can live on love alone—oh, she can, anyone can, but for a limited time and not very well—so of course money would be welcome. But she's not looking for a life-altering amount, just enough to keep the subject off her mind a few hours each day.

Nita approaches the bar with collision speed. At the last second she brakes and gently places her tray on the bar. "Sorry," she says, face creased into a pained smile.

"Oh, I'm sorry too," June says. "I'm just . . . it's not your fault."

"My dad," Nita says. "He used that old saying 'Hard work never hurt anyone.' Except it hurt him. Before he died every part of his body had arthritis or bone spurs or damaged tendons. Doesn't hurt? You might get an argument from a few million peasants, serfs, sugarcane cutters, miners. In our lucky little spot—a fluke of the universe we were born here and not in the middle of a civil war or famine—working hard usually doesn't kill you, but working hard and making no money can. An older man I know who does volunteer work for Megaphone, the street newspaper, worked as a carpenter and was doing okay till a few years ago. Now he can't even get steady work as a labourer. The construction companies have been replacing their fulltime workers with temps. My friend goes to the hiring office at five-forty-five in the morning, sits there with the others trying not to meet too many eyes, waits an hour and another and another with only coffee in his stomach, maybe—a big maybe—a call comes and he gets on the bus and spends eight hours trying to hide his sore back while making it worse slogging garbage around a construction site in the pissing rain. After the temp company takes their huge chunk he walks away with less than what he used to make before lunch.

"The laugh is that when the stats come out, he counts as one of the officially employed, even though underpaid and completely unsecured. And unions are hanging on like everyone else. I can understand starting off low and building toward something, but isn't that what people have been doing for generations? Didn't our very lucky corner of the world get to a certain place and now have to watch it all being redirected to CEO bonuses and levitated from the street to the penthouse through tax exemptions and unfair policies? Hard work, sure. But no one should have to work hard to make so little money it can't do any work of its own, like buying groceries and clothes.

"So I'm happy for you. Money can turn things around. Even if it's not much, at least you can afford proper staff and stop having to hire slack-asses like me. And don't try to make it better, I know where I fit into the workforce—I don't. But that's my thing to deal with."

The stillness takes on its own personality until Al says, "Don't be too sorry. It's not like you went and tried to steal a barrel of beer on a bus or nothing."

Smiles are the most that can be managed, but with feelings repaired as best as possible—albeit with duct tape and operating without a warrantee—things return to normal. For about eight seconds.

"Where are you?" June says into the phone. "All I can hear is traffic . . . How did it go? . . . What's that supposed to mean? . . . She's standing right in front of me, ask her yourself . . . Hello? Hello?" June slides the phone on the bar. "The King of the Buzz Cut is on his way. He was checking to see if you were here."

"Did he say why?"

June shakes her head. "He wants you to meet him at the shop. He sounds pretty wound up."

"I have a shift to finish."

June shoos her away with a wave. "Let's not go back to being stupid, you and me."

Chapter 18
By Any Other Name

The meeting with the estate lawyer goes quicker than Louis had it figured:

"I need it authenticated," Louie says. "And some general legal advice."

"You're the executor?"

"None was named. I knew the deceased and it came into my possession. I'm not in the will but want to see it through. Properly, do it right, have all parties protected."

"Is the challenge to the will that it's an outright forgery?"

"Challenge?"

"You see, ultimately the authenticity of a will is confirmed or not by the BC Supreme Court, presumably when a disgruntled friend or family member brings a claim against the estate and argues that the will is not authentic. The Court considers whether the will was executed in accordance with the formal requirements in the legislation—signature of testator witnessed properly, whether it was stored properly in the years prior to the death of the testator, whether a wills notice was filed with Vital Statistics. A wills notice would be fairly compelling evidence that this person did in fact execute a will, even though, oddly enough, it's not mandatory in British Columbia."

"Better slow down," Louie says. "He signed the thing all right, but there's no witness signature, and there might be a problem with how it was stored, no question about that. The will itself though, I'm sure it's genuine."

"So rather than authentication you're looking for an opinion on its validity. The will's form and substance, whether it's been properly executed and rational on its face, any indication that the testator lacked the capacity to execute a will by reason of insanity or other mental impairment."

"One thing I'd like to get straight," Louie says, "is how much of what I'm going to say is between you and me. Other than that, keep going. I'm just hanging on for the ride."

"Once I'm on retainer my loyalty is absolute. Of course, I wouldn't accept a retainer until I was confident that I could properly address the legal aspects of the case."

"There are some kinks in the background," Louie admits. "But right now all I need is advice on how to . . . here, why don't you read this first."

Louie stretches and wanders to the window, where he gazes out on a scene of stasis. He knows from his years of things nautical and meteorological that land both heats and cools faster than water, so all other things being equal, the daytime heating of the city sends parcels of air soaring more quickly aloft, drawing from the ocean a cooling onshore breeze. In the evening, as the land loses its high-caloric injection of solar energy, the wind reverses. To be at the intersection, the fuzzy flip-flop from onshore to off, is to feel the day stand still and catch its breath.

He wonders whether he needs to bother with a lawyer at this stage. A private detective would easily serve the main purpose, or he could even start with someone with decent computer search skills. But hooking up with a lawyer is probably the way to go. Louie's been caught short in the past without counsel, predictably so for someone of his solitary decision-making temperament, and besides, this isn't his show but a family affair.

Family affairs in any form aren't Louie's strong suit. An only child of five when the black lung from the Nanaimo coal mines caught up to his father, six when his mother hooked up with a returned WW II veteran of the BC Regiment and left Louie behind with an extended family composed mostly of neighbours and government workers. Lifelong bachelor. Many loves along the way but any meaningful union failed to survive his feckless attempts to cram partnership into his lockbox of absolute self-determination. So he'll play it safe. Safe all-round, he might add, hence the incomplete photocopy he showed the Monks. And good thing he went with his intuition, since it was immediately apparent neither mother nor son were in on the extended version of Charlie Monk's story.

The lawyer's quickly through the document.

"What's the good word?" Louie says.

"The date. It was a long time ago. I assume the will just recently came to light."

"That's right. I was a fisherman on the Island, Charlie Monk was my deckhand. An accident ended his fishing days and he died here in Vancouver a short time later."

"Other than the time that's passed, I fail to see these 'kinks' you referred to. What is it you're looking for, counsel on how to distribute the estate? And while we're on the subject, what constitutes the estate? You mentioned a deal of money and there's no indication of that here."

"There may be money, there may not."

The lawyer raises the page, bringing it up close to his nose despite wearing lenses that could have substituted for Erwin Rommel's field glasses. "'Ask the boy.'"

"Buddy Monk knows nothing of it. To him the whole thing is a bolt out of the blue."

"What about his mother?"

"Same. Both are curious but aren't counting any chickens."

"These chickens. Are they of the legal variety?"

Louie fingers the cigarette pack in the breast pocket of his shirt. "They're definitely free range, out there running around."

"I can't be party to—"

"I'm not asking anything like that. For now I just need help finding the rest. I've already talked to Buddy and ruled him out, so the other boy must be the one to ask. Later on we can define your role, and if it all works out of course your services will be needed to advise the families."

"I see. So you don't know where the others are." Another glance at the will. "The Fairchilds."

"I never met them. Just what Charlie told me. And after the accident they never came forward. I've already checked his old address in Bowser you see there on the will, but there's no trace."

"The Monks?"

"I didn't even know they existed till now. I only started with them because they were first on the list and shared Charlie's last name. There was also that Steveston address to go by, and it turned out they had never left the lower mainland so were easy to find. I always thought Charlie's family was the one on the Island. But it looks like he was staying with this Norma Fairchild and her kids while he was fishing, and going home to his family in the off-season." Louie has a smoke out and is rolling it between his fingers like a close-up magician prior to making it disappear. "I'd like to locate the Fairchilds, find out what they know and where they stand before I get deeper into this Monk business. When it comes to the estate, you can see there's more than one dog in the fight."

"Of course, but let's hope there's no fight at all. These things can be impossibly sad and shabby."

"Maybe everybody knows everybody else. The explanation could be as simple as Charlie staying with mutual friends on the Island to save on renting a place."

"But you don't think so."

A long moment till Louie says, "I don't think so. All I'm sure of is that the first order of business is to find the Fairchilds."

"Were they impoverished? When they disappeared, I mean."

"Don't know," Louie says.

"Most small-town west coasters don't move far from the mountains and water. Another small town maybe, or if there was no money then Victoria, or here in Vancouver, someplace where there's work. If they're still alive they shouldn't be too hard to locate no matter where they went. This is the everything-everyone-connected era, not the days when people could make themselves scarce and stay that way."

"So you're good with this?" Louie says.

"Nothing illegal, you understand."

"You're the lawyer, you'll have to tell me."

Chapter 19

Fiercely Mellow

It's almost seven. What kind of numbnuts goes looking for a haircut this time of night? Buddy glares through the window and jerks a thumb down the street. The man on the sidewalk, a newly arrived refugee from Syria who paused to practise his English by translating the words on the glass, scurries away, wondering whether fleeing his homeland has changed anything.

Possibly Nita has no intention of showing, but Buddy doesn't give that line of thought much credence. She'll come if only to get out of work. So what's with the delay, let's go, shake a leg. He was twenty minutes away when he called, add ten for the time it took him to throw out a few bags of papers and garbage and make the shop look halfway presentable, and now another twenty standing here with his thumb up his ass. Late, Nita's predominant character trait, late for everything. He'd call the restaurant again if it didn't reek of desperation. As does his face pressed to the window, come to think of it.

The light's good this evening. Creeping up on the solstice, the days are near as long as they'll get yet haven't the harshness of July and August, still sport a little spring softener. Buddy normally reaps great strength from following the mood of the sky, but there's no time for that now, not with serious business ahead. Once Nita gets here, an amount of love and tenderness is bound to crop up because it never completely soured, but it's about time they got down to issues, a hundred times he's reminded himself to stick to actual issues. A shiver of doubt turns into a full shake. He's going to piss in the pickles, just watch. Too late to back out, though, so come on, Nita, come on girl. If for once she'd be in the right place at the right time he could get the backed-up words out before they clog up his throat completely. His throat? Never mind his throat, they'll destroy his insides, wouldn't surprise him to wake up tomorrow with a perforated colon. He might have rewritten his notes and done more rehearsing, but he anticipated she'd see through a rehearsed performance and there'd go the conviction he wants to convey. And it is conviction, honest hard conviction on actual issues, not some loosey-goosey . . . here she is. Way to go, Nita, sneak up on a guy before he's ready why don't you. Play it smooth, Buddyboy, be cool, put on the stray cat strut.

Dingle.

Nita's changed from work clothes into an ultralight mauve-and-khaki top that flows over her small breasts down to charcoal workout pants tight enough to reveal her mitochondria. Buddy almost cries. He's been without her for the three months since their separation and a good two before that.

"Thanks for coming," he says.

"I don't want to start right off complaining," Nita says, "but do we have to talk here? Let's go up to your apartment, I haven't even seen the place."

"Too dangerous," Buddy says. "This time of night Oxhead rules. He'd tear you to pieces the minute you walked through the door."

"Don't tell me you got a dog," she says. "After all the energy I wasted trying to talk you into it."

"My watchmouse."

"Mouse, oh. So you did give it a name." She flops down in the orange brocade armchair. "What do you call it again?"

"Oxhead." Buddy hands her a coolish Lucky Lager he pulls from a plastic bag of cans and ice. "How're things over there?"

"I don't know how long I'm going to last. I love your mum, I love Al. But at work they can . . ."

"That's why I'm a barber. I get to work alone and with a weapon in my hand."

Nita laughs. "You don't know why you're a barber."

"You might have me there," he says. "But I sure remember shops like this with my dad. I'd get a haircut only when he took me. My mum hated long hair on young boys but would let me get all shaggy till he'd show up from the Island. For the first few days he'd fawn all over us and talk a lot about finding work closer to home, maybe on a boat running right there out of Steveston—we were two short blocks from the docks—but pretty soon the talk would turn to how iffy work was in the port with the decline in salmon and the shutting-down of the canneries. It was getting so fishermen couldn't find buyers for their boats. It wasn't till years later I wondered why it would be better at any other place on the Island or up the coast. He was from the Island originally, just following his nose to his roots, I guess. I knew it was nearing time for him to leave again when he started with practical matters—butchering a half-side of beef or pork for the freezer, post-dating rent cheques, renewing licences and all that. And taking me for my haircut."

The pause is so long Nita wonders whether thoughts of those days have run him off the rails. It wouldn't be the first time.

"Funny old guy," Buddy says. "Paul the Dirty Barber, the mothers called him. He had all these magazines on a low table in the waiting area, out-of-date skin mags before porn became mainstream. *Oui, Playboy*, so innocent now compared to the internet. The conversation rarely diverged from his trade. He'd start with the observation that a child's development is incomplete without lessons in self-grooming. We're taught to wash, wipe, shave, shower, clip nails and comb. But hair cutting, he maintained, is normally—and properly—left to the expert.

"He gloried in the barber's role as a checkpoint on a young man's journey. Heard it all before, it's been romanticized to death, but it has some weight behind it. A boy's first trip to the barbershop is special. Other groomers we could easily do without. Manicurists, pedicurists, they could be outright persecuted and driven beyond the city limits without loss to society. But introduction to the barber is a necessary component of a boy's development. In the rites-of-passage game, Iron John is your everyday neighbourhood barber's bitch."

Nita laughs. "That's why you became a barber? Why didn't you just join Big Brothers?" When Buddy doesn't answer, she heaves from the depths of the sprung chair and puts her can on the nearest table. "Look at yourself in the mirror, your expression. You do this every time, Buddy. If I laugh and try to have fun, you claim I never take you seriously. When I accept what you say at face value, you act like it's all a big joke. You can't have it both ways. It makes me feel inadequate, groping around always getting your meaning wrong. I don't care anymore about your cheating at every stupid game, but play fair with me."

When the silence settles in as though to stay awhile, Buddy says, "I was trying to tell you about my dad."

"Now you open up. Nice timing." Nita will not make this easy on him. But she'll go a little way. "I heard you dropped the lawsuit against the lawn bowling club."

"Yeah, well, what are you going to get out of suing a bunch of seniors? How many cardigans does a guy need?"

"Good. You're my hero."

He can tell the word was chosen lightly—sarcastically?—but Buddy can't prevent the puffing of his chest. "So I met Louie Zimbot," he says to change the subject, or more accurately to home in on what he intended to start with all along. "He's staying at the Ivanhoe."

"I heard."

"What's your take on this guy?"

"Just what your mum told me. I was cashing out while they were outside so I never got his story directly. When they came in we talked about nothing for a few minutes, that's it. June filled me in once he was gone."

"He's got a lawyer, looks like." Buddy sits up straight. "I hope it's someone tough. A pain in the ass with steel for a spine. Clarence Darrow, Johnny Cochran, that type."

"Maybe someone living."

"Then that Toronto shit-disturber, what's his name, Clayton Ruby."

"They're all lawyers known for civil rights cases. Are you still thinking of the lawsuit?"

"I told you I dropped it. For this, I just want the best guy available."

"Or woman?"

"Yes, or woman."

Nita rises and heads for the door.

"Hey, no, where are you going, there's something else."

"I'm tired."

"Just sit down again . . . There, that's better, isn't it. Isn't it?"

"I'll take another beer."

"You bet." Buddy combs his fingers through the slurry of ice and cans till latching on to a winner. "Here you go, finally starting to get cold. Plastic bags are handy for small ice jobs. That little waist-high beer fridge I won at The Dime wasn't worth the bother."

"There you go again." Nita hopes a sip of beer will keep her from screaming. Or laughing, which could turn out worse. "Ten witnesses and staff say you accused the real winner of stuffing the raffle box with entries and tried to claim your 'rightful prize' by lugging it out the back door. Everybody's heard about it, and I mean it—someone posted it on Facebook and it went viral. You didn't win the thing at all. Then to make it worse, you left the fridge in the alley to go back to the bathroom and it was hit by a car. When you tell these stories don't you ever consider that people communicate with one another?"

"Before you make me out to be the bad guy here, let me ask you a question. If someone leaves a little fridge in an alley for two minutes and some half-blind woman probably on medication smashes into it with her SUV, who's to blame? Seriously, what if the fridge had been a kid in a stroller?"

"She'd probably be charged with manslaughter."

"I rest my case."

"And you'd be charged with kidnapping a baby from the bar and abandoning it in an alley."

She grins that grin of hers and Buddy takes advantage of the rosy moment. "Hey, this is all right, isn't it? Gassing around like we used to."

"I'm almost out of gas. Why did you want me to come over?"

"Something Louie said. I wanted your take on it before I tell my mum. She's hard to read lately."

"You have five minutes."

"Before I start, do you mind keeping this part quiet? I'll tell Mum myself." Speaking of CC with second-hand information from a stranger, introducing hearsay evidence of a father gone to sea and in a sense never fully returned, sounds thin and unreal to Buddy's own ears, as though he's relating the tale of a quasi-historical character. But it's all he has to work with so follows Louie Zimbot's version without adding his own margin notes.

"Drugs," Nita says when Buddy finishes. "What can I say? I never knew the man, and you've often talked *of* your dad but hardly ever *about* him."

"So you think he levered money out of these guys, kept the coke, what?"

"Who can say what was going through his mind. Pressure comes from all angles, and if it catches you at a weak moment there's no telling how you'll respond. When given the right provocation, our essential goodness or badness can split off and take us in wildly different directions."

"I wonder if there's a statute of limitations on drug money or extorted money or payoff money or whatever it would be called. If enough time goes by, is it considered clean?"

"Wait till you hear what the lawyer says."

"Wait," Buddy says as though it's the most ridiculous suggestion ever to spurt through human lips. After a slug of beer and a few seconds with himself, Buddy continues: "Every time my dad was due home I'd build it up to be a huge deal, like he was returning from grand adventures in exotic locations. I guess because that's how my mum played it. And for a long time it was probably true for her. But at some age I learned to recognize her enthusiasm was forced, probably around the time it changed for me too. She put on a good show but the air between them was raw. Till then I was a street urchin, no one to tell me to come in from playing to eat supper, allowed to mess around by the docks and the river, could tear all over the place while the other kids were inside for the night. But as my dad got sadder and my mum got madder I was expected to be like the other kids. Dress properly, wear shoes all the time, and whenever he came home I had to be with both of them at every opportunity. We were a family, and that's how families are expected to behave. They stay together through thick and thin, eat together, play together and all that. But I don't remember my dad really being involved in any of it. He was just sort of there. So no, he never really went after what he wanted, didn't seem built for direct action at all."

"Looks to me that if he got involved with something illegal it was to help you and June. Most people would be gnawed by guilt for being away so much."

"He could have just talked to her. And to me too. I was probably smarter then than I am now. But fuckall out of him. Even his final message—a will left on a boat that we're learning about twenty-five years after the fact."

"Whatever his motives, he paid the price."

"Yeah. Dying's not all it's cracked up to be."

Nita smiles thin-lipped. "Why haven't you told me any of this before? Why didn't . . . " She rises and circles the room, taking in the tools of the trade, the chairs smoothly spun with a touch of the hand, the magazines and litter, the photos of hockey players and sprinters, warriors and tycoons. One of the large mirrors is tilted slightly downward, allowing her a knees-to-noggin view of herself. She can see CC Monk's son in reverse, sitting with his back turned, the mirror cutting him off at the waist. Nita's father had no problem with direct action. Pushed her into schoolwork, shoved her into athletics, signed her up for a dog's breakfast of activities, volunteered her for any number of supposed character-building undertakings, constantly mistaking *faits accomplis* for encouragement. So of Buddy's experience—what does she know?

"What are you going to do with your share?" Buddy says, drawing Nita from the mirror.

"My what?"

"Of the money. You stand to collect on this too."

"I have no intention of collecting anything."

"Look, you want me to play fair, I'm playing fair. I don't care what you do with it. Quit the restaurant, donate your slice to charity, build Yogi Bear Yoga their own ashram. Seriously, think of what you could do with it on the Downtown Eastside.

Wouldn't it be nice to be able to sweeten the volunteer work with a good-size donation?"

"What if it really is drug money?"

"Then swing it around to harm reduction. Give it to the free injection site or some place."

Nita slumps in the chair and crosses her ankles.

"Okay," Buddy says. "I won't mention money again. But how about this—Mum told me about you and the allergy thing with your friend Bo. So that's what you were talking about when you mentioned the nurse. Anyhow, I checked up and guess who his sister is? Sally From the Alley."

"I already know. And I wish you'd use her real name."

"Sally Fairchild."

"That's a start."

"I gave Bo a haircut yesterday. Didn't charge him a penny."

"Makes sense. You came close to being his brother-in-law."

"Cute," Buddy says. "I just thought I'd mention it. Free, just as it says on the card. No scam, even gave him the card back."

"First the nurse and now this. Do you remember every single word I say? No wonder you find it so easy to drag old arguments in to service the new ones."

"I remember when I'm accused of something and I remember when I'm dusted off. Monday after yoga you mentioned Bo and a nurse, I politely tried to make conversation by asking about the hospital, and you acted like I was reading from your diary on CBC Radio."

Nita acknowledges the claim with silence. She's starting to feel comfortable and has only herself to blame. It's what she gets for showing up in the first place. "So maybe I was wrong about the free haircut thing. Accept my apology."

"Yeah, right in that chair there. My first pompadour, did him up like John Travolta in *Grease* and didn't charge a cent."

"Let's keep it under control," Nita says. "You're a gift to humankind, okay? You walk with kings and keep the common touch or however it goes."

"Walk with them? I *am* one. Ask Bo."

"Did you talk to him?"

"I don't know that you'd call it talking. He's not much of a conversationalist. But somehow he makes himself understood. A word or two and you get the whole spiel. Does that make any sense?"

"Yes, it does," Nita says.

"I like the guy."

"So do I. But I'm not sure we're in the same space. There are problems there."

"Do you know where he lives?"

Shakes her head. "But I can imagine."

They sit, the silence ballooning till Nita cocks her head to look around him. Buddy follows her move. "Howdy, howdy, if it isn't my favourite warhorse."

From the rear of the shop, Oxhead strolls with his swivel-hipped gait till halting behind the main chair and gobbling up a crumb missed by the barber's broom. With nary a flicker of concern for the proprietor and the stranger at the front, he searches to no avail for further morsels before showing them his bum and exiting at a window-shopper's pace.

Nita's tingling. "Is that him?" she whispers as the creature, his cameo concluded, vanishes into shadow. "Where did you find him, her?"

"Him. And he found me."

"He's all . . ."

"Deformed," Buddy says. "You just saw his walk. Up close he has a squashed melon and a patch of long hair on his back."

"Isn't he afraid? Mice are supposed to be afraid. If it weren't for mice, there'd go our main metaphor for *timid*."

"I don't know what he is. He's just Oxhead."

"I love him."

"He's a beauty, all right."

The liquid cast of her eyes and the easy athletic grace as she shifts in her chair and redirects her attention from mouse to man has Buddy all hopped up. *C'mon, Nita, you can do it, girl.*

"Ten minutes," she says. "One more of the cold ones. Just one."

Yes!

★

Buddy is dawdling. The shop lights are off, and the view through the window is of a street wound down. Any pedestrians abroad are moving through the rain with the relief of being on the very last leg of a very long day.

Vegetation slumbers, awaiting sunrise when the heliocentric members of the community will swivel their heads to the east, providing a wake-up call for the shrubs to shake a leg and the night spiders to seek the shade. No crows are airborne, all abed in the rookery. They've given over their territory to the local nocturnal flyers and the out-of-towners trying to negotiate the downtown core without dashing their brains out on the foolishly lit towers of glass. Through the short grass and the rough concrete, up sidewalks and alongside front-yard hedges, waddle striped skunks and masked coons, bold as brass. In the alley, a stray cat struts. Comfortably protected from the elements, Oxhead is on the mooch, having a look-see at what's going on in the walls of the old building. Mindless of whether the Big Things in the smelly room downstairs settled anything, he's fixing to head on up to the second floor soon to grab something wholesome to eat. The snack he gobbled earlier without taking time to check had some blue stuff on it that made him spit up, and he's kicking himself for acting like such a greedy guts. How desperate can a guy get to bolt down anything he comes across? He ain't no rat.

Buddy's glad he and Nita got down to issues. After sailing through the shallows of CC and Louie Zimbot and money and sundries, eventually the sails tightened in the wind and the talk made for deeper waters, where dwelt the scaly personal issues, where be dragons. Nita might disagree, but Buddy feels he has a lot to be proud of, broaching subjects for months taboo, speaking freely with no thought of gaining the advantage. And if they didn't really cut to the heart, if he's fooling himself just enough to get to sleep tonight, at least they talked. They sat and talked and laughed a little too. So he was right after all. He'd picked the perfect time to invite her over to start cutting their way through the confusion and the sorrow. The other matter about which he'd been right, despite managing to dodge it till right at the end, was his finding a way to fuck it up.

If only he hadn't tried to kiss her.

Chapter 20

Tapped Out

Bo tosses his hat on top of the wardrobe trunk and wriggles his feet from his booties.

After an excellent visit yesterday with his friends at the SPCA—a new Jack Russell had him laughing so hard a staff member familiar with epilepsy rushed to investigate—he decided to keep the warm-and-fuzzies going and spent the rest of the afternoon with the birds at Lost Lagoon. He still needed a replacement for the rest of his Jester costume, so his plan for today was to check out the Salvation Army and a couple of other used clothing dealers. After all that, he needs a rest.

He lowers himself to the mattress on the floor. Rolling his UBC sweatshirt into a crumpled cylinder, he slips it under his neck and with a sound of relief gives himself over to the comfort of his bed. Spreading his feet into a V allows him to see his latest Vancouver sketch where it's propped against the trunk. It looks better from a distance. Up close, the lines show how his hand was shaking. He hasn't had much practice with the mechanical pencil. It's fancy and nice to the touch but isn't rough-and-ready like his yellow 2Hs and HBs.

He cheated a tiny bit with the drawing. From his perspective on the Fraser River delta, to get the look he wanted of the mountains took some fudging. As an artist, he offers no apology. The sketch might not be true to life but that's never been as important as transferring what's in his head to a piece of paper. The drawing is slipping down, and as soon as he rests he'll mount it like the others on a stiff piece of cardboard. Chilling quickly as his sweat evaporates, he rolls over, tugs the bedspread out from under himself and covers up.

For exercise Bo mostly likes walking. As a boy, he'd tramp for miles and miles, sometimes with his dad but usually all alone with his thoughts and the sounds of the forest and the water. People found it strange, but he never let it bother him, and eventually they quit asking where he was going. He knew from books that all sorts of people had walked much farther than he ever did. To the top of mountains, across deserts, through jungles. This one time on the back of a sketch he did of blowing grass and thistles, Bo printed a Spanish proverb from a book in the Carnegie Library:

Traveler, there are no roads. Roads are made by walking.

His handyman friend said there was a beautiful walk on the dike in Richmond, where he's been working on a house renovation. And as a bonus, his friend said Bo might find a new costume in the Thrift Store in Steveston, the old fishing village along the water. At the end of the SkyTrain line, somehow in the rush of downtown Richmond's shopping malls Bo got completely turned around and took three wrong buses before reaching his destination. By then he was tired and hungry and tingly and his feet were swollen like crazy, but it wasn't long till he found something that perked him up. It was the cutest bargain place he's ever seen, a little old converted church with a small slatted bell tower and a ramp leading from the sidewalk up to two red doors. The place was staffed by a whole bunch of older ladies attached to the Richmond Hospital Auxiliary, and in ten minutes he was on his way with his new outfit, black with bold red accents, and to carry it a small pack they threw in for free.

There sure were some big houses in Richmond. And not just there. All over the place these days. Every piece of property filled with bigger and bigger piles of wood and stone and mortar and drywall and wires and shingles and furniture and carpets and appliances, monster houses with parking for fleets of gigantic vehicles. He imagines little aliens looking down from a spaceship and being scared. *Wow,* they'd think, *they must be giants!* Bo's sure it's an adult obsession. For kids, a house is either where you go for safety, even if just to pull the covers over your head, or just the opposite, your house being the place you avoid.

Home can be a tricky thing to think about. There was a city job last year, where his handyman friend was hired to clean up an abandoned lot awaiting commercial development and hired Bo for the day. Garbage all over the lot. Pee-stained mattresses, abandoned fridges and chesterfields, crushed toys, clothing used as toilet paper. His handyman friend was on the way across the field, jouncing in his pickup with the trashcans over the rutted ground. At Bo's feet was a crumpled ocean of plastic and wet cardboard. He tugged, only to have the surface ripple and a man burst out from underneath. Skinny as Bo himself, and wild, eyes unfocussed on anything in this world. Barked twice like a dog and ran. Pulling away the discarded packing material revealed the man's home—two paperback books, a stove-in hardcase travel bag with broken wheels, a Tupperware container filled with something green that hadn't started off that colour. Bo felt like a home-invader. He and his handyman friend left then, and never got paid by the city.

On his back on the mattress, he can feel a pressure point building in his neck, and he shifts the rolled sweatshirt. The sketch turned out nice. Sneakily, he puts his feet together to shut off his view then pops them open to reveal the drawing as though coming around a corner and seeing it in a gallery. He tries it again, and the sketch stands up. Good. Not perfect, but it will do. Once he gets the hang of the new pencil, he can touch it up and switch to something thicker for shading.

He'd sure like some sleep. Getting up six or eight times to go to the bathroom down the hall chops his night into short segments, and sometimes the next day he's too tired to visit the pound or run his errands. He'll just lie here. It may not be sleeping but at least it's resting, and Mummy used to say that was better than nothing. Being still is nice all by itself for no reason, just being still. He's close to dropping off when the scattered workings of his thoughts are cleared away by people talking in the hallway. They stop outside and one of them tries the door. He hopes it's who he thinks it is.

"You gotta lock the door," Devona says. "In this building you lock your door, that's only what. It's a safety thing."

Somehow he's twisted the covers off. Good thing he kept his underwear on or Devona and his sister would get an eyeful. He'd like to stand for the ladies, but the trip to Steveston took way too much out of him. Instead, he scooches on his bum till he can sit with his back against the wall and pulls the bedspread up to his chin. Sally's wearing the pants Bo likes her in best, loose cotton from Nepal she found on sale at a Commercial Drive shop. They make her look dressed up even when that's not what she's trying for, and they cover the rough red scaly patches she gets on the backs of her knees. As for Devona, wow! She looks gorgeous. Her hair is really curly and all sorts of colours, and her big handsome face is smiley. With her bright salmon shoes she kicks her way through socks and a couple of costumes he was checking for holes.

"Hi, Bo," Sally says, "hi there, brother. Devona, can I show him?"

"Did we bring it to hide it? And lock the door behind you, it's a safety thing."

Sally dramatically sets down a recycled shopping bag with a string handle. The front is splashed with an interlocking design of stylish swirling letters that draws silent appreciation from her brother the artist.

"Come on, girl," Devona says. "Pull that old thing out." She whips her eyes to Bo and adds, "I'm not talking to you, mister, you keep your dirty hands where I can see'm." She's laughing to herself, burps of self-satisfied mirth rising through her throat like bubbles in a water pipe, when Sally reaches into the bag and comes up with a kitchen tap. "What you think about that, Mardi Gras?" Devona says.

Bo likes it a lot. One of the nicer examples of sink hardware he's seen. All one piece, no hot and cold taps, just a lever that turns left and right above a fancy faucet arching high from a ball-like contraption on the base. Sally's holding it out like a strange vegetable she's just pulled from the ground, twisted copper roots, patches of verdigris betraying its origin in places dark and moist.

"Marty picked it up at the Habitat for Humanity place," Devona explains. "That ReStore where they got all kinds of recycled whatever-it-is turned in from house renovations and that. He was thinking I don't know what he was thinking, after getting Bonita to pull his weenie for a month I was gonna take'm back? And this is how? A sink tap? No flowers, no dinner, no card with a poem. Fuckin faucet. On Bonita he lays a whole kitchen sink full of loving, and after she's done with'm all I get is this spout, which as if I didn't know he probably stole. Okay, I been bugging his ass before he left to fix the place so maybe he thought I don't know what he thought, I'll bring her something that shows for once I was listening. Anyhow, fuck him and the whores he rode in on."

Devona has many more pieces of her mind she'd deliver to the man Marty in absentia, but her impromptu joke has her in agony and searching for something to lean on. She supports herself with a stiff arm on the counter, groaning to keep from losing it completely, her large firm bottom stretching flat the pleats on a knee-length orange skirt. "Ow, ow . . . you hear that? Whores he rode in on . . . ha-ha . . . ow, owwwww . . ."

"So do you like it, brother?" Sally says, raising the contraption to eye-level for proper viewing. "It's way nicer than the one I have."

Bo's starting to tell her how much when Devona scoops up his pants from the floor and tosses them on the mattress.

"Hey," Sally says when her brother stands to fit his legs in the pants. "Where did you get all those bruises?"

Bo always has bruises. Sleeping on hard surfaces, bumping into things, getting pushed down. They don't hurt and his clothes cover them up.

"Yeah, I know, but those ones are almost black and they're all over the place."

"Get over here," Devona says to him. "Stand up straight." After a turn around him, she doesn't know what to think. He's purpled up real good, no question about that, but she could wave a bar of gold overhead as a finder's fee and not come across anyone on the streets around there with unblemished skin.

"Somebody been bothering you? Bothering you regular, I mean?" She gets a nip of chemicals she can't place, an unnatural blend of fake fruit and the type of alcohol the real hard-luck cases swig, all overlain with Street. "Whoa, that smell coming from your head?"

Bo bobs his head shyly. With all the gel and the lying down over two days, his hair must look awful. He works his fingers through in the way he's learned is best to get the John Travolta look, grabbing handfuls to puff up the front and patting the surface smooth. It doesn't smooth very well. The goo from the barber has dried from follicle to hair-tip, consolidating into hard crystallized hanks that spike out in all directions.

"The fuck's that hairdo?" Devona says. "Like you took a beachball crammed with hair and whacked it with a hockey stick till it split, huh-huh-huh . . . no, like you took a pillowcase filled up with hair and run two cars head-on from opposite directions into . . . nope, that ain't it, hold on, just wait a . . . got it! You went to Save-On-Meats, right? And you told the counterman you want a pile of them sheep intestines they use for sausage casings. Then you found Lilly and said to her, huh-huh, you said to Lilly, huh-huh, 'Lilly, I'm gonna borrow thirty-eight of them shit-ass wigs you wear.' Then you stuffed them wigs in the sheep gut and laid it down in the curb lane, and when the 20 bus came along . . . huh-huh-huh . . . when the fuckin 20 bus . . . hee-hee-hee-hee, no, no . . . the 20 . . . aaaahh-ha-ha-ha-ha, aaaahh-ha-ha-ha . . . whoa! can't breathe, gotta catch my . . . when the fuckin . . ."

While Devona recovers with her head down over Bo's cracker cupboard, Sally steps up into the leadership role. She loves Devona almost as much as Mummy, and doesn't feel too bad about it because Devona is a second Mummy, that's all, not better or worse just second in order. One thing, though, Sally sure doesn't get her sense of humour.

At the sink, brother and sister are equally confounded. A kitchen accessory. Faucet, copper tubes, they get it, but now what? In the place where it's supposed to go, the corked pipe juts horizontally from the wall. Sally plucks out the cork and plunks down the new device overtop the old, not expecting magical soldering but hoping to stumble across a solution to the installation while in the meantime enjoying a peek into the future at the completed renovation. After forming his own mental picture, Bo takes the tap from Sally, assures her and Devona it's beautiful and that his handyman boss will have it hooked up in two minutes flat. He gives Sally a long hug till they're both blubbering and laughing through tears. They've always been blubberers together, the brother and sister. They pull back, then they dance, Sally turning Bo in small circles, a minimalist waltz with her leading.

"Never mind what anyone thinks," she says. "I love the new haircut." Apart from the rigid stalks threatening her eyeballs, she does love it, and asks him about the barber.

Bo retrieves the coupon the King allowed him to keep for another visit.

"Buddy Monk!" Sally shrieks. "This is like, amazing. Remember when I told you I was going to England?"

He remembers. He was happy for her. Bo would love to go for a visit himself. He's heard you can walk around London for days and see so much you'd forget half of it.

"It didn't work out," Sally says, "but I can tell how good a barber he is. You look like one of those old movie stars from the magazines Mummy used to read."

Mummy?

Devona, over her laughing fit, hurries over, all bustle and jiggle, far better equipped than Sally for diversionary action but road-weary from years of dissembling, the grind of over and over assuring Robert that his mother loved him, loves him still wherever she is. Sometimes people have to go away, that's all. Her Bobby, Devona's Bobby, her costumed crusading Mardi Gras. His mummy still lives inside him.

"Never mind all that," she says, bumping Bo with her hip. "The only thing, how come you two left me out of the dancing? You think I can't shake a leg at my age? Lemme tell you the biggest tragedy in TV land is they didn't have them *Idol* shows when I was in my prime. *Dancing With the Stars*—don't make a girl laugh. The so-called stars'd be so out-shined they'd never show their faces in public, paparazzi wouldn't give piss on a pork chop for a Hollywood Bowl full'a them." She pauses while the injustice of her career's timing sinks in, as though one of history's great conquerors—who's that one she's thinking of, the barbarian, real mean cocksucker . . . Attila!—had the misfortune to be raised in a '60s Haight-Ashbury communal house with flowers in his hair. "I could move on the stage, that's only what," she continues. "Should of seen me on that pole, practically invented the upside-down flying beaver."

The gentleman takes the hint and extends his arms. Devona laughs, a delighted sound unrelated to her usual heavy artillery, and steps into the dance. Bo would like to try leading, but can't untwist the logic behind having a leader and a follower when two people are up to something together. His partner—a proud solo performer was Miss Devona, none of that lezzy stuff onstage in the clubs she headlined—does no leading of her own, and they shuffle around like mismatched draft animals trying to coordinate their efforts regarding a wooden cart.

"Almost forgot," Devona says. "Woman came looking for you yesterday over at the Carnegie. You must be doing something right to draw action like that. Gave her name—Nita. Seemed all right and she's no stranger around so I passed on your plans, the Value Village and the pound and that. What's her story, anyhow?"

"I know Nita," Sally says. "I do, I know her, she's my friend!"

Devona keeps her eyes on her dancing partner. "What's up with you and her?"

Bo fills her in best he can, and not for the first time is puzzled by how a connection with another person can be so hard to explain.

The dancing stops.

"She told me about you being sick," Devona says. "Didn't know someone else was mixed up or I wouldn't of given you a hard time about not being careful with your allergy. Truth of it is I was probably feeling pissy for being out and about when the hospital called and I dumped some of that onto you. Good thing

Sally came to the rescue." Overtop Bo's shellacked dome, she gives Sally a good firm nod of approval.

"But I know you, Bobby," Devona continues. "You probably ate whatever was put in front of you 'cause you thought it was polite. Polite only goes so far, you know? Polite is a kind of lying, so you got to treat it with respect, use it only when it won't make things worse. How would you feel up in the clouds talking to the Lord he asks you why you got yourself shot helping a hold-up man carry his bag of money to the getaway car? 'Being polite,' you say, and the Lord ships your ass straight down to Hell on the new SkyTrain line he builds for dummies. The Lord don't want to wake up every morning and find a flock of people bumming around Heaven getting in everybody's way trying to be polite, fighting to help each other on with their white robes instead of paying attention to some lady down here praying for a miracle to help her sick kid or something. Mean spirits all over the world cutting and blowing each other up, while up top Robert Fairchild de-fuckin-ceased is giving compliments on everybody's wings and trying to help out where none's needed." Devona stops dancing. "Look at me, see me laughing? I'm not, for your information. Polite, everybody being polite right when they're lying in each other's face and they both know it. Guess what? Mummy was polite. And see where—"

Sally looses a squeal and rushes Devona from behind, throwing her arms around the much larger woman and rubbing her face on the stout back. Left and right, bending her nose near flat to her face with each pass. Devona seems to shrink slightly, the anger boiling off and taking with it the poison of memory. "Okay," she says. "It's all right." She holds the hands clasped across the swell of her belly, pushes up the long sleeves of the shirt and rubs Sally's forearms.

When the air's fit to breathe, she smiles at Bo. "Might as well jump back in, Mardi Gras. Make us a three-part dancing machine."

To the music in their heads, the knot of irregularly sized dancers moves with the coordination to be expected, rather than hoped for. But nobody's complaining.

Chapter 21

Danger In Numbers

Al's out back with June in the delivery area when the hollering starts. He heads back in and arrives just as an elderly woman dressed in black announces her intention to leave. Sheesh! Only five minutes ago Al had to counsel Nita on her customer-relations technique, and here she is at it again. "Anything I can help with?" he says.

"Mr. Al." The old gal is visibly vibrating. "I try to support the neighbourhood, you know? Local shops, all that." A pause to point a curved finger at Nita and mutter an Italian curse. "But this one, what is it? Pushing, pushing—'Sit down, whatcha want?' I ask one little question about the menu and it's, 'Everyting, everyting we have, whatcha think?' And look at her—like a skeleton, how do you sell food when you never eat? She needs a good spanking . . . with a shovel!"

Al's left alone with Nita, who shoots him a look of bewilderment.

"Aww, c'mon," Al says, "all you gotta do is . . . you know."

"I'm just a waitress, Al. You figure it out. You're the hero living out his dream."

Hero? Living out his dream? "Don't make me laugh. You don't wanna know what I'm going through these days."

A long pause while Nita weighs the merits of answering honestly. She should want to know. This neighbourhood is her home, and June and Al are family of a sort. Community. It's about coexisting contrasts. Community without contrasts is a cult. And tolerance, she'll shout tolerance from the rooftops. But where does that leave the individual? Her, in particular. And at the moment, Al.

"Yeah," she says. "What you're going through."

"What's that voice like the end of the world it's coming? You heard something?"

"Nothing, really. Sorry about the old lady, but she was getting impossible."

Al shrugs. "Yeah, well, I gotta admit it can be tough. That old saying, the customer's always right? I figure it's the same as anyone else in an argument—on average, about half the time."

"Thanks."

"Hey, here's a laugh to lighten things up, heard it from Lippy this morning. We're at Caffè Roma, right? He looks around the corner at the sign for that Spartacus gym and says this, what the weight-loss expert said to the Mexican at the Jenny Craig Clinic—'Adios, adipose.' I thought you'd like that one, you been to Mexico, right?"

Nita gives him a free pass. "Sure, Al, that's a beauty."

"It is? You never thought Lippy was funny before."

"Lippy . . ."

"What? You heard something. I can tell."

"The neighbourhood," Nita says. "People talk."

"And what are they saying, these people?"

"Is June around?"

"She's having a smoke, that's how slow around here, having a smoke break every two minutes without it hurts anything."

"At least you make a living."

"Restaurants," Al snorts. "Too close to the edge all the time. You know what they got now, what they're eating now in this stupid town? Chow mein sandwiches. I'm not making it up, something how old, sixty, seventy years from the east coast of the United States, why did they eat it back then who knows, probably poor and put together anything they found in the pantry, whatever they could get their hands on. Now they're sticking it in their faces from the food carts on the sidewalk right in Vancouver." A sweep of his arm. "And look at this, lunchtime and June can hang around in the alley blowing smoke rings. And when they come in what do they do? Earlier three people ran out on their bill, if you can believe."

"Did you recognize them?"

"Recognize. Two guys, one girl. Some days, you know? Makes you wanna get up in the morning and say, 'Today's the day I start spitting in the soup.' But what are you gonna do, could have been worse."

"Like how?"

"They could've ordered chow mein sandwiches," Al says. "Now. No more messing around the bush—what is it you heard?"

Nita looks over his shoulder. "Maybe we should—"

"Never mind June. Give."

"All right. A friend in real estate called last night."

"This friend, would he be that cousin you talk about you don't trust for nothing?"

"This time there's no money in it for him, he was just passing on what he's heard about changes on the Drive."

When the pause extends, Al says, "Don't let's be a superspy."

"Apparently there's an offer in on the building with the yoga studio and Buck-A-Slice Pizza. He can't find out whether it's just the building or whether the businesses are part of the deal. But the owners are treating it like a nuclear secret."

"From your face, I'm guessing this friend, he says the offer's from Lippy."

"Not for sure. But Lippy and the commercial realtor involved have been meeting at Merchant's for oysters twice a week."

Al raises a shoulder that his ear tries to kiss. "It's the Drive. Something comes, something goes, so what's the problem? One less yoga place, a few more people walking around who can't touch their toes. And Buck-A-Slice where it's two bucks or three for the fancy toppings, their name don't even make sense. Tell the truth or get outta here, it should be for guys like that."

"He filled me in on some other stuff."

"How much stuff?"

"A rough sketch of the meetings between you and the other owners."

Al feels the start of a chill in his head. Like gelato on a hot summer day, you take a big spoonful and barely escape the killer headache, you go on spooning but careful of how much you stick in. "Keep going."

"If I have it straight, I mean if my cousin does, there are ten businesses involved. Cicalone and Lippy's five others around the country, and the four of your group."

"Ten, yeah, what of it?"

"And it takes a two-thirds majority vote to change things. Policy, direction, even who stays open or how they operate."

"Sure. But six outta ten ain't two-thirds. Us four got the hammer."

"My cousin's wondering how many more can join."

"Ten, I told you there's ten."

"Is that in the contract? *Limited* to ten?"

Gelato. Al's just been fed a giant spoon of rock-hard frozen gelato and it's on the way to his brain.

"Because if it doesn't," Nita says, "what if others sign up separately with Lippy? Like ohhh, let's say the owners of a yoga studio and a pizza joint. You see what my cousin's getting at. A two-thirds majority vote is great when you're four of ten and can do something about it, but if Lippy controls yoga and pizza, then you slip to four of twelve . . ."

Al wrenches his neck checking for June, and whipping his eyes back to Nita doesn't ease the pain. "But hold it, why would Lippy want us on board in the first place?"

"I have no idea. But let me put it this way—do you really think you and the other three have managed to out-manoeuvre Lippy Delillo, your personal business hero?"

"But—"

"There may be nothing to worry about," Nita says. "But you at least have to let June in on it. You know you do."

"Anybody else you told about this? The baloney artist?"

"I wouldn't dare." Nita's frankly scared of rousing Buddy into action. His disdain for Lippy Delillo and his band of boobs—with a reluctant concession to Al—is well known. The three others in on the deal at least have actual assets and a grasp of finance, but the remainder of the flock are so full of hard-luck stories it's impossible not to conclude their failings are necessary to their characters, existential underpinnings that if pulled away and replaced with good news would leave them adrift in the wilderness where the sun always shines, espresso flows from public fountains and there are no taxes on cigarettes, which is to say perfect, ergo terrifying.

"So we could be outnumbered," Al says. "Or could be soon if the two new ones are in Lippy's pocket."

"I'm not sorry I brought it up," Nita says.

"Don't be sorry."

"I said I'm not."

"Oh, okay then. You shouldn't be." Al thinks a little and continues at a measured pace: "I didn't think about it this way but you know what? I could have. I could've thought about it. But I already got no say in what happens, understand? If somebody else makes all the decisions, at least I get to keep this place. What, June and me, we're going to start over? Maybe go to UBC like we're eighteen? Sell the house and move to Regina where it's cheaper? Open a new business and compete with that place down the street that sells baby clothing with jokes on? And I'm telling you right now, you bet Lippy wants to be in charge. That's what he's good at, and guys good at being in charge end up being in charge, 'cause when the guys bad at being in charge are in charge there might as well be nobody in charge . . . wait, did I get that straight?"

"You're good."

"Thanks. Anyways, it'll help us too. Usually the world works out that one side gets what they want and the other side don't. So it's not so bad when one side gets what they want and the other side gets *sort of* what they want. I know what you're thinking, about Lippy and that, but we're not talking about no big corporate criminal screwing everybody around the clock. A guy like Lippy don't chuck people out on the street. How could he do that? You wanna know how he does it? I'll tell you how he does it, this is how—he don't."

The tone of finality leaves little wiggle room but Nita can't let it drop entirely. "It's time to tell June."

"I know, I know. I've been such a . . . no guts, that's me. But I wanted to go to her and say, 'Look at this, honey, everything's okay now.' These days she don't get time to enjoy. Maybe a holiday would be nice before we're finished forever. Anything except back and forth between here and the house."

"Before I go, let me say that as long as you're together you'll always be okay. You and June. Together you'll be okay."

"Maybe you're right, you're pretty smart."

Nita slides in close and kisses him on the cheek.

"Go on, get outta here for an hour," Al says. "Go save some abandoned puppies."

The door's just closing behind her when she hears: "Gravy! On the chow mein sandwiches! Can you believe? Gravy, they put on!"

Chapter 22

Unsolicited Opinions

Buddy hasn't enjoyed work this much in a long time. One in the afternoon and he's already blazed his way through eighteen heads, a pace if maintained till closing will easily allow him to set a new personal best. Opening time saw two young men waiting at the door, and with the lights on and the action in the chair cranked up, by some coincidence or eerie social reinforcement customers began filing into the shop in an uninterrupted stream.

Buzz, clip, whisk, over, over, over again. It's playing out nicely, the metronomic pace of activity bringing a kind of meditative peace. Nita used to describe her distance runs something like that and Buddy can relate. Once on a bet he chopped wood for eighteen hours straight—straight, baby, no breaks, had a sidekick feed him energy bars and squirt water into his mouth, chopped one-handed when he had to scratch or blow the dust from his nose, pissed his pants five times on the fly. Since the bet called for a full twenty-four hours, he lost to cramps and dry heaving and had to fork over a hundred bucks, yet still staggered away on a high.

He likes barbering. That's one thing he's never been able to impress on Nita, that he plain likes it. The boys and gents and a few girls and women leave feeling cooler, cleaner, more handsome, more butch, tougher, hip, rad, bad. Changed. Set Buddy to work on someone in a chair with a crisp cape around the neck and conversation itching to be let loose, and the grooming becomes a grooving. He swears the customer visibly calms down once in position, helped along maybe by the hands being hidden, a mild restraint on that part of the body which, aside from the cock-and-balls, is at the root of most troublemaking in the world.

An amateur meditator's mind will wander long before reaching enlightenment, and his settles on his roommate, *Mus musculus*, Oxhead's scientific handle. To say Buddy's worried might be too severe, but he's not hosting a desert tortoise either, a critter that would naturally outlive its owner. Most serious is Oxhead's nonchalant attitude. A careless city mouse without street smarts isn't long for the world. So in place of the recent full-service routine Buddy has decided to start scattering the food around. The hunt conditions both the mind and the body. And he'll put in a call to UBC and SFU. Who knows, there might be a comfy sinecure as a lab mouse available so long as the researchers commit in advance to non-invasive testing. Running mazes, something like that, three hots and a cot safely away from mousetraps and neighbourhood cats, give the mutant freeloader some peace of mind and a purpose at the same time.

Buddy doesn't notice he's down to the last customer till whisking him off. A few weeks of that level of activity would go a long way to paying some bills and servicing his debt, and a new record would have been nice. But the rush was an aberration, and with the decks cleared he locks up and takes aim at Al Esposito's.

June's voice is audible through the restaurant door. Inside, a table of customers is gawking up at her as she splits attention between a description of the specials and sniping at Al, who's at the entrance to the kitchen looking roughed up around the edges. Buddy recognizes one of the customers. Kayla, a girlfriend of Nita's. But before he can say hello his mother flashes him a heated eyeball and he carefully skirts the battle site, arcing around the table as the guests rise and huff their way out the door.

"There," June says. "See what you did? Satisfied?"

Buddy and Al aren't sure to whom the remark was directed, but decide discretion is the better part of valour and duck through the arch into the bar, where they hunch like Cold War operatives negotiating a defection. "Who's she mad at?" Buddy says in a tight whisper. "You or me?"

"I don't know," Al says. "But it's one of those days."

"We'll give her a couple of minutes."

"She's coming?"

"I can't hear anything. Maybe she's out on the street chasing those people who ran away."

"Those cowards," Al says.

They're still giggling when June rounds the corner.

"Very funny, laugh it up." She glares at one then the other and lights a cigarette.

"Umm," Al says. "You know . . ."

"What do I know, Al? What? That someone's going to complain about the smoke? That the health board will shut us down? You have all the answers, O Keeper of Secrets, so you tell me."

Al's answers. A pot full of holes that won't hold water, that's his answers. A colander or some of that what is it, cheesecloth. He follows Buddy behind the bar, where the barber helps himself to a draught. June takes a seat out front, heaves on her cigarette and straight into their faces blows a duster the men have sense enough not to notice.

"Are you in on it?" June says to her son.

Buddy turns to Al. "Did you finally tell her?"

"It's nothing you know nothing about."

"The deal with Lippy Delillo."

"Who's been feeding you lies?"

"So you are," June says.

"I'm not in on anything," Buddy says. "But word gets out quick in this neighbourhood in case you haven't noticed." June tries to interject but Buddy's quicker to his holster. "And before you start, Mum, I kept my mouth shut because it was between you two. Everyone has secrets and they keep them for their own reasons. Even if the reasoning is 180-degrees out of whack, a secret is one of the few things an individual actually owns."

The men wait till June says, "We'll finish this at home." She reaches over the bar and drops her butt into an empty glass. Buddy tips in some lager, and the *fzzzt* and the waft of beer-tobacco pungency marks the end of the first round. The second starts without a breather.

"I'm gonna go check the kitchen," Al says.

"What in the world for?"

"Because you never know!"

"If you two are going to start up again," Buddy says, "let's get this out of the way." He swings out to the middle of the room and casts about with the gaze-at-infinity eyes of a film director visualizing the next bit of action. "We can put the table over there along the side, or under the windows if that's better . . . no, off to one side, high visibility to pull in the walk-by trade but where I won't have my back to everyone on the street. I checked with the Legion and it's okay, they're not having one Sunday on Italian Day so we won't be stepping on any toes."

"What are you talking?" Al says.

"The meat draw. We already went over this."

"Went over. What kind of word is that for something you brought up once for two seconds?"

"It's perfect for this place."

"I don't think its gonna work," Al says. "Only three days away, not much time to put it together." A streak of panic makes him check with June, who with a nod affirms his call, though Al figures if they're back on the same side it wouldn't kill her to throw in a smile.

"What's to put together?" Buddy scoffs. "A bunch of meat, a roll of tickets."

"First of all, where you get the meat for one of these things is you buy it." Another glance at his wife. "No money, isn't that what we been saying? And what if nobody shows up? There we are stuck with a bunch of meat."

Buddy snorts. "A restaurant can't be stuck with something edible. It's not like having too many cowboy hats."

"Mr. Organizer, Mr. Social Director." Al's growing more emboldened the closer the environment approaches normal, which is to say with Buddy as his adversary in place of June. "How do you like this—the cops bust us for no licence?"

"A meat draw shouldn't require a licence. Hell, all of *life* is a raffle."

"Got to get a licence you want to go to the bathroom these days." Al laughs to himself. A licence for the bathroom, not bad, another one for Lippy . . . aww, there goes the subject back in his head again.

"Fine," Buddy says. "I'll check into the licence today."

"Later is better. Not ruling it out for another time, later in the summer is all. Take it slow and steady. That's what wins the race, am I right?"

Buddy supernovas. "Not the tortoise-and-hare bullshit! How many millions of children have been led astray by that fable? Let's get this straight—slow and steady doesn't stand a chance against fast and steady. It only works against fast but lazy. Quick but easily distracted. Swift but farts around. Speedy but drunk—"

"Aright-aready, you don't gotta—"

"How did Aesop manage to inspire people with that nonsense in the first place? It holds no hope, no risk, no . . . jazz! Check this out, Al. Let's say your boss discovers you stole a bunch of money from him. Okay? He gives you the rest of the afternoon to come up with it before he calls the cops, right? The problem is you have only two bucks left from the money you stole. Things aren't looking so good but you have one hope, the thoroughbred track. You love horses, love playing the ponies, and can get to Hastings in time for the last race. You following me, Al? Good.

"You go to the track and find there are two longshots with identical odds that'll pay off enough to cover what you owe and keep you from being arrested. You don't know anything about either of them except what you read from the numbers, which show they're pretty much equal. The windows are about to close and it's crunch time. You ready, Al? You ready to bet? One horse is called 'Slow and Steady'. The other is 'Crazyass Streak-of-Shit Hightailing Motherfucker'."

Sick.

"Come on, which one do you go with?"

"You're sick, you baloney artist."

"Never Aesop me, Al. Besides, where's the harm in a game of chance? Scratch out a little fun around here for once. Maybe then you two can stop fighting. It's a proven fact that meat draws generate fewer arguments than bankruptcy. And we sure as hell can't sit around hoping Dad left us a big pile of his drug money." Oh.

The slip brings black silence, a natural response Buddy accepts and for which he wears the blame. "I didn't want to, I mean I wasn't trying . . ." He transfers full attention to his mother and offers: "There's more to the story than just finding a will."

"Sounds like it," June says, ejecting a cloud of smoke.

"Louie passes on his apologies," Buddy says. "He wanted to bring it up the other night, but he didn't know how you'd take it."

"Doesn't affect me one way or another." Cloud of smoke.

So much a part of Buddy's mind has the story become that this time around the more flimsy features stand out as insufficient to maintain the overall structure. So he provides support, buttressing the tale with embroidered speculation that rounds into an entertaining narrative but ultimately provides no enlightenment.

Al is horrified. He follows the tale of drugs and a savage beating as though he's been mistaken for a witness and the whole cast of criminals are on their way to dogpile him. As for June, Buddy can't completely decipher her look. But there's a forlorn hitch in there that makes him regret the enthusiasm he poured into the narration.

"I know one thing," Al says. "Now for sure going with Lippy is the best move. We can't keep no drug money even if we wanted. And while I'm talking, I'm tired too of the dead husband and dead father talk and the meat draw talk too. Drugs, dead guys, gambling, what's this all of a sudden? Pray to God we can live without."

"If God doesn't have a sense of humour and isn't up for a little adventure," Buddy says, "we have nothing to say to each other."

"What you call adventure, I call looking for trouble. Here's one, there's this TV show I watched about this guy he's got about a hundred sled dogs up north. He raced in the Yukon Quest years and years and took some of the dogs to Russia, had them pull him around, and he figures these two old ones he's got with him on TV, this Bozo and another one Streaker, they hauled him on his sled I don't know something like ten-thousand miles in his life. So what he does when them and the other old dogs can't run so good anymore, in his big storage place with gear like a tack room he puts electric heat in the concrete floor. The old dogs get to hang around with the other ones on the property, this huge yard cut out of the bush, but when the weather turns bad or they're sick or you know what I'm saying they can't stand the young ones yapping, they can go right in the big house and lay themselves down on the warm floor and rest their bones. So adventure, sure, I had adventure since my family moved from Palermo I was twelve. But now maybe a rest. Looking for trouble that wasn't there all along?"

"Nice story," Buddy says, "a real tear-jerker, Al. If it makes you happy we'll give half the money to the pound for electric dog blankets. And we can throw in all that meat you're going to be stuck with."

"You know sometimes, mister, you can be a real—"

They're interrupted by a concussion of happy sound from the front door, out of which emerges the voice of the truant waitress: "Where is everybody?"

An animated group with Nita Randolph at its head sweeps into the room. Nita's in her black-and-white work wear. The dress of her companions, three women and two men, hints at a celebration. An old school tie, a scattering of upscale scarves and accessories, salvage-store chic, down-at-the-heels boots, a T-shirt with something in Arabic script, all of which looks calculated for effect, intended to announce the arrival of Good Times.

"You're everybody," June says. "Apparently the only one who counts around here." Out comes a cigarette she lights from the last.

She tries, Nita tries, isn't she trying now? Passing over the insult, half-breathless with excitement: "I've been rounding up the gang." Pointing at the tops of individual heads, she recites, "Carolyn, Jyllean, Beth, Dave and Scott."

Large grins and loud hellos till a cumulus from June raises coughs.

Nita persists, this time roping in Al—*oh my God, she didn't see Buddy back there*—by explaining, "Sorry for being gone so long, but I had to help Kayla." Dreads flap as her head pivots.

"Hey, where is she by the way? They were due here long ago. Nobody came in?"

June has shut down so it's left to Al: "Maybe there was a little problem. Five people came in but they had to leave. Sort of an emergency or something. Nothing serious, just one of those you know, a guy might die or, uh, I can't swear."

When Nita can offer up nothing more than a weak smile, the others, having lost their merry, trail out onto the Drive with the same baffled disappointment as the advance platoon.

"What was that?" Nita snaps. "June, what was that all about? I rounded up two batches of customers, ten paying customers with money and more friends and contacts and who twenty years from now will probably sue you for giving them cancer. What happened earlier with Kayla and her friends? What did you say to them? Oh, never mind. This isn't working out, is it? I'm a bad employee and now I'm mad at you and you're disappointed with me. I should have picked something at random from Craigslist. A camp cook in the tar sands making bitumen burgers or whatever. Steel toe boots in the kitchen, a cigarette dangling out of my mouth like you. No, I didn't mean that, it's only." She stops for a breath. "I guess I'm trying to say thanks, but the job's not for me. You too, Al, I'm sorry."

The silence absorbs some of the hurt, as it will among good people with the patience to learn from it. Until, that is, June pinches off the end of her cigarette the way CC used to with his roll-your-owns, carving through with the thumbnail under the coal to the index finger on the opposite side and flipping the glowing shag-end in the air like a tossed coin. "Let's see," she says. "You've been with us four days for a total of something like fifteen hours. I'll have to check, but I don't think that leaves much in your pension fund. Oh, and will you be expecting a severance package?"

Nita's through the arch by the time Buddy can scramble past Al and give chase.

"Wherever you do," June says, "don't come back with meat. That stupid idea is off the table for good."

Outside, Nita's nowhere in sight. Buddy passes on looking up and down the street. He'll never catch her if she's running and probably wouldn't be welcome to if he could. Running, the whole world's running, to or from or formlessly, loved ones neither more nor less than the enemy. Running dry of options and ideas, running at the seams, running loose, running at the mouth, an incoherent assemblage of individuals running wild with none to watch over them.

What now? His first thought is that his mum will need a decent amount of time to calm down, his second that his hanging around waiting for it to happen, or worse, trying to hurry it along, would be trying to ease an itch by scratching it with a cheese grater. Maybe he'll re-open the barbershop. That was some string he had going, a mean streak of cutting and styling, so why not open up and see what happens? Who can say the run of good luck has played itself out? Could be at the first dingle of the bell the rush will be back on. Buzz, clip, whisk, over, over, over again.

Moseying down the street, taking it easy-peasy, he reminds himself to ask Old Kim about a deal on a pile of meat. Al and June will surely come to their senses before Sunday, and if not, it'll be easy enough to sneak in after closing on Saturday and set up in the middle of the night. There's the matter of the licence, too, though that's less pressing. Pretty doubtful at a big shindig like Italian Day the cops will be looking to raid a meat draw. Charging down the street on horseback scattering visitors, tipping over kabob stands and the racks of grilled sardines in front of the Portuguese Club, smashing through displays just to confiscate a bunch of meat. Although you never can tell. Most cops are normal law-and-order types, but a few, well, he'll just say a thorough tasering of a citizen over a Maple Leaf dinner ham wouldn't raise unanimous surprise among the populace.

CHAPTER 23

OF BABIES AND BATHWATER

The apple-nose man doesn't see Nita coming. He paused in front of the barbershop to roll a joint, a lumpy colossus like a herniated eel, and is firing up when she pushes past, spoiling his aim and scorching the belly of the tremendous doob. Undaunted, he applies another match to the same spot and sucks the smoke from the middle of the thing, holding it by the tips like a miniature cob of corn.

At the *dingle*, Buddy catches a flash of dreadlocks in the corner of his eye and jerks the clippers.

"Hey!" The customer angles his head in the mirror. "Look at this—you carved out a big chunk."

"It's only hair," Buddy says. "You think if I cut it too short you'll lose your power like Samson?"

"Just fix it, will you?"

To disguise the slip, Buddy starts carefully reducing the length of the hair in general, while keeping an eye on Nita, who's plunked herself down at the front window beside the customer's son. "How about your boy over there," Buddy says, "is he next?"

"Naw," the man says, "his mother takes care of that."

"I'm sure she's good at it," Buddy says, "but if you'd let him get a cut he'd walk out well on the way to adulthood. Doesn't look too young for his first barber experience to me."

By the time Buddy reclaims the cape, whisks the customer clean and thanks him for the generous tip, Nita and the boy have made friends. "This is Sidney," she says.

"Like Sidney Crosby?" Buddy says. "Wow."

The boy grins and grabs his father's hand.

"Usually I only give treats to customers." Buddy pulls a pepperoni stick from an empty Barbicide jar on the old jewelry display case. "But here you go."

"What do you say?" the father prompts.

"Thank you," says the boy, peering at the leathery pole in his fist, trying to deduce its purpose through sheer youthful enthusiasm for the problem.

"You're welcome," Buddy says. "That's better for the teeth than candy."

The kid sniffs the stick. Oh. Dog food.

"Get your dad to bring you back when he figures you're old enough for your own haircut. Should be around your third year of college."

The father takes the jab on the chin, grins, and gives it back: "By then this place'll be gone so long all anyone'll remember is a dive with a bunch of junk in it. Out-of-towners will ask what that abandoned building used to be. 'Nobody knows,' the local-s'll say. 'Legend has it that men used to run out bleeding from the head and ears.'"

Buddy laughs his ass off, waves them out the door and is left with the problem of where to start with Nita.

He'd like to let her lead the way—she did, after all, take the initiative of dropping in on him at work, and there must be something in that—but he can't totally abdicate his position. An anglerfish female, he reminds himself, is vastly larger than its opposite number. When the male bites onto a mate, its mouth and the female's skin dissolve, fusing them together, and over time they gradually start sharing nutrients and eventually even blood vessels. The male, having lost any possibility of an independent existence, shrinks further, his life reduced to being a portable on-demand sperm supplier, a tiny wart on the female's hide beneath notice and beyond consultation. Buddy putters around with the clippers, arranges the guards, aligns the combs.

"I don't mean to be a nag," Nita says.

"You were never a nag."

"About why I'm here."

In the mirror is a man who resembles Buddy if it were possible for him to look fifteen and frightened. He has an underhand grip on a pair of scissors, holding them belt-high like a knife-fighter. He eases them down beside the combs on the clean white folded towel.

"It's about the storage unit on Terminal," Nita continues. "I have a few things I'd like to get at in the back, and your stuff is in the way."

"You should have mentioned it last night, I would have disappeared it by now."

"I forgot."

"Yeah, with all the other issues."

"Issues?"

"Issues. We finally got down to the important stuff. What took us so long beats me. If we'd been able to discuss things like that when we were . . . never mind, it's all, I don't know, spilled milk."

"There weren't any issues. You introduced topics, that's all. A list that sounded memorized in advance. And then you grabbed my tit."

"Eh?"

"You grabbed my tit."

"I didn't do any such thing."

"I can't believe you're denying it."

"Categorically."

"Then what's your version? How would you describe it?"

"I tried to kiss you."

"Yes, you did."

"I rest my case."

"With your hand on my tit."

"Well, yeah," Buddy says, "that's how it works. Sometimes they go together, those things."

"Except in this case the tit came first. The sequence shows what you wanted—first grab the tit then go for the kiss. The tit part was on your mind all along."

"But there was no *grab,* nobody was doing any *grabbing*. It was a caress. Like . . . like we used to . . . you know. . ."

"You don't really think that's going to get you out of this."

"Out of what?" Buddy's entire body is in a state of cramp. "I can't get out of something I'm not in. That's the whole problem—I'm not in anything. I haven't been ever." Anything. Ever. Not part of one bloody thing. And now his dad has even come back from the dead to remind him of it.

"Of course not. That's been your choice all along."

"How can you—"

"Forget the storage unit." Shit, now she's crying.

"Where are you going? Don't leave."

"Just like it started, you throwing me out of the shop."

"But that turned out to be a great move. The second time we got together we laughed our heads off about it. Don't dirty that part, don't make the good parts live in the same place as the bad. We have to have something beautiful to come away with."

Dingle.

Out on the sidewalk, Nita snaps, "Gimme that."

There's not much left of the mammoth joint. The apple-nose man in the sharkskin suit has smoked it right through the middle and it's come apart. Nevertheless, he hands the beautiful lady the larger half.

Nita tokes while regarding him. The man from the 20 bus yesterday. She's been carrying around the Bud Osborne poem he passed her.

For his part, the apple-nose man remembers seeing her somewhere before, hard to nail it down with all the moving around he does, the gigs of happenstance, the speechifying and preachifying. Foreign blood in the lady, a presentation all over the place with an athlete's body but with angry eyes—no, not angry but hungry, hungry for something. But he'd better move along. It wasn't wise to stop in front of the shop to twist one. From what he's seen from chance encounter, the barber's as lost as anyone else and can be a righteous wild man about it. If he finds out who's behind the *YOULYSSES* tag, there'll be lots of 'splaining to do, Lucy Ricardo. A moment to centre—

May all beings be happy, content and fulfilled,
May all beings be healthy and whole,

May all beings be protected from harm and free from fear,
May all beings be awakened, enlightened and liberated,
May there be peace.

—and when he opens his eyes the beautiful lady is gone.

The beautiful lady could use some centring of her own. The weed is helping, but it can do only so much. As a child and running right up to the present, Nita has had female friends she imagines as occupying separate rooms of a mansion, sisters young and old. On one floor are those who make her laugh, on another the day-to-day confidants, down that hallway are those with whom she shares secret longings, a few mothers fill up the kitchen and pantry, her wilder sisters run loose on the grounds and shout from the widow's walk, in the great panelled library hunch writers over their desks while nearer the windows artists transform canvas and dancers test the limits of space, in the carriage house wait two or three she's done more than kiss. She draws on the sisters and they on her, exchanging their—she always has trouble with this one—*specialties*, which sounds clinical, but what else fits? She needs each of them at different and overlapping times for different and overlapping reasons and puts pressure on none to be the one-and-only-all-things-at-all-times. But a marriage, the stress of two people trying to match One Everything to Another Everything, what arrogance to think she and Buddy could have pulled it off. And it's not just her husband, the father in the barbershop is evidence of that. If there was more than one Buddy in a single room then there must be millions out there in the world. And if there are millions of Buddys there must be millions of Nita Randolphs unable to connect with them.

If she was in training shoes she'd aim for the mountains and run straight up their sides till the air was cold and clean and she was high enough to see the mansion where her counterpart sisters live and learn. Except high up there on the mountaintop would be Buddy, climbing a tree or trying to throw a rock for a new record or just pissing off a forest creature.

Most distressing is that Nita might just possibly, in moments of weakness, maybe, on the outside chance, who can tell, never say die . . . love him.

Chapter 24
Warm Pursuit

Before entering Joe's Cafe, Louie engages in a leisurely reconnaissance of the surrounding portion of Commercial Drive, finishing with the coffee shop itself. There's no formal patio, but several customers have dragged out chairs to sit and smoke, and on the William St. flank the sidewalk is wide enough to accommodate a number of locals idling with a contented lack of purpose, faces raised to the early evening sun.

The interior space is marked by comfortable disorder. Small international flags on the walls, bullfighting posters, chrome-and-melamine tables and chairs, a counter without stools where beer and wine is served. Louie orders an espresso and takes a seat midway to the back, where partitioned off by a latticework fence are a couple of pool tables, more of which are visible in an adjoining room accessible through a doublewide walkthrough.

Waiting is no punishment when the coffee's black and strong, and Louie quickly finishes his espresso and scores another. He has low tolerance for mild liquids, prefers his beer skunky and near freezing, wine harsh and peasanty, coffee that needs diluting to flow. Water he generally enjoys fresh and clear, but won't turn up his nose if it's a little froggy.

Is this her coming through the door? No, this woman's heavier in the face than the one in the picture, though with the same large round eyes.

Louie's not one of those octogenarians who catapults into catatonia when faced with new technology, but neither does he actively seek adventure through the keyboard. So it was easy to give himself over to the barmaid at the Ivanhoe, who via Facebook found a Sally Fairchild just off the Drive. A connection, a question, a brief exchange of messages and a phone call. Ah, and here she is—yes, this is the one, standing in the doorway with a kind of sorrowful look.

An enquiring tilt of his head her way frees up a smile that changes her whole presentation, and she starts for his table. If nothing else, Louie's expecting an interesting talk. The Monks were Charlie's actual family, but what place did the dead man occupy in the history of the Fairchilds? To Norma, the mother, if she's still alive, he surely must be just another old boyfriend now lost in time. But for the son and daughter it would partly depend on how long Charlie was in the picture. Given enough time at an impressionable age, it's possible they held him as a surrogate father. If Louie's going to be dancing around the subject, he'd better do it lightly.

"Gee," Sally says, "you look just like your voice."

Louie's stuck for an answer to that, but he comes off his chair and says, "Please join me."

Sally carefully sets down a cloth bag, pinches at her jeans as though holding out a skirt and lowers herself primly.

A shout from outside delays further introductions. Through the window, Louie makes out a bit of a kerfuffle on the sidewalk, where a pit bull pup in full tail-wag mode is racing back and forth butting its head into smokers and newspaper readers.

Sally follows his look and says, "That's Arf-Arf. Maybe I should shorten her leash."

"Seems friendly enough," Louie says.

"She sure is." Sally ducks her head. "I'm really sorry . . . I forget your name."

"Louie Zimbot."

"Wow, what an excellent name!"

"So nice of you to meet with me, Sally." Her handshake is firm, and if a handshake can be happy, Louie figures hers is a prime example.

Sally would die for an iced cappuccino, and when Louie returns from the counter they settle in.

"So this is pretty weird," Sally says. "I mean, I guess I always knew he was like you know, wasn't alive anymore. It's been so long, right?"

"Oh," Louie says, stumbling over both his tongue and his prepared opening. "I didn't get that from you on the phone. My fault, I didn't realize you hadn't . . . gotten a confirmation."

"Uh-uh. Not for sure. Is it really for sure now?"

"I don't want to raise a whole lot of feelings you might have dealt with long ago, but yes, Charlie died twenty-five years ago, and I'm very sorry for that. He was a good person and I'm sure he was good to you kids and your mother."

Sally agrees he was a good person, and tells Louie so, but he was in and out of their lives so often and for such long spells that when he was home all she remembers were things being rushed and blurry. Mummy was angry with him a lot, that's for sure, but she also said the world is so hard that people need to find their own way to go through it. "I have to say something. Is that all right? If I say something?"

"Please, anything."

"You said on the phone you want to meet my brother too. I told him about it, that you were the boss on the fishboat when we lived on the Island, and that there was a will. He might not remember some of what I said, so when we go see him, I mean it's better that we're talking first. Umm, a really important thing is it wouldn't be so good if you brought up our mummy. Is that possible? Like according to the law and everything, that we could just keep it about the will and us without talking about her? Me and him are all that's left, because both of them are gone now, right? Our dad and our mummy too."

Our dad. There's Louie's surrogate-father theory confirmed.

Sally's looking out the window up at the sky, but she soon enough picks up the thread. "It's not like our mummy abandoned us or anything, or had a choice, I don't want you to think that. Devona says bad things happen and then you have to deal with them. Nobody knows for sure what happened to her. But it's not good for Bo to start thinking about her too much. Devona would like kill you if you brought that part up."

"This Devona . . . ?"

"A really, really good friend. Her and Mummy were friends first."

Louie leans in to raise a shield of discretion. "I'll check with you at every stage, I'll never step over the line, I'll do everything in my power to have this turn out exactly as you want. We could leave Robert—you call him Bo?—"

"Uh-huh, but he's Robert or Bob too, to some people anyhow."

"We could leave him out of it altogether until everything is settled, except that we need his help." He slides a photocopy across the table. "Here, there's not much, but have a read."

Sally pores over it as though it requires translation, and eventually passes it back. "So the part about leaving all of it to his family, how come you think it's money?"

"That's a good question," says Louie, edging out on the thin ice of deception, "and I can't answer it very well. All I can say is I have a feeling, but that could be wrong too."

"He didn't have any before, that's why he had to go away so much even when he wasn't fishing. Mummy had to work all kinds of jobs."

"The best I can guess is that if he came into any money it was right near the end."

"That would be amazing."

"Can I ask how old you were when you moved to Vancouver?"

"I was nineteen and Bo was a year older than me. He's still a year older—ha!"

Louie smiles. "Before that, back on the Island. Did your dad ever talk about anything like a hiding spot? A special place you had?"

"Nope. But it says 'Ask the boy,' so I guess that means he told my brother something, right? Him and Bo were closer than him and me. Devona figures our dad had a problem with women, but she says that about everybody, even other women. He never hit me or anything or yelled, and he didn't try any of that stuff guys try." She casts an apologetic smile at Louie, who hastens to assure her she's being a lady. Sally raises her hand like a school kid. "What if my brother can't remember anything?"

"It doesn't have to be a hiding spot," Louie says. "It might be connected to something else, something that wouldn't make you think of money. You know what it's like, you'll hear a song and it reminds you of a car trip or a favourite aunt, anything. Even the simplest thing could be a clue."

"I can't think of anything right now," Sally says. "Umm, I was wondering if we can, like, go on to the next step and maybe see my brother now? It's suppertime and there's a big mac-and-cheese in foil in my bag. If we hurry, I can get it to him while it's still be a little bit warm."

"I didn't think I'd get to meet him right away but sure, absolutely. The sooner the better."

"Great." Sally quickly stands. "You know how to ride a bike, right?"

"Uhhh, yes . . . but it's been—"

"Ha! I'm kidding, we'll take the 20 bus, it gets us really close." She springs up from her chair.

Good sport Louie gives his head a you-got-me-there shake.

"So we can go now?"

"One more thing."

It sounds serious, so Sally slips back into her seat.

"This is for legal reasons, and obviously I don't want to bring it up in front of your brother."

"It's okay," she says quietly. "I know what you want to ask. They declared her dead. Nobody really knows what happened like I said. But it happens to a lot of women where we used to live downtown, and officially like in a court of law she's dead, yeah, on paper and everything."

Louie is starting to like this Sally Fairchild very much.

"Now can I ask you something?" she says. "This doesn't have to be right away, and we have to get going anyhow, but if you're going to be in town for a few days or something, maybe you can you know, tell me some stories about fishing. Wait, not fishing, whew, okay, now I'm nervous . . . maybe about you and my dad? On the boat or whatever?"

"I don't have to go home any time soon, Sally. I'll be happy to tell you everything I can remember about your dad and about our adventures."

"Yay." She reaches out and lays a hand on his cheek.

"Have you told your brother we're coming?"

"Oops," Sally says. "I'll do that right away."

After a couple of minutes on the phone Sally makes the rounds of the joint, saying her goodbyes. It looks to Louie that she knows everybody in the place. When she's covered the room she hurries to the door and holds it open. "You're the guest, Mr. Zimbot, you go first."

"Thank you," Louie says, and steps out onto the sidewalk. "*Ow!*"

"Arf-Arf!"

Chapter 25

Weather Gauge

What a day! A trip to Steveston, a visit from his sister and Devona, a new Jester body leotard, and now Sally's coming over again, this time—Bo can hardly believe it!—with a man who knew their dad. He smoothens his checklist and clicks the mechanical pencil. The graphite slides out as though lubricated and he holds it up to the light. Twice he's left too much poking out and snapped off the end, but this time it looks just right. Excellent. On to his list:

1. HAIR √ Way better than this morning. With a little experimenting he found just the right amount of water to mix with the remaining gel and recreate the pompadour. The clots and tangles resisted, but after he cut two out of every three teeth from his comb it passed through fine. Not as good as the King made it look, but pretty nice.

2. FAUCET √ You don't just leave a gift lying around when the person who gave it to you is coming over, so he temporarily secured the new sink tap in place by strapping the tubes to the copper pipe with duct tape, a trick he learned from Red Green on an old TV show. The fancy new faucet isn't working yet, but water still flows out of the corked pipe, so like his dad used to say, he gets to have his cake and eat it too.

3. REFRESHMENTS √ Two oranges, one each for Sally and her guest. There was a third, a mandarin, Bo's favourite, but he couldn't resist and ate it while he was putting out the others. He kept his hands off the graham crackers, though, and they're sitting out with margarine and honey in a saucer on top of the cabinet. If anyone's really hungry he can dip into the supply of canned food he's been saving for an emergency. To drink there's

a large bottle of ginger ale he got on sale at the Washington and a Coke from helping a friend take her plastic bags full of bottles and cans to the recycling depot.

4. TIDY UP √ All his costumes are put away, his newer drawings are neatly stacked so they won't get stepped on, and everything's been wiped. He checked the toilet down the hall, and so far it's presentable. If Sally or the visitor has to use it, he'll double-check in case someone's tying off or throwing up.

That's it for the list. He thought there was a number 5, but it's either on a different piece of paper or was just in his head. Nothing to do now but wait.

He doesn't want to lie down and risk falling asleep, but it sure is tempting. The trip this morning took more out of him than he thought it would, and after getting lost in Steveston and spending half the afternoon running around on transit, he's pooped. But he's not complaining. He wouldn't have found the new Jester suit at any of his usual hand-me-down haunts. He runs his fingers down the sides, rubs his shoulders and arms and chest. The lady at the Thrift Store said it was donated by the parents of a schoolboy who switched sports from track and field to computer gaming. It's called a compression suit, and Bo's never seen anything like it. The way it squeezes is like he's being hugged real tight. At first he had some trouble getting it over his swollen feet and ankles, but after he slit the lower part of the legs it fit perfectly.

A knock on the door and here they are. A squeal and a kiss from his sister, then she introduces the guest.

"Thanks for having me," says Louie.

Chatting away, Sally sets a foil-covered casserole dish on the counter, counselling her brother to eat some of the mac-and-cheese while it's warm. Bo is more interested in showing Louie the Rube Goldberg contraption over the sink, and the two of them *ooh* and *ahh* while Sally watches. Once the tap demonstration is over and further pleasantries are exchanged, Louie sits on the storage trunk Bo pulls out from the corner and toys with the orange the host plops in his hand. He agrees with Sally that her brother's new outfit is stunning, and finally realizes the dingling he's been hearing is coming from the bells on Robert Fairchild's booties. This could be difficult. Sally described her brother as best she could, but as an acquaintance of Louie's put it on returning from his first trip to India—there was no possibility of being adequately prepared for the experience.

Bo and Sally take the mattress, knees drawn up, backs against the wall, and wait.

"I guess we should start," Louie says. "What have you covered so far on the phone?"

Sally turns to Bo. "Didn't I say he looks like his voice?"

Yup.

Louie smiles. "Did you tell your brother what we talked about?"

"Not too much," Sally says. "And you know something? It was, um, funny hearing about all that stuff after so long, and I guess I got some of it mixed up."

"That's fine. I'll start at the beginning."

The brother and sister shift and wiggle as though settling in for a movie marathon. They link fingers. Bo glances down at their hands and the matted forebody of the pompadour flops out from his hairline. Sally giggles and pokes it. Bo straightens his head and the mat flops back into place, prompting much sputtering and snickering and jiggling all over. Louie waits while they run through the routine a few times—head down and the mat flops forward, head up and the mat whaps back. Down, flop. Up, whap. Since this thing with Charlie Monk began, laughter has been a rare treat, and Louie joins in once or twice till the siblings are flushed and content. When they refocus attention on their guest, a grave look comes over the brother, something commensurate with the physical depth of his eyes that gives Louie pause and makes him upgrade his opinion of the man he's dealing with.

After listening to a bare-bones account of the will's discovery and Louie's personal opinion on the contents, Bo thanks him and quickly reads the few lines. The document doesn't really say there's money involved, but Bo understands why his visitor might believe it. Money. Bo doesn't know what to think about that. Some would be welcome, but if there's a big pile, then what? People say it gives you options. But beyond a certain point he's not so sure having options is the best thing. Practically infinite money makes for all kinds of questions: Would there still be such a thing as comparison shopping? Would you ever feel buyer's remorse? Do the rules in that universe allow you to actually have your cake and eat it too? Bo keeps the paper in front of him, puzzling over how an opportunity can be liberating and oppressive at the same time.

Sally tiptoes to the counter. While her brother's busy talking to Mr. Zimbot, she'll serve up the mac-and-cheese. There's enough for six people, plenty of leftovers to keep Bo going awhile. She ate earlier, so it's all for him. Oh, and Mr. Zimbot if he's hungry. She peels back the foil from the ceramic dish and . . . tuna casserole? She brought the wrong dish! She glances at Bo and pinches the foil back around the top, trying for an airtight seal. A doctor once told them there's no way her brother can be so sensitive to seafood that the smell can trigger his allergy, and the same goes for being splashed with sea water that had fish in it. But Sally disagrees. If it's in your head that it's true, then it is.

She snatches up the casserole, and with a strained voice says, "Could you please get the door for me, Mr. Zimbot? I won't be long."

Louie comes off the trunk. "Anything I can help with?"

"No. I just, um, forgot the ketchup in the car."

"We took the bus."

"Door, please . . . Thank you very much, everyone, I had a great time. I mean I'll be right back."

Louie watches her flee down the hall, closes the door and regains his seat on the trunk. Wonderfully kind and personable, these Fairchilds. But, well. Louie gets his elbows on his knees. "We can wait for her," he says. "Unless you have any questions or something to add. Anything that comes to mind."

Bo could tell him about the Renaissance Faire.

Louie listens closely, but the story is so discursive as to be incoherent. A day-in-the-life gambol among lords and ladies, minstrels and jugglers, a sword-fight with the clanging of steel-on-steel, the cheers of the spectators. Frequent ellipses have Louie on the verge of interrupting, for continuity's sake if not outright cross-examination, but the passion in Bo's telling gentles his impatience.

Bo sure hopes this helps but can't imagine how it can. But "Ask the boy," it says in the will. And since he's the boy, he keeps talking until running out of breath.

Louie scratches the back of his neck. How to begin picking it apart? Certainly he remembers the Renaissance Faire, it ran in Courtenay from the mid-'70s to the mid-'80s. But it bore no resemblance to Robert Fairchild's description. It was a time of artistic renewal in the Comox Valley, and the name referred to a cultural renaissance rather than any mediaeval reconstruction with knights in shining armour. Artwork, jewellery, pottery, craftwork, along with weed that would dip its head in homage to the power of present-day BC Bud. The convergence on the town of artists, artisans, musicians and busloads of hippies truly tied the collective local shorts in a knot. Nude women splashing about in the Puntledge River, tie-dyed legions of dropouts, hilarious reports of behaviour suggestive of reefer madness. Louie participated the second year, in Lewis Park, where it moved after the inaugural year's art sale outside the Sid Williams Theatre. Operating from a small floorless tent, he sold a few of his sketches and a dozen printings of his poems, chapbooks of handmade paper with red arbutus-bark binding. As a hook, he played up the grave man-of-the-sea thing by wearing a sou'wester and offering a selection of whalebone scrimshaw from a friend willing to split the profits. Louie had a high old time in the dual sense, and the second the direct sun hit the tent he discarded the sou'wester, which anyway looked foolish on a man in a Keep on Truckin' sleeveless T.

None of it fits with Robert Fairchild's version. And the Faire's last hurrah was long before Charlie filched the crab pot and started this whole business. Robert must be conflating separate incidents, who can say how many spread over how much time. Sonofabitch—Louie's run out of boys to ask. "Sounds like quite the adventure," he says.

Yes, it was. Bo and his dad took in all the colours and sounds and smells and cheers and laughter and kept going right to the river. Instead of following it down to the bay, they went the other direction towards the mountains. Once they were past the picnic spots and couldn't hear the music from the Faire, they went into the woods and had a real tricky time getting through, scratched and poked by branches and brambles the whole way. At least Bo was partially protected by his costume, but his dad was scratched so bad he had smears of blood all over his arms. When the bushes thinned, his dad had Bo sit beside him on a flat spot. The river was right in front of them. His dad had a lot of things he wanted to say, Bo could see that in his face. He started two or three times, but in the end just finished his cigarette and tossed the butt into the river.

"Try to think," Louie says, "think hard. Was there ever any place he said was special? A place he showed you, maybe?"

Didn't Bo tell the part about being by the river? When their bums were wet from the grass?

Louie gets off the trunk. He's always thought better when on his feet and—"*Ow!*"

The door rebounds from the back of his head. Considering the dog-butting and door-pounding he's been in for today, Louie felt safer when his boat was going down. The door's coming back for another try, and he leaps clear just as a large animal with a multi-coloured mane blows in looking ready to pick a fight. Louie doesn't speak, and off Bo's introduction learns the animal is a Devona.

"She was going right past," Sally says from the hall. "Yay! How lucky is that?"

When Bo starts to climb off the mattress, Devona waves him back down.

"I take it you're a friend of the family," Louie says.

"You can take it or leave it."

Hard and earthily attractive. No stranger to life, in Louie's quick assessment, been around the block but it hasn't left the mark of despair.

"Who you supposed to be?" Devona continues.

"Louie Zimbot."

"Bo already said."

"I was a friend of—"

"I heard all that. You nervous or something?"

"I don't know what you want to hear."

"Like it best if I never heard from you at all."

"I'm here in good faith."

"Glad you got faith in something and you better start praying is all I can say. Let's take this outside in private, you and me. Is that the so-called will, Bobby? Gimme that for a couple minutes, I'll check out this good faith."

"It's all above board," Louie says. "I've hired a lawyer who can vouch for my bona fides."

Devona snorts. Look at him—why are so many of them small, them fishermen? Runts. She snorts again to terminate the examination. "Sally, come on in out of the hall. Go around that way, keep to the other side of the trunk if you don't want to catch this motherfucker's bona fides."

Sally hasn't seen Devona this mad in a long time. She makes Mr. Zimbot go first and they clomp down the stairs. Sally moves to the window and through the distorted glass watches them emerge from the building and stop on the sidewalk below. They aren't very far down, she can easily make them out, one head thick with grey hair and the other like a watercolour of a rainbow that was messed with before it dried. Sally tries to get the window open but the frame is sealed with old paint and dirt.

Out on the sidewalk, Devona moves a green plastic bag of garbage out of the way, shoos a pair of strutting pigeons and takes the up-sun position of advantage so Louie has to squint against the lowering western rays. Clearing the decks, preparing for sea action.

"Relax, Leonard," she says, "don't let me chase you away."

The Leonard in question, a stick figure with skin lesions for arms, levers himself erect from his sitting spot against the wall. "Naw, naw, I'm full anyways, I eat any more probably bust a gut. Tell Sally she could be a chef on TV." He wanders off, switching the casserole dish from hand to hand to get at the remnants of tuna on his fingers.

Lengthening shadows. Devona has the weather gauge, but Louie's inching toward the street hoping to get the wind at his back. A couple of old dogs on the way home who should be doing some perfunctory bum-sniffing as they pass, not circling each other with their hair up.

"Not the real thing," Devona says, fanning the air with the photocopy.

"All you did was glance."

"Sally told me. And I read enough."

"I'm getting tired of people jumping down my throat when all I'm trying to do is help."

"Jumping?" Devona twists this way and that in exaggerated pantomime. "Who's doing all the jumping? I don't see no jumping. Sally's not the jumping kind, neither's Bobby, so who else?"

"It's just a term."

"Serious, how many people you been spreading the news to?"

"Only a lawyer."

"Never heard of no lawyer jump down the throat of someone writing the cheques."

"Can we drop the jumping?"

"You brought it up, now you want to drop it. Not much stick-to-it for a fisherman."

"Call the lawyer if you like, I wrote his name and number right—"

"Hey, don't go snatching, I'm not done with this. And keep your distance. I don't want any'a your bona fides all over my new top."

"I just wanted to show you the part where—"

"Don't have to show me nothing. I got eyes in my head and in case you missed it I got two big feet'd be happy to jump down your throat, talking about jumping. How'd that look you show up at Emergency a pair of ham hocks like this sticking out your mouth?"

"If we can we both just relax I'll start at the beginning. Please."

Devona cants her head back and sights down her nose. "Going to tell me everything just like that, huh? Wills're supposed to be private, everybody knows that. Family business, and now you're ready to spout off to a stranger. You don't know who I am, mister. I could be one of those psychos runs around collecting human heads to put in the freezer."

"And I could be an undercover cop closing in on you."

Devona rolls it around in her mind. "Sorry, but that don't cut it. I'll give you this, you at least put in the effort. Just not funny." More silent evaluation but with the edges sanded. "Louie, right?"

"Louie," he confirms.

"I am so a friend of the family. I do some looking after."

"I can see that. And admire you for it."

"Don't be tickling my tits, mister."

"All I'm saying is that Robert seems to have . . . excuse me, is there a disability involved?"

"People around here have enough labels pasted on'm."

Louie nods. The area's nothing like what it was in his day. *Downwasting,* that's the term it calls to mind, the erosion of the land or the thinning of glaciers. "No labels."

"Don't beat yourself up," Devona says. She checks the fisherman out again, more carefully this time, brazen in her appraisal. "You're different yourself, old man. Looks like to me you never mixed much with people scared of being different, am I right? That's why it's so hard to get along. You got everybody trying to be the same, dressing, looking, behaving, it's easy enough to scare'm into thinking that's the only way to go and to shut their stupid faces less they get kicked off the team. Motherfuckers don't ever ask themselves if the team's any place they should be the first place. Round here most of us already been off the team awhile. I seen the way it's gone. But what it is, it's not simple as just making the right moves. When you got no history of being allowed to make your own decisions, where you going to pick up the smarts? And if you're already born good at decisions, how do you pick right from wrong when the only choice you ever been given is between wrong and wronger? When that's the way, thrown on your own don't you do anything? Everything?"

"I'm not the enemy, Devona."

"Well, well, you finally said my name. Trying to win my heart or something?"

Louie risks a smile, and both captains order the cannon port lids closed. "You've known the family for a long time?"

"Since they come over to Vancouver. Met right here on the street, them three used to live up there in Bobby's place if you can believe that. Me'n their mummy ran together awhile. That's maybe something I can ask you about. What went on over the Island back then? Norma, she—you know her name, right?"

"Norma, yes," Louie says. "Norma Fairchild."

"Scared out of her skin, just told me some people probably looking for her and the kids and hot-footed it. The old man, that Charlie, left'm high and dry."

"There was an accident, did you know about that?"

"Norma said he got busted up and soon as he got out the hospital grabbed his ass in both hands and bolted, left'm to work the rest out on their own. He was thinking I don't know what he was thinking, that a kid like Bobby might not need some extra help?"

"He died a short time later."

"I got eighteen bucks on me and I ain't spending a nickel of it on flowers."

"I don't have enough facts to blame you."

"Just so you know, Bobby's smarter than you can guess." She casts about and stoops for a pigeon feather. "See this? The bony part down the middle? He told me that's called the *calamus*. Told me all the other parts too but that's what I remember. His mummy said the schoolteachers over the Island tested him out like almost a genius IQ. Beat the kids three-four grades ahead in scores. Hard to I don't know how you say it, hard to reach, I guess. Which tells me the teaching part is what came up short in that game, not the learning."

She stops dead, no transition to her retreat into the past, and Louie gives her all the time she needs. When she's back: "Good looking, their mum. Real, real pretty. Like Sally but with more red meat in there and eyes like Bobby make you think you're looking into some dark part of the Bible." Another halt, this one with signs of a dive deeper than the first, to a place harder to pull out of. "She got used up, if that's your next question. Used up. She did whatever she could. Me'n her, and I got to say she took to it like she'd sampled some of it before, didn't handle it like a rookie. All kinds of . . . don't matter now, don't matter at all."

Louie eases his way through the sludge of remembrance and says, "I'm glad we had a few minutes alone."

"Go ahead and get back up there. I was on my way someplace. Ask Sally for my phone number if you got anything to say. And don't go passing it around, it's a privacy thing. One more—don't bring up their mummy. I mean it old man, Sally's got a grip on the thing but Bobby can get himself strange. You all right but don't go thinking I don't have my eyes open. 'Ask the boy,' it says. You start getting all in Bobby's shit, you'll be the boy, 'cause I'll pull the *man* part right off you."

"You have my word."

"When I get done you won't have no boner to go with your fides. Huh-huh-huh . . ." On the precipice and about to tip too far, she shuts up her mouth, nothing funny about this at all, too big a thing to be laughing about . . . "Heeheehee, ow . . ."

"One last thing," Louie says. "They refer to Charlie as their father. They must have been close."

"What you mean?"

"I assumed it was a seasonal boyfriend type of thing. Did Norma ever describe the relationship in detail?"

"Detail, relationship, I don't fuckin know. She only ever called'm their kids. Theirs together."

The stairs aren't terribly long or steep, yet Louie finds the climb up to the second floor an epic march. Back on the trunk, he accepts a graham cracker and munches it absently. That about does it. Duty has been served so what's to keep him here? Front desk at the Ivanhoe said a slew of backpackers would be checking in, and it's always entertaining to meet young people afoot in the world. And cheque day was yesterday so there might be some residual action around the pub. Louie's stirred up for some reason, and though it's been a long while, there's no harm in being friendly to any uncritical mature ladies open to comparing activity levels. The brother and sister are sitting patiently across from him on the mattress, at ease with the dead air. Would it be rude of him to leave? Small talk, he's never been good at small talk. He could comment on the gadget over the sink.

His interest picks up when Sally sits beside him and delivers a stack of sketches. Each is mounted with tape or glue to a piece of cardboard. The artist, petrified with embarrassment, remains on the mattress.

"They're really good," Sally says. "And he's got way more."

Louie makes his way through the collection, pausing, considering, drawn in. Hard to compare them to his own work. His might be technically better—not that he's claiming any real talent—but these . . . raw, scorching, including the pastoral subjects. A muscular and fiery grace. Louie makes suitable noises of appreciation before carefully setting them aside on the trunk and getting to his feet.

Bo lifts himself off the mattress and goes to the cracker cupboard, where he slides out the top drawer that holds his valuables—coupons, safety pins for repairing his costumes, bird feathers, interesting rocks, evergreen cones—and pokes around the offerings a few seconds before settling on an appropriate way to thank Mr. Zimbot for all he's doing.

"Please," says Louie, "a gift isn't necessary." The name leaps off the surface of the card and acid-etches itself into his receptors. "Oh. All right. Thank you, thanks so much."

Bo hopes it comes in handy.

"It will, thanks, it's very nice of you. Just out of interest, is this the, uh, your regular barber?"

Not regular, only once.

"Isn't it great?" Sally says. "He got a free haircut from a guy he never met before and it turned out to be Buddy."

"What?" Louie snaps.

Sally full-moons her eyes. "Is something wrong?"

"No, uh, I was surprised at the coincidence, that's all. You both knowing the same barber." Louie scrutinizes the card as if trying to get his tongue around a foreign name. "Buddy Monk."

"For sure," Sally says. "King of the Buzz Cut."

"Right . . . from the neighbourhood. You must know all kinds of people."

"All kinds," Sally says. "But Buddy's special."

"How's that?" Louie says.

Sally ducks her head shyly. "We were sort of engaged."

Chapter 26

Pile-up On the Human Highway

A puff of smoke drifts aloft from June's perch on the front steps before getting lost in the glare of the streetlight. Though Al's been asleep for hours, she looks over her shoulder to ensure he isn't trying to sneak out before returning to her study of the surroundings. The rhodos and the azaleas, the old mossback chair-for-two. Backlit by moonshine, the monkey puzzle tree's reticulate branches chisel the sky into cruel geometry.

As though it's buried in deep geologic time, June can't place the transition point, the age of her son when she made the switchover from being mother to mother-friend. Perhaps there was no sharp discontinuity. From the days her little Buddy was joined to her inside and she was literally house-and-home to him, through tempests and teapots and his years of roving and seeking, they were friends right the way along. June would like to think of herself as a brave woman. But to have any self-awareness is to know the fear, to remember in a long life every psychic prompt to duck, dodge, dissimulate, anything to keep your head above the high-water mark. The fear can be contained through courage, but in real life more commonly by a greater fear. To be a mother is to have the greater fear personified in the child—protect at all times.

★

She was pushing forty that day on the Island, but what of it? She could rip off a ten-mile hike along the Fraser River dike, play-wrestle her teenage son to a standstill, pull a double shift at the Buccaneer and still indulge in the daydreams, selfdreams, lifedreams that were her . . . escape? recreation? . . . her art, that's it, her art. And upon arrival of the supposed middle-age marker of forty, why should her worth suffer? How sad at any age to think your best years have passed.

It wasn't a large place, the Fanny Bay Inn, a waypoint alongside the small highway on Vancouver Island's east coast. Oyster country. Of a summertime weekend there might be a dozen or more motorcycles out front, but this first day of her holiday the lot was empty of chrome and leather, just a handful of dusty cars, trucks, and jeeps sprouting kayaks and surfboards from their exoskeletons like scaled-up insects. And there, just off the narrow gravel shoulder—CC's old Mercury half-ton.

A start of recognition and a quickening of possibilities before the slow deflation back to reality. Her husband must have lent the truck to a friend. She and CC had talked twice in the past ten days, and he'd be up in Prince Rupert for at least another three weeks. Ugly fishing season, the way he'd described it, pathetic catches, most of the men he knew would be lucky to make the payments on their boats. And now his own skipper was laid up with an infection from an untreated cut, unable to stand on a swollen and inflamed leg. *No problem, don't worry, June honey. I'll go out myself. People say I'm the best damn solo fisherman they've ever seen. The minute I hit shore I'll wire the money home, every penny after food and gas. Hard fishing, though, no guarantees for anyone in this business, but I'll do my best. Don't I always come through? Bloody right I do, June honey. How's the kid? . . . Awww, good, that's good. Tell him a grey whale surfaced right beside the boat last week, if it comes by again this time I'll get a picture and send it home in the envelope with the money. Sorry, not thinking straight, working too hard, I meant by wire, I'll wire the money to get it in your hands ASAP and send the picture by mail.*

June pulled off the road and parked beside a car with Oregon plates and a mohawk of bicycles strapped upright on the roof. Checking out CC's truck, running her hand over the primer on the right wheel well and peeking inside brought him a little closer to home. And at least it cleared up where he was based. Between stories of Rupert, the Charlottes, Port Hardy, Ucluelet, she had lost track of this season's home port, and the truck narrowed it down to mid-Island. Since he was rarely ashore it hardly mattered, but in a nice conjunction she'd get to meet one of his friends. A pat on the hood of the truck and a boot in the tire like an old-timey motorist.

She hadn't been to the FBI in years, but it was instantly familiar. Entrance under a projection of the second floor, modest-sized bar and eating area, easy and friendly, neighbourly as can be. A bit musty, wood and wallpaper, a dark floral carpet that could have come from her grandmother's parlor. Her friend had offered to come down and provide an escort back to Hornby Island, but if June needed that level of hand-holding she shouldn't have been travelling at all. She picked up a menu from the bar and let the waiter know she'd be out back on the "terrace." They had a laugh over that, and she continued outside, where the terrace was a country back yard, an uneven expanse of turf sprouting a few weathered picnic tables and fenced-in with wire, beyond which was rough pasturage, weather-scarred trees and farther out the drop-off to the bay.

Hungry. She'd skipped breakfast and couldn't bear to join the restaurant line on the ferry from the mainland, the boat still loading vehicles and the crowd already impatiently jostling, craning their necks to see what the holdup at the hot food section was all about, wrangling their children away from the windows lest they be diverted by an orca or a sea lion and fall behind in the race to pack on a few pounds of lard for the harrowing adventure of conquering Vancouver Island by recreational vehicle.

When the waiter returned, she didn't need to consult the menu. Oysters, goes without saying. Six naked Fanny Bays and an order of lightly breaded pan-frieds. The house white, chilled to a burning frost.

The breeze was singing in a different dialect than it did at home, and to interpret the lyrics she moved to the fence to listen undisturbed by human static. She was working again at the hotel in Steveston, as she had off-and-on over the years to supplement what CC sent home. Tolerable for a while each time she returned, this go-around was a constant chafing trial, and if proof was needed, here she was in a beautifully scruffy grass yard waiting for wine and oysters and thinking about work. She's never been afraid of change, but was starting to wonder whether that bit of boasting covered up a fear of trying to effect change herself. Even today, does she not just adapt to the altered circumstances forced upon her? She hasn't much formal education, which can be a hindrance. Not the lack, but knowledge of the lack—being afraid to alter the status quo for the most part comes from thinking you don't have the proper tools. The most cursory glance at those in charge of near anything shows that both their self-confidence in, and qualifications for enacting effective change are greatly overblown. Yet still she's paralyzed by reservations, hesitations. Fear.

At a friendly call from the waiter, June returned to the table. He left the tray in place while he slipped around with full glasses and bottles and returned with empties, using her location as a distribution hub for the surrounding customers, which carried the advantage of drawing June's way friendly nods and pastel comments: *Travelling alone?—Love the sandals—Have fun on Hornby.* She enquired of those in her vicinity, but CC's friend was not among them and no one recognized the truck.

June was away. Just that. Buddy was staying with a friend, the son of one of the other waitresses from the Buc, a woman who claimed the fourteen-year-old Buddy made her laugh. If she was still laughing at the end of the five days, June had promised her a free head examination and a full pension.

Away. Sky of crying blue. Quartz-edged mountains and conifers. The amniotic smell of the ocean, the smell of life. Oysters, those amazing give-no-fights going down. White wine cold to make the teeth ache. No husband no son no house no work no her—beg your pardon, no regular her, no worker her, no home her, just *this* her. She dallied over her lunch, played with the food, scribed a smiley-face in the crumbs. She hadn't seen her friend in a year and needed the interaction so badly she could taste it through the horseradish on the oysters. Yet this could be it, June could chop it short right there, sleep in the car if she had to and go no farther.

Walk long and lovely-lonely along the shore, dig in the sand, pad through the forest duff, paddle out onto the salt chuck with music in her head.

Done and on her way. The bartender looked close to her age, a warm pacific sort who complemented the old-fashioned wallpaper and would likely end his days with the same flywhisk ponytail if it was the last hair standing. Hand-built cabin, she'd bet. Baked his own bread. He was reason enough to linger, but by now she was in motion. The bill was light, and with the understanding of one in the same serving boat she piled a generous tip on top. She thanked her waiter, waved, and was out the front door into the parking area.

The mottled overlay of sun and shade confused at first, and only after her eyes adjusted and she made a conscious effort to parse the scene—vehicles left and right, small highway backed by trees, two motorcycles cutting in off the road, yes, it was all real—could she confirm beyond reasonable doubt that against the front fender of the Mercury half-ton was her husband kissing a woman with her knee up between his legs. When they separated to get in the truck, June had just enough presence of mind to turn quickly and slip back into the FBI. Through the window she watched them pause at the edge of the road before joining the uneven flow of traffic and disappearing south.

⋆

Al's stirring in the house. June flares another cigarette and looses the first puff without will, allowing the smoke to leak out and crawl up her face to the top of her head, where it encounters a mini-jet stream and evanesces. More sounds of scurrying from inside. Hall light, toilet, fridge door . . . *please, please don't . . . keep going, Al, go lay down again* . . . Quiet. Dark.

The grossly fat racoon she hasn't seen in weeks is back, emerging from between the house and the fence to her right and cutting across the grass beneath the monkey puzzle tree. He doesn't spare a glance, and his cocky waddle carries him across the street for a browse of the north side garbage.

It's not as if she assumed CC spent each fishing season celibate. Hitting a far-off port after so much time afloat with nothing for company except your skipper and a load of dead sea creatures would almost demand release. Even though it was all suspicion, and June didn't like it, still she avoided a confrontation. Besides, although she hardly considered herself a fallen woman, over his long absences she'd stumbled enough herself to jar loose a few flight feathers from her angel wings. To maintain the dignity of wifely primacy June had tried to hold in her mind an interchangeable sampling of fictional faceless sluts from Dickens, or a story set in some 18th century. English port town: Down the cobblestone alley staggers CC, drunk and cursing, reeking of gin and fish guts, careening off the brick walls till falling into the arms of a barefoot strumpet who drags him into a one-room flat, beds him in front of her misshapen bastards and betrays him to a Royal Navy press gang.

But the woman CC was kissing up against his truck was nothing like that at all.

*

After quietly slipping back into the FBI and assuring the barman all was well—she'd changed her mind, it was so nice here and she was in no hurry—June took a seat at a table-for-two away from the windows. Numb, and as though just out of the womb all things around her registered as new. The chair rail along the wall fascinated. The sound of walking across the creaky floor, footsteps abruptly damped on transition to the carpet. What was that fragrance—old wood? tobacco? male musk? Her waiter entered from the backyard terrace and greeted her with mock astonishment. She laughed because that's what you do.

Short lunch rush over, the place quickly cleared, people aflutter with lives aclutter unwilling to waste perfectly good vacation time sitting around doing nothing but relaxing. At the bar, she asked for needless directions to Hornby Island and received an extended geography lecture that in normal times, that is to say any other time at all, she would have lapped up.

Casual now, easy girl, easy as can be: There was a truck out front. She thought she recognized it. An old high-school friend. She missed him on the way through to the terrace but he must have been in here, probably using the washroom.

Happy to help, the friendly bread-making barman with the flywhisk ponytail: *You mean Charlie. Him and Norma live down around Bowser—Oh, Bowser, June says, we lost touch over the years—Yeah, they've been around longer than me, and I moved from Toronto so long ago I don't keep track anymore—Ha-ha, June laughs, my mum used to say time gallops away when you're not pulling back on the reins—Just thought of something, the ponytail barman says, hope I'm not being too forward, but if you have a day or two at the end of your Hornby trip, here's my card—The Breadnoughts?—Yeah, my band, we're gigging in Cumberland next Friday, please be my guest—I'll try, June says, but I can't promise anything—Try hard. You can make it part of a high-school reunion. I don't have Charlie's number, but I'll keep an eye out for next time they're in—No! June barks. I mean, it's okay, please don't mention I was here, seriously—Uhhh, sure, you got it.—Bowser?—Yeah, the bread-making barman says, him and Norma and the kids.*

CHAPTER 27

HE COMES BEARING GIFTS

Ridiculous. Half an hour before opening and Buddy's already in the shop. What's he thinking—catch the early birds? Next thing you know he'll be putting in a normal workweek. And look at this, now there actually is an early bird, some wingnut looking through the glass with his hands binoculared around his eyes.

Dingle.

"Hey, it's you," Buddy says. "Stopping by for a touch-up?"

Nope. Bo was on his way to see Sally and got off the 20 bus a few stops early, that's all. On Hastings, a man started screaming so the driver pulled over and there was a long wait till the transit police arrived. Bo had never seen the man before. There are so many new faces on the Downtown Eastside he can't keep track. Most of them are young, some because they've heard of the safe injection site and other harm-reduction programs, some getting away from home, a whole lot of them just restless—kids with guitars, backpacks, dogs. Others of all ages show up before winter hits in the rest of the country, heading here to the west coast where if they have to sleep rough it's harder to die from exposure. Once the bus was underway again, a lady who'd been sleeping across from Bo jerked awake and added her own series of screams—maybe she and the man had gotten hold of the same stuff—and scrunched up against the window. A lot of the riders were getting fed up by then. Bo himself was drawing some long looks, so when the 20 turned onto Commercial, he left before the impatience reached the tipping point and someone got hurt. He's seen it before.

During the lengthy explanation, most of which Buddy has to compose in his head from snippets, our barber gives him the once-over. The business end of Bo's pompadour has come apart and juts out in stiff stalks, and no mane-shucker on earth would believe the owner of such a mess would stop by a barbershop just because he was passing. Buddy snaps a fresh cape and says, "Jump up in the chair, let me straighten you out."

Bo explains about giving away the One Free Haircut card.

"Don't worry about it, your head's still under warranty."

Bo's shoulders heave.

"Think that's pretty funny, do you?"

He sure does.

"Grab a seat."

Bo leaves his day pack at the front. A cardboard mailing tube juts from the open mouth at the top, and he carefully props it against the window frame before scaling the barber chair.

"What's this, bubble gum in there again? I'm thinking to fix you up with something easier on maintenance. A good buzz cut or a fade is what the young guys are going with these days."

No thank you.

"All right, all right, you like the old look, fine with me. But I'll have to take it down some, cut out the sticky stuff." Buddy goes to work, keeping as much of the main body as he can. A blaze of sun reflecting off a storefront window on the west side of the Drive trumps the dispassionate fluorescence of the shop, and the place starts to warm in thermometer degrees and hospitality both. "Got to admit I like the pompadour. My dad used to wear his hair like this."

Funny, Bo's dad did too.

"No kidding."

With the remediation project complete, Bo turns his head this way and that, getting a good look at the scaled-down cut in the mirror. He presses his lips in acceptance if not outright approval. A pompadour, but barely. He'd like it fluffed up more on top, but doesn't want to keep Sally waiting. Once the cape is whisked away, in his hurry he misses the chromed footrest, steps down hard and lets out a cry.

Buddy catches him by the elbow. "Hey, when was the last time you had those feet looked at? How do you get around with your ankles swollen up like that? Look at them, you had to slit the legs on whatever you call that."

Compression suit. And his feet aren't always so bad.

"There are three-four clinics right on the Drive, why not stop in while you're here?"

Bo explains that Leonard, a friend from the Downtown Eastside, returned Sally's casserole dish, and since she's cleaning up this morning after a late-night event at the Legion, Bo's on his way there to deliver it. As a bonus, Bo finally thought of a present for Nita—that's it there, in the cardboard tube sticking out of his pack—and decided to combine the errands to save on bus fare. He really appreciates the free trim and the joke about his head being under warranty and the suggestion about the clinic, but now he's running behind schedule.

"Nita mentioned that," Buddy says. "About you and her being friends."

And Sally mentioned that Nita and Buddy were married.

"Yeah, well, that's in the shitter."

Bo checks himself out in the mirror one last time. He won't mention it, but the King definitely took off too much.

"So how did you meet Nita? Are you with a what would you call it—a group? She does a lot of work downtown."

Bo starts to tell him about Nita at the bus stop and his suspenders and her commenting on The Only and Justice Rocks in Strathcona Park and the seafood place and—

"You're chatty today," Buddy says.

Sniffing the same impatience as on the bus, Bo cuts the account short and collects his pack.

"So how often do you see her?" Buddy says. "Nita."

Bo already tried to explain, but somebody in the room, and it wasn't him, didn't want to listen.

"Heh, sorry about that. Just, uh, has my name ever come up?"

Only from Sally.

"Tell you what, give me that pack and let me lock up. I have to check with the Legion about something anyway."

Bo's happy to have someone do the carrying for a while. The pack has no padding and he can't find the right way to arrange the casserole dish so it doesn't dig into his shoulder blades.

They're barely past Take-A-Number Deli when Buddy says, "So this gift, is it a secret or can you tell me?"

Just a sketch Bo did. One of his old ones.

"That's thoughtful," Buddy says. "You going to drop it off with Sally? Or is Nita meeting you there?"

A smile.

"At the Legion, I mean."

Bo knows what he means.

For the rest of the way they're content to let the Drive do the talking. It speaks in iridescent bubbles, quivering globes from a woman in Grandview Park with a supersize bubble wand and a tub of soapy water. Communication from deeper in the park is by djembe drums, a semi-circular phalanx of young men with hammerhands making their point bop-bop-boppingly. From spots along the pavement rise baby cries, long-time-no-see-ums, what time you got? spare change? red light motherfucker don't text and drive! *Bop-bop-babababababop!* Spheres, circles, round and round.

When the door to Legion 179 opens, Sally almost jumps into the ceiling tiles. "Wow, I can't believe I left the door open. Anybody could have walked in. Donna was supervising for my first day, showing me where all the cleaning stuff is and where the garbage and recycling goes, but then some kid of her friend's ate a whole bottle of paste at daycare and she needed help." She pulls the door closed and tries the locking bar a few times.

Sally's glad for the visit. It was time for a coffee break anyhow. It feels good to hug Bo, and the same when Buddy hugs her. Sally doesn't know how to describe how being engaged to Buddy was so right even if it wasn't a real engagement. That's something most people who heard about it can't understand. She's tried to tell them that the nice part is Buddy liked her enough to ask for her help, and he's always been good to her way before that. Which isn't all that far away from love, just not the romantic kind. About hanging on to the pretend part, sometimes she just forgets. And when she remembers, she can't explain it very well. Pretending's not so bad anyhow. Everybody does it. If a question is really bothering her, then answering the way it *could* have been makes it feel right the way myths, even silly ones, at least stop the chatter in your head so you can move on. When the hug from Buddy is over, her brother pulls out the casserole dish.

Sally lets out a cheer: "Yay! Thanks, I forgot where it went."

Bo's pleasure.

"It'll sure be funny if it turns out you and me get a whole bunch of money and I was worried about a fifty-cent dish from Value Village."

"Something's come up?" Buddy says.

"Probably not, but it's fun to hope, right? Like carrying a lottery ticket around a long time after the draw without checking it. No way you won against all the odds, but until you check, it might be true."

Bo excuses himself for interrupting, and lays out the second part of his errand.

"Oh, I can show you where Nita lives," Sally says. "Up the street from our place on Graveley but I can't remember the number. Do you have to go right away or can you wait till Donna gets back?"

"I can take him," our barber says. "I know where she lives." Of course he does. The day Nita moved in Buddy followed her. At a distance, it goes without saying—he's no freak. At the destination, he lurked up the street trying to concoct a plausible reason for happening upon her as she lugged her few boxes up the steps, but the only thing he could think of—out jogging—was precluded by his cowboy boots. He shoulders the pack. "Let's beat feet, Bo."

Didn't Buddy want to check on something to do with the Legion?

"No rush, I'll come back another time. Let's get you to Nita's."

Bo keeps the smile to himself.

Over the top with her new job and the best coffee break she could hope for, Sally's all-over warm and fuzzy. "Kay, bye!"

Buddy can hear the rattling of the Legion's locking bar from across the street, but past 6th northbound the tire-hum and muffler-thrum and barrage of crosswalk and vehicle backing-locking-warning beeps and signals and alarms prevail. He's hot and bothered for no reason he could explain were he so inclined to try. Itchy, that's all, itchy. It isn't till he stops for the light at 1st that he realizes he's outstripped Bo and retraces his steps.

"Come on," Buddy says, "there's a clinic over there in the Mercato. No arguing, goddamn it, or I'll carry you in. How would you like that, eh? Stuff you down the front of my shirt like a scared puppy on the way to the vet. Put you on the floor and you hide under a table, the nurse has to get down and coax you out with a doggie treat."

Yaksputz-figsack-korfle!

*

Buddy's stretching out his legs to keep up. He never ceases to be amazed at how Nita can move so quickly so smoothly. His is a herky-jerky form of locomotion that grabs footfuls of pavement and chucks them out of the way, while hers is liquid straight from a creamery.

"You shouldn't have left him alone," Nita continues.

"Alone with a dozen doctors, desk staff, a waiting room full of people and clearly visible from the street."

"Without someone he knows."

"He wanted me to get your gift to you. Best I can tell that makes it your fault."

"Hilarious."

Buddy pictures Bo in the waiting room. Leaving aside the dubious quality of the food he probably takes in, the lack of vitamins and minerals and anything like a proper balance, in sheer quantity he has to be down a field of wheat and a hefty cow. "How do they do it?" he says. "You see them out there looking a hundred years old and still at it. No regular food, horrifying hygiene, addictions, exposed to the elements and near every hand against them. How do they keep going?"

"Practise," Nita says. She wipes the word hard off her lips but can feel it rising again. "They become very good at hanging on through years and years of practise."

Buddy nods. "Must be tough to practise that long and never get in the game."

"That's not funny."

"It wasn't meant to be."

"Look, you did your duty and delivered his gift. Why don't you just leave it to me from here on. Go home, have a beer, break down completely and go back to work."

"At least I have work."

A sideways glance.

"I didn't need to say that," Buddy says.

"I'm beyond worrying about it. I've had jobs that ended quicker."

"My mum would have you back in two seconds. And what's Al going to do for a fantasy life without you around?"

She deflects the suggestion with a cocked shoulder. They've been over this before. Her ex can walk away from anything. He doesn't appreciate the consequences of failure. In her rush through time and space Nita has undoubtedly disappointed, angered, offended, insulted, distressed any number of people, her mother and father foremost among them, and the great majority of times has dealt with it as the unavoidable consequence of being a human. But this go-around it's June and Al she's let down, for no other reason than . . . ?

"It's just a job," Buddy continues. "You let that get between you two and my mum will think you've lost your mind."

"Maybe I have. Your ringtone just threw me back to my own mother listening to *The Shut-in Hour*."

"I've been waiting for a call from Louie Zimbot, let me get this."

Phone to his ear, he scoots away to the north side of Norman's Fruit and Salad, where he's backdropped by a stucco wall given to a mural of mostly long-wavelength colours, the reds, oranges and yellows that never fail to rosy Buddy away from the high-frequency blues, indigos and violets of the day. He wanders along the narrow paths between the outdoor produce stands, listening closely, trying not to interrupt, and at the climactic moment halts, blocking the aisle. Forgive him for being inconsiderate of the morning grocery shoppers, for who wouldn't be? Who wouldn't with this pouring into his ear? His stomach churns, and the protests of an elderly black-clad lady with her eye on the sweet peppers—*That one standing in the way, he needs a good spanking . . . with a shovel!*—are scarce heard amid his guts below.

"So?" Nita says when Buddy has emerged from the labyrinth of green goods and rejoined her."

"It wasn't Louie. Someone else, another matter."

"Yeah, right, Buddy. It's none of my business anyway, you don't have to feed me a line."

In the clinic, for the second time in under a week Nita's best intentions are frustrated by a health-care professional. "Now what?" she says to Buddy on the way out.

"You heard her, Bo left under his own steam and seemed in no pain. Maybe I was making too much of it."

Nita systematically examines the street up, down and around. "He might have gone back to the Legion."

"He could have," Buddy allows. "Do me a favour, will you? I got stuff on my plate."

"All right. And sorry for all that earlier. You did good by taking him to get checked out."

"Call if you need help. With Bo or anything. Furniture picked up to save on delivery charges, painting your place, something with the yard. A fence, you need a fence put up? The owner might give you a break on the rent. I could . . . never mind." He struggles a second. "There's something very strange going on these days. I'm learning about you the way I couldn't before, learning in hindsight. That's not a good way to put it, what I mean is things you probably said a hundred times are only now starting to come clear. Like I was listening all along but it had to percolate through instead of penetrating all at once. But hey, this isn't the time. Just keep in mind what I said about helping out."

"Whatever I need?"

Buddy jangles. Her fingers are on his shoulder. If only she'd leave them there a little longer. A touch, that's all, light-pressure contact. "Name it," he says. "If you want, next time Ted Nugent goes bear hunting I'll waylay the ignorant bastard for you."

"Just tell me everything's going to be okay."

Buddy sucks air through his teeth. "That I can't do."

"So little?"

"Not right after you asked me. It's like this—let's say you mentioned I never bring you flowers. I couldn't just react, could I? Rush right out and buy you some on the spot? I'd have to wait a few days, a week or two, then show up with a gorgeous bouquet like I really thought about it, came to my senses and turned over a new leaf."

The impish look on his face wrings from her a small bright laugh. "Good enough. But at least tell me what Louie had to say."

"That wasn't him on the phone. I've heard nothing from him since Wednesday. One meeting, that's it."

Buddy has just spoken the crystal-clear truth. And since Nita need know nothing about the call from the East Vancouver Lawn Bowling Association, he'll keep it to himself. Now the only problem is lack of time to go online and do some research. For all his bravado and threat of a lawsuit, he doesn't know the first thing about lawn bowling.

Chapter 28

Postcoital Decompression

By the time Louie left Robert Fairchild's room last night and reached the Ivanhoe, the hostel pub was well into it, a mass of people riding a trajectory with the potential for any manner of trouble. That the possibility of boredom had been left safely astern was only to have eliminated the middle passage, and with no suitable captain to steer them through the fog of drugs and alcohol, the passengers had given it over to fate to keep them in open water. Trying to avoid the drifting ship of fools, Louie rowed his way to the bar and ordered a shot and a beer.

"Eight-ball, that's only what."

The owner of the voice was hidden by a moving screen of four or five backpackers with their gear shouldered, shifting their feet and turning in quarter-circles in front of the pool table as though having mistaken the pub for a dormitory room and wondering where in the press of people they were expected to lay out their sleeping bags. Louie ducked down, and made out a pair of shiny salmon-pink shoes.

"What we got here?" Devona said when the backpackers parted. She granted Louie a split-second of her time before cracking the cue ball hard enough to launch the eight over the rail, where it was snatched mid-air by her opponent.

"That'll be a scratch and the match," said the man with tattoo tears at the corners of his eyes and a big yellow grin.

"Not no legal scratch till the ball hits the floor," Devona said. "What you did is like one of them fans reaching over the wall to grab a fly ball out of the fielder's glove and fuck up the World Series." Despite the obvious injustice being visited upon her by this bear-toothed bastard, she rooted in her fanny pack and slapped down a toonie on the table rail. "There you go, buy yourself a hand job at the massage parlour, huh-huh-huh . . . no, save it up and start your own place, huh, jack off the police sneaking in on their lunch breaks, huh-huh, wait in the hallway till the hard work's done then come in for the finish." Bent over the table, hands on the rail, particoloured hair shaking and dancing. Familiar as the proposed masturbator was with her fits of laughter—the overflowing of the eyes, the gradual loss of language skills—the sheer magnitude of hilarity coaxed a smile from him.

Louie and Devona hung around the bar awhile, drinking a lot and laughing carefully, as near strangers will do when unexpectedly finding themselves attracted to each other. Louie met a scattering of regulars who failed to impress themselves into his memory, introduced to them by Devona as her "runt fisherman," and when the two of them moved to a table, the talk grew legs.

Interesting, the ebb and flow of attraction. Sex is something they didn't address ahead of time, no flirting or outright propositioning, just a result of finding themselves a little bit inside each other's skin, the sense of some inexplicable overlap in the animating force. Upstairs in the shaggy-saggy old room, approaching the bed, Louie hesitated. Not performance anxiety—yes, it had been a long time, but he's never been one to falsely equate the occasional failure with lack of masculinity—rather a fear of pressing too much on a wounded constitution. He'd have liked to let it rip like the old days, fall in love for a day or a night or the length of a song, but to share of oneself is to invite reciprocity, and who was he to ask such a thing from a woman whose history could be glimpsed through the bottom of her glass, darkly? But within about fourteen seconds it occurred to him that he was up to his old game of overthinking every bloody thing, which goes partway to explaining why he's been alone most of his life, and very soon all was well above the Ivanhoe-ho-ho.

⋆

The return call from estate lawyer hauls Louie's mind away from last night's laughing and lovemaking back to Monk business. "Thanks for getting back so quickly. I was hoping you could give me some advice over the phone."

"I'm afraid that's not the way I work."

"This thing's getting screwy and I don't want to do someone an injustice just because of my lack of knowledge. Simple question, that's all I got."

At least there's a pause, and Louie rides it without opening his mouth.

"Simple question."

It emerges from Louie in a rush and clatter: "First, since our meeting Wednesday I've learned Norma Fairchild is dead. She went long ago. So it's down to the brother and sister, and it looks as though Charlie Monk spent enough time with them over the years to become very close. I'm wondering how that will affect their legal position. Not being direct relations but a large part of his life."

"This is billable time."

"Got it."

"All right," says the lawyer. "The brother and sister are named in the will, so I can't see them being shut out completely. In fact the closer they were, the more it could bolster their standing if it ever comes to a challenge. But it complicates things. A man lawfully married to one woman, a sort of loose common-law arrangement with another . . ."

"Have a pen handy?" Louie says.

"Go ahead."

"Here's some stats. Sally, her brother, dates of birth and all that, social insurance numbers, the date of their mother's disappearance, the year they moved from the Island to the mainland."

With the information recorded, the lawyer says, "Very impressive. How did you happen upon all this?"

"Friend of the family with shiny pink shoes. Never mind, long story."

"Do you know whether the Fairchilds are aware of the Monks' involvement?"

"I haven't told either side about the other."

"Do they strike you as the type to raise difficulties?"

"The Fairchilds, no. I can't foresee any problems there."

"From the other side?"

"Probably not from the widow," Louie says. "The son has something of a wild hair up his ass, but at least asks thoughtful questions. He's not stupid, but then stupid people don't have exclusive rights to it. Stupid gets around, common enough it might be spread by sneezing. The main thing gnawing at me is that they know one another."

"Which ones?"

"All of them. Robert Fairchild just recently ran into Buddy Monk, but Sally's a friend from the neighbourhood and she also knows June Monk, the mother."

"I think it's time for full disclosure. In my experience, the larger the secret, the less it serves the interested parties to keep it. You don't want this to blow up in the courtroom."

"I'm meeting Monk at his barbershop later," Louie says, "we'll see how it goes."

Louie punches off and stares out the window. While trying to focus on what he's told whom and when, and of the small lies he's been using as garnish—technically omissions, sneaky things that eat away at credibility every bit as much as deliberate falsehoods—he finds the thread of events unravelling under the pressure of a fresh erection, which is calling attention to itself with the insistency of a class clown already assured of repeating the grade so with nothing left to lose. He can't tell whether Devona's scent is lingering in the air or has transferred to him, and he sniffs around in circles awhile.

On the way up the stairs last night, with Devona bumping him with her shoulder and squeezing his hand, he was anticipating the sex turning into something of a scrap, a deal of rough-housing that in men of his age often leads to minor injuries that never quite heal completely, receding just long enough to fool a fella into holding up a trophy fish in one hand for the photographer before the shoulder or elbow or back gives out, after which fisherman and fish are in the same boat, so to speak. But it didn't play like that. He enjoyed her body, the firm strong ass, the strength of her hands, and for her part she spent extra time over his hoary chest and whiter-on-white scars. They lingered on each other's face, looking and kissing and probing and they might have kept on forever if she hadn't smelled the banana that had been rotting since Tuesday.

With the forgotten fruit in a plastic bag out in the hallway and the lights off, they sat at the window looking down on Main, the street sombre and mostly sober at four in the morning.

"Smoke?"

"Called it quits five years ago," Devona said. "Tell you, it was harder than stopping all the rest of it. Don't want any type of smoke in me now, don't go near nothing burning case I run out and buy a pack and start right up again. Won't even suck on a joint. Present company excluded, huh-huh."

A quiet laugh, Louie noted, hardly one at all. The draft from the cracked-open window winkled the smoke from its hover over his head and freed it over the sidewalk. "At the risk of breaking the mood, have you met the man Sally was engaged to?"

"There's the mood broke," Devona said.

"Robert knows him too."

"Buddy Monk, the one that put that padded toilet seat cover on Bobby's head and called it a haircut. But forget about him and Sally. All kinds of wicked hurt can come out of a breakup, but it wasn't no real engagement."

"There's such a thing as a false one?"

After Devona ran through the aborted Dunmow Flitch incident, or at least her version, which tended to scatological commentary on the nature of win-at-all-cost culture, caveman attitudes, women as accessories and disregard for the sanctity of marriage, all liberally decorated with observations on the lying cocksuckerage of the male half of the species, Louie finished his smoke, flipped it out the window and led her back to bed. They didn't see each other's face this time, for Louie was behind, firmly against the great meaty mound of her. When they were done and side-by-side, Devona laughing at this second instance of orgasmic good timing, Louie said, "So you're the one who put a stop to the whole thing."

"You got it. Right in his barbershop in front of three customers. Take Sally to England, my ass. You ever run into'm, check out the left ear. Gave'm a clout that mashed up the top part like the freaky cauliflower ears on them UFC dummies."

"Not to stand up for a total stranger," Louie said, "but other than planning to cheat on the contest, was he doing much harm? Sounds like he and Sally are friends. And didn't you say he paid her?"

"I get it," Devona said. "But guys like that. The kind that'd steal a car for a Christmas present, lift a diamond to get engaged. Fuckin men."

"You forget you're talking to one?"

"I don't ever forget one thing."

Louie ran a hand through her streaky paint-pot hair. "Thanks for going to the trouble of bringing me their records."

"That was for them."

"This isn't."

She trailed her nails through the thicket on his chest. "Huh, funny thing about sex," she said. "Sometimes it's hard to know if you're sharing your happy part or your sad."

Chapter 29

Bring Me the Head of Al Esposito

First thing this morning, Al was cutting through Victoria Park. Everything was wet from an overnight drizzle, and the smell of the grass and the tamped-down sandy dirt of the bocce courts had him feeling pretty darn good.

Not perfect. There were a few things eating at him. The subject of money, which of course had everything to do with Lippy Delillo's business proposal, leading him to dodge the morning rounds with the entrepreneur and the boys in case his uneasiness slipped out. And then there's June. Al's getting concerned about his wife's state of mind, wondering whether, God love her, that menopause business she went through is one of those deals you never really shake and comes back like malaria. Another thing—if he ever gets his hands on any of those graffiti guys running riot with spray cans all over the neighbourhood thinking they're artists or anarchists or whatever, he won't be responsible. Oh, and one more thing—never in his life has he been anything but perfectly regular no matter what he eats, but for three days he's been all bound up fit to explode. You know something, now that he thinks of it he wasn't feeling too good after all.

Al's in the kitchen, wrapping up a survey of the equipment. Much of it could use replacing but that's the way it goes. You want to work, you gotta have the tools. It's always been about work. Finding it, holding on to it. *Got work*—something you can say just like that and have everyone know you're going to be okay. *How you doing?* a guy will say. *Got work,* you say. The paycheque goes straight into the gas tank and onto the table and clothes for the kids and with luck a little left over for a couple bottles of beer and something nice for your wife. *Got work*. Say it out loud, sounds good, no? Makes you want to catch it on its way past the lips and paste it in a scrapbook. Back in the day, the men would go at it Monday to Friday for however long, weekends if it was put out there, and on the days off still pitch in to help someone on the street fix their place up, didn't have to be no close friend or nothing. And you couldn't keep the kids from hanging around wanting in on the action either, ready to work for the sake of measuring up in the older men's eyes. Helping a neighbour building a porch or pour a concrete driveway—an honour. Now so many people make bad money in bad conditions that the old community thing about working just to help is poisoned. Who's got the time? The energy?

Al's not saying things were all rosy back then, don't think his head's in the clouds. The unions were stronger so it was harder to lose your job, but it happened, there wasn't always protection. And just like now, not all jobs gave you much beyond a cheque. Anything that takes up such a huge part of your life's got to hold rewards or you're headed for the bottom, and the only things hanging around there—he's seen it too many times—are the bottle and trouble. The fear. The fear is one thing that's never changed, it was the big one then and the big one now. Piss-poor job you never wanted in the first place and still scared of losing it. But for now—*got work*.

He takes a look over the kitchen service counter. At a table on the far side of the room, a guy and his wife who come in now and again are into their usual pissing contest about who got the worst meal. They're not even from the neighbourhood. How far does somebody want to travel just to complain about food? Look at her—who orders a tomato-and-avocado sandwich then picks out the tomato and cuts off the crust? Food, eat it how you like, but she's got that look, no? Like she goes around sniffing every meal before she'll touch. Both of them. Mrs. Allergic-to-Everything and Mr. Gluten-Kills. Sheesh! Butter is poison, sugar why don't you shoot me, all that. Either one eats a wiener by mistake, the cops'll have a double suicide to deal with.

It looks like they've had enough food and atmosphere both, so Al hustles out front and presents the bill to Mr. Tree-Nuts-Give-Me-Hives. As the couple leaves, there's almost a full-frontal collision with June, who blows into the room like a hurricane trying to escape a newsman's camera. "Am I the only one in the neighbourhood in the dark about this proposed deal with Lippy Delillo?"

"Aww," Al says, "I never signed nothing yet. And I brought it up once, you didn't want to hear. Be honest, now—we were home on the porch and you said it's up to me, you didn't want to hear nothing to do with Lippy. You got to be part or don't be part."

"Thank you, Al. I want to state in plain English where I stand. Lippy Delillo is not a man I would ever want to be involved with in any way, shape or form. People with no social conscience I can do without."

"I got it, I got it. That plain English you're using? You used it forty-five-hundred times already. Years, it's been, there's no more surprise left."

June winds her neck in and rocks back from her toes onto her heels. "Still, let me go on record by saying that no matter how much I personally think the deal is getting in bed with the devil, I'm behind you fully. One-hundred percent. We'll ride out the consequences as we've done since the day you found me on the sidewalk and squashed one of my oranges."

Hey, that's right, Al forgot he stepped on one of the oranges she dropped when she was trying to juggle . . . Wait a minute, did she just say—

"This news about the will," June says, "we both know it's a longshot. It might give us the breathing room we need, but we'd be crazy to start counting on anything at all. Doesn't matter. Go ahead, let's try it your way."

"My love, I don't even know what 'my way' means no more."

June puts her arms around Al's neck and he holds her tight around the waist. Al's had his fill, and by that he means Lippy and everything. He loves June more than ever for backing his play, but how much will it take out of her? Already she's spending more and more time alone with a smoke on the front steps at night, and if that's not a bad sign he'll eat a chow mein sandwich. June's shaking a little bit so he'll hang on to her till she's better. Then it's time to put the brakes on. That's all there is to it—pile it on his shoulders and take it on the chin. They'll find a way, they always have. And you know what, anybody who's listening? It makes him feel pretty good thinking that way. Better than this morning anyways.

Chapter 30
The Bind That Ties

Come on down, they told Buddy, *happy to have you, no hard feelings.*

Getting back to work isn't helping keep thoughts of the debacle at bay. Humiliation is hard to neutralize without a certain serenity in your surroundings, and this kid's contributing exactly none. "I'm staying open late for you," Buddy says to the mirror while holding the boy's head in place with a sample of the extra squeeze he puts into wringing out a dishcloth. "So don't give me the gears."

"Gears," says the kid. "What kind of word is that?"

"My dad used to say it." Buddy swings his attention to the kid's own dad, who's parked in the rank of chairs along the front window. "Everything changes, even the language."

"Yeah," says the boy's father. "But some things got to stay the same. After you took out the chunk of my hair yesterday—that woman who came in, yikes, I don't blame you, I'd jump out of my whole skin—I decided on the way home that my son was grown up enough for his first visit to the barber. And there's something about your place here. I mean, I could have gone anywhere."

"Dad, can we go anywhere now? I'm scared. I don't want the gears."

"Scared is part of being a grown-up," the father says. "You think I don't get scared sometimes supporting you kids and your mother? What if I got hurt and had to ship you all off to work in a Bangladesh factory making crap for Joe Fresh? With my job that can happen. And that's the least of it. Running a hammerhead crane, five miles in the air wondering if this is the day she topples.

One day down she goes and there's you peeking over the edge of the coffin at your dad mixed in with asphalt and Tim Hortons cups. How'd you like that? You wouldn't. So sit still and be quiet."

"Pleeeease."

"Now look," Buddy says. "You got your own kid crying,"

"That's all right. I was brought up it was supposed to be for babies, but I'm starting to think go ahead and let it out. We had this guy at work, they say he never cried once in his life till the day he slit his wrists."

"Who says he never cried before? And how do they know he died crying?"

"Beats me. But you got to believe somebody now and again."

"My ex says you got to start with yourself," Buddy says. "I wish I was better at it."

"Or learn while you're young, one step at a time." The man nods at his son. "Getting a haircut. Step on the way to adulthood, just like you said. Solid. Tried-and-true. Everything else is about change. Phones are already smarter than you and me, and there's going to be way more than that before our time's up. Look at my son, changes before your eyes. We did too at his age. Along the way we tighten up or something, go into suspended animation like in sci-fi, hoping when we wake up everything's been taken care of. But you know what? Even if all the change is good, which I doubt, we still got to hang on to the things that went before or we'll never be able to figure out how we get from one place to another."

Barber-grin in the mirror. "Cheer up, son, I'm all done."

Before the whisk can do its work the boy's out of the chair, thrashing about under the cape and heading for the door. He's intercepted by his father, who untangles him from the cotton sheet and hands it over.

"Thanks," Buddy says. "And keep your wallet where it is. First cut's an initiation rite."

"Hey. That's real good of you. I mean it. Don't see that these days."

"Can we go, Dad?"

Buddy passes a palm over the kid's stubble-field scalp. "What do you want to be when you grow up?"

"A super hero. Then I could, like, laser this whole place till it explodes."

"Yeah, well, eat your Kryptonite or however that works."

"Thanks again," the father says, and after the boy seals off the evidence of his initiation with a Seattle Mariners cap that comes down over the tips of his ears, off the pair trots.

Buddy checks the time and steps outside. *Come on down,* they said. Bounces on the balls of his feet, waves at Old Kim sweeping up a dust devil next door. *Happy to have you,* they said.

The light post banners trumpeting Italian Day look good this year, the temporary no-parking signs are wrapped on the meters in anticipation of Sunday's street closure, and everything else within the barber's visual arc passes inspection.

Come on down, they told Buddy, *happy to have you, no hard feelings*. If you ask him, lawn bowling is an asinine pastime to begin with. At least similar games have something going for them. Curling with its broom work, up and down the ice shuffling and sweeping, getting the old circulation going, with the bonus that there's usually a bar overlooking the rink. Bocce in Victoria Park, friendly arguments and mix of languages, loaded with personalities and characters. But lawn bowling? Parading around in whites, no raised voices, all goody-goody. The politeness, the sportsmanship, the bloody smugness.

"Mr. Buddy."

"Kim. What's up?"

"Found yo note. What kind o meat you want fo the meat draw?"

"Haven't made a list yet. The grand prize should be a big ham or turkey, something impressive like that. The rest of it, a few steaks, a bunch of sausages, bacon, I don't know, smoked meat?"

"How many prize you give out? How many draw?"

"Haven't got down to details."

"I ask yo mum."

"No! I'm handling the logistics, it's a birthday surprise."

"Yo mum birfday in October."

"Anniversary present."

"Yo mum and Al not marry."

"Give me a break."

"You have no permission from yo mum, I think."

"Let me handle that."

"You have licence to sell ticket?"

"Of course. It's on my driver's licence along with the motorcycle endorsement."

"Dis not professional, Mr. Buddy."

"It's not meant to be. There's no money involved. Just pure, wholesome, amateur fun—like the Olympics."

"I try. No delivery till tomorrow, come tomorrow ten o'clock."

"Thanks, Kim. You're the best." Buddy holds up an open palm.

"Doan high-fi me, please."

Buddy returns his attention to the street. A ruckus has broken out near the entrance to Britannia. Young man, older woman, youngish woman, two dogs, guitar, no danger of violence but plenty of huffing and puffing. There was none of that earlier on the grounds of the East Vancouver Lawn Bowling Association. All was hushed, peaceful, grass so green under sky so blue.

The 20 bus pulls up and disgorges Louie Zimbot, who picks his way through the sidewalk scene and cuts across the street. He's ushered inside, and once the old fisherman's aboard the barber chair, Buddy surprises himself by sharing his story of shame.

Yes, grass so green under sky so blue. Civilized, an oasis of good will. *Happy to have you, no hard feelings—Tea? Coffee?—The cowboy boots will put you at a disadvantage on the grass, here are some sneakers to wear—Would you like a list of the rules in case you have to brush up? All right, pardon me, didn't mean to offend. But if you have any questions along the way, feel free to ask.* The denture-plate smiles, the doting appreciation for Buddy's dropping his threat of a lawsuit, the lofty sentiments of fairness and preserving community relations.

All for the camera, as it turned out. All for the local news crew shooting human-interest stories to insert between ads for high-energy drinks and impossible claims for shampoo. How fun for the TV viewers, how sweet of the East Van lawn bowlers to have arranged a match between Buddy Monk, King of the Buzz Cut, and a club member, an ancient woman from the blurred transition between *Australopithecine* and *Homo* who, while moving at the speed of a yawn, demolished the local barber without allowing him a point. Not a single tally. Shutout, 21-0, twenty-one shots to zilch in just seven ends. And after the match—this was right to camera, Buddy would like to emphasize, the old geezers rubbing it in like horse liniment—he was presented with an East Vancouver Lawn Bowling Association sun visor, which he was forced to wear above the pained smile of a loser, while behind him the golden-agers cavorted like colonial villagers over the corpse of a man-eating lion. Once the crew departed—*Tune in Sunday morning to see yourself on TV!*— backs were turned and the antediluvian bowlers returned to their business. Outside the grounds and on his way home, running as hard as he could to punish himself, Buddy was overtaken by his wrinkled sack of an opponent, who slowed her BMW, honked, ran down her window and flipped him a one-finger salute before speeding off up the street.

Louie finds the story hilarious. And by the time the fisherman's out of the barber chair, Buddy has settled into reluctant acceptance. "When you saw me on the sidewalk, I was just about to come inside. It hasn't even been on TV yet and already I felt like everyone was avoiding eye contact. It must be what actors go through after a lame performance."

"At least actors can rise to greater things," Louie says. "Where do you go after getting your ass handed to you lawn bowling?"

"I appreciate your support."

Louie poses in front of the mirror, chin up, chin down, tries a couple of paces back and forth. "Nothing halfway about this cut," he says. "I guess that's why you're not just a prince." He fishes in his pocket and hands over the card.

"One Free Haircut."

"I'm not looking to cash in."

"Another one. Where'd you get it? I haven't gotten around to passing out more than a couple of these things."

"It was a gift."

"Don't give me that look, just come out with it. The last time I was surprised was when I discovered pajamas don't all have built-in feet."

"You and your mother aren't the only people mentioned in the will."

"Of course not," Buddy says. "I reached that conclusion from the partial photocopy." He studies the old fisherman in the way of a teacher grading a stylish term paper on the accuracy of its research alone. "Must be a woman involved. Only makes sense, away from home every season, hard job, stands to reason he'd have gotten lonely."

With a grunt Louie seeks refuge in the brocade armchair.

"You're not exactly yakking your head off," Buddy says, "so what, there's more than one? A bunch of women? A string of them tucked away in every inlet from here to Alaska?"

"Just one that I know of. Her name was Norma. She died some time ago."

"What else?"

Louie's searching for the right toehold when the vibrations start. "My phone, I have to take this . . . Hello."

"Mr. Zimbot?"

It's the lawyer, and Louie blinks at his tone.

"Are you there?"

"I'm in a barbershop, just let me step outside." Louie shrugs an apology to Buddy and is waved along. Once on the sidewalk, he says, "All right, we can talk. Thanks for getting back so quickly. Has something come up?"

After a pause long enough for concern, the lawyer says, "Hold onto your hat."

"Let's not be dramatic," Louie says.

"All right, how do you like this—officially registered as the birth father of Robert and Sally Fairchild is one Charles Clarence Monk."

A few moments later, back inside, concern screams from Louie's face.

"What's going on?" Buddy says warily.

"The estate lawyer I've been in contact with. He seems to be up on his stuff. He's no tiger, but don't tigers miss their prey more often than not?"

Buddy visibly jerks. "You trying to Aesop me?"

"I don't understand the question."

"An animal lesson. I just found out my dad had a woman on the side who meant enough to him to put in his will and you're Aesoping me with tigers?"

"If I were you," Louie says, "I'd get Aesop off my mind and pay close attention. This puts you in a bit of a bind."

"Bring it. Anything else isn't living at all. Life without binds is just lawn bowling."

"All right," Louie says. "Hold onto your hat."

Chapter 31

Entre Chien et Loup

Our barber spent most of the night on the roof.

At twilight the clouds over the North Shore Mountains transformed from the grey of a drowned man's skin into smutty black, rearing on their hind legs in violent updrafts, and Buddy climbed the fire escape to play host to the squall. Leaning back against an exhaust-fan housing that last saw use in the days when the barbershop was a Jamaican jerk joint, he rope-a-doped there letting the storm have at him, taking every fistful of rain full in the chops. Wild but brief. Soon the wind slackened and the rain dropped into a dull pitapat. When it stopped altogether, a crease to the west allowed the sun to tag the sky with a slash of red before sinking from the public eye.

Then came the crows, the cocky black beasties converging for the evening commute back to their Burnaby rookery. The surge of the loose formation, the pulsing waves of bird after shiny-coal bird did much to massage Buddy back into a loose equilibrium. When the shivering wouldn't stop, he changed into dry clothes and was soon back on the roof, above the street, above his living space and working space, pacing the flat surface, skirting pipes and a defunct a/c housing, treading on loose flashing, finally choosing a dryish patch on which to sit, arms around drawn-up knees, till sometime in the middle of the night. Back in his quarters he slept like a fossil, waking rested but sedimented into a rigid cramp.

He slowly lowers from the waist and hangs until his hamstrings relax enough for him to get his knuckles on the floor. His bare feet detect uneaten oats on the kitchen tiles. Buddy hasn't seen Oxhead since Wednesday when Nita dropped by the shop after work, and though two nights shouldn't be cause for panic, who knows the mind of a mouse and how long a translation it makes of two days? The malformed little fart may have gotten himself lost or be lying injured somewhere wondering why he's been forsaken by his guardian for all these years. Maybe it was as simple as Buddy's putting out the wrong food, but what if not grain and such do you feed a house mouse? For that matter, how are you to nourish any foreign body, any unreadable soul?

He needs a workout. He can't take Louie's news to June all pinched by confusion. A man needs a clear head and his feet on the ground. Clean underwear, socks, gym shorts, muscle shirt under a sweatshirt. Heavy day, power all the way, clear the mind with squats, ass to the grass. With his daypack filled with towel, lifting belt, knee wraps, shaker cup of whey protein and 1500mg of micronized creatine, Buddy's out the door.

He walks the Drive, oblivious to externals. Grant Street. Entrance to Spartacus Gym. Down the stairs he goes, checks in, stows his valuables in his locker and returns to the entrance area. Just ahead is the small aerobic section: runners on treadmills, urban alpinists scaling step climbers, stationary cyclists pedalling their way through an indoor *Tour de Drive*. On a typical day all of them would be fixated on the bank of TVs to their fore. But today serves up a more riveting spectacle, and all faces swing toward our barber like heliocentric flowers seeking light from the sun. Happy to oblige, Buddy breaks into his pre-workout psych-up poem:

I will ask thee, thou blood-drinker, of the mead
of the Bearserks, what is given to them, men
daring in war that plunge into the battle?

He scans the ranks of inferior athletes aboard their machines and at great volume continues:

Wolfcoats they call them,
that carry bloody shields in battle,
that redden their spearheads when they come to fight,
when they are at work together.

Although convinced nothing on earth could actually stop him in his tracks, on arrival at the lifting area Buddy stops in his tracks. It's Bo, head-hands-and-feet sticking out from an oversize cotton sweatsuit. He's being skirted by men and women heading from one machine to another, dumbbell rack to the mats, bench to the water fountain. Out of politeness he's spinning in circles trying to get out of everyone's way, which has him wound up in the excess fabric like a Sharpei pup on a lazy Susan.

The clinic was so crowded yesterday that Bo went back to the Legion, barely catching Sally on her way out. And he's sure glad he did, because they spent the rest of the day and night together at her place. It was almost like when Mummy would go to work and he and Sally had the downtown apartment to themselves. Bo demonstrated his new pencil by making a small sketch of the living room, Sally sang a song, for fun they went outside to see how the clematis was doing on the trellis. A little later Sally hard-boiled some eggs, cut them in half, mashed up the yolks with mayo and spooned the mixture in the depressions left in the white halves. She didn't have paprika to sprinkle on top, but otherwise they were exactly like the ones Mummy used to make for special occasions.

It was early when the storm arrived. He'd only been sleeping a little while, and Sally was making soft noises in the tiny bedroom. Quiet as can be, Bo snuck off the sofa and crept outside. From in front of the trellis he watched the clouds shift and shove one another while pouring rain down on the city. Wild and exciting, fresh and fierce. He went to the curb and let the storm pelt him with rain. When the rain stopped, the crows came. Bo waved and waved at the pulsating flight, waved and waved till his arm ached. When the last bird was too small to pick out from the dark background, he went back inside. His sister had just woken up and was ready to go look for him, and he was shivering so hard she brought him a blanket. They were both wide awake by then, and it was still early, so Sally made some herbal tea and they talked and talked. When he told her about wanting to get more healthy, she clapped her hands and said she remembered getting a coupon in the mail for a free introductory visit to Spartacus

Gym where you could be introduced to "total fitness" by a professional trainer. Neither of them had ever thought about joining a gym, but free is free, and maybe Bo would learn something that would make his shoulder feel better. They both laughed because once again their love of coupons was paying off.

"Hey, what's up?" Buddy says, breathing hard from nothing physical. "Didn't expect to run into you here."

Bo explains about the coupon.

"So where's this trainer?" Buddy says.

He's supposed to be here in five minutes. Bo doesn't know whether to continue the light conversation. His friend Buddy looks funny and is shifting his eyes all over the place.

"Okay. Well, uh, stay warm. I'll be over at the squat rack—that thing over there—if you need anything."

Our barber has no hope of mustering the concentration needed for heavy lifting. He does some half-hearted stretching between two trips to the water fountain, all while surreptitiously following the principal character in the floor-to-ceiling mirrors. Where to start? He and Bo share no physical similarities, if it needs to be pointed out. And what of Sally From the Alley—correction, Sally Fairchild? Was it some kind of sibling recognition that drew her and Buddy into the same orbit? But hold on just a second here. Before he gets caught up in some magical mystery tour of spiritual connectedness, isn't he skipping something? Whatever happened to due diligence or even rudimentary fact-checking? Buddy's no detective, but all those years of formal schooling—as much as his mother pooh-poohs them as wasted effort—at least taught him to reason scientifically, logically. So let's see: According to Louie, the information on the Fairchilds originated with that friend of theirs, Devona, the gorgon who bashed Buddy in the ear. Hard as it is for him to favour her in other areas, she obviously isn't lacking in protective instinct, so up to there he'll trust the information. The lawyer, though, how deep did he dig?

But hold on. Only the genes can say for sure. Until a DNA test has been properly carried out it's all irresponsible speculation . . . Look at him over there with the trainer. Could it be?

One minute an only child and now Buddy has a brother? And a sister? Both older than him, too. What, suddenly he's a fucking *baby* brother?

Bo is already tiring. The trainer has him standing in one spot, elbows crooked and out to the side, forearms parallel to the ground, rotating his torso left and right. All kinds of splintery noises are coming from his neck and spine, and though unaccompanied by pain, to Bo's ears it sure is creepy. Each sweep through the frontal position gives him a glimpse of his friend the barber, who seems to be warming up just fine without all this turning and twisting. His friend, yeah. People can be called all kinds of different things because they are all kinds of things. Walker-Talker Man, King of the Buzz Cut, Nita's husband, Sally's *fiancé*, Bo's friend Buddy.

"Slower," the trainer says. "Pretend you're swinging a big weight back and forth at the end of a rope."

Who needs to pretend?

The trainer laughs. "Wait and see, in six weeks you'll think this is nothing."

If Bo stops right now it'll be nothing.

"All right, get some water. And when you come back take off the sweatsuit, it's just getting in your way. Wait, you wearing anything under there? . . . Okay."

The water is fresh and cold and Bo gulps from the fountain till he splutters. Someone's waiting so he moves. Oh.

"You going to be all right?" Buddy says.

In a minute. Just water up his nose.

"Do me a favour. When the trainer's done with you, don't go rushing off. There's something I want to talk to you about."

Buddy can tell him now if he wants. Aren't they friends?

"Yeah, for sure we're friends."

So?

"Uhhh, sorry about the haircut, I took too much off." True as far as that goes. From a barber's perspective, the head on the end of that skinny neck looked better with the unsheared pompadour.

Buddy doesn't have to apologize. The King gave both haircuts to him for free so how can Bo complain? Like his dad used to say—beggars can't be choosers. Bo knows that doesn't make much sense, but then how many of those old sayings do? Here's one: business is business, like it's a separate part of the world like a lake or a mountain and doesn't involve people. Another one: it's not the money, it's the principle. That one really makes Bo laugh because like Devona says, how hard would anyone fight to get back a pail of sand someone borrowed and didn't return? Most of those old sayings are called "common sense." But that's a tricky thing. Bo knows from the Carnegie Library that before Marco Polo returned from his travels, common sense in Europe said asbestos came from salamanders that lived in fire.

"You're pretty smart," Buddy says.

Was the haircut all the barber wanted to talk about?

"There's this other thing. Later."

Buddy returns to his shilly-shallying at the squat rack. Out on the floor, Bo strips down to his compression suit. The mirrors lining the perimeter of the room reflect a dozen sets of eyes riveted on the shrink-wrapped curiosity.

The trainer gathers the discarded sweatpants and top. "Have a seat on the bench there, I have to check on something."

Our barber's draped over the unloaded bar positioned just below shoulder-height in the rack. "Having trouble with motivation today."

"Never mind about that," the trainer says.

"Why the whispering?"

"I saw you talking to him. Friend?"

"Sort of."

"Has he ever been to see a doctor?"

"Yesterday. I took him to the clinic, dropped something off for him and when I came back he was already gone."

"You left him there alone?"

"What, I'm his keeper?"

"Look at his ankles—don't look!"

"You're going to have to pick one."

"It's called *pedal edema*."

"Yeah, fluid retention, one of the reasons I took him to get checked out."

"He's like a street guy, you know?"

Buddy nods. "Not quite. He's got a little place on the Downtown Eastside, but I know what you mean."

"Listen, man, I got a cousin lives down there, and with all the drugs and stuff, I don't think he's into any of that, but the way he talks I just don't know. And it's not just drugs. Malnourishment for a long time can bring on that kind of swelling. Liver disease, kidneys, could be anything. Hep C is all over the place that part of town. Your guy here, Bo, who knows? If he's been taken to St. Paul's before, maybe they know he has a history of liver disease but missed something else. Or they might think it's a kidney infection but it's cancer. Or he's redirected because the ER is full and he ends up where they're not used to seeing guys like that, the doctor runs a few tests and they leave him on a bed in a corner. I'm not trying to scare you, but you should get him looked at properly."

"Yeah, I know. And I will. His sister lives on the Drive, I'll have a talk with her."

"Look at him in that suit," the trainer says. "Other things need attention before he starts on an exercise program or it's just inviting injury."

"Don't I know it," Buddy says.

Chapter 32
Bycatch

Buddy's on the far left rear seat of the 20 bus, pressed against the window. "It feels like I'm going behind her back."

"You are," Nita says. "But you don't just dump it in your mum's lap on the word of a man you met three days ago."

"I trust Louie. But how smart is asking this Devona character? Looking for help from a woman who flattened my ear?"

"Who else do we know who's close to Bo and Sally?"

"Bo and Sally."

"Right, like you're prepared to break it to them directly. Pull the cord, we'll head back to the Drive."

"Yeah, yeah . . . I still feel like a sneak."

"Being a sneak's your biggest worry? Jesus." Never down the middle, her man. It was from him she learned that some people achieve moderation only through averaging high-and-low asinine extremes. She looks past him out the window, and the whir and bounce of the passing stretch of Hastings manages to tranquilize. "You're lucky. I never had what you and June have."

Buddy, too, tries for calm by watching the buildings and citizens sail past, but on catching a reflection snaps out of it in time to capture the hand in mid-air before it can reach Nita. The apple-nose man in the sharkskin suit explains that everything's cool, he wasn't going to touch. Putting the hand out this way makes a connection without physical contact. It flows both ways, the palm drinks in the love while giving back some of its own. He never touches, it's a thing with him never to touch. Fingers just jam up the world's flow. Poking into your business, grabbing for money. Squeezing triggers.

"We've met," Nita says.

"I'd be more careful,." Buddy says, unclamping the man's wrist. "Not everyone reads palms the same way."

The apple-nose man takes a moment to evaluate the two riders. He saw the love-style-fire in the stormy woman with the jungle hair when they shared the joint outside the barbershop. As for the barber, it's easy to read the words but difficult to translate the meaning. Only thing to do is keep tagging the barbershop window, helping the journey. With hands cupped inward like parentheses he urges them closer together, and as the bus cruises to a stop takes his own sweet time getting to the exit. The door's hesitation in opening is helped along by a passenger chorus of "Back door! Back door!" and off steps the apple-nose man in the shabby sharkskin suit.

Buddy enjoyed that. More accurately, he enjoyed Nita's reaction, which was more along the lines of none at all. He's always been attracted to women with a good deal of constitutional robustness, who aren't given to faints and flutters, don't run from strange animals and nasty bugs and doubtful-looking foreign foods, who take the world as it comes in all its improbable manifestations and back down from none of its unfairness. At some point from meeting-to-marriage-to-breakup, he probably should have told her so in just those words.

Nita enjoyed that. More accurately, she enjoyed Buddy's reaction, which was more along the lines of none at all. Was a time he would have had the man upside down by the heels for attempted assault. To some degree she carries a secret envy for Buddy's belief that the world can be imposed on, that sheer strength of will can make it behave, and moreover can be accomplished by the individual. At some point from meeting-to-marriage-to-breakup, she probably should have told him so in just those words. She might even try now, but here's Main Street.

On display at Main and Hastings is the usual traffic—vehicular, pedestrian, illicit, an aggregation of strollers, slouchers, observers and shopping-cart pilots, most of them patrons on one level or another of the services provided by the Carnegie Centre.

"There she is on the corner." Nita waves.

Buddy tries, sure he does, has a smile on his face and everything, but the minute they hit the corner and before Nita can provide a smooth opening it just comes out of him: "No getting behind me, stay right where I can keep an eye."

"Don't be giving me *behind*," Devona says. "You were looking in the mirror when I laid that belt in the ear on you, so either you're blind or one of them whip-me kinds begging for it." Over her shoulder is a striped carry-all, the heel of a single salmon-pink shoe hooked over the mouth. On her feet is a pair of worn black high-top Chuck Taylors ill-mated with her short skirt. "If you can't behave, us girls'll handle this on our own." She turns to Nita and cocks a hitchhiker's thumb at the man in question. "How does this one fit into it? Alls I know is he tried to kidnap Sally to England."

"I didn't mention on the phone that Buddy's my ex. Sort of. We live apart. Married but separated."

"I get it," Devona says. "I'd congratulate you on the split, but he's standing right beside you and might hear me. And let's not stop there, boys and girls. The whole story, please. If it's going to take long, then I don't know but I could do with a cold glass of beer to pour down my neck."

"Likewise," Buddy says.

"You buying? Business booming? Wouldn't mind getting in on the big haircutting bubble before it bursts. Broke the heel off my shoe, going to cost me good money when I pick it up."

"Promise to keep your hands in sight and I'll buy you a new pair."

"Fair enough. C'mon, might have to get hold of a friend. Let's take it down Main if you're up for a walk."

"As long as we sort this out," Buddy says.

"Don't get carried away wishing," Devona says. "Remember the old saying—it's always darkest right before it gets pitch fuckin black."

Buddy would be more than happy to hold the Ivanhoe door for his companions, so there's no need for Devona to hip-check him aside and do the honours. And you'd think that once inside, the barber would at least have a hand in the seating arrangements, but again Devona scoots past—if that's the term for the movement of someone so solidly attached to the ground—locks down a table and positions the barber and his partner close together and across from her, forming a short-base triangle with herself at the apex.

The Hoe opened just forty minutes ago, but being Saturday, yesterday's paycheques still have some stretch to them, and between a good crop of backpackers from upstairs and a number of regulars sheltering from the overly pleasant weather there's some life to the place, if only of a rheumy-eyed, cottonmouth sort.

"Same tab," Devona says when the waitress arrives with their order. Flicks her nose at Buddy. "Sunshine here is springing."

Glasses are hoisted, tipped and lowered.

"Whoever it comes from," Devona says, "I'm guessing there's a whole lot more to this than just Bobby's health."

"Like I told you on the phone," Nita says, "I made an appointment for him with my family doctor. He'll get a good thorough physical."

"And like I just told you in person, there's a lot more."

"It gets complicated. For starters, it involves the two of them, Bo and Sally both."

As for the recent business, Buddy sticks to the facts, which are few and easily presented. He pauses, and after some consideration and reading of the woman across the table quickly runs through a bowdlerized version of the background events on Vancouver Island.

Long seconds pass until Devona says, "That's some story."

"Uh-huh."

"Your own mummy. She alive?"

"Her and her partner have a place on the Drive, a small restaurant and bar."

"What does she have to say?"

"Nothing yet. I want to be sure before I tell her, that's what we're doing here."

"What's her name?"

"June. June Monk."

"That right." Devona drains her glass and holds it up to the waitress, twirling it to include the table. "She never learned the name. You got brothers and sisters? From the same mummy, I mean."

"Just me," Buddy says. "But hold on, are you saying their mother knew?"

"She had a name," Devona says with her first flash of heat since the Carnegie corner. "She had a name, too. Norma Fairchild. I'd like to hear you say it."

"Happy to. Norma Fairchild. I'm not blind to her part in this, but right now I'm understandably concerned more about one of my dad's partners than the other one."

"Which was which? Tell me that, how do you know which was the Other One?' How do you separate people into Ones and Other Ones in the first place?" A tight squint and her register lowers. "Norma knew. Not about you or nothing, I would've heard. And not the part about a wife, but another woman, yeah. June, by the way. Me too, I don't mind saying the names, it's good to say the names. June Monk. How Norma found out, go and guess, maybe that shit-ass confessed somewhere down the line, if you'll excuse my French talking about your daddy. Anyhow, by the time me and her hooked up he wasn't in the picture."

Buddy checks with Nita and returns his attention to the head of the triangle. "What's your take on the rest of it?"

Devona appears to spread out, as though her main mass has been held in by attitude alone and is suddenly free to reclaim its natural territory. "At least now I know the story behind this money talk. The crab-catching thing and the drugs is news to me, but your daddy died, yeah, I heard that part." A glance at the door. "I don't guess you've been getting any of your information from a fisherman about this high, have you?"

"Louie mentioned talking to you."

"And we'll be talking again," she says. "I guarantee that. Looks like there's a pisspot full of information he's been leaving out."

"Do you have any thoughts on this 'Ask the boy' business? I don't know anything, so it must refer to Bo."

"Even if it does, might never be able to pull it out, at least not in one piece. His drawings are about the only things that stick to stuff you'd recognize. They're like small stories or something, you know? Got a whole bunch on the Downtown Eastside, the people, the street, the community. I always heard that you only know what an artist is thinking by their work, not their own selves."

"He draws?" Buddy says.

"That was the gift he gave me yesterday," Nita says. "It's beautiful. Soft and . . . I don't have the words of an art critic, it's just peaceful and a little sad. It reminds me of Emily Carr, like one of her totem poles in a clearing, a handcrafted thing backed by trees with a story you don't really understand but that won't leave you."

Buddy drops his eyes. "I guess I have some catching up to do. But for now all I want is to confirm whether they were my dad's real kids or adopted."

"Adopted is real," Devona says. "Don't think different."

"That came out wrong. I mean are we related biologically as well as what would you call it, situationally? Cross-family-wise? I can't find the term."

"Like I said to the runt, she only ever called'm Charlie and hers kids."

"Tell me everything. You've been in their lives since they hit Vancouver, take it from there and fill in whatever you can remember hearing from Norma."

"I'll decide what gets filled in. It's a privacy thing."

Buddy comes nearly off his seat. "There's no room for privacy, you're going to have to let go of the very notion of it. It's been ripped out of our hands and the absolutely worst thing to do is to prolong the doubt and confusion by hiding. We're talking about two people who could be my brother and sister. Even if they're not, we've been swept up together in this thing."

"You want *swept up?* I'll give you *swept up*. It's never no control, it's running scared. It's having a story just like anybody else except it don't count. Your story isn't the one that makes people happy at the end, so it plain don't count. Nobody wants to hear it—no, that's wrong, it's that nobody believes it when they do hear it. Don't want to believe 'cause it starts off too much like their own story. Starts off the same so it could've been their story right the way through except it got changed somewhere along the line, and nobody wants to think that could've happened to them, that bad luck and selfishness and not looking out for people could've toppled them down to the ground, that easy as anything they could've turned out like you.

"Got most of my friends sweeping up their kids to go to the Vancouver Food Bank. Their kids, you got it? Bless their hearts all them people helping out down there and the ones dropping off food, but what kind of country needs such a thing as a food bank at all?

"*Swept up* is flat-out disappearing off the face of the earth. Woman after woman after woman gone from the streets or that highway up north or anywhere, everywhere. And the worst part is the monsters aren't what I'm talking about. Murder-of-the-week or trial-of-the-fuckin-century, the only side anyway of those stories people care about is the devil side. They fall in love with the real-on-earth devil like they do with one in the movies, and once the devil's gone, everyone's back to being blind it happened in the first place. The real unhuman part is the whole picture, women and men and kids, the every single day rot and poorness and hand-to-mouth and dying by yourself and real live human beings with scrambled brains who need fulltime mental help.

"With all that, whatever gets you through the night, right? Just gets you through the days and nights. What kind of place we living in? Something like I don't know, ten-fifteen bucks for a gram of crystal meth—and five fuckin hundred for a hockey game. Pick your poison, baby. Do the math and pick your poison."

Chapter 33

Nurse Stump

"There's more," Buddy says. But his mother's already blowing out of the office. He gives her a decent lead then follows at his own pace.

Al nods to himself. Good, this is good. Whatever's up, from the look on Buddy's face and the way June's all jumpy, better they take it outside them two. "Your mother, she had to stop in the ladies room."

Buddy pulls up beside Al and waits. A minute passes as the men follow imaginary gnats flitting through space, and another two or three as they shuffle their shoes to remove nonexistent chewing gum from the soles.

"Lemme ask you," Al says. "You ever think of, you know, being a hero?"

"Where did that come from?"

Shrug. "One of the guys from our morning walks. We're having a small thing later for him. Nobody knew him much, nobody knows what to say."

"Sorry to hear it, Al. How did he die?"

"Don't even know that, just sick or something." Al contemplates the tiles on the floor. "Peaceful in your bed would be best, no? Go to sleep and don't wake up. I was a kid I dreamed about going out a big hero. Saving a baby in a buggy that rolls out into traffic, catching an old lady in a header off a balcony, swimming out in English Bay to save some kid's dog, stupid thing bites you but anyways you haul it out of the water and die right there on the beach. Now mostly I want it simple."

"Here's hoping."

"What about you, Buddy? How you want to go?"

"The same as most people, I guess. In long drawn-out agony full of tumors and spite."

Sick. And Al would tell him so too, really mean it this time, put an end to those kinds of baloney jokes and for all. Except here's June back.

Early afternoon under clear skies and a cheery sun. Buddy slows and slides off into echelon to study his mother in motion. Still the purposeful stride. A hitch here and there, the accumulated aches and knots of years on the feet, a lifetime of resisting gravity's attempt to pull her under. Worry in the mouth, but head up and a firm tread. Aware of the scrutiny, out of the corner of her eye June's returning the favour, and when they pass Yogi Bear Yoga and Buddy stops to check through the louvers of the venetians she says, "Nita doesn't go on the weekends."

"Can't a guy look through a window?"

"Can't a mother tell her son he should know his own wife's schedule?"

"Can't a son tell his mother that his wife might have changed her schedule the way she changes her mind?"

"Good point," June concedes. "She called half an hour before you came by. She wants her job back. Come on, keep moving."

They enter Grandview Park by the cenotaph and pick their way through the curved concrete benches that serve as a wildcat street market for goods foraged, fabricated and filched. Mother and son move slowly along the pathway to the children's play area, where three young ones in the prime of toddlerhood are racing back and forth through the squirts of the water feature, happy little indigenous animals well-adapted to the west coast temperate rainforest. Buddy and June peel off the path and pull up a patch of grass.

"What are you thinking about, Mum?"

Fanny Bay oysters, freezing white wine, a barman with a flywhisk ponytail. A truck and a kiss. Much as June and her friend blabbed those five days on Hornby about everything under their hats, June took a pass on the incident at the Fanny Bay Inn. She barely talked to herself about it, and the short holiday unreeled as though specifically called to duty for the restoration of self. Healthy food, unhealthy drinks, freedom that fairly shone and pulsed around her like an aura, the breed of deeply satisfying fun that has little to do with the word's connotation of simple play. Her friend had a schedule June was invited to join or not at her will, to weave in and out with the sense of the moment or the mood of the day. Alone or together, handicraft fair in the woods, a magnificent primal evening naked on the peninsula in Helliwell Park as a storm swept through seemingly bent on filling the hollow of Tribune Bay. Each day a long hike along forested escarpments and ridgelines, up and over and around the hump of the island. Trees of all types, healthy or failing, hard and upright, pliable and tangled, old and semi-reclined, nurse stumps and deadfall supporting a profusion of new growth.

"When CC was home," June says, "when you couldn't sleep, what did he make you do?"

"Thanks to him," Buddy says, "I could whip off fifty push-ups with strict form by the time I was twelve."

"What did I do?"

"Read me stories."

"Which worked best?"

"They were the same, in a way. Your parents, the Great Depression, fighting just to eat. World War II, fighting to survive, to safeguard freedom, the fight of a generation. And after. Unions battling for halfway decent treatment. And ever since. Women, Blacks, Indians, immigrants, gays, all of them having to scrape and claw. So what about those stories of yours? The fairy tales and fables and the Bible—every one of them about trying to get even, tricking, deceiving to get out of the mud, go to the ball in a white dress, finish on top, one-upping, revenge, slaughtering giants, cutting off heads, pulling down temples. So Dad training me to do push-ups? Can't see too much difference. Preparation, that's all. Just preparation."

June's last day on Hornby. On her friend's boat, a modest vessel that could have used more cover from the elements, but then rough exposure was partly the point. Casting off from the marina at Ford Cove, putt-putting out and around the breakwater. In forty feet of water not far from Hornby's shore, slowing to a crawl to approach Norris Rocks, a slash of exposed crust barely peeking above the waves that June wouldn't have spotted until they were right upon it had the sky above the site not been filled with seabirds. Gulls wheeling, swooping, keening. On the beach a scavenging bald eagle stripping a salmon, background player to the rocky outcropping's stars, a rookery of Steller sea lions. The mature males fat and lordly, proud, styling and profiling on their front flippers, the basking females lolling about and . . . wait, what's this rushing off the rocks? A wave of juveniles plunging into the water and swimming for the boat, ten, a dozen, thirty, forty, surrounding the bobbing craft, roundly pointed snouts in the air, barking, growling, eager, desperate for play. June's friend had played with them on dive trips, scuba gear on, settled on the bottom or hovering just above while the young sea lions had at the small groups of divers, tugging on fins, straps, hands, anything floating loose or sticking out, swimming between legs, gently biting the neoprene hoods, chasing, rough-housing with the visitors to their saline playground. Behind on the rocks the parents waiting, watching. Waiting, watching. Watching.

"You knew," Buddy says. "Didn't you?"

"Yes."

"Since when?"

"Doesn't matter."

"How did you find out?"

"It does not matter."

"About the kids, too?"

"I knew there were children involved."

"You couldn't tell me I had a brother and sister? How do you keep that to yourself?"

"Brother and sister, *pff!* Don't blow it into one of those fairy tales that I find out now you hated all along." A cigarette provides punctuation. "I knew the woman's name was Norma. I knew she had a couple of kids. I wasn't going to dig any deeper. End of story."

"Not the end, nothing like the end. Back in the office you cut me off before I was finished."

The old bandstand is gone from Grandview Park. It was a tatty old thing half-lost in a back corner, launching pad for celebrations, speakers corner speeches, protests. The present incarnation is out in the open not far from where mother and son sit on the grass. The riser is subtle, a semi-circular pad of concrete where paths meet, naked to sky and open to foot traffic. No claim to history as the old one but the same attitude, purpose unchanged, and there's no clamshell above the words and music, no proscenium arch to block clear perception from any and all directions.

"Keep talking," June says.

Chapter 34

Every Picture Tells a Story, Don't It?

Al wasn't expecting more than the boys from the morning walks, but look at the turnout. He better cut off the free drinks at two apiece and after that start ringing them up. He's no cheapskate, but what are you gonna do?

Times have changed. In some ways you'd hardly know a friend had passed. Al's not much for big displays of grief, saw enough of that growing up whenever a family member died. The wailing, the weeping, grandmothers and great-aunts going through the sufferings of the damned, weigh sixty pounds but got fourteen nephews and grandsons built like wrestlers holding them up like the old dames are going to collapse and go right through the floorboards. Worse in other places, he guesses, and in ancient times. Knocking out your own teeth, cutting and whipping yourself. Over there in India, Al wonders why the wives show up at all. You wouldn't catch him hanging around a bunch of people looking to chuck him on a bonfire with the dead husband. Lickety-split gone, that'd be Al, ninety miles away the minute after the doctor shook his head.

Anyways, he's said a hundred times that it's good to celebrate when people pass, to focus on someone who maybe got a little blurry in your mind while they were alive. Build up the good and never mind the bad, make the deceased more handsome or pretty than in real life. Funnier, smarter, kinder. And who says that ain't the way they were? We go through life not half-knowing one another, including the ones we love. Holding a grudge against some family member who wasn't aware he did nothing wrong. How come the wife's upset, who knows 'cause you never bothered asking. But this is working out different, here it hasn't been so much about the dead guy good or bad, but about Lippy Delillo. And if the stories flying around reach Lippy's ears, a bunch of Hindu wives getting thrown on a campfire will be small potatoes. Or rice, if that makes more sense in Al's example.

He's been spending so much time running back and forth to the kitchen that a couple of the guys have taken over pouring the drinks, and some of the women are doing him a big favour by stacking empty plates and platters in the kitchen. It's good of everybody to help, but where's June? When she went off with Buddy, Al didn't count on forever. But he tried her once on the phone and left it at that. When things aren't going so good, Al finds having people around makes all the difference. They beef you up just by being there and letting you know you're not alone. June's different, June's like her son, sick or scared and it's under the porch like a dog. Not that he's comparing June to, you know what he means.

To get back to this Lippy thing, some of the rumours are jealousy plain and simple. Like the one about Lippy being close to broke. Don't make Al laugh. Who goes chasing after a bunch of other businesses when the bottom's falling out of your own? And if Lippy's shop on the Drive really is in trouble, how about his other joints around the country? What, they're all going down the tubes at the same time? And here's another one—somebody checked on the internet and didn't find nothing about Lippy being in no Olympic Games for Italy like he said. That one don't count in Al's book. Guys and sports, you can't believe nothing. Tell him again how many goals you scored when you were sixteen and got screwed out of a tryout with the Canucks. And remind us how far that home run was you hit in the charity softball against the Blue Jays. And once more please about the five Frenchies you knocked cold in the Montréal Golden Gloves. Blah, blah, blah, guys and sports, same everywhere—baloney artists.

Al should get back to the kitchen, but there's something about this old guy who's standing at the door.

Louie Zimbot could hardly have anticipated the scene. A full room but with no music, TVs all shut off, half the people mingling, a few looking wrung out, others hunched together as though planning a revolution. June Monk isn't in sight, but a waiter's approaching.

"She stepped out. I'm Al Esposito, like the name on the front. June, she's my wife."

"Ah, so you're Al. I'm Louie Zimbot. Pleased to meet you."

"There's a handshake a guy can respect."

"This might be easier all at once. With your wife here, I mean."

"Hey, wait a minute, wait just a minute, you gotta be that fisherman guy, right? You must be here about—" Al eyeballs the room for spies or busybodies. "I don't want to go spreading it around."

"Is Buddy around?" Louie says. "Over at his shop maybe?"

"Don't got a clue. He never tells me nothing, that one, except where to get off. Just wait around here. Sooner than later."

"I'll do that."

"Can I ask you something? Outta the blue, I know, but . . ."

"Fire away."

"You ever think about dying? Like how and all that? Peaceful, that's the way to go, am I right? How about you, how you want to go?"

"Never really thought about it."

"Go on, everybody thinks."

"Fighting a white whale."

Al's face drops. Another one. What, can nobody take nothing serious no more? "Anyways, there's beer in the tub by the bar. Plates at the end of the room there, help yourself to what's left of that buffet looks like trench warfare. I'll give June a call."

Louie's glad this Esposito isn't full of questions. He's almost reached the limit of his involvement. Make sure the key players are up to speed on who knows what and let them deal with it, that's what Louie would like. Get himself back to the Island and bail his pickup out of the compound. But the owner still hasn't moved.

"So, uh, Louie," Al says. "You were his boss, no? This CC character?"

"We fished together."

"But you were the boss."

"It was my boat."

"Right, the boss." Al looks up and away as though addressing the ceiling. "So, uh, what do you guess the chances are, this money? Buddy, he doesn't know nothing. Trust me, that one would've figured out a way by now. Hook or by crook, him, crook if he gets to pick. I'm not counting on—hey, look who snuck in. How you doing, kid?"

Nita hugs him and kisses the top of his head. For a second Al wonders if he's going to get one of those things guys get, but there's too much going on for anything to develop down there, even if he wanted.

"Look here," Nita says, "Louie Zimbot in the flesh."

"Nice to see you again."

"June here?"

"Her and Buddy." Al says. "One of their big powwows."

How much would Nita like to be a fly on the wall at that meeting? She wouldn't care if the price to pay was having her wings torn off by a sadistic child.

"So you gonna hang around or you gotta run?" Al says. "Get Louie another beer if you're helping yourself."

"Now that we're sort of on the subject," Nita says.

Al pulls himself upright. "Mincemeat for brains, that's me. June told me but I forgot. Sure you can have your job back. Come, go, all the same. You're family, you can never have too many of them."

"I'll stay late to clean up, as long as it takes."

"Don't matter so much about late or early. Comes to time, nobody's perfect like Lippy."

"How do you mean?"

"Lippy. I told you about that. Nailing his appointments and everything right on the head. Like magic."

"Come on, Al, you don't know how that works? All he does is give a time he's guaranteed to beat. Let's say he's twenty minutes away. He tells you he'll arrive in exactly thirty-one minutes. He gets there early, stays out of sight for however long it takes, then walks through the door at the exact time he predicted."

Al quickly runs a few numbers through his head. "So if he tells you like maybe eighteen minutes . . ."

"He knows he can make it there in ten, fifteen, doesn't matter so long as he has time to spare."

It still whiffs of magic to Al, gives him the same goosebumps as watching a guy get out of his wheelchair and walk around on one of them Sunday TV sermons. "Lemme think about that some more."

Nita reaches into her daypack. "I'm on my way to get this framed at Dr. Vigari's gallery." Holding the drawing by the edges of the mounting cardboard, she flashes it at Louie. "I'm not a fisherman or an artist. What do you think?"

Louie takes the sketch in his hands. A small boat in a forest clearing. Hard to gauge the length, but the impression is of something no more than twenty feet. Unfinished, barely much more than a start, lying partly on its side, angled toward the viewer. If the artist has captured anything like the actual dimensions, the disproportionate vessel is best off forever resting right where it is. Wheelhouse too tall for stability, beam not wide enough, deck too far below the gunwales. Just visible off the prow is what could be part of a boat stand. Clearly the craft was built amid the trees. It certainly wasn't thrown into the woods by storm action. But perhaps Louie's overthinking. The sketch needn't be an attempt to represent reality. It could as easily be something from the imagination.

"Peaceful, isn't it?" Nita says. "Makes you feel it had great meaning to the artist."

"Do you mind if I ask where you got this?"

"A friend."

The style is instantly recognizable but takes a turn from the others. The drawings Louie was shown in Robert Fairchild's room were hard, forceful pieces of work that aroused, provoked. They were the storm, this the lull. "Do you have any idea when it was done?"

"No. But from the condition and the yellowing of the paper I'd say years ago."

"Would I be familiar with the artist?" He flicks his eyes at Al, who's busy scribbling numbers on a napkin: Twenty, thirty-one, eighteen . . .

"I doubt it." Nita says.

"Maybe we can have a talk."

"Definitely, but right now I have to get to work."

Okay, Al's not stupid, something's going on. One of those I-know-you-know-that-I know things. But he's too tired to start. June will be back soon, and once the freeloaders and everybody else leaves there'll be plenty of time to get to the bottom. And you wanna know something? Even with a dead friend on his mind, and whatever's going to happen with June's dead husband, Al's smiling. A little bit outside, lots inside. When there's people around, right? Good people around.

Chapter 35

Entre Loup et Loup

Buddy's across the street behind a chestnut. To some degree the tree's canopy is deflecting the rain, but after thirty minutes of lurking he's soaked. The long delay has been to confirm that Bo and Sally are the only ones home in her alley apartment. And if you don't buy that rationalization, he won't press it.

A raccoon passing behind him deflects his attention, and when he turns back to the building the lights are on. Through the drapes two silhouettes approach, cross, recede, combine. Indefinite as they are, Buddy feels he can match each to its owner. When they merge, their shared circumference contorts. Perhaps they're dancing. He'd like that, if they're dancing.

Buddy needs sleep. Physical exercise creates micro-tears in the muscle fibres, which then must be rested to heal and grow. Likewise the competitive spirit, so after each fever-pitched day he gives the night over to a solid six-hour stretch of shuteye before jerking awake to monitor the sun's rebirth. Sleep, rest, peace—the night stretches out before him with nothing of the kind on the horizon. Sky a deep black plum, twilight long lost. *Entre loup et loup*. Dogs all gone now, just wolves to deal with back and front. Friendly wolves, he's hoping for friendly wolves.

He'd like to die at the climax of his life, that's what he should have told Al. None of this fluky, unheroic business about ending at no particular place in the narrative. But enough with the end, what he's involved with here is a beginning. Buddy pictures himself ringing the doorbell. From inside the question, anxious: *Who is it?* From outside the answer, comforting: *Don't be scared. It's your brother.*

He steps out from underneath the chestnut into the rain. Crossing the street, the stray cat struggles to find his strut.

Chapter 36

Love Is In the Heirs

"I can't talk just to talk," June says. "And I'm not going to spend my life trying to remember what I haven't told you just so you don't feel left out."

Al gets it. Except the part about talking just to talk. June's pretty good at that. "To be carrying something like this around by yourself so long."

"Up till now it wasn't hard. It hurt at the time but somehow I rationalized it away. The other woman had children. I didn't know CC was their father, I just thought he was a substitute. If the real one wasn't there . . . I don't know, maybe she needed him more than I did, maybe the kids did. Trust me, it wasn't a burning love-fest of a marriage in the first place. But all of this is hindsight. I can't remember thinking that way at the time. I can't explain, Al. I can't recreate the *me* from back then. It's like we're not related, the *me* then and now."

Al rearranges the bed sheet so he can slide closer. They've just finished making love, and if you ask him it was the best in a long time. The only one in a long time and the best. About kids, Al can't comment. But he don't have to be one of them Dr. Spocks to get how hard it must be.

"Sally." June swings her legs off the bed and sits up. "Her brother. Or is it her two brothers? Where do I start?" She reaches back and strokes Al's head.

He scooches closer. It's about the forty-eleventh time she's repeated the same thing, and all he can think of to do is curl an arm around her waist and press his belly against the spread of her hips. "They got tests can tell for sure, DNA like on them *CSI* shows and everything."

"Buddy says he's sure," June says. "I've never heard conviction like that in his voice."

"It'll probably come up when this business about the will catches fire. That's when the lawyers and the relatives we don't know about yet'll start circling around. We'll have to put bars on the windows like them underwater cages on National Geographic so they can take pictures of the sharks."

"Please, love. There's not going to be a fight about anything, especially over money. I won't have it."

"When's Buddy gonna tell them?" Al says. "Sally and this other one."

"We didn't get that far. We'll talk about it tomorrow."

"Italian Day. Gonna be busy."

"Then the next day. Or the one after. Jesus, Al." June beats down the craving for a cigarette and rolls back on the bed.

Al's doing pretty good. Not quite ready to go again, but like anything extra you want, it takes some work. No hurry, though when the phone rings he's thankful for the breathing room. June doesn't do much talking but Al gets the idea, and after she hangs up he says, "So Buddy opened the can of worms with them two. Good? Bad?"

"He didn't go into detail. He'll fill me in tomorrow."

Just as Al's about to announce a personal triumph in the arousal department, *ring-ring* all over again like the phone doesn't think people have stuff to do. Luckily it's a short conversation, during which Al decides that one of Buddy's problems is growing up an only child. It's easy to explain by Al's can-of-worms theory. The way he looks at it, the larger the family, the more the worms get spread around, everybody gets the same pat on the head and the same kick in the ass but in small doses. With an only child, all the worms get concentrated in one can. A lot of pressure can build up, if you follow him. "Hey," he says, "there's a smile. I guess no big tragedy yet."

"He called to tell me he's on his way to Nita's."

Al's eyebrows arch. "Sheesh—out of the family and into the frying pan."

★

It's some dreamshimmer time of the morning and Nita can't let him stand out there looking like that. Past the raincoats, gumboots and transition-season apparel in the foyer is a narrow staircase, and Buddy follows her up to the second floor. After a quick assessment of the near-empty room, he says, "That's a nice loveseat."

Nita lets the needless comment hang from the noose till it stops kicking. She'd been looking forward to an early night, but Louie Zimbot's theory concerning the sketch left her wired, and on returning to the bar she stayed till closing. By the time she walked home she hadn't much energy left, though the sight of her husband has recharged her some, positively or negatively yet to be determined. Other than looking a little gnawed on, he seems to have dropped years. It might just be disorientation on his face and in his movements, but Nita reads an almost childlike wonder. "Do you want some of this wine?"

Buddy shakes his head and moves to the front window. Through the branches of a magnolia he can just make out the street. "I can't coordinate my thoughts. Can't tell you how I feel about it."

"Feeling and thinking are different things. How did Sally and Bo take it?"

"Happy, yeah, that's good. Surprised. Some crying. But overall it was as if I'd just been away for a while. Back from having lived somewhere far off. But now what? Tell them travel stories? I don't know where to start filling in."

"I wish I had known your father. It would help explain so much."

"Don't kid yourself. We're not talking about a guy who was easy to read. Good man, as far as a kid could tell. Didn't talk much. Broad on homespun philosophy. His favourite piece of advice was the old saw that it doesn't matter what you do in life as long as you try to be the best at it."

"I heard enough of that growing up."

"Yeah. What if there's nothing you're any good at?"

"I mean I wonder why people think it doesn't matter what they do."

"You're rare. Not everyone wants to be the best charity fundraiser, the best bike-lane advocate, the best whatever, slumlord basher. Most people realize you have to look after yourself before you take care of someone else."

"Only till you need less help than someone else. And you don't have to try to be the best anything. Just do."

He turns to face her. "Where does that leave me? How do you do *brother*? How is it done? What school teaches *brother*?"

Nita can no better answer that than Buddy can. He's back to staring out the window, and she leaves him to garner what peace from it he can.

After a time he says, "How do you know when something's true? I look at them, think of them, and they're my actual brother and sister. But the question is whether it's from desire. Does wanting it to be true make it so?" He's halfway across the floor. "I desired you, right? I chose you. You're beautiful, soft without being silly, strong without being hard, you're . . . you're fucking weird, and I love that, I love weird. But what would make me want to be Sally and Bo's brother?"

"The two of them." Nita sits up. "There's, uh, some damage there."

"Sure there is. And thanks for keeping the hint subtle, but I realize I'm damaged too. Big deal. Everyone's damaged. Our genes make none of us mentally and emotionally perfect. We're damaged in shipping and come out of the crate that way. Immediately after, we start picking up more dents and scratches from our environment till we're mauled so thoroughly we should be put on special at Value Village. But if that's all it took—damaged people to relate to one another—we'd be living on a seven-billion-member commune with everyone wearing the same T-shirt. But here's the thing, a two-part answer to my own question. First, I know they're my brother and sister. I feel it like the genetic memory of *place* some people claim to have on visiting Africa for the first time. Second, if I'm wrong—it doesn't matter. The convergence makes us family, sharing the common ground of Charles Clarence Monk."

He retreats to the safety of the window. After a few seconds he turns and makes his way to the armchair. One heartbeat, two heartbeats, three heartbeats, four. "So!" he blurts like a great white hunter contracted to clear the room of its elephant, "what's this my mother says about you still being in love with me?"

"Jesus, Buddy. That's no way to ask a question like that."

"She let it slip once or twice and I thought I'd clear the air."

Softly: "What do you think?"

"What I think has never brought clarity to anything."

Softer: "Tell me what you think."

"Well . . . I guess maybe . . . yes?"

"That's real positive, honey."

Buddy glances at the door to the stairs as if to assess its worth as an escape route. "You know how I feel."

"I could wake up one morning and disappear just because I hadn't heard it out loud."

One heartbeat, two heartbeats, three heartbeats, four. "Yeah," Buddy says. "That'd be the shits."

Nita manages not to laugh and refuses to cry, and so they sit. They sit. They sit for an age of agony on the brink of the screaming meemies until doing nothing becomes more intolerable than action and they meet in the middle of the floor. As though new to the game, they share an awkward bony hug—knees-to-knees, elbows out, wrists-to-shoulder-blades, foreheads bumping. As they flounder, hopes fade, but once disentangled they venture another embrace, this edition with the fleshy bits, the skin and muscle, the parts with blood running through.

Buddy fights for an explanation. A rover must rove, a knight must be errant. So why this degree of need? Springs to mind Schrödinger's Boozer, his college friend with a scientific defense for all matters great and small. But there's no science here. Correction—science there is, but it's not strong enough all by its lonesome to explain his feelings.

He's been without her for the three months since their separation and a good two before that. If it didn't involve Nita, such a gap would be no cause for alarm. Buddy's appetite runs more to periodic gorging than regular browsing. In the pre-Nita years, when arousal could no longer be suppressed with wind sprints or enervating gym workouts he invariably found a woman in a similar state, as though they'd been sucked together by pheromones of desperation. Nothing wrong as far as that went, all in good fun. But in almost record-breaking time neither could have picked the other out of a police lineup, and other than some testimonial masturbation in its honour the relationship was added to the long list of experiences from which he would never learn. Until Nita.

From beginning to almost the end they regarded each other's anatomical parts as unique features other people didn't possess, and somehow it carried over to the way they related emotionally and intellectually. Her heaving beneath him or Buddy on his back with her walking north on her knees—after that what was there to fight about? Or was it the other way around, did it start with the heart and soul and spread to the cock and cunt from there? Either way it was madness that first time, back at her place after the mountain hike. Hard and soft with exquisite explorations and happiness. That was the key—they were happy in the sex and the love. What happened to the happy? That's what Buddy's most indignant about, that the happy just up and beat feet.

So no science, not now. For how to explain what happens when Buddy removes Nita's top and discovers anew that her skin isn't simply smoother than his but of another quality altogether? She's trembling under his hands, synapses running amok, nerve ends dancing an uncoordinated jig. Now she's removing his shirt and Buddy's knees will not put up with this another second, keeping upright is asking far too much, he'll sweep her off her feet and carry her into . . . but his legs are completely gone, and there go the sandals and the pants and now he's down on his knees with his face at her waist, hands running up the back of her bare beautiful legs.

Nita doesn't function well in a formal relationship. So why her need for a man at all, never mind this specific man? Her fingertips are digging into Buddy's scalp through his buzz cut while he holds her legs apart, his tongue licking, probing . . . this is insane, the shivers, tiny rash-bumps all over like pebbled leather, she has to lie down. And he's so far away down there, too far away, she needs to see his face. He's standing and urging, directing her to the love seat . . . No, their love needs a larger canvas . . . Good, he's changing direction for the bedroom. The mattress is on the floor, unromantic but there's no stopping except to kiss, sweet and desperate, aching. Is this it all over again? Is she caught? Think, Nita, think. No, that spoils everything. Wrong, definitely think, we're talking about your life here. Think! What's this off to the side, a doorway, a dark hole. With a cry she wrenches free of his arms, leaps into the tiny bathroom and slams the door.

For a second Buddy wonders whether Nita was trying to bolt from the house and mistook the bathroom for the stairwell. It doesn't make sense she'd run off naked, but his logical apparatus is undergoing severe attenuation under the assault of . . . what exactly? Well, exactly love. But how many times can it be endured? Some can handle falling in and out only once, others any number of times, and he has no idea where he fits on the sliding scale. Before Nita, he rebounded from breakups disgracefully quickly, but the cumulative effect has him plain exhausted. He'll run away while he has the chance, launch himself into the night. No, impossible, he'll not turn his back. It was there from the very first. They'll talk, he'll get her take on it and factor that into the equation—ah, right, an equation. He's always found it difficult to manoeuvre when science clashes with feeling. But a leopard doesn't change its spots—what the fuck, now he's Aesoping *himself!*—and a loose interpretation shouldn't be out of reach.

Bang-bang-bang! "You all right in there?"

Nita flinches. What's with the pounding on the door? As though sitting nude on the edge of a bathtub hiding from the ex-husband she still loves doesn't make her enough of a loser, now she's helpless? Maybe she is. This feeling, the giddy-sickmaking, the absorption in the moment that obscures more than it reveals.

She stares at the top of the bathroom vanity. Beside the sink is where, in their place together, he would leave his shaving kit. Razor, foam, toothbrush, deodorant, sundries. Not in the cabinet like someone expecting to be around awhile but in a small zippered carrying case. Ready to roll.

What a feeling. How is it possible to be so horny when you're hiding behind a door from the hornymaker? Hornymaker! Now the giggles are coming. Buddy's going to think she's gone out of her mind. Way to go, girl, you're in love with Lieutenant Horatio Hornymaker. Oh, shit, now she's losing it, squeaking, weak-limbed, silly and dizzy and reckless. Another knock on the door. It's not locked, why doesn't he just open it? Can't he see she needs rescuing? Can't he see? She pushes off the edge of the tub just as the door swings inward.

A raw red collision. Crying from regret and confusion and wanting and lacking, they stagger about in a lusty grapple, reaping bruises from towel hooks and drawer handles while emitting low moans and high wails, fiery and fierce and heedless. They race along the hallway toward the bedroom, a vortex of legs and arms mauling and scratching, pornographic roller derby, till stopping in the doorway a mere arms-length from the new mattress to kiss. Kiss and hold each other. They pull apart slightly and share with their eyes: *Are we good? Are we safe?* The unspoken answers must fit each to his and her need because the surge resumes, and at a clumsy four-legged stumble they hit the mattress, slam down and are immediately joined, foreplay having worn out its welcome and been banished to the romance section of the Carnegie Library.

From Buddy a few murmured apologies for clumsiness matched by as many pardons and merciful light laughter from Nita. Then, inside her up to the heart and with his fingers tangled in his love's wild Medusian hair—both of them close to it now, very close—comes to Buddy a revelation blinding in its simplicity.

"What is it?" she whispers up at him. "Is something wrong?"

"Wrong?" he says as the waters part.

"You went away there for a second."

"Don't you see?"

"See what, my darling man?"

"Science is predictive and practical. Art is contingent and sublime. Ergo, Love is Art."

Chapter 37

Italian Morn

He's pretty sure there's a pot of water on the stove. Sally does that every night before going to bed so in the morning she can just boil it up and put in the oatmeal. But Bo's stomach feels full already. Water would be good, though. He's thirsty as anything.

Yesterday was mixed. Very tired after his trip to the gym, good most of the day, bad for a while around supper. Buddy's visit chased away the dark things, but the pain has snuck in again while Bo was sleeping. From the pullout bed he can hear Sally in the kitchen. By his sister's tone he can usually read her mood and sometimes even the subject, but this morning she's almost turned off her voice. That's all right, it's pretty easy to guess what she's talking about. If his legs weren't so cramped and twitchy he'd join her so she had someone to talk to.

They're supposed to drop by the barbershop today at three o'clock. Buddy's closing early for a game at a neighbourhood restaurant, and he'd like them to be his guests. After he left last night, Sally explained about the restaurant, and Bo's excited about meeting Mrs. Monk, someone they're almost related to. He's a little nervous, that's for sure. He hopes he feels better once he's up and moving around so he can get home to change. He doesn't want to be out of costume when he meets his new brother's mummy. Sally loaned him a pair of her jeans and a kittycat T-shirt, and his belled hat and booties are here, but he can't fit into the compression suit anymore without cutting the fabric so far up the legs that the outfit will be ruined.

Lately he's been feeling the press of time. He was pretty good in science at school and thinks time is like water, able to exist in nature in all three states. Gas as it leaks away when you're not paying attention, liquid when finding its own level, solid when it won't budge from the path right up to death. Slippery, too. How often have people bought something extra to save the time of another trip and never noticed where the savings went? Or wasted time by taking the long way somewhere but are able to find more time for almost anything?

He pushes up on one elbow and tries to see out the little window. His neck aches, making it hard to keep his head up. As he manoeuvres to the edge of the mattress to try sitting, he's butted from behind and knocked clean off the sofa bed. By the time Sally hits the room, Bo's on his back flailing his arms.

"Arf-Arf!"

Energized by the roar of the hometown fans, the puppy throws a head fake and evades the defender's moving guard. Through a basting of canine saliva, Bo squeals his good morning to his sister before covering up. Sally drags the dog off, and Arf-Arf settles into a self-satisfied pant.

Sally crouches. "Are you all right?"

Bo's fine, thanks. Actually, he's more comfortable than a minute ago.

"You don't have to let her on the bed with you."

He didn't know he had. Not until she butted him onto the floor and started kissing him. That's a pretty sneaky dog, getting all the way under the covers without waking him up.

Sally tows Arf-Arf into her bedroom and closes the door. On her return she finds Bo sitting on the edge of the sofa bed looking like a bone licked cleaned of the last scrap of meat. She's used to her brother's various costumes, but right this moment Bo reminds her of one of those sad kids from the Oxfam commercials. Good thing the doctor agreed to rearrange his Monday appointment schedule. "Sit at the table," she says. "I'll make some breakfast."

He'll sit here a couple of minutes if that's okay.

"No hurry, we've got all day." Sally's glad he's listening. Or understanding her, if that's a better way to put it.

Last night after Buddy left, Bo went outside hoping for a repeat of Friday night's storm. After a while, with no rain coming, Sally had a bad feeling. She found him down the way standing in front of someone's cedar hedge that separated their backyard from the alley. He was talking to himself. Or maybe it was to someone on the far side of the hedge, because he started walking back and forth like he was looking for an opening. Poking his head into possible openings, pulling aside branches. Sally was glad it isn't one of those huge dense hedges on the West Side, because Bo was determined and might have still been out there trying. But he got tired and saw his sister and followed her back inside. Sally couldn't get him talking after that. She made up the sofa bed and said goodnight and went to the bedroom. She plugged in the blue nightlight she found at the Salvation Army and stared at the soft glow for a long time.

Bo's doing some talking this morning. He must have had a good sleep because he feels pretty good. In the tiny kitchen he sits at the table in a chrome-legged chair with a green vinyl seat and back cushion, the only thing left from when Mummy was with them. Bo offers to help with breakfast but Sally says the porridge won't take long, and besides, she has to keep busy.

Sally can't get last night out of her mind, she just can't. It's like the car trip with Mummy when they sang along with Blood, Sweat and Tears doing the 'Hi De Ho' song over and over and over. When Buddy told them the news, Sally thought he was joking. He says she has a pretty laugh and he does that a lot, using funny voices and horsing around to make her laugh. But this time he was serious. Her brother—Bo, her old one—was confused and asked their brother—Buddy, the new one—if he could stay the night with them to sort things out. But Buddy had to get going, and promised to tell them the whole story after all the Italian Day stuff was done with.

When he invited them to the restaurant for today, at first Sally was scared about what she'd say to June. Buddy must have read her mind because he stepped right up to both of them and said—Sally remembers exactly—"You're my brother and sister. You never have to worry about anything ever again." Bo told him the same thing back, and that's when Sally started crying and threw her arms around Buddy's neck, which she's never ever done, not even when they were engaged.

She's crying again just thinking about last night, and drops the bag of brown sugar on the floor. Bo gets up and hugs her and wipes her nose with his shirt. She tells him she'll take it to the laundromat as soon as she has a full load. Calmer now, she stirs the porridge with the wooden spoon to keep it from burning. Tastes. Just right. Mummy used to eat hers the old-fashioned way with butter and salt-and-pepper, but Sally and Bo like it sweet, and this time she's careful handling the sugar bag. Once breakfast is on the table, she takes a spoonful right away and swishes it around with a mouthful of milk. Bo looks at his. Sniffs the rising steam. "Sorry," Sally says, "I didn't make it right."

Yes, she did. Bo dips in a spoon and licks it. Sally plays with hers, laughing, encouraging, hoping to get any amount of food into her brother. But the tactics are pointless, and when she's full she adds both bowls to the empty pot, which will need some soaking to loosen the burned parts she didn't notice on the bottom.

Sally centres on Bo, holds him tight in heart and soul and starts laughing through a shimmering veil of tears. It's all there is to do. Sally and Bo . . . and Buddy.

Chapter 38
Drive Time

"Go, just go. I have to work and if I don't get some sleep I'll be a wreck all day." Nita has more to say, but when she pulls the duvet over her head all Buddy can make out is a muffled volley of high-and-low swear words. A spread of brachiated dreads is abandoned outside the duvet and dangles over the edge of the mattress. He waves goodbye to them while calling out his love for the lump under the covers.

Buddy takes a walking cruise along Graveley. Off the port side, greenery and scenery. To starboard, passing vehicles that receive a good-morning salute. Abreast Sally's alley he resists the impulse to burst through the door for an impromptu hug and continues on down to the intersection with Commercial, where he heaves to for a look-around.

Italian Day.

The forecast is for clear skies and a high of 22°, near perfect, and preliminaries are underway. A small corps of traffic authority constables are ready to swing the barricades into place. Pickups, flat decks and cube vans are being rid of their loads. Musicians are unreeling cords and stacking cases of equipment. The pace is accelerating all around, occasionally jumped up by a minor emergency—supplies forgotten back at the muster point, misplaced truck keys, a malfunctioning open-sided tent, a disagreement over the dimensions of a choice spot beside the Italian Vespas and Fiats fronting Grandview Park. At the north Main Stage on Grant, a call comes in from a missing bass player who left with some audience members after last night's gig at the Fairview and awoke reeking of booze and bad decisions on the paving stones in Whistler—but now he's on the shuttle bus approaching

Squamish, no shit, and will meet the band on the Drive and did they bring his guitar?

It's all much more complicated than the three-in-the-morning setup at Al Esposito's. Nita had the keys from locking up, and since their first attempt in three months at making love had been enough of a success to corrupt sound judgement, she agreed to help Buddy sneak in the unauthorized meat draw gear. On holidays and for important celebrations Al forgoes the rounds with the boys, and he and June open the restaurant together. By now they'll have seen Buddy's computer desk and the empty ice-cream bucket with the rolls of tickets. And to retreat a step, they couldn't have missed the poster taped to the front window. Buddy's particularly proud of the poster, an enlargement of one of those animals-of-the-world conglomerations from junior-high nature books. Birds in the air, mammals on the savannah and in the forest, reptiles and amphibians in desert and swamp, fish in the sea, the whole works crammed cheek by jowl as if Noah & Sons bungled their carpentry and the Ark went all cardboard on them at the first drop of rain. Across the top in felt pen: MEAT DRAW — 4:00PM SHARP.

Any time now Buddy will be getting a blast from his mother, so he picks up the pace and thirty minutes later is scrubbed, shaven and presentable, if not as by-God gorgeous as he feels. He packs a box with the microphone and small amp from the storage unit, and totes it down the stairs.

On the sidewalk, a squad of young crows is receiving tactical instructions from their briefing officer: *Lightning raids only, in-and-out fast . . . No landing to scavenge in the dance areas—remember last year's trampled martyrs . . . Under no circumstances strafe the open barbeques with shit and bring shame to the whole squadron!* The opening of the door fragments the minimurder into individuals who wander about staring at the sky like total strangers until the human enters the barbershop, whereupon the briefing is renewed using as many code words as the young ones can remember after being up half the night with excitement.

In the shop, Buddy dumps the sound gear on the reception counter, rests his eyes on the reverse image of YOULYSSES on the front window and takes the main chair by the shoulders, rotating it back and forth like a dance partner while scatting nonsense lyrics to himself in the mirror. It's a work day, absolutely. He's part of the neighbourhood, part of the city, a citizen. The plan is to keep the shop open from ten till three. Unlikely there'll be much business, which is fine. He'll prop the door open, keep an eyeball on the surge of festive humanity and wait for his new family members to arrive. By then June will have called in a panic or a rage and he'll have talked her down.

It's going to be a full day, and Buddy should eat something to see him through. There's nothing upstairs in his fridge, so maybe some pickings from the Drive. He could gobble a couple of protein bars or . . . Jumpin' Geriatric Jesus! The meat!

Next door Kim braces. "Mr. Buddy. Good to see you."

"Kim, my friend, sorry about yesterday. You wouldn't believe."

"I believe you in trouble. The Portugee Club, he forgot a big party coming in yesterday. He got yo meat."

"Got my meat?"

"You no pick up yo meat and you no answer yo phone. I call and call. So the Portugee Club got yo meat."

"It was a hectic day," Buddy says. "That's no excuse for letting someone steal my meat."

"Not steal, he buy."

"Come on, Kim, seriously. We've been friends for years, you and me and my mum and Al, sort of an extended family. And in hard times family steps up, right? Like when your wife passed away."

"Ohhhhh, that mean, Buddy."

"I apologize. Really. But I'm desperate, here. Hard to explain, but now it's more than just another meat draw."

"One more thing no license?"

"Listen, forget the meat that was stolen from me. Give me whatever you've got." Buddy hunches and rakes his eyes over the lumps of animal products behind the glass counter. "There, that black forest ham that's been cut into . . . and the prosciutto and what's left of that smoked meat . . . all the sausages you have, split them up I don't know, half-a-dozen to a package . . . turkey loaf, that'll work, and that ugly thing over there." He leaves the counter to check out the shelves opposite. "Pickles. Won't that surprise them—yes! Another excellent idea from the King of the Buzz Cut."

"You sure in love with yoself." Old Kim's behind the counter awaiting a final decision before starting the cutting and wrapping.

Buddy has swapped listening for reminiscing. "My mum used to put down preserves every year. Mustard pickles and pickled beets—fantastic. She'd let me have the first jars all for myself. I'd eat them with my fingers and walk around for days with yellow and purple stains on my hands like I'd been strangling circus clowns. Only thing we're missing now is a grand prize, something big and impressive." Kim tries to interject, but Buddy puts his hands atop the counter and yells, "This is fun, eh!?"

Kim grins. "Wait, please. Maybe I have one big meat in a cooler room."

When Buddy sees the baron of beef, a great goddamn ton of bovine arse being wheeled out on a stainless-steel serving table, both in the vernacular and literally he almost has a cow.

"Not real baron-a-beef," Kim says. "No sirloin attach. This call steamship round."

"Who cares? No one'll quibble about winning something the size of their grown children. Thanks, Kim, thanks so much. I was getting scared there for a minute."

"Friend and family come together." Kim swallows to suppress the quaver in his voice and says, "Like yo family when my wife pass."

Buddy's head lowers under its own weight. "Sorry again for trying to use that as leverage."

"It okay. Only most time you stupid, not every single time."

"Heh. Keep it in the cooler and don't let anyone from the Portuguese Club through the front door. I'll be back in a few minutes."

"That leave you no time to practise lawn bowling." Kim's face doesn't so much as twitch.

"Don't you know watching TV in the morning rots your brain? Mind your own business."

"Binness fine if people doan forget pick up they order."

"*Gamsahamnida.*"

"You welcome, Mr. Buddy. Doan high-fi me, please."

Buddy ducks out the door and into his own joint. And there's his brother. His brother in a kittycat T-shirt, belled hat and booties. Buddy flicks a hat bell and conquers the urge to lift him onto his shoulders. "Where's Sally?"

She went to the restaurant. Buddy's mummy asked Sally to help out with the meat draw.

"She what?"

Sally's really looking forward to calling out the numbers.

"That's my job!" Buddy scrambles under the counter for the box of sound gear. "Come on, hurry. I'll drop you off then pick up the meat next door."

Bo can go by himself. It's close.

"Okay. Tell Sally I'll be right there. Let's beat feet."

After Buddy peels off to the deli, Bo waits for a good-sized break in the pedestrian traffic before entering the turbulent flow. Jam-packed as it is, he finds everyone very polite and has no problem picking his way along the street. He can smell grilled sardines and hamburger and chicken and something sweet. He'll have to remember to check around later—surely somewhere along the route there's a stand with graham crackers. People are wearing all kinds of colourful clothing, a hodgepodge of styles that reminds him of the Renaissance Faire. On the walk here, he and Sally passed a trailer with a radio DJ playing songs and some brand new shiny Italian cars and a black man with an accent juggling and doing balance tricks with another man backing him up with music. All sorts of stuff, and even more now, variety in all its colours. Not far along he comes across a pit of play balls full of kids screaming and diving and tumbling about, and there across from it is Al Esposito's.

Up till now Bo hasn't been nervous about meeting June. He figured any lady his dad picked must have something in common with Bo's own mummy. His sister sure likes her, and Bo always agrees with Sally's choice of friends. He hasn't cried over the situation yet, but the whole thing gives him a hollow feeling all the same. With two mummies involved and two sides to the family, there's sure been a whole lot of stuff everyone's missed. Times when someone was sad and didn't have the right person around to explain things to. Times when someone was being picked on and didn't have help. Times when someone just wanted to walk along thinking about nothing but knowing the person you're with was on your side.

Bo steps gingerly over the curb and onto the sidewalk in front of the restaurant. He'll have to remember to tell his brother about the mouse. When Bo was getting close to the barbershop, he saw the tiny thing squeeze out of a hole in the brick and scurry along the seam of the buildings before disappearing around the corner. It was funnier looking than any mouse he's ever seen, but was going so fast he couldn't be sure what was wrong with it. Most people don't like mice as much as he does, especially ones right where they live, and he doesn't know his new brother well enough yet to say whether that goes for him. Bo smoothens down the kittycat T-shirt, adjusts his Jester hat just so, swallows really hard and reaches for the door.

Chapter 39
The Meat Draw

Buddy plunges the wheeled serving table into a gap in the pedestrian flow and immediately has to swerve for a tremendous desert tortoise. The grand old beast likely would have emerged no worse from the collision, but it would have been the end of the party for the chihuahua on its back, a shivering specimen outweighed by the Grand Prize at roughly the ratio of a corncob to a Cadillac. When the dog begins to scrabble around on the reptile's carapace, the pair's owner touches up the dome of bony plates with a shot of spray adhesive and on the trio plods.

A unicycling clown in a curly red wig, upstaged by the dog-and-tortoise show, allows a decent separation to build before continuing his unsteady way a metre above Commercial, waving, tooting a toy horn and passing out two-fer and three-fer coupons for one thing or another to people concerned mainly with getting their children out of the way before he topples.

The street is engorged with thousands of people surging north and south. Working hard to keep pace with Buddy is Old Kim, pulling a wood-slatted wagon laden with packaged meat and Buddy's sound gear. Kim's passing up the potential for a good day of business, but if keeping the deli open means missing out on the entertainment then there's really no option. June's reaction alone will be compensation enough. All he has to do is keep in the background and deny any association with whatever Buddy has planned, assuming his friend has a plan, a safer assumption than the continuance of the earth's rotation.

By all means Buddy has a plan. Simplicity itself—arrange the meat draw so his brother wins. Rig the game, if you must put a name to it, and like it or not it's the way Bernard Clarence "Buddy" Monk bebops through life.

The two men wrangle their loads over the curb in front of Esposito's, reseat the packages that are close to slipping onto the street and barge through the door.

"Hey, Mum."

"Glad you're so upbeat," June says without a dram of glad in her voice. For free, she tosses in a withering glance at Old Kim that stiffens him to attention like a border guard under inspection.

"That's some poster, ain't it?" Buddy says.

"So far it's attracted exactly three people, and they didn't stay. I had no details for them other than the four o'clock start time, which was fifteen minutes ago." She glances back and forth between the delivery vehicles. "If all of this is meat, you'd better get a vet to stitch it back together and give the animals another chance."

"The crowd will pick up," Buddy says. "People like to arrive fashionably late to meat draws."

"*Pff!*" She backhands the serving table. "What's this under the tablecloth?"

"Baron of beef."

"Steamship round," the Korean border guard corrects.

"Leave it here with the rest," June says. "I'll get it into the cooler."

"Thanks." Buddy drops his voice. "Are they, uh . . . ?"

"Sally's out back trying to calm down. Bo's at a table by the far wall."

"My main concern," Buddy says, "is the pressure on Sally. Running something like this, I mean. It doesn't leave her time to enjoy the contest, plus it makes her ineligible to win. So I'm thinking—"

"Stop thinking," June says. "That's the solution. I'm serious. I don't know exactly what's rattling around that head of yours, but you're not allowed behind that desk."

"Just looking to help."

"Isn't that nice." She transfers her full attention to Old Kim. "Maybe you can give us a minute."

The border guard's stomach churns as though the North has begun pouring through the DMZ. He abandons the wagon and slinks for the archway.

Mother and son are left with each other's eyes. One heartbeat, two heartbeat, three heartbeat, four. "I love you," June whispers.

Buddy extends both hands into the sunlight pouring through the window and they lock fingers. He leans in, kisses her hard on the cheek and ear and temple and forehead, sidesteps the serving table and follows Old Kim's spoor into the bar.

June lowers her arms. Sixty-four years old and look at her life-house—all the grooming and patching and painting and decorating and it's still a fixer-upper. But it's her house. No home is just right and June has always been able to deal with that. It's about adapting. At twenty-four years old she wasn't setting out to be a mother until she got pregnant. It happened and June responded naturally. She doesn't see how the lack of intent would or could lessen the love for the child. Then as a widow, she had no interest in looking for another partner until the day she tried to juggle three oranges for Al—and look at how beautifully that swung her way. She's accepted and modified and doesn't for a split second think some counterfactual rewiring of her history, including the most recent turn of events, could possibly change who she is.

There are two more occupants for her life-house now. June already knows Sally, and the love from the girl when she walked through the door had them both in tears. The brother is a new and different type of addition. Time will tell. And what of the other mother? Did she know? Were Norma Fairchild and June Monk, counterparts across the Strait of Georgia, each clasping the same secret tight to the chest through the dark nights? Running through it all is a possibility that nags. Till now, June has been holding CC's Island family to be a spinoff on her and Buddy, the indulgence of a lonely man and definitely subordinate. But what if it was just the reverse?

June props open the door and lets the warmth of the street creep over her shoulders and around her body and between her legs into the room. She'll pass on phoning Nita to see what's keeping her. Wounded but on its feet, her and Buddy's relationship staggers on, and if Nita has to play the delinquent to find her centre, June will leave her to it. Al's calling from the kitchen, so June goes to check on what problem it is this time that only she can solve.

Al doesn't consider it a problem so much as confusion. The guys have been dropping in since this morning with different versions, and Al doesn't know what to believe. The only thing for sure is that Cicalone is closed on the Drive's busiest day of the year. One of the guys did some digging and it turns out the head of the six stores around the country is some guy in his nineties who lives in Toronto. According to another guy, Lippy's not even a partner, just owes the old man money and has been working off the debt in Cicalone at no salary. Nobody knows half the truth yet, but the icy feeling is that Lippy don't have the authority to clinch any kind of a business deal at all. So what's up? Everybody's running around looking for a lawyer, including the guys from the stores in the other cities

Then there's this one guy—actually two guys, one pretty trustworthy, the other not so much—who think all that talk's a bunch of bee-ess and aren't scrambling trying to pull their money out of nothing. *Loyalty*, they're calling it, a word that sounds good coming out of your mouth till you think of all the people brown-nosing around Hitler or Mussolini or that poison Kool-Aid guy, or even just that baloney artist with the Scientology, what's his name, Elroy Hubbard or something, the goofy wingnut who signed up that actor from *Top Gun*.

Anyways, now that the twists and turns are coming fast and furious, Al can't decide whether it's a relief or a disappointment. He was far from putting his signature on anything, but the potential alone gave him that almost high feeling, you know? Funny, no matter who has the right answer, if the whole thing was so flimsy that it's collapsing into rumours, you gotta wonder what Lippy was thinking. Greedy, sure. Desperate, could be. But stupid not so much. Nah, something like this Al figures Lippy just reached too far. Probably that's why all the stories. Guys who gotta be big shots on the outside are usually small shots inside. Anyways, Al's got only himself to blame. He saw something he wanted and grabbed it with both hands before checking to see whether he needed oven mitts to keep from getting burnt. He won't make no money but at least he didn't lose none.

June's happy as heck, but Al's take on it is more complicated. It's good to have people you know standing at the top of the heap. Like you never made it past kicking the soccer ball around the playground but one of the neighbourhood guys signed with Juventus, there he is right on the TV. Which anyways is better TV than this morning's local news, watching Buddy get handed his jockstrap by an old lady with one foot in the grave. Huh. Lippy. One thing, Al's sure gonna miss the excellent jokes.

"Are you all right?" June says.

"Oh, hey there June honey, how you doing? You know something? A hug wouldn't hurt nothing." Heaven, in her arms. "Right all along, that was you about Lippy. But who cares about win or lose like a contest." He pulls back and captures her eyes. "You were backing me all the way even if you thought I was being a stupid so-and-so."

"Any time," June says. "Forever and ever."

Al wipes his eyes with a clean corner of his apron. "I heard some people."

"A few, and others are coming in quick. I could use help."

The door swings, and in pokes a bouquet of dreadlocks. "Late, sorry, I'll get right on it."

Al grabs a last hug and says to his ten-times-better-than-any-one wife, " Nita, she's good on the floor. You on the bar, and me, I'll keep an eye on this side, a day like this probably nobody wants no big sit-down meal anyways. We'll push the chicken wings and the veggies, sandwiches, snack stuff. Thanks for cheering me up. Go ahead, my love. Let's have some fun today."

In the bar they're almost ready to go. "Test, test." Buddy taps the mic. "Test, test." Without interference from the street a plain speaking voice would serve the modest space, but a sax player up the way and a guitarist down the street are ripping it up while a brigade of djembe drummers bangs away in the background. Buddy turns up the amp. "One-two-three, one-two-three. Can you hear me at the back?"

Mumbles of affirmation fail to convince, so Buddy checks with his mum, who shoots him a thumbs-up from behind the bar. Nita, hard at work taking orders from the stream of regulars who have their timing down pat for special days and are just arriving, gives him a nod of approval. Over the course of Buddy's explanation of the rules, the regulars are joined by new faces from other parts of the city and environs, suburban outriders and visiting outsiders and the like, and by the time Buddy relinquishes the mic to Sally the room is full.

"That went all right," June says when he reaches the bar.

"Look at the crowd. Didn't I tell you? So much for your measly three people who didn't come back."

June steps out from behind the bar. "Here I come bearing arms," she says and wraps him up. They roll around the vertical in a sloppy waltz that draws shouts of encouragement. June bows.

Buddy waits for his beer, slings it down, and with the second joins Old Kim at their table. "Where's Bo?" he says while positioning his chair for maximum coverage of the playing field.

"Baffroom." Kim starts to giggle.

"What's so funny?"

"Not funny, just nice. Hear a man next table say, 'Rising tide liff all boat.' Sally bruvver say, 'Not boat at anchor—those boat get swamped.' Pretty smart. I like him."

They're set up against the far wall, close to the front where Sally sits with the basket of tickets. Old Kim has the meat wagon parked beside him ready for the winners. The prizes are wrapped in butchers paper and include several unlabeled "surprise" packages, the contents of which are perfectly safe but Kim would advise be refrigerated promptly and not put up too long before consumption. *Caveat carnivore.*

At forty minutes past the advertised start time, the mood of the room is darkening.

"Better start soon," Old Kim says. "People want they meat."

Buddy heads for the front. "Everything okay, Sally?"

"Just waiting for you to tell me when."

"My mistake. You're a hundred percent right. I forgot. If you're ready to go, then on with the show. And keep in mind we have a lot of meat to give away. If you get uncomfortable, I'll be right over there ready to take over if necessary."

"Thanks," Sally says. "But I'm not as nervous as before."

When June called and asked her to run the meat draw, for a minute Sally thought she might put on some lipstick. But she doesn't feel good in makeup, and anyhow she knows lots of the neighbourhood people here so there's no need to get fancy. Because everything's changed between her and Buddy and her and June, her big fear was being too scared. But for some reason it hasn't turned out that way. She's fine. Really fine.

"Hi, everybody," she screeches just as the music from outside stops. "Eeee, that sounds real loud. Is it too loud, does it sound too loud?" Buddy darts up and repositions her chair so she doesn't seem to be chowing down on the mic's foam windscreen. "Sorry about that," Sally says, "it was too loud. We'll start over . . . Hi, everybody."

"Speak up!"

"Hi, everybody. Buddy explained the rules, right? It's like a raffle. When you bought your tickets you kept one half and the other half with matching numbers on it went into this basket from Paranada down the street. I love their store, I got an excellent pair of like pirate pants except with elephants from India on them and . . . What? . . . Sure, let's get started. Is this too loud? Good. Okay." Into the basket dips her hand, a ticket is drawn, the number called.

"Wooooo!" The first winner is Kayla, the friend of Nita's who apparently has forgiven June's part in driving her and her party from the restaurant Thursday. After her ticket is checked at the desk, to applause and shouts of congratulations she proceeds to where Buddy and Old Kim are policing the meat. She selects the nearest package and to more cheers raises it overhead like the Stanley Cup.

"Come on, Kayla, no speeches, keep it moving."

"I didn't say a word, Buddy."

"Tell it at yoga."

"I'll think of you when I'm feeding the scraps to the dog, you big dink. By the way, I saw you on TV this morning, and in case you don't know, in lawn bowling you're supposed to roll the balls, not heave them up in the air so they slam into the ground and leave craters."

Buddy's already indifferent to criticism of his lawn bowling skills. The EVLBA visor has pride of place on his hat rack, awaiting the fading of memories and a ration of bullshit to turn the debacle into a personal triumph.

He takes another look at the wagon. Lot of meat in there, thirteen more prizes not including the goliath in the cooler, and how to pull off the swindle still has him stumped. If he could find a matching basket at Paranada, fill it with tickets identical to the ones . . . hold on, that's ridiculous . . . okay, how about he . . . nope, cut that one off at the knees, his own mother would call the cops. He can't keep the baron of beef aside and give it to Bo outright because he touted the thing in his introduction. Besides, that would pervert the essence of the experience. It's not a handout, it's a contest. His brother has to win fair and square. Or foul and triangular, whatever. The obvious solution is for Buddy to replace Sally at the desk, but how? Or maybe he's missing something.

Sally is turned in her chair, eyes closed, hand in the basket mixing the tickets for the next draw when from the back booms a gravelly male voice: "Point of order! The Legion traditionally starts with a 50-50 draw. Why are we rushing into the meat?"

When Buddy comes off his seat, the man reconsiders his position. "You raise a good issue, sir. Consider my objection withdrawn. Carry on." He nods wisely to those in his vicinity.

Sally plucks the next ticket and calls."

"Wooooo!"

Buddy gets his elbows on the table. "It's that fucking Kayla again," he says to Kim. "Two in a row right out of the gate. Quick, get something on top we can afford to waste."

"One minute, please." Kim roots through the beige packages. "Ah. Tofu wiener."

"You brought tofu to a meat draw? You trying to get us killed?"

Kim nudges the package to the lip of the wagon, where Kayla snatches it on her way by. The deli owner flashes Mr. Buddy a sparkly grin. "High-fi me, you want."

Kayla falls short of the three-peat. The third prize goes to a Washington State man who has a few words on riding his bicycle up from Sedro-Woolley to raise awareness for lupus. The distance is greater than the crowd collectively has peddled since the invention of spokes, and the visitor's remarks garner respectful applause from those not busy Googling *lupus* on their phones. When the smiling young American arrives for his meat, Kim has manoeuvred to central position a large, clearly labeled filet mignon.

"Nice touch," Buddy says approvingly after the man's departure. "You're fast with those hands."

"Long time I butcher," Kim says. "Also I play card. One time I show you some magic trick."

Buddy is transported through time and space to his thrashing on the lawn bowling greensward. So what if that's not his thing, his style. He has his own game. "Kim, my old friend. Let me tell you a family story to swell your heart. Then I'll suggest a good use for those magic hands of yours."

Thirty minutes later the meat pile has been stripped of most of its mass. Nita's back at the bar for another order. June's been working hard and their exchanges have been limited, but on this round she stops her before she's finished filling her tray. "How many more draws?" June doesn't have to utter his name or state the nature of her concern.

"They're down to four," Nita says. "No sign of trouble yet. I've been keeping an eye."

Tray at capacity, Nita is about to make off with it when June says, "Maybe we're being unfair. Buddy could use some room, given what he's gone through this past week."

"It's been more than a week that he's been trying to replace his father."

"That's what I used to think," June says. "I've carried it around for so long. But I've had it wrong. Not replace him—make up for him."

Round Twelve: Old Kim has been calmly rebutting Buddy's every suggestion. On principle the deli owner is not against playing fast and loose with the rules. Since landing in Canada as a young man, the rules have been used mostly to make his life difficult. And no one can say it isn't for a good cause because when it comes to family, all's fair. But Buddy's not getting it. Twice Kim has explained that without rigging the game in advance, personally running it or having the person drawing the tickets in on the scheme, there's not much to be done. The draw is too simple to be manipulated at this stage. It comes down to luck, a commodity of which the good version is distributed to very few people. Kim's cardsharp fingers would be better employed reaching into his wallet to see whether the money to pay for all the meat has magically appeared or whether he'll still be hounding Buddy for it at next year's Italian Day.

Our barber's watching his brother cross the floor, marking every step of his arrival. "You were gone a long time."

"Congratulation," says Kim, sliding his chair to make room. "Buddy tell me everything."

Yes, new brothers, it's very good news. So good Bo can't . . .

"Way to go, Kim," Buddy says sotto voce. "Make the guy cry why don't you."

"You cry two minute ago when you tell me."

"That's different."

"Same."

They're interrupted by the Round Twelve winner, a middle-age man with wavy hair Buddy spots as permed, who happily picks up his prize, a generous package of what Sally described as "little porky baby ribs."

Bo leans on the table and lowers his head on his hands, raising a *dingle* from his hat.

"You okay?" Buddy says. "You were gone so long. You missed almost everything." He doesn't know how to help. It looks as though even a hand on his brother's arm could break a bone. "My place is right across the street. You want to lie down for a while? How about the clinic, it's just a block away."

Bo's fine. It's just all the excitement. And the rush. Everything's happening so fast.

"Wait'll you get a load of the baron of beef," Buddy says while raising an admonitory finger to Kim, who for accuracy's sake mutters the correct name under his breath. "It's like in *A Christmas Carol* when Scrooge wakes up in the morning. Remember? He yells out the window at the kid to go get the goose in the butcher's window and the kid says it's as big as him."

Bo remembers. Except he's pretty sure it was a turkey.

Cutting off their exchange is Sally's call, and when Kayla arrives to pick up her third prize of the day, completing the hat-trick, Buddy's ready to file a formal grievance with the courts, a stay-of-meat order or some bloody thing. He refuses to look directly at her, but she lingers long enough to catch a corner of his eye before flouncing away like a ten-year-old on her way to hopscotch.

"Okay, everybody," comes Sally's amplified voice. "Draw number fourteen, last one before the championship grand humongous prize. Yay!"

"After this I'm going to get her to call a break before the finale," Buddy says. "Time to get serious. Bo, you didn't lose the tickets I gave you, right?"

Nope. Bo pats his pocket. Through the bathroom door he could hear the numbers being called, and he hasn't won yet. He shows Buddy the tickets.

Buddy blinks, blinks, blinks and inches out his hand with the quiver of a boy after a butterfly, the thrill of the hunt tinged with regret for robbing such elegance of its freedom. Bo passes the tickets to his brother. Buddy meticulously folds the double strip down the centre to soften the perforations and tears from top to bottom, dividing the whole into two columns of six tickets each. He hands one strip back to Bo and waggles its mate.

"This half was supposed to go in the basket or there are no numbers to match up with the tickets you keep. I guess Sally missed it." He begins plucking them into singles.

"Draw fourteen winning number," comes Sally's voice. "Three-eight-five-three-two!"

The roar that emerges from the winner, a forty-something man with a newsboy cap, crashes on the ears like the opening salvo on the Somme. To prolong the moment of triumph he takes a roundabout route, weaving between the tables, doubling back almost to the start, past the bar, chin up, ticket raised overhead. Such is his arousal, so excited is the state of the good red blood racing through his manly frame, that once in front of Sally it takes a full thirty seconds for the news to register that he misheard the call.

"Wrong number," Sally repeats, comparing the ticket with the one from the basket. "See? Three-eight-five-three-two. You have three-eight-*nine*-three-two. I'm really, really sorry."

For a few seconds the hapless contestant remains rigid, as though searching within himself for the means to return to his seat with a shred of dignity intact. But he's urged along by shouts of support conveying more commiseration than ridicule, and off he goes, albeit on a more direct path than his trip to the front. At this point, Kayla steps forward and claims her fourth prize of the day.

From the archway, Nita joins in the clapping. The drink orders have tailed off, and with the grand prize about to assume centre stage a sort of fuzzy puzzlement pervades the space, as though the guests are experiencing an undefined unease and have yet to link it with sitting in a bar gambling for meat mere steps away from several thousand people celebrating a glorious day outside. Nita checks the clock behind the bar and gets a whiff of herb. A glance over her shoulder is rewarded with a smile from the apple-nose man in the sharkskin suit.

"Hello," Nita says. "Here by yourself or joining friends?"

Because the apple-nose man is friend to the world he accepts the beautiful lady's question, but on the way here he blasted some equally beautiful local weed and can't locate a spot in his mind for an answer.

"Can I get you a drink? On the house."

The apple-nose man politely declines the offer. He can't stay long. He was down at the Kettle Society and couldn't resist the pull of the music from around the corner on the Drive. Smiles on faces, communal energy. He crooks a finger to bring her closer, then straightens it and sights along his arm till it's lined up with our barber at the table against the wall. He cups his hands like parentheses, one each for Nita and Buddy, brings his hands together till they meet, and slowly flattens out the brackets till the palms kiss. Now if she'll excuse him, he likes to keep on the move. Just before he goes:

May all beings be happy, content and fulfilled,
May all beings be healthy and whole,
May all beings be protected from harm and free from fear,
May all beings be awakened, enlightened and liberated,
May there be peace.

Before Nita can process the encounter, at Buddy's direction Sally announces a short break. The floor immediately fills with stretchers and talkers, racers to the washrooms and smokers aiming for the outdoors.

Ten minutes later Old Kim and Al are wheeling the serving table from the walk-in cooler. Once over the crevasse in the concrete floor Al has spent seven years not getting around to repairing, they head up the short hallway that debouches into the main room. Their arrival is greeted by *ooohhs* and *aaahhs* that change from theatrical to genuine once Kim slides off the tablecloth. The floor is jammed with players ordering up, topping up and shaking it out, and the restaurateur and the deli owner bushwhack their way through, slapping at the hands reaching out for a reverent caress of the carcass.

"Some piece of meat," Al says. "Should've bought a ticket myself."

With the wheel locks applied, they relinquish custody to Sally. On the way back Al has a stroll, greeting a stranger here and there, keeping his distance from a couple of his morning-walk pals because who wants to talk about Lippy Delillo for the rest of his life? Al's lording it, and why not? The place is packed, and he couldn't care less if the meat draw wasn't his idea. The way he figures, the President of the US never pulled the trigger on no cruise missile, but when some terrorist gets one up the rear end the Prez takes a bow, don't he?

Kim's cutting back to his seat when he hears his name. He finds room at the far end of the bar and waits.

"Where's Buddy?" June says.

"He go outside," Kim says.

"I can't see him in the window."

"Small window, big world."

"All of a sudden you're a philosopher. Just go check on him. Please."

"He say doan follow."

"At least let me know if he tries to sneak back in." She slides him a draft. "Consider that a bribe."

"One beer. Some bribe. Now I tell you every single ting. Mr. Buddy, I see him on Lion Gate Bridge. On top art gallery. He send letter from Toronto. Phone from Lamaramadingdong."

"Piss off, Kung Fu."

Outside, Buddy's leaning against the painted brick of the building, scoping the street. Heat waves still balloon from pavement, grills, bare shoulders, overheated imaginations. But the light is waning and the daytime crowd has summited, taken a mass selfie and is on the descent, leaving the cleanup to the sherpas. Exhaused children are being wrangled up side streets or into vehicles to be transported home, where they'll be stripped of dirty clothes and hosed of sweat and tears. The main stages yet blaze, but all around tents are being folded, racks denuded of merchandise, booths disassembled, displays dismantled. The blood-flow of foot traffic continues, the systole-diastole of human interaction up and down the vein-artery system of the Drive, the evening being transformed by the lowering light and the hum of energy, shapeshifting into something less tame, more jungle.

When June was out of sight, Buddy checked with Sally, and as expected she would be happy to have her new brother help her draw for the grand prize. He smiled at her then, and brushed back some lanky strands of hair that had slipped from behind her ear. She smiled back and waggled her fingers at him. Now it's up to Buddy. It doesn't take a sleight-of-hand man like Old Kim to hide a ticket in the fist while rooting around in a basket.

Inside, Bo is heating up again, worse than earlier when he had to press against the cool tiles of the bathroom. The kittycat T-shirt seems to have turned on him with actual claws and he's pulling at it, plucking and twisting to get it away from his skin. Itchy, twitchy. His feet are like puffballs, his hands like bladders. And he hurts. He hurts pretty bad. Can't think right. Overlapping images—knights in armour, a boat on dry land crafted by an unskilled hand, his sister, Sally-Sally how does your garden grow . . .

. . . Buddy didn't know. He didn't know, you see. When he was ten, the age gap between he and June seemed immense, conferring an aura of strength on his mum. In his mind it was impossible for his mother to be scared. And how about years on, when CC died? June was almost forty. How would Buddy deal with news of that sort now that he's forty-one himself? If Nita died he'd—no, get away from him with that thought, take it away. But while he's on the subject, how about his forty-year-old mother? Bring her back, please, so he can look into her eyes with the understanding of a man of equal years and experience. And if we're bringing people back, stop for his father. And pick up his wife along the way before she's gone. Before she reaches 11.2 km/sec. If go away they must, they'll all find a way to reach escape velocity. . .

. . . Bo can't see out through the window. His vision has tunneled, a grey centre graduating into a black surround, contracting. Is it just that? His vision? Or has Walker-Talker Man gone away? Bo can smell himself, swampy vinegar and bile. Then comes a pulse. He lowers his internal eye and there it is deep in the earth below, not a single point source but multiple cores like raisins in a cookie. Closer, closer, changing into light, here it is, like a tickle but bright, so bright, illuminating his floppy boots, surging up through his feet and legs, travelling his trunk—wait, another burst is taking him face-on, another slanting in obliquely from out on the street, other shafts of light arriving from all quadrants. A brief suspension allows him to snatch some air into his lungs before the infusion renews. Bright, his skin, bright as the sun. Is there real magic in him? Some magic works at a distance, the kind that comes from Heaven or Hell. But the truly mysterious magic, the wrenching need and aching pain of love and family, needs proximity. Bo has to get to his sister and his brother. Explain that he can't help them, doesn't have the power to make everything right, can't erase time or make people forget or make them do good. It's too much . . .

. . . Maybe Buddy will stay right where he is outside the bar. At some point explanations break down, usually right where the question changes from *what?* to *why?* One of the first things he learned from science, really. Elementary particles and forces exist and behave in explicable ways, even if new mathematics has continually to be invented to predict the quantum critters' actions. There are quarks, this is known. But from top to bottom, with all their ups and downs, strange and charming as they may be, *why* are there quarks? Beats the hell out of Buddy and, not incidentally, everyone else. And while he's entertaining the notion of unanswerable questions, allow him to tack on the entire mystery of love and family and friendship and connection. And with that addition, our barber reaches the limit of his philosophy, or at least his patience for it. So he'll stop the questions and let things play out. Calmly, if possible. At peace, provisionally. But for now with his signature on a non-interference pact.

"Well, well, look at the baby brother."

"Devona."

"What you doing here with your hands in your pockets—squeezing the worm?" That didn't sound funny to her own ears, and she doesn't much feel like trying for an improvement.

"I'm relaxing," Buddy says.

"It's working. You sound like an all-night deejay got hold of some Prozac at two eh-em and just filled his pants."

Buddy glances down. "You got your shoe back."

"Uh-huh. Cobbler only charged me ten, saved a fin." She sticks out a leg and appraises the salmon-pink specimen on the end of it. "My old sneakers would be better for lawn bowling, but don't matter, I'll probably never be good enough at that to get on TV."

Her eyes are on the level of Buddy's nose but seem to be staring down at him. The barber returns the stare and says, "Where's your guy?"

"What guy?"

"Louie."

"He's not mine, and anyhow I left him holed up in the Hoe."

She told Louie. She told him we got to talk. That's the next step after you fall in love, even if you just think it's love. She didn't want him to get all worked up, it wouldn't last long. But it didn't have to last, just had to be. You got to fall in love. World being the world, it doesn't help in the long run but it does for the time being. Day, two, a week, just got to be done. It was a nice night, Devona has to say, the whole time with him was nice. Usually *nice* is one of those froofy words without the muscle to describe what she's feeling, but in this case the weak word is the strongest. The fisherman treated her not exactly like a princess or nothing, she'd never lay that kind of Disney talk out there, but he made her feel like a . . . sure, why not call it a lady? Except what they did with each other isn't something a lady would use as a conversation starter with a nun. Or even a social services officer, comes to that, huh-huh-huh. All in all, the love wasn't the forever-and-ever type, but the subject does raise questions. Like what if she'd met a man from a different world before her own world was set? Just before it was set, you see? Different place, maybe. Anywhere, small town with fishboats and hand-made quilts and little kids chucking rocks in the ocean instead of through drugstore windows to rob the prescriptions. Anyway, she'll miss him. He's got the *bona fides,* you know?

"The runt might be by later," she says to Buddy. "He's making a couple phone calls to Comox. 'Overseas,' he calls it, thinks he's a comedian. But never mind him, I come here to support Sally. She's calling a meat draw while the Eyetalians celebrate getting chucked out of the old country."

"Here it is."

They back off and take in the sign.

"Al Esposito's," Devona says. "Louie says Al's what, your stepdaddy?"

"Something like that I guess," Buddy says. "If you're going to get in on the game you better hurry. Grand prize is being drawn in a couple of minutes."

"I don't gamble. I like to piss my money away where it makes a bigger splash, huh-huh-huh."

Behind them on the street, the desert tortoise is on the return. All by his lonesome he's following the centreline southbound, grateful for his time in the temperate rainforest of the northern Pacific coast but sorely missing his home in the Sonora, where he was kidnapped from his family these eighty-five years ago. An hour back, his owner was struck by a diversion or an accidental encounter or an epiphany or any of a thousand other reasons to up stakes and head for new territory, leaving the tortoise to keep on keepin' on. The Chihuahua bailed out somewhere along the way to wait for the office to open Monday so he can apply for the temporary foreign worker program.

"I guess your mummy is in there," Devona says. "She knows Bo and Sally, yeah? Your mummy, I mean."

"Don't worry, you look great."

"Not trying to impress nobody."

"Okay. Just don't have to worry, that's all."

Devona hesitates. "You coming in?"

"I'm good. But here—give these tickets to Sally to put in the basket. They're Bo's. If he wins, it'll be legitimate."

"Why wouldn't it? And what're you doing with the tickets anyhow?"

Seconds slough off with the speed of a saline drip while the I-know-that-you-know-that-I know game plays itself out.

"I'll be along in a couple of minutes," Buddy says.

At the door Devona takes a last check of her shiny salmon-pink shoes and feels her forehead and cheeks.

"Go ahead," Buddy says. "You're safe with my mum."

"Don't push a person."

"Just open the door and walk on in."

"I said don't push." She ventures a try at the door. "Huh. Cocksucker's locked."

"Must be jammed. Let me." Three pulls is enough. Buddy leaps back to the window. Hands beside his head like horse blinders, nose on the glass, peering . . . over there at the archway, June and Nita staring directly back at him.

Sally's returning to the desk. She's on the mic but Buddy can't hear her over the street noise. Looks like his brother can kiss the baron of beef goodbye, and ain't that a bite in the ass for Buddy's having switched allegiance to the God of Fair Play. As if to hammer home the irony, the djembe drummers are back at it with a will—hammer, hammer, *bababop*, drum-drum-drumming. Buddy locates Bo at the table on the far wall. *Bop-bop-babababababop!* What the hell . . . he tightens his hands into a tube around his eyes, blocking the light. His brother. Right there, right over there, doesn't anyone see? Open your eyes, he's right in front of you, can't you see? *Bop-bop-babababababop!*

The people around Bo appear to be moving very slowly. He's alive to a nauseating odour that seems to have bypassed his nose and infiltrated osmotically through skin, blood, bone. The smell of confusion, of loosened structures, of failing expectations. He's dappled with light and bombarded with alternating doses of heat and arctic cold, temperature extremes with no transition phase. And what's this, what's this now, an acceleration, people darting and jerking, a speed-up of time itself in great streaks and sheets.

"Check your tickets everybody, the grand prize number is four—four—two—"

Buddy's screaming at the window, bowing in the pane with arrhythmic blows of his hands. Right over there, but no one sees, no one hears, no one's home in the house.

Bo feels the strength. Not providing support but in direct opposition, actively fighting against him. Why does it hurt, it's never hurt like this before, why does it hurt so much and . . . now it's out of his control, he feels it slipping through his fingers, breaking free like a trained animal suddenly grown self-aware. A hitch, a blink, a burp and it's out, out there in the room. Faces distort, bodies contort, illusory music, hysterical laughter, swords clashing, puppies by the bushel basket, phantasms looking on as Bo spasms, jerking, burning, he hurts, it hurts so bad, he's never felt such hurt. Mummy . . . Mummy . . . deep breaths, deep breaths and pushhh, pushhh . . . Mummy . . .

"—six—"

Mummy . . .

"—seven!"

"Wooooo!"

MUMMY!

*

It takes Sally a long time to sort everything out. The next morning, when she goes home to shower off the smell of the hospital and get some sleep, she can remember only three things clearly: She remembers calling the last number. She remembers being really, really glad she wasn't closer to the window when Buddy threw the bicycle through the glass from the sidewalk. And she remembers right near the end looking over at Bo, and just for a second—this is totally weird and sad and beautiful and makes her cry every time—she could swear he was glowing like an angel.

Chapter 40

Treasure Island

Louie avoided a legal mess for abandoning his truck at the ferry. But after fines, impoundment fees, towage costs to a garage in Nanaimo and a few bucks to learn that any more spent on the old beater would be throwing good money after bad, his feet and the kindness of friends will have to get him around till a few government old age cheques accumulate.

Five minutes into the trees he stops to orient the laminated topo map to the direction of travel. He's glad he phoned from the mainland and asked around. Robert Fairchild's story of his boyhood trip with his father wouldn't have gotten the fisherman within guessing distance on his own. Up the Puntledge River from Lewis Park—that much fits. But the destination point is halfway to Comox Lake, too far from either of the old Faire sites or any other launching point in town to take a young frail boy on a hike. Charlie Monk must have driven here, parked and they walked in, the way Louie has in the borrowed car. The Renaissance Faire he's already dismissed as having any relevance beyond a vague geographical reference point from which to start. The celebration undoubtedly held deep significance for Robert Fairchild as a link to the past, to a father now long gone. But in the opinion of his sister, who after years of playing audience could recite the account almost verbatim, whatever special information their father bestowed on her brother would more likely be connected to the part of the story dealing with their walks up the river.

Rain has fallen over the past three days, temporarily stifling hopes for a long hot summer for the tourists and quieting fear of drought for the farmers and wildfire fighters. Green predominates, with a richness almost libidinous. A ferric pine-fir tang accents the smell of decaying deadfall and duff. Louie sidles past a baby hemlock sprouting from a nurse stump and judges the surroundings wet enough for him to safely cop a smoke. The bill of his ballcap shelters the match. He appreciates the forest, but the second he ducks under its canopy he feels as if he's cheating on a jealous ocean. Nothing pulls him like the sea, nothing can furnish that deep-level confidence of knowing he's home. Some see only the beach, some the surface or for what it holds for recreation, some slight the water completely for dreams of the far side. Louie feels the body of the sea, its substance. But this is fine. Quiet, comforting, and in the hush and the damp the cigarette tastes good.

"No rush," Buddy says.

No problem. Louie won't be rushed. He makes an unnecessary display of poring over the map. Left-centre-top is a sloppy circle in grease pencil.

"Relax, finish your smoke," Buddy says.

Louie can do without the blessing but nods his appreciation anyway.

Buddy can't stop himself. "Can we get going? This could take a while. That circle on the map isn't very specific."

"My friend told me it's easy, a natural clearing fifteen minutes from the road. He was a surveyor and says anyone who spent any time in the bush had either come across it or heard about it. I remember the story going around town, too. A kind of running gag. But I never thought to connect it with Charlie. It's still a longshot, but it's all we have."

Buddy stares at Louie's cigarette to make it burn faster, tilts his head and assesses the cloud cover from under his Seattle Sombrero, digs in a toe and flips over a flap of wet red cedar bark. He has to say Nita was wonderful. She took over the arrangements as though she'd been on retainer all these years and was finally cut loose to show her stuff. Negotiating through the bureaucracy, coordinating with the hospital, clearing out Bo's room in the SRO building—she handled it all, leaving Buddy free to be with Sally. A champion, Nita, a winner. There's no clamor from either of them to move back in together, but the topic, like some tropical parasite, is at the larval stage just below the surface of the skin. Provisionally reconciled more-or-less—that's about as close as they've come in their heads without either of them saying so.

Louie extinguishes his smoke in a watery depression and carefully field-strips the butt. There's no travel-worn path, but the patchy understory is easy to negotiate. Buddy follows in his footsteps.

The blood type matching was a cinch, both Buddy and Bo being type A. They share four HLA antigens, not the best but a decent tissue compatibility. The crossmatch, which will be repeated just before the surgery, was negative. Stage 5. ESRD, End Stage Renal Disease.

"If they match," Buddy said to the doctor, "take one of mine. Two kidneys are too much to keep track of anyhow. I'm always leaving one on the bus, or wandering around the apartment trying to remember where I set it down like my reading glasses."

"Very good," said the doctor, "but being a living donor is not without risks. I'd be happy to explain—"

"It's always bugged me, the second one." He turned to Bo in the bed. "Just be glad you don't need my liver. You'd be screwed, brother."

Feebly: *Yaksputz-figsack-korfle!*

Louie leads on, and their trek takes them over a swampy patch that sucks at their feet. The boat does, or did, exist. The practical part of Buddy would say all they have to operate from is a pencil sketch of an amateur attempt at boatbuilding and Bo's muddied remembrances of excursions with his father. But on they go, the barber and the fisherman through the forest. Because it must be true. Of what are dreams made other than hope and hunch?

Twenty-five years of botanical encroachment has nearly effaced the clearing. There's no boat left to match Robert Fairchild's drawing, just rotted wood amid the undergrowth. A quarter-century of decomposition without ever being afloat. Can an object be called a thing without having been the thing? Can a boat be a boat if never afloat? Can a brother be a brother?

Buddy goes to work on the patches of silvery wood visible through the saplings and ground cover, stripping vegetation and pulling out boards. Louie circles the remains, examining what Buddy unveils, calling his attention to pieces with potential. The planks are too thin for anything much larger than a canoe, and Louie figures they were chosen so one man without proper tools or experience could bend them onto the hull's ribs. With the surface layer cleared from the entangling growth, Buddy comes across the craft's name plate—*Ocean Jester*—and tosses it aside. Soaked now, he digs deeper, heaving boards, flimsy sheathing cut for portholes, a clump of stairway that falls apart at a tug, an iron handrail he launches into the bush like a spear. Deeper, working like a beast through the disintegrating wood slimed with age. After a time he stops.

Grandview Park, when Buddy told his mother the whole story, or at least what he had a handle on. He can't remember her exact words, but the gist was that any given point on your timeline can be broken down into two parts—how you feel you should be living your life, and how to explain to yourself why you're not doing so.

Karma can kiss his royal ass. His destiny is nothing more than what he can create from serendipity and the predispositions fed him by his genes. Said and done. At least it would be if he could fasten on what part of his life so far he's created. Possibly none of it. Something happens to which he responds, then something else happens and you can already see where he's going with this. Again and again like shampoo directions—rinse and repeat as necessary. He thinks some on his family new and old, and has a glimpse of a future that finds him expanding out of himself and into their world. What's in store? He can scarcely imagine there's even such a thing as a state of blissful accord. True, at mid-life he's already registering signs of increased tolerance and patience, but he puts it down to age, like hair in his ears, things over which he has no control and shouldn't beat himself up about. So if the day comes when he's in perfect harmony with his loved ones, his friends and neighbours, himself . . . well, he'll burn that bridge when he comes to it.

Buddy continues his labour at a pace more likely to see him through to the end. When he reaches the bottom and digs out a fibreglass footlocker from where the collapsed boat has pinned it, he rests. The box is heavy, but much of the weight is from mud and grasping roots, vines and tendrils, most of which he claws off. He pushes the box across a plank to Louie and struggles out from the confused pile of debris. Once on secure footing near the trees, Louie invites Buddy to do the honours. Rusted as it is, the padlock resists his attempts to blast it open with a rock, but when he retrieves the iron handrail, forces it through the hasp and levers it sideways, the entire hinge lock pulls free. The barber steps back from the footlocker to make room for his father's old skipper. Louie carefully pries it open, glances inside and in turn steps aside for Buddy.

Pictures. Hundreds. *I kept all of it.* Babies, a woman holding them singularly and together. A hunchback boy with a baseball glove. A girl holding up a shell on the beach. The woman again, Norma surely, in a tight pantsuit and with her hair up. And here in front of the Steveston Cannery is Buddy's mother. He forgot how jet-black June's hair used to be. And one of him, how old would he be there, and what's he holding—look at that, the ribbon for winning the Grade 6 crokinole tournament. *I leave it to my family.* Copies of birth certificates, vaccination records, school report cards, a page in minute script of heights and weights. *I kept all of it.* Two women and three kids. Pictures and papers, crossovers and parallels. All of them.

Louie allows him the time he needs, which is not too long, considering. They retrace their steps through the bush, carrying the footlocker between them back to the present.

⋆

"Have any plans?" Louie says on the way to the Departure Bay ferry.

"Got the urge to hit the road after the operation," Buddy says. "I'll be travelling lighter with one less organ."

"Except you have some catching up to do."

"I have some catching up to do."

The sun's out in the open, tired of having its intents and purposes disguised by cloud. Louie zips down both front windows and lights a smoke. "Why would your father build the boat? He must have known he could never make it seaworthy."

"He never meant it to be," Buddy says.

They reach the ferry with plenty of time to spare. From the passenger deck railing, Buddy rests his eyes on the trail of foam spreading astern, superintended by seagulls alert to targets of opportunity. He follows the steel deck forward and peers through the rain toward the mainland.

Epilogue
Flaming Datum

The overnight storm was long and violent. This morning sees trees down on roofs and vehicles, power out for much of the valley, windrows of debris along the main roads. In contrast, the world beneath the surface appears untouched. The ocean rocks and rolls, and the sunken troller, long accustomed to the inexorable pressure of something much greater than her, endures.

The two young divers kick their way past a familiar forest of plumose anemones and follow the slope into deeper water. They've gained much in experience over the past year. Diving with the sea lions off Hornby Island, participating in the annual lingcod egg mass survey, starting their tech diving course. Best of all, they've accumulated hours of digital footage toward their documentary on the underwater charms of the northern Pacific coast. After drifting for twenty minutes along a wall of rock encrusted with sea life, they check their pressure gauges and decide to reverse course while beginning a gradual ascent that will bring them close to shore. The plan changes when they come upon the wreck.

The publicity over last year's rescue didn't last long, but at least it shamed the RCMP into returning their camera. The video of the trapped diver is jerky and hard to follow and when posted on YouTube failed to garner much attention. But fleshed out with their new footage, including an awesome sequence of a sixgill shark and with background music from their band, The Seahorse Jockeys, the documentary is ready to be pitched. Or it would if the dude at Discovery Channel would get his act together and answer their email. Now, with a higher quality camera more appropriate for serious filmmakers, they move in on the wreck.

It's been only three days since their last dive, so the air-sea interaction from last night's storm must have penetrated deeper than they thought. The old troller is dramatically altered. The false bottom has separated completely and lies with the remnants of the deck under the half-dome of the hull, which has lost its stomach for the quarter-century fight and spilled its contents onto the seafloor.

After a slow pan they'll use as the establishing shot, they zoom in on a sprinkling of incongruous objects dominating the foreground. At this juncture, the video camera is left dangling from a wrist strap while the divers rise to the surface with the first of the polyethylene-wrapped parcels of white powder.

Acknowledgments

With love and gratitude I'd like to thank my wife, Tracy Rideout, who's been instrumental throughout, as has Anna Gustafson, comic, writer, speaker, and dear friend who put together the website to spread the word about the book.

Also great thanks to Vancouver's Keith McKellar (aka Laughing Hand)—a master of caricature sketches and the artist who created the wonderful cover. My copy editor from Toronto, Glenda MacFarlane, is the most thorough of any editor I've worked with and a new friend to boot.

And of course Chris Needham, the publisher of Now Or Never Publishing—a pleasure to deal with right down the line.

To wrap it up, hitting the stage now as co-headliners are: my mother, Irene Reid (R.I.P.), from whom I got my joy in stories. And Gordon Pinsent, my father, from whom I got my need to tell them.